Prai

WINDS OF MARQUE

"Bennett R. Coles ranks among my go-to list in SF. Entertaining and intelligent storytelling and terrific characters. In *Winds of Marque*, Coles may well have invented a whole new subgenre that has me scrambling for a description—Steam Space? Whatever you call it, [it's] a blast to read. Here's hoping that many more adventures are in the offing for Blackwood and company."

—Steven Erikson, *New York Times* bestselling author

"Science fiction fans of the Hornblower or Aubrey-Maturin sailing sagas will likely thrill as the cannons are run out for battles in space." —*Publishers Weekly*

"The kind of authentic-feeling space navy action that you'd expect from a master like Jack Campbell. Outstanding action that will keep you turning the pages with enough twists to keep you guessing until the end. Looking forward to the next book in the series."

—Michael Mammay, author of *Planetside*

"*Winds of Marque* maintains a brisk pace from the get-go. . . . Coles cleverly preserves many of the naval traditions that have become synonymous with historical seafaring adventure stories. The leadership structure aboard *Daring*, the divisions between the sailors and the officers, and even the commands shouted out in the middle of a battle feel ripped from the pages of a Patrick O'Brian novel." —*BookPage*

Praise for

BENNETT R. COLES

WINDS

— OF —

MARQUE

Blackwood & Virtue

HARPER Voyager
An Imprint of HarperCollins*Publishers*

WINDS OF MARQUE. Copyright © 2019 by Bennett R. Coles. All rights reserved. Printed in the United States of America. No part of this book may be used or reproduced in any manner whatsoever without written permission except in the case of brief quotations embodied in critical articles and reviews. For information, address HarperCollins Publishers, 195 Broadway, New York, NY 10007.

First Harper Voyager mass market printing: July 2020
First Harper Voyager paperback printing: April 2019

Print Edition ISBN: 978-0-06-302268-3
Digital Edition ISBN: 978-0-06-282036-5

Cover design and illustration © Damonza.com
Cover images © Shutterstock; © Bigstock
Sword © Barks/Shutterstock

Harper Voyager and the Harper Voyager logo are trademarks of HarperCollins Publishers in the United States of America and other countries.

HarperCollins is a registered trademark of HarperCollins Publishers in the United States of America and other countries.

20 21 22 23 24   CWM   10 9 8 7 6 5 4 3 2 1

To Captain(N) Edward Hooper, Royal Canadian Navy.
The pluckiest space engineer I know.

WINDS
OF
MARQUE

CHAPTER 1

Save the rum.

If nothing else, Subcommander Liam Blackwood thought to himself as he hung on to the arms of his chair, save the rum. He steadied the bottle on the wardroom table as the entire deck shook again. If artificial gravity failed, every untethered object on board would become a missile. And rum was just too precious to risk. Ignoring the concerned glances of the other officers, he pulled himself to his feet and placed the bottle back in its cupboard. All around the tiny space, dishes and other formal trappings of officer life rattled against their restraints.

The door slid open and he heard the thumps of someone entering the wardroom.

"XO, sir." There was a pleading in that voice, he could hear. "The captain intends to continue with full sail."

Yes, he did, Liam thought quietly to himself. And the stupid, arrogant bastard was unwilling to listen to his propulsion officer. Why did Liam always get saddled with the idiots?

"Sir," came another voice. "Do you think the ship will hold together?"

Having finally succeeded in neutralizing his expression, Liam turned to his officers. Lieutenant Mason Swift, who had spoken first, stared at him from the wardroom doorway. His complexion had gone ashen, from the tip of his chin to the top of his shaved head. Half a dozen more officers gripped their chairs around the dining table, all dressed in full blue coats and ruffled shirts as befitted a formal dinner. A pair of liveried stewards hung on to the fixed shelves on the forward bulkhead. The meal had started out as a pleasant affair, but what had begun as just an uncomfortable swell of solar winds had grown over the past hour into something far more dangerous.

Liam cast his eyes around the room, knowing that none of the officers or crew present were senior enough to truly understand how the nobility worked. Military professionalism was what they were used to, and that wasn't what they were dealing with here. The captain was from one of the great houses, and he wouldn't listen to anyone. He didn't know how to.

If the lord captain wanted to get them all killed, that was his prerogative.

But Liam was the executive officer, and it was his duty to advise the captain whether he liked it or not. Sighing inwardly, he adopted a stern expression and clambered around the shuddering table to grasp for the door. "Sails, with me."

Lieutenant Swift followed him out as requested, shutting the wardroom door behind them. He was *Renaissance*'s propulsion officer, and a damned smart fellow. But he had no ability to filter his speech when speaking to senior officers.

"Did you brief the captain on the sailing situation?"

"Yes, but he wouldn't listen! He doesn't give a—"

Liam silenced him with a sharply raised hand. It lost some effectiveness when Liam had to suddenly use that hand to steady himself, the ship rolling heavily. Swift stumbled, but his expression of righteous anger didn't fade.

"If we don't back off the sails," Swift hissed, "we're going to lose a mast. In the next thirty minutes."

Liam knew that his propulsion officer didn't exaggerate.

"I'll talk to the captain. Get back down there and hold things together."

Swift's look of gratitude helped. But it didn't change any of the facts of the situation as Liam staggered aft along the main corridor of what had been his floating home for the past six months, the cruiser *Renaissance*. Fine, swift, and well armed, she was barely a year out of the builder's yard—a newness clearly portrayed in the polished surfaces and pristine control panels illuminated in the dim passageway that stretched fore and aft most of the length of the vessel. This passageway was the only place inside the hull that gave a true sense of the vessel's vast size. Impressive, but right now all Liam could see in his mind was that long hull twisting and finally snapping under the unrelenting pressures of the solar confluence.

He passed a handful of crewmembers as they lurched from handhold to handhold. Their expressions were fixed in professional determination, but Liam could see the fear brewing in their eyes. Even they knew that this wasn't just another storm.

Up a single ladder, and then Liam stepped forward onto the bridge. Even through the tinting effect of the broad transparency that formed the bridge top, the glare of a dozen suns forced him to shield his eyes. Long clouds of superheated gas glowed among swirling, dark streams of dust that twisted in the solar winds. Stellar movements in the cluster were well documented and, these days, rigorously tracked, but the vagaries of solar storms were impossible to predict. Quickly studying the bank of consoles to starboard, he saw the false color images of the nearest stars and their current activity levels.

In that moment, the entire deck heaved. It wasn't the sluggish rolls of before: it was a hard movement, like a smack against the hull. Members of the bridge crew, strapped into their seats in a semicircle forward, glanced nervously at each other. One of them spotted Liam and looked back, fear reflected on his face in the glow of red and yellow warning lights on his console. Liam gave him a stern nod, then indicated for him to keep his eyes on his station. An XO couldn't show fear, Liam knew, despite the icy pit in his stomach.

Liam straightened his uniform and stepped into the central command ring, turning his gaze immediately to the young man seated in the command chair. Captain Lord Silverhawk gave him a disinterested glance before facing forward once again. His narrow, youthful features were molded into what many crewmembers took to be command confidence, but Liam knew to be the fundamental, unshakable arrogance of a lifetime of privilege. A lifetime of only twenty-nine years so far, but more than long enough for Silverhawk to believe in his own omnipotence. If the captain was concerned about the strength of the solar confluence into which his ship sailed, he'd never show it.

"Bit of a blow, sir," Liam said with as much casualness

as he could muster. "I'll send the roundsmen to secure for storm sailing."

"Very well," Silverhawk replied.

Renaissance tipped to starboard as another wave of solar wind particles smashed invisibly into the hull. Antigravity compensated quickly, but not fast enough to stop Liam from slamming into the command chair. His eyes instinctively shot up to inspect the top mast through the transparent canopy, stretching high above the hull with a full sheeting of solar sails. The mast swayed visibly even as he watched, the giant sails straining in the flow of particles. That last wave had struck the top mast hardest, based on the motion of the hull, but even a cadet could have read the mast status board by the captain's left arm and seen the building pressure on all four. Looking out to his left, Liam could see the taut sails of the port mast, and to his right he saw the wild dance of the starboard sails as they caught random eddies.

Captain Silverhawk paid no attention, either to the visual chaos outside or the intricate readings on his consoles inside. His eyes were forward, staring toward the distant pocket of darkness ahead that indicated where *Renaissance* would break out of this particular subcluster and back into open space.

"That fop Longridge thought he could get the jump on us," Silverhawk said suddenly, "by detaching *Celebration* from the squadron while we resupplied. Bet he thinks he can claim the first dance with Her Royal Highness."

"I'm sure that won't be the case, sir," Liam replied, steadying himself as the ship rocked again. So that was the captain's motivation for this suicidal run—a dance with a bloody princess.

"I can picture his jaw hitting that polished floor when

he enters the ball and sees me already standing there."
Silverhawk's wolfish grin turned momentarily curious as
he finally looked at Liam. "Does the local lord have a
ballroom with a polished floor?"

The ball was taking place at the home of Lord Grandview on Passagia, which also happened to be Liam's
home world.

"Yes, sir."

"I hope it's hard. For when Longridge's chin hits it."

So it was a race, Liam realized. And Lord Longridge's
Celebration was too far away to be actively tracked, leaving *Renaissance* nothing but dead reckoning to try to
guess her position. No doubt Longridge was taking the
longer, safer route to reach Passagia—so *Renaissance*
was cutting the corner through an area of the cluster rou-
tinely classified as off-limits for sailing ships.

Liam noticed the main screen of the command console
in front of Silverhawk was a navigation assessment of the
two warships, with projected arrival times for each ship.
What a bunch of nonsense.

The deck rattled once again. Liam studied the mast
status panel.

"Looks like we might need to break out a replacement
set of sails, sir."

"So long as we don't reduce speed, Lord Blackwood."
Silverhawk turned threatening eyes toward Liam. "I've
already told that odious little man, *Swift,* that we are not
slowing down."

"Of course, sir."

"*Renaissance* is the newest, fastest ship in the fleet,"
Silverhawk continued. "I will not question her might just
because of a storm. We will carry on at full speed."

Here in deep space, the ship didn't really have a "speed" that could be accurately measured, since there was nothing close enough against which to measure it. What Silverhawk really cared about, Liam knew, even though his captain didn't, was *Renaissance*'s velocity relative to its target, Passagia. And even that was only relative to the main star, not the second planet—Passagia II—upon which the royal ball was to be held. The only number that actually mattered in this fool's game was the computer-calculated time it would take for *Renaissance* to reach orbit around Passagia II—and whether it was less than the estimated time for *Celebration* to do the same.

Liam glanced out through the transparent deckhead again, assessing the now-steady lean of the top mast as solar wind from a dozen stars channeled into a maelstrom against it. Silverhawk hadn't even noticed.

But now that Liam knew where the captain's main focus lay, a plan coalesced in his mind.

"Sir," he said, "I recommend we batten down completely for this transit. I wouldn't want *Renaissance*'s lines to be marred by wind damage, especially if we end up being moored next to the royal yacht."

"Good idea, Blackwood. Let's keep her looking pretty as we set a new speed record for the Navy."

Liam barked the order to one of the bridge crew, who in turn relayed it to propulsion. Battening down meant that an outer layer of plating was extended over all exposed areas of the hull, including the bridge canopy. At least that would help secure the ship against the maelstrom—until she was ripped in half.

Liam knew there was no further point in him being on

the bridge. He needed to get somewhere that could actually affect the ship's fate.

"I'll supervise propulsion, sir. Make sure they don't slacken off."

Silverhawk didn't reply. That usually meant he didn't object, and Liam didn't wait for more. He lurched forward to ensure that the crew had begun deploying the thin shield of armor over the bridge's transparent canopy. Once that was done, the captain wouldn't be able to see what Liam did next.

Propulsion control was three decks down from the bridge and forward—in the exact center of the ship's hull. As Liam scrambled down the last ladder he could hear the swell of noise growing from the orders and shouts of a crew working frantically over the steady, awful creak of the masts shifting against their braces. Here, in the heart of the ship, the four masts came together into a massive, cross-shaped thrust block where all the forces pressing into the sails were transferred into the forward motion of the ship. Each arm of the cross was designed to have some, usually microscopic, flexibility as the forces differed on each mast. As Liam descended the ladder he heard a mighty, metallic groan as the highest arm of the cross visibly shifted.

He stepped down to the hard deck and pushed his way forward.

Lieutenant Swift was hunkered over his control panel in front of the main display. The sailing table was a broad surface where a tracing of the ship's hull and all four masts was dotted with a galaxy of sensor lights meant to give an overall survey of the health of the propulsion system. Liam expertly noted the series of lights up each of the four masts and the sail points strung along each yardarm. There were far too many yellow readings on the projection, and a growing number of reds.

"Sails, XO," he said loudly, clapping a hand on Swift's shoulder. The gesture caught the attention of most people in the room.

Indignant surprise melted into relief as Swift turned to look at him.

"Sir, good. Have you talked some sense into him?"

The comment was much too loud with sailors present. No officer could be seen to question the captain—even if the captain was a buffoon like Silverhawk.

"Don't waste my time with stupid questions!" Liam roared, getting right into Swift's face. "Get this ship battened down and ready for the storm!"

Crewmembers scurried at his command, thankful that the XO's wrath wasn't being directed at them. Another shake of the deck knocked many off balance, but they frantically continued their work. Behind the mass of bodies, the heavy crosspiece of the thrust block groaned dangerously.

Liam turned back to Swift, leaning in close.

"Don't say things like that out loud," he muttered. "Now give me your status."

"Battening down is forty-five percent complete, and security rounds are sixty percent complete. In about four minutes this ship will be as tight as she can be. But that won't solve this."

He gestured broadly at the main sailing table. Liam's eyes followed, noting again the multitude of stress indicators.

"Top mast is already past allowable limits—it could snap at any time. Bottom mast is not far behind. Port and starboard are strained but holding, but if we lose top mast, it'll drag us hard to starboard and put unpredictable stresses on the other three." Swift lowered his voice. "If we don't short those sails, we risk losing all four masts. And port in particular could pierce the hull if it cracks."

Liam looked down at the main panel display for the ship's internal damage-control condition. He recognized the signs of battening down in effect, but didn't have the expertise to pick out individual actions.

"Master Rating," he said to the sailor seated at the display. "Has the bridge been shielded yet?"

"Yes, sir," she replied immediately, continually tapping in changes to the display as reports came in through her headset.

She wore, Liam noted, the shoulder patch of a supply tech, not a propulsor. But she spoke into her headset with a practiced efficiency and manipulated the display controls like she'd designed them.

With the bridge shielded, the captain couldn't physically see the top mast, even if he happened to look up.

"Short-sail the top mast," he ordered Swift. "Enough to get the strain under control but not so much as to leave it with no tension."

Swift was barking orders even as Liam's final words were uttered. Propulsors leaped into action, scrambling up through the access chutes that lined each mast. Far above, Liam knew, they were reeling in sails and tying off loose sheet. The massive thrust block groaned as tension fled from the top mast. Slowly, on the main projection, red indicator lights for the top mast began to switch to yellow. Or at least enough of them did to reduce Liam's worry that he was going to lose a piece of the ship.

"That should do it," Liam said.

"For now," added Swift quietly. "But with three masts

still at full sail the imbalance from the top is just going to create new stresses. We need to shorten all masts."

"The captain requires us to get to Passagia with all haste. Short sailing will surely be noticed, even by him."

Swift hung on as the deck rocked again, but Liam could sense his mind churning the problem. The propulsor's eyes flicked between a variety of display boards.

"So what we need," Swift said slowly, "is a way to maintain the bridge's perception that we're at full sail?"

Liam glanced down at the master rating still seated at her display. She probably couldn't hear the conversation with her headset on.

"Ideally, yes," he replied to Swift. "What I really need is for our estimated arrival time to stay ahead of *Celebration*'s."

Spotting a general-purpose console, Liam brought up the navigation assessment that the captain was monitoring on the bridge. It showed ETAs for both ships. *Renaissance*'s was being fed by real-time information and fluctuated every second, but even in its fluctuations the ETA remained sooner than its rival's.

"You're kidding me," Swift muttered. "That's our mission—to beat *Celebration* to the ball?"

"Shut up," Liam snapped. "We have our orders. Tell me how we can do it and get there in one piece."

Swift considered.

"Internally, I can manually go into the sail parameters and reset them so that the readouts will make it look to the bridge like we're still at full sail even if we aren't." He tapped the navigation display. "But I can't change the laws of physics—our ETA will still be delayed."

The thrust block creaked again. New red indicators flashed to life on the bottom mast.

"Change the settings," Liam ordered, "but incrementally so there isn't a big jump on the bridge displays. Start with top mast, then adjust the others from there."

"What about the nav estimates?"

"I'll figure that out."

Swift stepped away, issuing orders before busying himself at a console.

Liam stared at the nav screen. The figure for *Renaissance*'s ETA at Passagia changed by the second, but stayed within a broad range that varied by no more than twelve hours. Even the short sailing of one mast had made an impact, a lengthening of the voyage time that was likely already tickling the captain's notice. When the shorting of the other three masts took effect, those numbers would take a dramatic turn. And even under current conditions *Renaissance* was only tracking ten hours ahead of *Celebration*.

Liam stared at the numbers, not yet sure how he was going to rewrite physics and preserve *Renaissance*'s perceived lead.

"Sir?"

The voice startled him out of his reverie. He glanced around, then down at the supply tech. She was staring up at him, her expression shy but determined.

"Yes, Master Rating?"

"One of the things we monitor in stores is the number of days left for each critical section of supply, which is dependent on how far we still have to go and how long it will take. We adjust it all the time—can't you do the same for the navigation?"

So much for not being overheard. As executive officer, he reviewed the estimated stores endurance every day. But he knew it was quite different from navigation.

"Those figures change because we adjust our burn-through rate of stores—my nav estimate is pure speed-time-distance. I can't adjust those."

"Sure you can! We adjust distance constantly, depending on where in its orbit our destination planet is."

The words to dismiss her suggestion were already forming in his throat. But then something made him pause. The nav estimate was by default based on the destination star, not the actual planet. If he could somehow change the distance parameters to reflect the planet . . .

"Do you know how to do that?"

She rose from her seat at the damage-control board and moved to stand next to him at the nav display. She opened up an obscure submenu and began typing in new values.

"I assume you want me to put the planet as close to us in its orbit as possible?" she asked.

"As close as the planetary limits will let you."

Within a dozen keystrokes, Liam saw the *Renaissance*'s ETA suddenly jump forward by six hours. It was a sizable jump, but still within the range of reasonable possibility. If Captain Silverhawk was watching, the new ETA would likely please him too much for him to question it.

The supply tech finished her manipulations and straightened, admiring her handiwork with a smile. A sudden lurch of the deck knocked her into Liam, who automatically steadied her in his arms. She held on for a brief moment, then regained her stance; she was still smiling as she looked up at him.

"Will that help solve the problem, sir?"

A sailor, even a senior rating, holding the XO's gaze for so long caught Liam off guard. But it was the warmth of her gaze that really caught his attention. He felt his pulse pick up slightly, and he looked away, nodding at the nav display.

"Lucky you were on watch."

She gave him a curious look, then glanced back at the damage-control board.

"Oh, I'm not, sir. I just couldn't sleep with all the pounding, so I came down to see if I could help."

Liam knew that supply techs often manned critical displays during battle stations, to free up the propulsors to do technical and emergency work. He noted the name tag sewn onto her uniform.

"Well, Master Rating Virtue, you've helped out a lot more than you know."

"Thank you, sir."

"And if you tell anyone about what just went down, I'll run you out of the Navy."

"Yes, sir."

The deck heaved again, the crosspiece groaning against sudden stress. Liam indicated for Virtue to retake her seat.

"If you have nothing else to do, Master Rating, I'd like you to stick around. It's going to be a long night." He wouldn't be moving from this spot. The crew needed to know that he was leading the charge to get *Renaissance* home safely.

"I'd rather be here," she said, "than strapped in my bunk and trusting the mast-monkeys to get me home."

She nodded at the propulsors all around her. Greasy, sweating, and scrambling to fulfill their duties, they cussed and shouted at each other but worked with diligent efficiency. He leaned in close, speaking just above a whisper.

"Watch your language, bin-rat. These mast-monkeys are the ones who're going to save your skin."

She turned to face him, large brown eyes glinting. "Like this bin-rat just saved yours, sir?"

He tried to frown, but it twisted into a smile.

"Call the galley," he ordered. "Have a rum ration sent down for everyone in propulsion."

"Yes, sir."

He surveyed the chaos of the scene around him. It was all madness, but they would make it through.

CHAPTER 2

"So, Mason," Liam asked, casting his eyes around the ballroom before turning back to Swift. "Knocking out a prince or knocking up a princess—which would be more fun?"

Over the rim of his third drink, Swift cast his eyes across the crowded ballroom. The polished, wooden floor was filled with small circles of chatting nobles as servants weaved with trays of drinks. Tables of food were laid out discreetly against every wall, beneath the banners of every noble house in the sector.

"I suppose, sir, if you did it in the right order you could do both."

Liam burst out laughing, and clapped his friend on the shoulder. "Well said."

The usual fops and dandies were prancing and parading in their extravagant outfits all around the great room, the men wearing more product than the ladies they worked to impress. The women were little better, wrapped in impossible ensembles that, through their very complexity, likely served as the best defense of chastity. In their small groups the ladies held court, the subtext of eye contact and subtle gestures easily overwhelming the dim hubbub of spoken words.

Captain Silverhawk was distinguishable from the fops only because of his naval uniform. He was in top spirits, having indeed beaten Captain Longridge to the ball, and in the snippets of conversation Liam had endured, *Renaissance* had apparently set a new speed record and weathered the most titanic solar storm in a century. The posturing was in full swing, with much false laughter and increasingly bold claims.

But in the middle of it all were the real stars of the show. Nothing less than an actual princess and her brother the prince, arrived from the home world just yesterday to oversee some series of local celebrations. Neither was a close heir to the Imperial throne—children of one of the Emperor's younger offspring, apparently—but they were still considered royal, and therefore they commanded the evening simply by showing up. Their pure white clothing stood in stark contrast to the obsidian quality of their royal skin, and even in the crowded ballroom there was a deferential distance maintained around them. He was a reedy, petulant thing who looked ready to take offense; she was pretty enough and didn't seem yet of an age to have become jaded by the constant attention of suitors.

"But then," Liam said as he sipped the last of his rum, "you'd probably be hanged, and that wouldn't be fun."

"Me? I thought you were intending the escapade, sir."

"I learned my lesson long ago, Mason. Leave the shenanigans to the great nobles and the foolish youth."

"Aren't they one and the same?"

"Mind your acid tongue," he said with a smile.

"If you insist on dragging me to these things, sir, acid is part of the deal."

Swift was definitely more at home in the grubby bowels of a ship in space than at a foppish ball, but Liam had long ago learned to appreciate his friend's unfiltered view of the world. He'd done a damn fine job getting them through that storm, as always, but as Liam's mind drifted back to the hellish scene, he kept picturing the moment Master Rating Virtue was thrown into his arms by the swells.

"Perhaps I should have brought that bin-rat who was so helpful to us during the storm," he mused.

"Virtue? I get the feeling she'd eat that prince for breakfast."

"She did have a rapier wit."

"Shame she's not in my department. If we even have a ship anymore."

Liam glanced over, knowing that there was no one in the fleet who better understood the damage to *Renaissance* than Swift.

"Quite."

A new burst of laughter caught his attention and almost against his will he looked over to where Captain Silverhawk was trading gibes with a new arrival—a younger man, also in uniform. They were likely related, the youth sharing Silverhawk's impressive height, sandy hair, and sharp features. Despite their vast difference in military rank, the two men carried on like old friends, their collective wit apparently hilarious to the surrounding suitors.

Silverhawk suddenly looked over at Liam. Their eyes met and the captain motioned him over.

Cursing himself for even looking in that direction,

Liam silently smoothed his dress uniform and wove his way through the crowd.

"Good evening, sir," he said with a slight bow.

"Ah, Blackwood. Allow me to introduce my cousin, Lord Highcastle. He's just arrived here on Passagia and is looking for a good ship. Naturally I'd bring him aboard *Renaissance,* but I fear we ran her a bit hard, eh? Find him another one—a ship that's going to see some action."

"And I'm not sailing with that beastly Longridge," young Highcastle added. Liam noted his rank of cadet—not even a graduate of the Naval Academy yet.

"Oh, stars, no!" Silverhawk laughed. "Blackwood, don't send my cousin anywhere near that blowhard."

Amid a scattering of mean-spirited laughter, Liam bowed again.

"I'll look into it right away, sir."

"That's all." Silverhawk had already forgotten Liam was there, beginning some new tale for his cousin about adventure in the Navy.

Liam slipped away, finding Swift over at one of the tables laid out with pastries and sweets.

"I remember now why I agreed to come," Swift said, mouth stuffed with cake. "Good food."

"And the free drinks," Liam muttered, catching the eye of a servant and motioning for another rum.

His own status as second child of a minor lord here on Passagia didn't count for much in this crowd, although he couldn't help but notice a pair of ladies hovering nearby. They giggled behind their fans and glanced at his and Swift's uniforms with barely concealed admiration before flitting away.

"And the pretty girls," Swift added, reaching for another treat.

Liam's past enjoyed the occasional sweet treat, and he certainly wasn't averse to the company of a pretty girl; but he'd always figured it would be through naval service that he'd earn his reputation, and it was for this reason, he knew, that he'd really come to this party.

Liam's gaze chased the crowd until he saw the host of the ball making his way through the crowd, his uniform dark and elegant amid all the foppish finery of the civilians. Rear Admiral Lord William Grandview was also a second son, but his noble house owned more of Passagia than all the others put together. The young nobles seemed to part before him even as he made to move. In middle age and at the height of his influence, Admiral Grandview was a man worth knowing.

"Ah," Swift said, finally looking up from the dessert table, "your patron approaches."

"Make yourself scarce, Mason."

"I'll entertain those pretty girls, sir. Permission to carry on?"

"Yes, please."

Liam accepted his new drink from the servant and watched as Grandview somehow managed to offer compliments and due respect to everyone he passed while barely slowing his pace. His eyes were on Liam, and in that gaze, there was a military focus rarely seen planetside.

"Subcommander Lord Blackwood," he boomed while still several courtiers distant. "How nice of you to join us this evening."

Liam straightened instinctively, his slow nod practically a bow as he noticed the sudden, jealous eyes of various ambitious dandies shift to him.

"You honor me, Lord Grandview, with your invitation."

Barely checking his stride, Grandview took Liam's elbow and led him clear of the crowd. They walked at a casual pace, but the tightness of the man's grip made Liam suddenly wonder if he'd broken some obscure social protocol and embarrassed his host.

"Sorry to hear about *Renaissance*," Grandview said amiably, barely glancing down at him. "Thanks for bringing her back in one piece."

"Captain Silverhawk is an excellent navigator," Liam answered automatically. "It was a bold maneuver."

"It was idiocy of the highest order," the admiral muttered. "I'm grateful to you, Liam, that I don't now have to explain to the Imperial court why their newest warship was destroyed on a routine passage."

"You're very kind, sir."

"There's someone I'd like you to meet," the admiral continued, steering them toward the edge of the room. "Could be a good opportunity for a talented officer like you."

Liam felt a rush of relief. Despite his best efforts, *Renaissance* was badly damaged, and would likely be out of active commission for several months. Her refit could be hidden as a routine work period, but questions were likely, and Captain Silverhawk certainly wasn't going to take the blame. Liam knew he needed to get as far from that mess as possible.

"Lord Grandview," came a new voice. Liam felt the admiral slow to a stop, still holding his arm. Glancing toward the voice, he saw an older gentleman dressed in a ribbed surcoat of the finest red velvet, adorned with a gold sash. His hands were nearly lost in white lace as they reached out to grip Grandview's extended palm.

"Lord Redfort," Grandview said with genuine warmth. "Thank you for coming."

"Your generosity exceeds all protocols, as always," the older man said. The crest on his sash revealed to Liam that he was a senior member of the Imperial diplomatic corps. "Although your attempted theft of my finest naval officer is hooliganism of the highest order."

The gentle smile on Redfort's face robbed the words of any malice, but Liam still looked quickly to Grandview for a response. The admiral beamed indulgently.

"My lord ambassador, it's impossible for me to steal someone who never belonged to you. An officer of the Navy is sworn to serve the Emperor in battles of cannons, not words."

"And I fear that cannons are very soon going to replace words in our dealings with the Sectoids." Redfort's diplomatic façade was in full force, but even Liam could see that the ambassador was not pleased.

Grandview suddenly released Liam with a gentle push toward one of the arched entrances to the ballroom.

"Head to my study, lad—first door on the left—and wait for me there."

The admiral placed an arm around Redfort and led him away, speaking quietly but with earnest.

Liam didn't hesitate, and strode out into the cool dark of the corridor. Not twenty paces and he saw the study door, held open, dim lights glowing from within. As he stepped inside, he breathed in the pleasant scents of wood and spice. One of the moons sparkled through the tall windows on the far wall, a fixed point against the scattering of moving lights in the sky. At this time of year

Passagia's orbit took it to the dark side of the system, where the eerie blackness of deep space consumed the usual brilliance of the sky. The Grandview estate was perched high on a plateau, above the fog so common at the surface, and Liam took a moment to appreciate the beautiful, dark clarity of the night.

In front of the windows he saw the dim shapes of the admiral's workstation, his eyes drawn to the moonlight that glinted off a scale model on one side of the desk. He recognized the familiar lines of the battleship *Vigilance* wrought expertly in glass, and he stepped forward to observe it more closely, entranced. The vessel was displayed in full sail, of course, all four masts extended and the dozens of sheets billowing forward in an eternal stern wind. The chaos of the cluster rarely allowed for such simple sailing, but it was the classic image of a solar sailing ship and no doubt how Lord Grandview wished to remember his final command.

"Dreaming she might be yours, one day?"

The low, female voice startled him from his examination of the model. To his left was a cluster of armchairs, flanked by several table lamps emitting warm pools of light. And in one of the chairs, watching him with a neutral expression, was a woman in a naval uniform.

She didn't rise as he slowly approached. Indeed, not a muscle in her body shifted in her upright posture, hands resting in her lap, one leg crossed over the other. She was in full dress uniform, as he was, and her decorations and qualifications indicated a rank of commander—a step above him.

"Good evening, ma'am," he offered. "I was asked by Rear Admiral Grandview to come to his study."

"Are you Subcommander Blackwood?" she asked. At

his nod she lifted a hand to gesture at the chair facing her. "Take a seat."

There were no name tags on dress uniforms, and as he settled his drink on the side table Liam studied her face, trying to recall if they'd met before. She looked about his age, perhaps slightly younger, though there was little sense of youth in her olive features. Her black hair was tied back efficiently, revealing a square face that would have been attractive if it wasn't set in a heavy frown. Her brown eyes were bright, but hard, and they remained fixed on him in assessment.

"You're old to be a subcommander," she said, accent revealing enough to mark her as nobility. But she was not from one of the major houses, and not from here on Passagia.

"In this sector of the Empire I'm actually considered young for my rank." Her expression remained frozen, and Liam was irritated by the flush in his own cheeks. "Perhaps your own rise is exceptional, ma'am."

"Not particularly. What was your specialization as a junior officer?"

"I was boarding party, in addition to my regular duties."

"Have you ever fought hand to hand?"

"Yes, ma'am."

"Did you ever conduct intelligence gathering?"

"Yes."

"How does a nobleman hide effectively amid the common folk?"

"With great care, ma'am." He felt no need to explain himself to this woman.

"You're a member of the local peerage, though. Why has that not seen you already in command?"

Liam paused, fighting down his growing resentment.

"Noble titles aren't a consideration to advancement in this sector."

She rested a finger against her chin, studying him with an intensity that made him uncomfortable.

"I'd naturally be suspect of any noble-born officer still at your rank at your age," she said. "Have you ever been charged with a crime? Were you demoted?"

The weight of Liam's tunic seemed to close in on him, the heat rising in his chest. Being passed over for promotion because of highborn fops being dropped into command didn't technically count as demotion, but it certainly felt like it.

"Out here in the Halo, we actually get promoted based on merit." He meant to stop there, but the three drinks already in his bloodstream pushed him on. "If you don't like that, you can take it up with the admiral. I don't give a damn what you think—I've earned my rank, unlike a lot of more senior officers. Ma'am."

He was only heartbeats away from rising and making his exit, but the sudden softening of the commander's features held him in his seat.

"And from what I understand from the admiral, you've done a good job of keeping those senior officers out of trouble. Although I understand Captain Mistvale still holds a grudge."

Silverhawk wasn't the first idiot Liam had bailed out of a jam, but being a fop minder wasn't really how he wanted to be known.

"I just do my job, ma'am."

"By incurring the wrath of your commanding officer?"

"I'd rather that than lose the ship."

She sat back, her expression amused. "Empire before self?"

"A lesson I think many of our noble peers would do well to remember," he snapped.

"I agree."

That surprised him, and his next retort died on his lips.

"You serve the Empire above all, Subcommander Blackwood?"

He wasn't sure if she was smiling at him, but the entire tone of the conversation had suddenly shifted.

"Yes, ma'am."

"Have you ever dealt personally with the other races?"

"I've met plenty of brutes, but the bugs I've only seen in their ships from a distance. The others, no."

"What do you think of them? The other races?"

He shrugged. "What's to think? The brutes are mostly harmless if they're making money, and the bugs need to be held at bay."

"Why do the Sectoids need to be held at bay?" Her use of the race's official name wasn't lost on him, nor the narrowing of her eyes.

"We don't know much about them," he said carefully, "but it seems like every interaction we have with them is violent. It's probably best if we stick to our space and they stick to theirs."

"Is that how you deal with every unknown in life? Just push it away?"

"No, ma'am, but you were asking me about the Sectoids."

"In your role as Captain Silverhawk's executive officer, how do you deal with the unknown?"

"Each case is different. I assess what our mission was, and how best I can work through the unknowns to succeed."

"Are you command qualified?"

"Yes, ma'am."

"Are you married?"

Liam's fingers closed on the armrests with an iron grip. He seemed to be facing yet another entitled noble, with an easy arrogance and no sense of personal boundaries. But even so, he sensed something in her that held his interest. She was clearly intelligent, and she was watching him with specific intent, which he struggled to fathom.

"Why?" he said. A sudden smile crossed his lips. "Do you have a proposition for me?"

Her laugh was surprisingly musical, and the coldness in her eyes sparkled away. "I think the admiral has one for both of us, if he's managed to convince Lord Redfort to let me go," she said as she snapped a communicator free from her belt and typed a brief message. "But are you tied down here planetside?"

"No. I'm actually looking for a new ship, since *Renaissance* is going into refit."

"I hear you set a new speed record—why not slow down if the ship was at risk?"

"You'll have to ask Captain Silverhawk."

She nodded, her eyes dangerously close to rolling.

He swallowed the last of his drink, noting the wet bar in the wall behind her. "Can I get you a brandy, ma'am?"

"Yes, thank you. And pour one for the admiral too."

Rising from his chair, he crossed the hardwood floor and reached for the decanter of deep amber liquid. "I didn't catch your name, ma'am?" he asked as he measured three generous glasses.

She rose from her chair and came forward to take the proffered glass. She was nearly as tall as he was, and walked as though she was used to commanding attention. "Sophia Riverton. Commander."

Her emphasis on the rank wasn't lost on Liam.

"Liam Blackwood," he said, touching his glass to hers, "subcommander."

They drank, but before he could think of something witty to say, he noticed a flourish at the study door. Rear Admiral Grandview stepped into view. But instead of the typical room-filling pronouncement, he simply nodded to them both before gesturing for them to sit. Liam handed him a brandy and did so.

"I gather you're getting along," Grandview commented.

"Yes, sir," Riverton said. "He'll do fine, thank you."

"Good."

Liam was used to senior officers talking over and past him, but he appreciated it less and less each year. "I'll do fine for what, sir?"

"A new kind of mission, Subcommander. One which requires able, freethinking officers who aren't afraid to take risks."

"I think I fit that description, sir."

"Because there will be risks," Grandview continued as if Liam hadn't spoken, his face hardening. "And not just the kind you're used to."

"You intrigue me, sir."

Grandview glanced at Riverton. The commander set down her drink and sat back. "I think we're both ready to hear the details, sir," she said.

The admiral pulled out a palm-sized device and placed it on the table between them. He activated it. A soft crackle pulsed through the air, followed by a faint whine that grew higher in pitch until it vanished beyond audible range. Liam recognized the effects of the dissonator as it masked the room from any surveillance equipment.

"You've both probably heard rumors, but let me state

it plain: war with the Sectoids is imminent, and we aren't ready. The Emperor has ordered every warship to be prepared for action, and all supply lines to be cleared.

"We're having particular difficulties in the Silica sector. Intelligence suggests that there is a coordinated effort among the pirates to disrupt His Majesty's commerce, and that they're operating from a fixed base somewhere within Silica. Their attacks are becoming more brazen—and more damaging—but whenever we send in a large warship to investigate, the pirates vanish. This suggests that either they have spies active within our own hierarchy or they have a way of detecting our major vessels at a distance. Whatever the cause, our traditional methods are completely failing, and we no longer have the luxury of time to figure out why.

"What I'm charging you with, Commander Riverton, is to quietly take command of one of our test ships, *Daring,* and undertake a very unconventional kind of mission. And you, Subcommander Blackwood, will be the executive officer."

Liam kept his face neutral, fighting down a long-burning frustration that was getting difficult to ignore. Second-in-command, again. Assistant to another captain who would take all the glory, again.

"Does this mission involve fighting the Sectoids?" Riverton asked, with a sudden edge to her voice.

"Your mission is to clear out these pirates and open the trade lanes so that we can reinforce our fleet if war comes." He leaned forward, expression grim. "Which it may sooner rather than later, and if so, there will be plenty of opportunity to fight the bugs."

"I'm saddened to hear that," Riverton said quietly.

Liam glanced sideways at that curious comment. Was

she saddened to hear that she might have to fight Sectoids, or not have the chance to? There was an intensity in her expression that struck him as misplaced in this conversation.

"There will be the usual risks you would expect in a Navy mission," Grandview continued, "but there is one more risk which you must understand. This mission is top secret, and it has been debated considerably among the admiralty. Many of my peers don't agree with it, and if it fails then they will do everything they can to denounce you as rogues, and denounce me as mad. The Emperor has given his consent, but only if we succeed. If this mission fails, it will be the end of our careers."

Liam froze. Even members of the nobility could be dishonorably discharged from service if their actions embarrassed the crown—Grandview's comment was more than an idle exaggeration. He glanced to Riverton beside him and noted the cold set of her features.

"That's quite a risk," she said slowly. "One I'm not sure I'm willing to take . . . unless adequately compensated."

"I agree," the admiral replied. "Which is why I convinced the Emperor to grant those of us involved in this mission a very special motivation, ideal for taking down pirates."

Riverton's stony expression shifted into a predatory smile. "Prize money?"

Grandview nodded.

"According to the traditional split?" she asked.

"Yes."

Liam glanced between them. Prize money? As in, the crew kept the value of the cargo seized? He did a quick calculation of what an XO's share might be. It might even be enough for him to buy his own ship . . . He cleared his throat. "But, sir," he said, "there hasn't been prize money awarded in a generation. How can we make a claim like that?"

"I have a letter with the Imperial seal stating that it shall be honored, for this mission." He sat back. "None of us here are going to inherit our ancestral estates—what better way to secure our futures than through service to the Empire? Take down those pirates, and you will be both honored and rich."

"But if we fail, we'll be dishonored and destitute," Liam pointed out.

"Risk versus reward, Liam. The question is, do you think you'll succeed, or fail?"

"I don't think I'd be sitting here if you thought I'd fail."

"I'm betting my own career on this too. I'm betting it on you"—his gaze shifted to Riverton—"and your captain."

"What sort of support will I have?" Riverton asked.

"You'll be acting independently of Navy command, and posing as a civilian merchantman. Replenish on your own, and stay clear of other Navy ships. Your orders are directly from the Emperor, through me."

"Rules of engagement?"

"You have a free hand, Commander, provided you succeed in your mission."

Riverton turned her head, her gaze pinning Liam where he sat. Her eyes flickered down and up, assessing him once again. "Are you up for this, Subcommander?" she asked.

Liam paused long enough for his two superiors to think he was deeply considering. But he already knew his answer. Sit around on Passagia on half pay waiting for another commission while the threat of the *Renaissance* disaster loomed, or risk everything on a bold adventure that promised riches? It was hardly a difficult choice. "Yes, ma'am."

Riverton rose to her feet, extending her hand to the admiral. "Lord Grandview," she said quietly, "my executive officer and I accept this commission."

CHAPTER 3

It was the fog that she hated the most. Huddling under her cloak, Amelia Virtue quickened her pace along the wet cobblestones, weaving through the mass of shuffling townsfolk. On either side, the buildings sagged inward; the glow of lights escaping from behind curtains, and the occasional streetlamp, making the street bright enough to navigate. Pools of water lay in the broken surface of the stone, splashing against her boots with each step. Her feet were already cold, and even with her cloak the damp chill of the fog was seeping into her bones. Life aboard a Navy ship might be cramped and sterile, but at least it was warm and dry. Passagia II was blessed with more water than anyone knew what to do with, but Amelia wished it would just stay in the oceans and not hang about in the air like soup.

Through the gloom, she spotted the hanging sign of the Laughing Boar. Flickering light spilled out through its iron-framed front windows and as she approached the heavy wooden door swung open to disgorge a trio of merrymakers. She slipped past them, reveling in the wave of warmth that engulfed her as she stepped into the room. She breathed in the mingled scent of tavern fare and ale, of smoke and unwashed people; the large, dim interior was bustling with activity, tables crowded and a mass of patrons hugging the bar on the far wall. Sailors, mostly, Amelia reckoned, based on the general air of bravado and the number of empty flagons littering the space. *Renaissance* wasn't the only ship to have recently returned to port, and the Laughing Boar was a fleet favorite.

Amelia dropped the hood of her cloak and wiped the moisture from her face. She spotted her friends after another quick scan of the room and angled toward them. At her size, there was no way she could muscle other patrons out of her way, but she had long ago learned the fine art of dodging through a crowd. Staying low and quick had kept her alive many times growing up, especially when she'd clasped a fat purse recently liberated from a market toff.

Emerging at the table, she spotted a slight opening between the stools of a man and a woman. Placing a hand on each of their shoulders, she grinned down at them.

"Any space at the table for a poor, drowned bin-rat?"

Mia Hedge returned the grin, shifting over on her stool and patting the exposed wood. She looked much more relaxed than when Amelia had last seen her on board *Renaissance,* her dirty-blond hair spilling over bare shoulders. And there was something odd about her attire.

"Are you wearing a dress?" Amelia blurted in shock.

Hedge rose from her seat and offered a half curtsy, laughing as she sat down again. "I always do on the first night ashore."

"Why?"

"Because I can," Hedge said triumphantly, reaching for her tankard and taking a deep pull.

Amelia squeezed in next to her, wrapping an affectionate arm around her friend's shoulders. She glanced to her other side and saw Atticus Flatrock peering down at them. His girth spilled over both sides of his own stool, his wry smile barely visible through the mass of dark beard hiding most of his face.

"What I really want to see," Amelia said, "is this old space dog in a dress!"

Flatrock barked a laugh. "Not saying it's never happened," he retorted, "but only for the right audience."

A rumble of laughter erupted around the table. Nearly a dozen men and women were crowded around, ranging in age from the young lad who'd probably be passed out after two drinks to the grizzled old coot who kept smoothing the last silver wisps on his bald head. Amelia vaguely recognized only a few faces, but she joined in the banter like an old friend.

Some of the sailors were discussing how they had signed on with *Inspiration,* the cruiser docked just aft of *Renaissance* at the orbital yard high above them. She was preparing for a deployment against a reported Sectoid incursion into Human space.

"You really think you're going to see combat against the bugs?" Amelia asked.

"Maybe," one of the women answered. Her face seemed permanently fixed in a scowl.

"You better hope not," the old coot warned. "I've heard enough stories of the bugs to make me never join a ship which plans on chasing them."

The *Inspiration* sailors scoffed, but Amelia knew there

was truth in the old man's words. At least, if the rumors she'd heard were true.

"What kind of stories?" the young lad asked, downing the last of his ale and reaching for a new tankard.

"I've heard," the old coot said, leaning in, "that the bugs have arms like swords, so fast that you don't even see them strike. If you still have your head on your shoulders, the only thing you'll see is one of your arms hitting the deck."

"That's if they get close enough for blades," Amelia added, enjoying the look of fear growing on the lad's face. "Apparently they can spit acid from five paces that will burn your flesh to the bone."

"And they come in such numbers," Flatrock added, "that even if you kill ten of them, ten more will be there to take their place."

"Nobody's fought the bugs in hand-to-hand in a generation," snapped the woman from *Inspiration*. "They just hide on their giant ships and interfere with our trade."

"Something's changed," the old coot warned. "There's a lot more bug ships being sighted in Human space. Why do you think you're heading out?"

A tense silence fell over the table for a moment.

"Well," Amelia said to break the spell, "maybe we can just pay the brutes to fight them for us."

This got a laugh from some.

"I think the brutes are cute," Hedge said. "Like really big dogs, but with no fur, and small heads, and big tails . . ."

"And scales, and claws, and walking on two feet," Flatrock added.

"Yeah, yeah—so just like big dogs."

"Except nothing like them."

"Shut up."

Amelia laughed. She'd been in the Navy long enough to see a few worlds beyond Passagia, but she'd never met one of the other races. They mostly kept to themselves, except for the odd brute looking to make easy money. And with *Renaissance* in the shape she was in after that storm, Amelia doubted there would be much travel in her near future.

"So what's this I hear about your captain dashing his own ship against the maelstrom?" the old coot suddenly asked, eyeing Amelia and her two shipmates.

Amelia heard Flatrock snort in disdain. As much as she might want to, though, she was under orders not to discuss the details of the incident. "Yes," she opined, thinking quickly. "When ship captains decide to do dangerous things, do they really understand the true implications of their actions?"

"What?"

"Consider syrup," Amelia continued, pausing for a quick sip of ale. "It might not sound like much, but it's a crew favorite. And as the section head of food storage, I have a lot of it."

"That's true." Hedge sighed, remembering.

"And when heavy weather causes the storage units to buckle, syrup escapes." Amelia smirked at the confused looks around the table.

"So, you're saying," Hedge said, "that Captain Silverhawk should have considered the syrup before taking us into that storm?"

"Don't underestimate it. That stuff is slow, but relentless."

"I hear you and Hedgie spent twelve hours scraping that stuff off the deck this morning," Flatrock scoffed.

"It was a slow onslaught of leaking, seeping sweetness." She was rewarded with smiles and a few guffaws.

"Stupid is what it was!" Hedge snapped. "Nearly got us all killed, and just so his majestic captain lordness could dance with a princess!"

Scoffs of disapproval sounded from around the table.

"Come on," challenged the young lad, high with drunken courage. "There had to be a better reason than that. No captain would be that dumb."

"Virts," Hedge said, elbowing Amelia, "tell 'em."

"It's true," she admitted, realizing that at least that part of the incident was already widely known. "The captain wanted to beat *Celebration* back so that he could have the first dance with some princess who's visiting."

"That's the craziest thing I've ever heard!" shouted the lad, rising to his feet in indignation.

"Are you insulting my captain?" Flatrock roared, bursting upward and sending his stool flying backward.

The lad started, obviously unsure how to respond. Amelia could see the amused gleam in Flatrock's eye, but she kept quiet, watching to see if the kid would take the bait. Finally, he sat down again.

"No, sorry."

"Oh, come on!" Flatrock guffawed. "I was looking for a reason to fight."

"Say"—Hedge leaned on Amelia and pointed past her to another table—"aren't those folks from *Celebration*?"

"Yeah," said one of the other sailors at the table, "I think they are."

Amelia felt Hedge's body tense.

"Hedgie . . . ," she warned, "you're wearing a dress."

"Gives me more mobility in my arms." She pushed up and climbed onto the table.

Amelia sighed; she was too tired for this tonight. Flat-rock was still on his feet, motioning the lad to stand up and glare at the other table.

"Hey, *Celebration*," Hedge screeched, loud enough to be heard across the entire tavern. "Nice to see you finally sneak into port!"

Some of the sailors looked up. One of them threw a vague cuss back at her. Flatrock stepped forward, calling him out for the insult. A few *Celebration* sailors rose to their feet.

"Oh," Amelia said, slipping down off the stool to crawl under the table, "for the love of . . ."

"All of us from *Renaissance* have been here for hours," Hedge continued, "and I bet our captain's already in bed with the princess. Your captain's probably in the royal kitchens, scrubbing dishes!"

It was a lame insult, but in the powder keg of the first night ashore, it was all that was needed. Amelia saw boots scrambling and stools tumbling as sailors charged each other. The roar of a brawl erupted. Amelia heard three quick thumps above her, then heard Hedge's battle cry as she launched herself into the fray.

Amelia gave it a few moments, then grabbed her cloak and crawled out from under the now-empty side of the table. More sailors were running to join the fray, but no one noticed her as she kept low and headed for the door. Throwing her cloak over her shoulders, she glanced back once at the melee. Flatrock was still on his feet, huge fists swinging, and Hedge was momentarily visible in a tussle across one of the tables. Whether she was fighting her opponent or kissing him wasn't clear from this distance. Amelia couldn't help but laugh. Flipping her hood up, she stepped out into the cold.

The roar of the tavern was silenced as the heavy door slammed behind her, and the quiet stillness of the foggy street was a shock. Amelia stood for a moment, watching as a few townsfolk shuffled or strode past, the last of the common workers heading home. The cold surrounded her in moments. The tiny room she rented above one of the shops was far enough away from Tavern Row to give her some peace, but on a night like this she wished it was just next door.

Dark forms huddled against the building fronts, curled up against the chill.

"Spare a copper?" one of them called to her. The deepness of his voice caught her attention.

Her eyes flicked down. The man was hidden under his ragged cloak, but his lean form was obvious beneath the sodden wool. He was probably starving, and with winter coming, he'd suffer terribly. She paused long enough to pull out a coin and drop it in the cup at his curled-up feet.

"Bless you, milady," he whispered.

She stepped away, not wanting to loiter too long as the streets were starting to empty. It would be a few hours before the hordes of drunken sailors spilled forth from the taverns, and she knew from long experience that it was this depth of the quiet night when single travelers were most at risk. Hearing a soft shuffle of movement behind her, she quickened her pace.

The beggars she passed were mostly lying down, curled up to sleep as best they could. She passed a few townsfolk without meeting their eyes, not wanting to invite or provoke any trouble. She noticed that a man was walking in the same direction as her on the far side of the street, a heavy cloak obscuring his features. He didn't

look up, and she eventually overtook him, but she kept
an eye on him the entire time. Something told her that he
was keeping an eye on her too.

She splashed through a rising trickle of water draining
down the street, quickening her pace. The fog seemed to
muffle sounds, but she could make out at least two other
sets of footfalls behind her. They were neither quick nor
close, but she tracked them carefully.

The fog was getting thicker, with several blocks still
to go. Normally when she was being followed she'd take
a random route and lose any pursuers in order to avoid
revealing where she lived. But all she wanted right now
was to get back into the warm and dry. She glanced over
her left shoulder at the man across the street, wondering
if she should just dash back to the Laughing Boar and ask
one of her shipmates to walk her home.

Suddenly hands grabbed her from the other side.
She was pulled into the entrance of a narrow alley, and
felt the hard slam of stone against her back as she was
pushed up against a wall. An angry-looking youth filled
her vision, his forearm pressing her back as he bran-
dished a dagger.

"If you have money for beggars," he hissed, "then you
have money for me. Give me your purse."

She fought down the shock and anger of getting caught
out, and reached under her cloak. Her hand closed on her
sailor's knife.

"Come on," the thief snapped, "or I'll cut your face."

She wrenched her arm out, slashing the blade of her
knife across his chest. He cried out in pain, stumbling
backward and clutching at the wound. She lunged forward, punching him square in the face and sidestepping

his desperate stab with the dagger. Her kick crashed down into the side of his knee, sending him staggering to the ground. His weapon skittered away across the cobblestones, coming to rest at a pair of boots.

She looked up, and saw the tall, thin form of the beggar she'd given the copper to. His ragged cloak looked ready to fall apart, but his stance was guarded and steady. One of his hands was reaching for what Amelia could now clearly see was a sword, but he froze as he met Amelia's eyes, and for a moment Amelia and the figure simply stared at each other over the groaning form of the thief. Then the man she'd spotted from across the street appeared out of the shadows, pausing next to the beggar. Glancing between the two of them, Amelia lowered into a fighting stance and raised her knife. "I want no trouble," she warned. "But I will defend myself."

The two cloaked figures stood in silence as Amelia's words were swallowed by the silence of the fog.

Then the beggar dropped the hood of his cloak.

"Master Rating Virtue," he said in his deep voice, "stand down, if you please."

She blinked, looking closer even as she kept the knife ready. The voice did sound familiar, but his face was shadowed . . . but as she studied him, she slowly recognized the elegant cut of his dark hair, short on the back and sides in the military way with a bit of stylish length at the top. The beggar wasn't thin, she suddenly realized as he stood up to his full height, but lean with muscle.

"Lord Blackwood," she said, unsure if it was appropriate to either curtsy or knuckle her forehead, considering the situation.

"You're clearly capable of defending yourself," he said. His tone was mild, and difficult to interpret. "Lieutenant

Swift and I were moving to your aid, but I see now our efforts weren't required."

The other cloaked figure dropped his hood, and she recognized the shaved head of *Renaissance*'s propulsion officer. He collected the dagger at their feet, then manhandled the thief out into the street. Blackwood didn't move, his gaze staying on her the entire time.

"Yes, sir," she said finally, moving closer so that she could see his expression in the dim light. His high cheekbones shone in the streetlights and above his sharp, smooth chin his smile was easy and confident, just as she remembered from *Renaissance*'s propulsion room. She felt her cheeks flush as his eyes held hers, but she quickly brushed it off as simply the adrenaline after the fight. "Thank you, sir."

"Thank *you*," he said, reaching under his cloak and offering her back her coin. "Not many passersby are so generous to beggars."

She took the coin instinctively, still trying to process the fact that she was standing in a dark alley with two officers, one of whom was a lord.

"How may I serve you, sir?" she asked.

"First," he said with a bit of a smirk, "I request that you stop pointing that knife at me."

She glanced down and saw that she still hadn't relaxed from her defensive posture. Cheeks flushing, she pocketed the knife and squared her shoulders.

"Do you have a few minutes to chat with us privately?" he asked.

"Of course, sir."

He gestured for her to accompany him back onto the street and he fell in beside her as they walked, Swift following a few paces behind.

"You didn't stay long at the Laughing Boar," he commented. "I understand it's usually a lot of fun."

"I wasn't in the mood for brawling this evening," she answered, then remembered she was addressing a noble. "I mean—there was a fight and I wanted no part of it, my lord."

"I find it's often a good way to release stress after a long deployment, especially after what we've been through, lately."

She kept her eyes on the street, not sure how to answer. The soft thud of their boots against the cobblestones was the only sound. He seemed content to simply walk beside her.

"Do you often pose as a beggar on a damp street at night, my lord?" she finally asked.

"I've discovered that beggars are the people no one notices, present company excluded," he said with a hand on her shoulder, "and it gives me a reason to wait outside a building without drawing suspicion."

"Why were you waiting outside the Laughing Boar?"

"To meet you." She stopped dead at this, turning to face him. His expression was friendly and serene, as if this sort of thing was commonplace. "Thank you for leaving early—it was getting a bit cold."

Lord Blackwood was looking for her? Amelia's pulse quickened, and she wasn't sure if it was in interest or fear.

"Am I in trouble, sir?"

"Not at all," he said.

Her gaze drifted down his tall, lean form. A grin tugged at her lips. "So why are you looking for me in the middle of the night?"

"I've been assigned to a new vessel," he said quietly, "and since she's just coming back into commission we're assembling an entirely new crew. I've been thinking about who from *Renaissance* I might like to keep serving with, and I thought of you."

Her eyes shot up to meet his. His rugged features were softened by an easy smile.

"You'd like me to go to a new ship?" she asked.

"As part of my crew. No doubt we'll be drawing from the manning lists to make up the balance, but the captain and I certainly have some choice in who we bring aboard."

"Is Captain Silverhawk taking this new ship?"

"No," he scoffed, just a bit too openly. His features settled back into a carefully neutral expression, polite smile returning. "We will have the honor of serving under Commander Sophia Riverton."

Amelia had never heard of Riverton, but she couldn't be any worse than Silverhawk. Her name suggested that she was nobility, but pretty much any ship captain had blue blood in His Majesty's Navy.

"May I ask what ship, sir?"

"The frigate *Daring*. She's an older vessel but she's just come out of refit with some new gear. I think it will be a very rewarding commission, and I need top people to join me. Are you interested, Master Rating Virtue?"

"Yes, sir," she said immediately, realizing that she'd done nothing but ask questions so far. "Thank you for thinking of me—I'm honored."

"You did tremendous work during that storm, far beyond what you were required to do."

He gave her an appraising look, and she was suddenly very aware of her matted hair, old cloak, and bloody knuckles. But his expression was still maddeningly polite, with no hint of any trickery.

"Thank you, sir," she finally said. "You're too kind."

"So do you feel up to running a department on your own?"

"Excuse me, sir?"

"I'm offering you the position of quartermaster aboard *Daring*." His smile finally turned into a genuine grin. He offered her a crisp, folded parchment. "And with that comes a promotion to petty officer. Are you interested?"

She opened the parchment, and saw to her amazement that it was a letter of promotion signed by Blackwood himself. Despite her best efforts, she couldn't stop her own matching grin from bursting forth. A ticket off *Renaissance,* a promotion, and the chance to get away from this damp chill?

"Count me in, sir."

THE NEXT MORNING, AMELIA THREW ON HER UNI-form and went straight to the Navy base. Fortified, stone walls ringed the entire facility, brick buildings emerging through the fog as she followed the morning gaggle of sailors reporting for duty. Her first stop was at the uniform shop, where she presented her parchment and was rewarded with the rank of petty officer. Then she headed for the sky-ladder.

The ladder cars trundled along their tracks at regular intervals, and with few sailors milling about this morning she was able to quickly secure a seat in the next utilitarian car. The doors hissed shut behind her and the car rattled along horizontally as it lined up for the ascent. Her stomach lurched, as it always did, when the car first lifted off the ground, but she took slow, deep breaths and adjusted to the strange feeling of flying. For the first minute the fog obscured any view. Then came the moment she loved most, when the car pierced the fog and broke free into the clear sky. The bank of clouds glowed pink in the morning sunlight and in the far distance she could see mountain peaks rising high above the lowlands. The car continued to accelerate, the view revealing more and more of Passagia even as details shrank away from sight. It was a blue and gray world, rarely noted in Imperial literature for its beauty, but it was Amelia's home and she felt a fondness in her heart for it—even if she was glad to escape it for a while.

The sky-ladder reached far above the life-sustaining blanket of air around Passagia, up into the cold vacuum of orbit and the Navy's dockyard. The car slowed, then jerked to a stop before sliding onto horizontal rails and shunting into position on the docks.

Amelia sprang out onto the hard surface of the broad jetty; all around her was the bustle of a busy port. Giant cranes trundled slowly past, ferrying huge nets filled with crates. Lampposts sprouted every twenty paces or so, illuminating the jetty to the equivalent of midmorning light, but high above the naked stars shone brightly.

Amelia always liked this time of year, when the blackness of the Abyss was visible between the suns, and the sky wasn't always awash with light. It wouldn't take long for Passagia II to rotate through its orbit and bring back into view the sky-filling brilliance of the Hub, the core of the cluster where all known intelligent life made its home—but Amelia was happy to enjoy the dark skies when she could.

She spotted the battered *Renaissance* tied up along one side of the jetty, and another cruiser astern of her, likely *Inspiration* getting ready to sail. But her prize this morning was a frigate. Across the jetty was a smaller vessel, her hull a mottled gray, and bulky, external storage containers jutting from the lower half of her hull. The bow was quite snub, and there were none of the flowing lines about her that defined modern Navy ships. The bridge was high and aft—almost too far aft, like a merchant ship's.

Curious, Amelia approached with a slowing stride. Despite appearances, it was a warship: there was a beam turret forward of the bridge, and yes, there were the trace outlines of gunports for cannon running nearly the length of the hull.

The jetty was deserted in front of this ship, with only a single gangway leading across to an airlock. Amelia wandered up and saw the ceremonial ring hanging by the brow: HMSS DARING.

"Huh," she muttered aloud.

She looked back across the jetty, at all the activity around the mighty *Renaissance*. The cruiser was a thing of beauty, she had to admit, and she remembered the pride she'd felt when she'd first joined the crew. But *Renaissance* was ugly on the inside, and was only going to get worse now that she was damaged and stuck in port. She turned back to examine *Daring*. A ship was only as good as her crew, and here was a chance to build a new crew from scratch. That could make this little frigate as beautiful as any ship of the line.

"Hello," she said to the silent hulk floating before her. "My name's Amelia, and I'm going to be your quartermaster."

With a new skip to her stride, Amelia headed off to *Renaissance* to collect her gear.

CHAPTER 4

Daring might have had lovely lines, but if so, they were well hidden. Liam stepped down onto the jetty and surveyed the dark shape of the frigate that was his new ship. Much of her hull was hidden behind bulky cargo holds that had been fastened down her length, mismatched and multicolored boxes that looked garish and clumsy. *Daring* was an older vessel, with none of the curving, molded surfaces of the latest generation of warships, and Liam had to admit that the cargo holds didn't look out of place. Admiral Grandview had promised them a ship that could pose as a civilian merchant, and this tub certainly fit the bill.

Directly across the dock from *Daring,* the cruiser *Inspiration* floated just beyond the polyglass, fresh from refit and looking lean and hungry. Forward of her rested the battered hulk of *Renaissance,* the dearth of activity before her only accentuating the cruiser's wretched appearance. Even from here Liam could see the unnatural bend in the top mast, which was still extended because it no longer fit in its stowage couplings.

Forward of *Renaissance,* a pair of huge battleships were tied up on either side of the jetty, an army of storesmen preparing them for an imminent departure. Liam had just read the new orders and he knew where they were going. He envied them in a way, but the sudden importance of *Daring*'s mission instilled him with a renewed sense of purpose. All those stores being loaded, he thought, didn't just magically appear on the jetty, and if *Daring* didn't succeed in ridding the lanes of this pirate infestation, the entire fleet would suffer. Both jetty cranes moved with graceful precision as they loaded the heaviest equipment through the polyglass gates, their towers stretching up out of the surface lighting to disappear against the blackness of orbital space.

Some of the brightest suns were still visible, but the dark sky out here in the Halo was even deeper than usual. Having grown up on Passagia, Liam didn't mind the darkness when his world swung through the outer portion of its orbit, but he knew that it caused great unease in many people.

One of Passagia's moons was overhead, and spotting it spurred Liam into motion. Tidal forces were critical to getting ships into space and sailing, and with the orders he'd just received, they didn't have much time to get the ship loaded. He looked over at the enormous pile of crates in front of *Daring,* and at the sailor moving efficiently around them.

Ignoring the rumble of forklifts behind her, Petty Officer Amelia Virtue was focused on her count as she finally reached the end of the stacks. Her uniform was grubby, her chocolate-colored hair was wisping loose from its bun, and her face was locked in a scowl. But Liam saw the sense of purpose in her movements, a determination entirely lacking in the pair of storesmen who stood idly by, waiting for orders.

Virtue was discussing the loading situation with her small crew as Liam approached.

"All three storage ports are open," one of them reported to her, "but it's going to take all of us just to man a single loading station."

Before she could answer, Liam stepped into the conversation.

"Quartermaster."

She turned, her eyes widening as she recognized him.

"Yes, sir."

"I just received updated orders. A fleet of Sectoid ships has been sighted on the border and all available units are being massed for action. We have an updated departure time—seventeen hundred. The battleships are going first, then *Inspiration*"—he indicated the cruiser across from them—"then us."

"Yes, sir," she said automatically, although the concern on her face tightened into near panic.

He stared down at her, wondering for just a moment if he'd been too hasty in bringing her over from *Renaissance*—with a promotion, no less—and trusting her with the role of quartermaster.

"What do you need, Quartermaster?"

"I need those jetty cranes and a squad of longshoremen," she blurted.

"Not going to happen," he clipped. "We're lowest priority for dockyard support, and there are three bigger ships in front of us."

She nodded, her eyes flicking down the jetty, then toward *Daring*. A moment of quiet descended, broken only by the distant bangs and clangs of crates being loaded onto the other ships. "I need," she said carefully, "our entire crew up here to help load stores."

Good answer, Liam thought. Don't wish for what you don't have—use what you do have.

"Some of the propulsors are busy in the rigging, but I'll get you the rest. Have a plan ready."

Ignoring her startled reaction, he turned on his heel and approached the sailor who was standing watch at the brow. The position of brow's mate rotated through the lower ranks, and this particular sailor was one Liam had met only once before, when he'd been signing up new members of the crew. Master Rating Flatrock, if he remembered correctly. The big man looked perfectly capable of handling the single access point between the jetty and *Daring* as she floated just beyond the polyglass. At Liam's order, Flatrock activated the ship's internal broadcast to muster all sublieutenants and below to the jetty.

The broadcast was still echoing through the airtight passageway connecting *Daring* to the jetty when Liam saw the first hint of movement from within the ship. He glanced down the passageway, curious to see who the keener was, and immediately snapped to attention.

"Pipe the side," he barked.

Flatrock pressed his bosn's call to his lips and shrilled the three-note signal indicating the passage of a commanding officer.

Just as Liam raised his hand in salute, and noticed Virtue and her storesmen instinctively doing the same, Commander Riverton stepped onto the jetty. She returned the salute crisply and motioned for Liam to walk with her away from the brow.

"I just got word that your previous commanding officer is on his way over," she said without preamble. "Any idea why?"

Liam felt his heart sink even as his mind raced. Silverhawk was coming here, hours before *Daring* was due to sail? Was his former captain coming under pressure to explain the damage to *Renaissance*? Liam could guess pretty quickly where that line of investigation would end up—and he wanted nothing to do with it.

"No, ma'am."

"I guess we'll find out in a moment." Riverton nodded toward a pair of tall, uniformed men emerging from a nearby carriage and striding toward them. A pair of servants followed, carrying civilian-style luggage. Liam recognized Silverhawk, and realized that the younger man next to him looked familiar.

"That cadet is Captain Silverhawk's cousin," he said, remembering the ball. "He's looking for a ship to sail in."

Riverton muttered something under her breath that sounded neither inspiring nor ladylike.

Silverhawk was upon them moments later. He returned their salutes and peered down his nose at them before casting skeptical eyes toward *Daring*.

"Commander Riverton, I understand you're sailing today for a routine patrol mission."

"Yes, sir," she replied. "Nothing interesting—mostly post-refit trials and some engineering tests."

It was the official line, an attempt to keep *Daring*'s departure as low profile as possible.

The cadet sighed heavily, his eyes passing over *Daring* toward the battleships.

"Not ideal," Silverhawk said, glancing at him, "but a start. It'll give you time to develop your bridgemanship skills in a slow-paced environment."

"But I want to be on the battleship," the cadet replied. Or rather, openly whined.

"In time," Silverhawk said with an indulgent smile. "Off you go, then, lad."

The cadet seemed ready to argue further, but after a moment he sulked off toward *Daring,* motioning for his servants to follow.

"Excuse me, sir," Riverton said icily, "but it seems that *my* ship is somehow involved with your discussion. As such, I rather think I should be involved as well."

"Yes, Sophia, of course." Silverhawk offered her his most engaging smile. "My cousin, young Highcastle there, will be attending the Academy next year and we both know how much better a cadet can perform if he has real operational experience prior to commencing his studies."

"And . . . this involves my ship how?"

"He's going to join your crew," Silverhawk replied, a flicker of irritation marring his easy expression.

"Surely, sir, he'd have a more educational experience aboard one of the larger vessels."

"No room aboard them," he clipped, just a bit too quickly. "It has to be yours. I'm sure you can find a use for him. Ava Templegrey is your medical officer, isn't she?"

"Yes, sir, but—"

"Perfect. She and Highcastle are well acquainted."

Riverton turned her head to stare at Liam. Her expression was very close to neutral, but her eyes betrayed her anger.

"Blackwood, supervise the loading of stores, if you please."

Liam knew a dismissal when he heard one, and with

great relief he saluted his superiors and returned to the ship.

Most of the crew had emerged, automatically forming up into three loose ranks on the jetty. A pair of officers stood off to one side, joined now by the towering, gangly cadet. The ship's assaulter, a powerful-looking woman Liam knew only by name and rank—Chief Petty Officer Sky—noticed his return and approached.

"Available crew mustered, sir," she said with a salute.

"Very good."

"We taking on a new cadet?"

Liam glanced over to where Highcastle was introducing himself to the pair of sublieutenants. "Not sure, Chief. We'll find out soon enough, I'm sure."

Petty Officer Virtue finished checking the last of the crates and moved closer, clearly not sure if she was allowed to interrupt the executive officer and the assaulter.

"Crew mustered, Quartermaster," Liam reported. "What's your plan?"

"Sir," she said, clearing her throat and trying to sound confident. "My team is currently marking each crate for loading into one of the three bays. I request that the crew be divided equally and spaced down through the decks next to each bay. I'm getting six lifters brought up and I need the crew to guide each crate down to the storage lockers as directed."

Liam nodded. "Chief Sky will direct the crew into position. Get these stores moving."

Sky turned and barked a series of orders to the crew. The ranks broke up as sailors scrambled on board to take up their assigned positions.

The three junior officers, Liam noted, were hardly as

responsive. Highcastle seemed more interested in watching the activity near the battleships, and one sublieutenant made a quiet remark that caused the other to laugh.

The storesmen appeared with lifters—each a meter square and ideal for taking the weight of a crate—and started handing them out at the loading bays. Under Chief Sky's direction, temporary airlock corridors were connected to all three cargo access points and sailors began deploying themselves into a chain for passing stores.

Sky returned, glaring at Virtue.

"You got a plan for those snotters, PO?"

It was a statement of Chief Sky's confidence in her position that she was willing to call junior officers "snotters" in front of the second-in-command. Liam had to assume that Commander Riverton held this assaulter in very high regard.

"They'd be useful as loading captains down below . . . ," Virtue offered, glancing nervously between Liam and Sky.

"Like hell." Sky snorted. "Ideally you want them as far away from decision making as possible, especially when their decisions will affect you."

"Well, they're young and strong. They'll be useful in guiding lifters down the hatches."

"Now you're talking."

Virtue relaxed visibly, until she realized Sky was still glaring at her expectantly.

"So get over there," the chief growled, "and make them do it."

Virtue jumped into motion.

Sky cast an amused eye at Liam. "This should be fun, sir."

Liam agreed, curious how Virtue would deal with the

officers. He wandered over to the brow and made himself look busy with the communications console while watching.

Highcastle still had his eyes down the jetty, looking wistfully at the battleships, and didn't even notice Virtue's approach. The two subbies regarded her with little interest.

Sublieutenant Charlotte Brown was one of Liam's picks for the crew, a no-nonsense commoner who had won a seat at the Academy through her sheer ability. She'd been one of the few shining stars on *Renaissance*'s bridge.

But it was the other subbie to whom Virtue spoke— one of the captain's picks. Liam had met Ava Templegrey briefly and knew that she was fresh out of medical school.

"Sublieutenant Templegrey," Virtue said. "We're really pressed for time to get everything aboard and I'd appreciate the help of all three of you."

Templegrey raised a single, doubtful eyebrow. Her pale features were smooth and fine, no doubt the product of generations of selective breeding, but her bright blue eyes fell on Amelia with disinterest.

"And what would you like us to do?" she asked, her cultured voice carrying a sense of superiority with frightening ease.

"You're probably the three fittest people here," Virtue said. "You'd be a great help guiding the lifters down between decks."

Templegrey laughed, real amusement laced with derision. "Well, Charlotte," she said to Brown, "I'm glad we're appreciated for our fitness."

Brown smiled, but her expression was less sanguine. She glanced over to where the rest of the crew was now bringing the first of the crates aboard.

"We should help out," she said simply, frowning. "If the ship isn't loaded and we miss our launch window, there'll be hell to pay."

Her common accent was laced with Academy intonations, making for an interesting cadence.

Templegrey surveyed the loading activities for a long moment. "I suppose I'll want to ensure that the medical supplies get to the right place." She turned back to Virtue. "Which storage are they destined for?"

"Midships, ma'am."

"Then I'll put myself there." She tapped the young cadet behind her. "Come along, James."

Highcastle started at the soft rap against his uniform. He noticed Virtue hovering for the first time and cast a querying glance at Templegrey. "Where are we going?"

"To help load the ship. They apparently need our strong bodies."

"No." His gaze swung back to the activity farther down the jetty. "I want to watch the battleships."

Templegrey rolled her eyes and wandered off, presumably to oversee the medical supplies. Brown took a couple of steps, then looked back.

"Mr. Highcastle," she said, "let's go."

Cadet Highcastle's uniform was so new it practically still had the tailor's marks, but the air of superiority in his cold expression was long-practiced. From his great height he looked down his nose at her. "I said," his voice cut with the clipped precision of the royal accent, "that I want to watch the battleships."

Brown's face hardened. "I don't give a damn what you want, Cadet. If you're part of this crew you'll pull your weight. Now get over to the forward loading bay and start helping." He looked to protest but she cut him off. "That's an order."

A cross between a scoff and a protest burst from his lips. He seemed genuinely perplexed for a moment, but Brown's glare didn't shift. Finally, seeming to understand she wouldn't relent, he pushed past her and strode rapidly toward the ship.

"Forward team," he called out with easy authority, "I want our bay loaded first, and there's a crown for each of you if we do it!"

Liam watched the three officers join the efforts, then glanced back to where Virtue still stood. The petty officer looked exceptionally uncomfortable, and rightly so; that clashing of officer egos was not really a scene any sailor should have seen. Liam made a note to speak to Brown about not being quite so blunt with the cadet. For a moment he dared to hope that Highcastle would soon be nothing more than a bad memory, but Commander Riverton was returning, and her black expression said everything.

"Add Cadet Highcastle to our crew list," she said, voice flat. "And assign him to understudy your commoner, Sub-lieutenant Brown."

"Brown can certainly handle him," he replied, "but do you not think, ma'am, that Templegrey might be a better—"

"I said Brown."

Liam was caught short by the sudden order. Riverton's angular features were taut with suppressed emotion.

"Yes, ma'am—I'll add him to Brown's watch right away."

She stalked across the brow without another word. She

was halfway down the passage before Flatrock thought to pipe the side, but her salute was more a flicker of her hand as she disappeared into the ship.

Liam nodded his thanks to the brow's mate and then stepped clear to take in the stores situation again. The forklift was shunting crates from the mountain to the three cargo doors, and the crew worked diligently to shuttle packages through the hull. But Liam had seen this process enough times to know that it was going to take more time than they had. Not a good way to bring a new crew together, he thought, missing their departure time. He watched as Sublieutenant Brown barked orders at her team of loaders, while Sublieutenant Templegrey simply stood and watched. Cadet Highcastle seemed to think it was a game he needed to win, and he shouted encouragement in that royal accent. Chief Sky simply stood back and watched, frowning over crossed arms. And Petty Officer Virtue ran between the crates on the jetty, scribbling marks on each one. None of them seemed in a hurry to take charge of the situation. So that left Liam.

Down the jetty, the first of the battleships was already departing. She released locks and drifted silently clear of the structure. A pair of tugs came alongside her smooth, massive form and nudged her up and away from the spar. A flash of thrust from her ion engines sent her gliding free into orbital space, and the first of her great masts—the top mast—began to unfold from the hull. It was a leisurely, elegant transformation—one that sailors rarely had the chance to see with the unaided eye. Liam stared, transfixed, as the bottom mast began to extend as well.

Standard Navy tactics were to deploy a squadron of ships whenever a Sectoid presence was detected, but the sheer number of vessels spotted by scouts had sent a ripple of concern through the admiralty. No one knew what the bugs were planning—when had Humans ever understood the motivations of this mysterious race?—but having *Daring* depart quietly as part of a group of much larger vessels was the perfect cover for her to slip away into the blackness unnoticed. They couldn't afford to miss this window.

But more importantly, he thought as he stepped forward, this ship was not ever going to slip her berth late. Not while he was in charge. He stalked over to where Brown was still shouting orders at her surly crew, gripping her arm to silence her.

"Save your voice, Sublieutenant," he said quietly to her, before grabbing the next sack and throwing it at the crewman who waited just inside the hold. The sack slammed into surprised arms, but Liam was already lifting the next box and heaving it across the open space. The sailors stared at him.

"That's the sort of effort I want to see," he said, loud enough for both Brown's and Templegrey's teams to hear. He picked up another sack and flung it at the now-ready sailor. "We have to slip this berth along with all our sister ships, and no one is going to wait for us. Now move!"

Behind him, Brown grabbed another sack and heaved it with all her might. It didn't go as far as Liam's toss, but another sailor stepped in to catch it and pass it along. Liam approached Templegrey's team and watched as they leaped into motion. The highborn officer raised a delicate eyebrow to him, but he had no patience for courtly charms right now.

"Break a sweat," he whispered to her, "or as many nails as you have to, but get this pile loaded."

Real offense darkened her well-bred features, but she grabbed a metal box and tossed it to the nearest sailor.

"I have medical supplies in here," she snapped to her crew, "so watch how we load them."

Liam lingered for a moment, to ensure that she continued her work, then made his way aft to Highcastle. The cadet was smart enough to have already followed the example, his exquisite tunic cast aside and his long arms in constant motion as he helped load crates. But he was frowning darkly as he did it.

"I say," Liam called out to this third team, "does anyone know any good working songs?"

Quietly, amid the clatter of moving stores, one of the sailors started to sing an old ditty about a gunner's lover. Liam knew it well and he took up the strain as he settled next to Highcastle and started flinging boxes. It was a lower-deck favorite, and it had the perfect cadence for guiding the steady heave of gear. All around him, the sailors warmed to it and started to sing, their movements settling into the rhythm of the song.

Behind him, Liam heard Templegrey's soprano voice suddenly ring out in the opening lines of a particularly bawdy song about a tavern wench. Her team took up the tune immediately, grins splitting their faces as they roared out the old classic with their classically trained officer.

Beyond, Liam could just make out Brown's team breaking into steady song. The words were different at each cargo opening, but the cadence was identical and the old work songs did their magic. Stores flew through the bays. Liam stalked up to Chief Sky, who was still hanging back. Her expression had lightened, though, and she nodded approvingly at the XO.

"Nice work, sir."

"I didn't do it to impress you, Chief," Liam growled. "Your job is to help out whichever team is falling behind. And by *help out* I actually mean fling stores, not just look mean."

"Yes, sir," she said quietly. He wondered if she was actually capable of *not* looking mean, but she moved to help shift a new pile of boxes that the forklift had just dumped next to Templegrey.

No, Liam thought to himself, taking a moment to survey the scene. We shall not fail. Not while I'm in charge.

Then, with a final glance to ensure Virtue had everything under control with her assignments, he moved to help Brown's team.

CHAPTER 5

"This isn't the way it's done, sir."

Liam smiled at the remark as he offered a glass of wine to *Daring*'s coxn. The ship had slipped her berth on time, and it had been an exhausted, sweaty, but happy crew who had cast off all lines and raised the masts of His Majesty's Sailing Ship *Daring* for her new adventure. There were more surprises to come, Liam knew, but it was an excellent way to start.

Chief Petty Officer Butcher accepted the drink, but his expression remained uneasy. He glanced around the wardroom with a mixture of curiosity and distaste.

"Thirty years in space, sir, and I've never heard of this before."

"We've never served on a ship quite like this one," Liam replied as he handed the next glass to Chief Sky, "and we have to make a few adjustments."

Butcher sipped his wine, his grim expression softening at the taste. "It's just damned odd, sir."

Throughout her years as a trials ship, *Daring* had undergone multiple reconfigurations, and it seemed little regard had been given to the demands of daily life in space for a regular ship of the fleet. Her propulsion space was larger than that of a normal frigate, with numerous direct access tunnels carved to weapons systems and storage bays from there. Several sections of the interior layout had simply been removed to accommodate these changes, one of which was the senior-hands mess. Which meant the room where the senior sailors might once have gone to relax and take their meals simply didn't exist. The only alternatives were the wardroom, where the officers ate, or the junior-hands mess.

"I suspect that this will be preferable to having you dine with the crew."

"Yes, sir. But I understand that everyone is on a first-name basis in here . . ."

"We'll suspend that custom, Coxn. Working titles are fine."

Chief Sky tugged at her starched, high collar. Her dress uniform looked about as pristine as Butcher's did. "And dressing for parade every evening, sir?" she asked.

"Once a week only, Chief. Otherwise duty uniforms."

Daring's two senior sailors glanced at each other and a silent communication seemed to pass between them. Chief Butcher turned back to Liam.

"Thank you for making us welcome in your mess, sir."

"It's our mess, Coxn, officers and senior hands. The wardroom will now be known as the senior mess." He indicated for them to begin mingling.

Sublieutenants Brown and Templegrey had already been briefed to be on their best behavior, and they greeted the approaching sailors with welcoming smiles. Templegrey even held up her hands for Liam's inspection.

"Not a single nail broken, sir," she said, a mischievous smile playing across her lips.

Liam took her hand and kissed it in the courtly manner. He nodded to both her and Brown. "Fine work today, both of you."

"All just a bunch of lollygagging," Lieutenant Swift drawled as he joined them, "while we did the real work."

A chorus of good-natured protests from the sublieutenants was met by an expression of supreme indifference. Lieutenant Swift wasn't quite as refined as some, but Liam was confident that his chief propulsor's grounded, no-nonsense style would play well in this crowd.

Standing stiffly on the far side of the room, Cadet Highcastle watched the interactions with a mixture of curiosity and distaste. His own dress uniform was impeccably tailored and he seemed perfectly at ease with the formality, but applying the practical niceties of hospitality seemed quite foreign to him. Liam turned to the steward manning the bar and told him to refresh Highcastle's drink. Liam knew from long experience that alcohol was an excellent lubricator in any social situation, and he suspected that this evening would require a fair amount all around.

Only one member of this new, combined mess had yet to arrive. Liam began to wonder if she'd realized that she was invited, or whether long habit had steered her down to the junior mess, to which she would have belonged only days ago.

As if in answer to his thoughts, the wardroom door opened and Petty Officer Virtue slipped in, eyes wide and collar awry. All chatter stopped, and Liam saw every gaze fix on the new arrival. Virtue froze in the doorway, looking for a moment like she might bolt right back out again. Her gaze flicked from one senior person to another. Then, in an impressive effort of will, she stepped forward and spoke in a loud, steady voice.

"Petty Officer Virtue reporting, sir."

Liam couldn't contain his chuckle, and he heard the chorus of guffaws behind him, mixed with scattered applause. He took a glass of wine from the steward and walked over to her.

"Welcome, Quartermaster," he said, offering her the glass.

She took it, clearly unsure at the reaction to her arrival.

"This is your mess now, Amelia," he said. "This is your home, and you're always welcome here. No need to report."

Chief Sky stepped forward, reaching to straighten Virtue's collar. "We don't actually bite," she said. "And in here we don't even bark that much."

Virtue's expression shifted from uncertainty to relief, until a smile finally broke through. Guided by Sky, she walked forward into the welcoming crowd. Liam hung back, amazed at how the ice had been broken. Butcher compared his dress uniform to hers, obviously noting wear and tear. Templegrey made a show of flexing her bicep, no doubt in reference to their conversation on the jetty earlier. Even Highcastle detached himself from the far bulkhead and joined the group.

After another round of drinks and conversation, dinner was served. Liam took the executive officer's customary seat at the head of the table, and offered the seat at the opposite end to Chief Butcher as a courtesy to the ship's senior sailor. Highcastle, he noticed, was the first to move after that, securing himself the seat to Liam's right. Swift, the most senior officer after Liam, took one of the seats nearest the coxn in a good show of welcome. Sky and Virtue took opposite seats at the center of the table. Liam made a subtle gesture for Templegrey to take the seat to his left, opposite Highcastle, leaving Brown to sit with Butcher and Swift.

He hadn't actually planned it, but Liam admired how the seating had resolved itself. The coxn would feel honored by the senior lieutenant's presence, but would also have an easier conversation over dinner with the commoners Swift and Brown to chat with. Highcastle was close to hand in case Liam needed to shut him up, and Templegrey was right there to carry on topics of aristocratic interest if the lordling couldn't debase himself to speak on general topics.

Dinner on the first night out was always a decadent affair. The stewards had arranged the Imperial silver down the center of the table—the ship having been in commission so long that the silver was stamped with the seal of the Emperor's late father. Full, multicourse place settings crowded the smooth, wooden surface. Liam watched in approval as Swift and Brown subtly indicated to Virtue, Sky, and Butcher which knife, fork, spoon, or glass was required. It even became some sort of game between Brown and Virtue in particular, and by the third course waves of giggles were occasionally erupting from mid-table.

With no shortage of fresh food, the cooks were able to indulge; over three courses of excellent fare, and at least as many courses of wine, Liam watched as the senior personnel of the warship *Daring* began the essential process of bonding into a unit. Indeed, this would be the last time all eight of them would sit at this table together, and the reason for this unusual circumstance kept him watching the time very closely.

Sooner than he would have liked, he rose to his feet and motioned for quiet. All eyes turned to him. Some of those eyes were quite glassy, he noted with satisfaction.

"Ladies and gentlemen of the warship *Daring,* it is an honor to sail with you. I'm pleased to have this unique opportunity to speak to the entire senior staff while in space—a fact made possible only through the generosity of the captain, who has for the past two hours been acting as officer of the watch on the bridge. Never before have I seen such a gesture, and I think that Her Ladyship Commander Riverton has set through personal example the kind of ship she intends to command. As her senior personnel, we are expected to be selfless, to be tireless, and to put our crew before ourselves."

"Hear, hear," echoed the coxn.

"And before we dispatch Sublieutenant Templegrey to assume the watch from our commanding officer," Liam continued, "it is my privilege to reveal to all of you the true purpose of *Daring*'s mission. We are not, as officially announced, conducting routine trials of a new damage-control system. And this ship is not, as officially scribed in Navy records, on reserve duty and designated a noncombatant."

He let his eyes wander across the seven intent faces staring back up at him. Joviality had been replaced by keen interest. He reached to the shelf behind his chair and recovered a strongbox. Placing it on the table, he removed the paper upon which their orders were written, with the Imperial seal clearly affixed at the bottom.

"Our mission is to search out and destroy the pirate threat in the Silica system. We are to pose as a civilian merchantman in order to gain intelligence, discover how and where the pirates are operating, and terminate those operations."

He spent the next few minutes providing more specific details of how they were going to conduct the mission, internally delighted by the new life he saw in their faces as he spoke.

"We're going to be operating outside of the regular Navy," he finished. "We are, in effect, a one-ship force with a free hand to do what's necessary to accomplish our mission. If we need supplies, we'll have to requisition them ourselves, but it also means we get to keep whatever we take. And share it among ourselves."

The coxn stared back at him. "Does that mean what I think it means, sir? Because I haven't seen that sort of arrangement since . . . well, not since I was an able rating."

"Yes. It means prize money. According to the traditional split, that will mean two-eighths to the captain, one-eighth to the XO, two-eighths divided among the commissioned officers, one-eighth divided among the other members of the senior mess"—he indicated Butcher, Sky, Virtue, and Highcastle—"one-eighth divided among the crew, and one-eighth to the senior officer who ordered this mission. We are assuming tremendous risk, and thus the Emperor himself has approved of this method of compensation."

Before the celebrating began, he continued briskly. "But war with the Sectoids is near, and we need to accomplish our mission and destroy the pirate threat and clear the supply lines for the Navy." He paused, wanting to convey the importance of his next words: "If we don't, then our fleet will be unsupported and at risk. And we'll eventually be seen as skulkers who contributed nothing and hid from the fight. If we fail, the Emperor will deny all support to us and we'll be hunted down by our own Navy."

Silence fell around the table, each person absorbing these new facts. Among all the commoners—Butcher, Sky, Swift, Brown, and Virtue—he saw a fire of excitement, lit by the possibility of riches they would never have dreamed of. On his left and right, though, the pair of aristocrats looked far more thoughtful.

"This mission is from the Emperor himself," Templegrey mused as she ran her fingers across the seal on their orders. Her vivid blue eyes lifted to meet Liam's. "If we succeed, we're protected from the very top?"

"Yes, we are."

She nodded, sitting back and folding her arms.

"Well then," Highcastle suddenly exclaimed with a grin, "let's hunt down these pirate scum and give them what for!"

His youthful exuberance broke the tension, and the table erupted in laughter again. Liam glanced at the clock again and realized that it was time for Templegrey to relieve the captain on the bridge.

"Ms. Brown," he said as he retrieved his wineglass, "the toast of the day, if you please."

Brown rose to her feet, her face alight. Liam didn't think he'd ever seen her looking so happy.

"On this, our first day in space," she said, "I offer a toast to the health and long life of His Majesty, the Emperor."

The officers immediately raised their glasses in return, followed quickly by the senior sailors. Several calls of "the Emperor" echoed around the table.

Templegrey made her exit immediately after the toast, and Butcher and Sky made their farewells shortly after,

Virtue following their lead with some obvious reluctance. Brown stayed long enough to finish her drink, but then announced that she had the middle watch and was headed for her rack. Liam reminded Highcastle that he was paired with Brown, and suggested that he would be well served by going to bed as well. Within ten minutes of the toast, it was only Liam and Swift still seated at the table.

"You conniving bastard," Swift said, raising his glass in salute. "My lord executive officer."

Liam rose unsteadily to his feet and carried his drink down the table to sit across from Swift.

"I couldn't tell you beforehand," he said. "We couldn't risk anyone knowing our real mission until after we were safely in space."

"I know." Swift sat back, folding his arms. "But prize money . . . Sir, you can't imagine what that means to folks like me."

Liam nodded. It was hard to remember, spending so much time in uniform, the vast gulf that separated Swift's circumstances from his own. What would be a useful sum of money to him would be life-changing for his propulsion officer's entire family.

"When word reaches the crew, I expect we'll have a very motivated ship."

"The challenge," Swift replied, "will be to direct that motivation toward useful ends. We can't have our sailors thinking they can steal or pillage any ship we come across."

"We must maintain our purpose," Liam agreed. "Otherwise we're no better than the pirates."

Swift drained the last of his drink, staring thoughtfully upward. "Any idea where we start our search for the bastards?"

"We're going to sail in as a merchant and get a sense of the sector," Liam replied. "With a bit of luck the pirates will come to us."

Swift shook his head with a sigh. "You and your bait setting. You know that's going to get us into trouble one day."

"I expect it to. But if the trouble comes to us, we're ready for it."

Swift gestured toward the empty seats around the table. "What do you think of the senior team, sir?"

Liam frowned, considering. "I think they're mostly a professional bunch, each bringing their own particular strengths. But as for that young cadet . . . time will tell."

"Isn't he Silverhawk's cousin?"

"Yes. Foisted upon us by the good captain himself."

Swift rolled his eyes.

"We didn't have any choice," Liam persisted. "And I'm sure the likes of you will keep the likes of him in line."

"Just once, I'd like to sail with a completely professional crew."

"Perhaps this is our chance to build that professionalism. It may just take a bit of extra effort."

"Then I'd better get some sleep while I can." Swift rose from his chair, stretching.

"Good night, Sails."

"Good night, sir."

The Imperial orders still lay on the top of the strongbox and Liam realized he needed to get them back to the captain's cabin. She was probably off the bridge by now. Gathering himself, he left the wardroom and headed up two decks. The ship was rolling gently in the swell, pitching smoothly against a head wind as she sailed inward toward the Hub. Even with the external cargo pods, she seemed to slip through the solar winds like a yacht, and so far Liam was pleased with how the old frigate rode.

The quarterdeck was the highest deck in the ship, and as Liam ascended the last, steep stairway he emerged into a dark, open space filled with damage-control equipment. Forward was the door to the bridge, and aft was the door leading to senior-officer country. It was a rather grandiose title, he thought as he stepped through into the short corridor with a single door on either side.

To be fair, on a battleship, this would be the home of the captain and all the senior department heads, with space set aside for any visiting admirals and/or royals, as well as humble lodging for the army of attendant servants. But in an old frigate like *Daring,* there were precisely two cabins—one for the captain and one for the executive officer. Liam's cabin was on the port side, and he chimed at the starboard door.

"Captain, ma'am, XO," he announced.

"Enter," came the reply.

The captain's receiving room was barely large enough to contain the briefing table with six chairs plus a personal workstation. Two portholes allowed narrow beams of starlight to add to the dim illumination provided by the single lamp on the table.

In the pool of lamplight Commander Riverton sat over her dinner, uniform coat discarded on the chairback beside her. The collar of her white shirt was unbuttoned, the frill hanging loose, but her hair was still tucked up neatly. She sat back from her plate, crossing her arms as she looked up at him.

"Good evening, Mr. Blackwood."

"Good evening, ma'am." He stepped forward and placed the strongbox on the table in front of her. "The officers and senior hands have been briefed on the mission. I sense a great deal of enthusiasm from them."

"Very good."

He waited for further comment, but she simply regarded him with a neutral, possibly expectant, gaze. She'd displayed skepticism at his idea of bringing the senior sailors into the wardroom but had granted him leave to try. No doubt she was curious as to the results. He decided to take the unspoken invitation, pulling back the nearest chair and sitting across from her. "I believe that the merging of the two senior messes will be successful, ma'am. The officers made our three senior hands feel very welcome."

"As long as proper discipline and decorum are observed at all times," she replied coolly.

"You're always welcome to join us, ma'am."

"And I will, if I feel that my ship is not being run with the proper respect for authority."

"Yes, ma'am."

"For example, I didn't give you permission to sit, Mr. Blackwood."

Her voice hadn't raised a decibel in volume, but her tone was like a smack across the face. He scrambled to his feet.

"You hide it well," she continued, "but I can tell you're drunk. No doubt my entire senior staff is as well. That may be acceptable aboard a ship on a routine patrol, but I will not stand for it here. Exercise restraint, or I will exercise it for you."

He had to bite down his immediate retort, that a raucous first evening in space was tradition in any warship. A drunken dinner set good morale and gave him a chance to assess his senior staff. It was a time-honored tradition dating back generations, but apparently Lady Riverton had different ideas about how the Navy should be run. Her cold stare brooked no discussion on the matter, though.

"Yes, ma'am," he said.

"I'm particularly concerned about fraternization," she continued. "It's bad enough among the officers on a regular ship, but mixing with the senior sailors like this is asking for trouble."

He doubted Butcher or Sky would be any trouble on that front. As for Virtue . . .

"I'll keep an eye on our new quartermaster, ma'am."

Riverton made to speak, then pursed her lips shut. The creak of the hull was the only sound in her cabin for a long moment.

"And the cadet," he added. "Young nobles like him are notorious for fraternizing."

"Subcommander Blackwood," she said, her voice like steel, "you might think yourself better than the lordlings who get foisted upon you, but before you climb too high on your own pedestal, I suggest you take a good look at your own vices. I will certainly be watching."

He flushed. "Yes, ma'am."

Any afterglow from dinner had fled. He'd been upbraided by a captain more than once in the past, but never with such calm certainty. Riverton's gaze felt like a blade skewering him against the bulkhead.

She unfolded her arms and retrieved her cutlery. "Schedule an emergency exercise for the third hour of the middle watch," she said. "I want to drive home to your senior mess the perils of excess while in space."

He kept his face stoic, but groaned inwardly. Setting up an exercise would take him several hours, right when he wanted to climb into his own bunk. And he doubted any of the senior personnel—or the crew, for that matter—would appreciate being roused in the middle of the first night out. And everyone knew who arranged these exercises: the executive officer.

Liam suspected he would be a most unpopular figure tomorrow.

Riverton was eating again, and he assumed that he was dismissed. But then, he'd also assumed that he could sit down moments earlier.

"Yes, ma'am. Permission to carry on?"

"Carry on."

He retreated from her cabin, crossed the flats, and entered his own small living space. As he hung up his formal jacket and loosened his collar, he forced his wine-fogged mind to focus on the task of creating an emergency exercise. Probably a simulated fire, he figured, but with all those extra access tunnels to propulsion, he'd have to double-check the ship's diagrams to ensure he didn't create a bigger problem than he intended to.

He glanced at his footlocker and considered the flask of rum sitting there. But Riverton's glare still hung in his mind's eye, and with a quiet curse he lifted the handset of his internal telephone and wound it up, calling the galley to order a pot of coffee. It was going to be a long night.

CHAPTER 6

Amelia read over the summary one last time, then found herself starting to read it again.

"Stop it," she said to herself. "It's good."

The stores office swallowed the sound of her voice, shelves of wooden crates muffling the echoes so common in a steel-encased ship. There were two chairs squeezed into the space, and a pair of terminals, but because of the watch rotations in space, she rarely had the company of her storesmen. This little room was her own private kingdom, and if she wanted to talk to herself, she thought with a smile, that was her royal prerogative.

But the summary was good, she knew, and the report that followed it was detailed, integrated, and easy to read. She clutched the tablet in her hand and took a deep breath: time to head for the bridge.

As she locked the stores office behind her, she heard the usual noises of a busy ship. Voices carried down the passageway and there was the thump of a hatch shutting.

The creak of one of the masts matched a sudden lift of the deck as *Daring* caught a solar gust. Amelia grabbed the bulkhead to steady herself, then proceeded aft.

She paused when she reached the ladder, as it was crowded with a line of gunners descending. Immediately she spotted a familiar, dirty-blond head and couldn't hold back her grin.

"Hey, Hedgie."

Able Rating Hedge glanced up as she reached the deck, her scowling face streaked with dust and sweat. When she saw it was Amelia, her tired face brightened. "Hey, Virts. I mean, PO."

It was still odd, being addressed by her new rank. Amelia had been delighted when both Hedge and Flat-rock signed up to sail with *Daring,* but it had made the transition both easier and more difficult at the same time.

"You look like you've been cleaning the cannon from the inside," she said with sympathy.

"Might as well have." Hedge sighed, wiping her fore-arm across her face. "We've been reorganizing the ammo stores to make them more accessible."

"Oh . . . did we not do a good job when we loaded from the jetty?"

"As well as we could, considering the deadline." Hedge glanced around at her fellow gunners. "If those idiots had given us the time we needed then, we wouldn't be using our off-watch hours now to sort everything out."

"We were under orders to sail," Amelia explained. "We couldn't miss that window."

"No, no," Flatrock boomed, stepping down off the lad-der. "The officers can't look bad. And they have us sailors to fix the problem later."

That certainly wasn't Amelia's impression of *Daring*'s officers, but she knew better than to disagree with a group of sailors in the middle of a healthy round of complaining.

"At least it's done now," she offered. "And I heard in the senior mess that the captain is very pleased with how our recent drills have been going."

"Well, you should know"—Flatrock smirked—"chatting over dinner with Her Ladyship as you do."

Amelia couldn't suppress her laughter at that. She hadn't heard Commander Riverton speak more than five words at a stretch. The idea of dinner conversation with her painted a painfully awkward picture.

Hedge jerked her chin at Amelia's tablet.

"Whatcha got there?"

"A stores report. I'm just heading up to the bridge to deliver it."

"Well, enjoy the cocktails and chatter, PO. I have to catch some sleep before my watch."

Amelia squeezed her friend's shoulder, then punched Flatrock in the arm. Leaving them, she climbed up past the gun deck and up to the quarterdeck. This highest deck of the ship wasn't officially off-limits to the crew, but no one ever ventured here unless on specific business. In all her time in *Renaissance* Amelia had never once made it this high, and even in *Daring* she still felt odd climbing that last set of stairs.

Although the rest of the ship's interior mimicked the changing light of day and night, *Daring*'s command center was always dark. Here on the bridge, the crew was always on alert and needed to be able to scan the blackness of space beyond the clear canopy overhead. The blackness had significantly diminished even in the past week as *Daring* sailed inward from the Halo. Light from thousands of distant suns brightened the bridge enough for Amelia to see with only a momentary blinking of adjustment.

A pair of sailors manned the helm and propulsion controls to port, the sailing table—identical to the one in propulsion control with which she'd become very familiar—revealing moderate solar wind force against all four of the masts. Another pair of sailors sat at the tactical station to starboard, ready to direct *Daring*'s various weapons systems in battle. Two lookouts wandered back and forth around the outer ring of the bridge, peering out with their handheld telescopes. Pacing the center of the bridge, the officer of the watch monitored the central console and those around it.

Sublieutenant Brown had the watch at the moment, her role immediately recognizable by the pistol and saber she wore on her belt. Amelia felt a strange source of pride as she watched the young woman's quiet self-assuredness. The fact that Brown, a commoner, was an Academy graduate would be enough to make her entire hometown boast—and while Amelia had no personal connection to the officer, it still gave her a boost to see someone from a similar background having achieved so much.

Cadet Highcastle was Brown's second. Standing tall, his uniform impeccable, he cut quite a dashing young figure, she had to admit. His sandy hair was longer than a typical sailor's, but styled back in a way that highlighted his high cheekbones and elegant jaw. The resemblance to Captain Silverhawk was obvious, and Amelia could only hope that the similarities were only skin-deep. After several weeks of intermittent interactions with him in the wardroom, she still didn't know what to make of him.

And, at the raised command chair on the port side of

the bridge, sat Commander Riverton, her eyes forward, her expression intent. Subcommander Blackwood stood just to the side. Amelia admired him for a moment, loving his easy charisma that could instantly command a room. He and the captain were conversing quietly, his easy smile and large gestures quite in contrast to her statuesque serenity.

Blackwood suddenly noticed Amelia, and she realized with a start she'd been staring. He gestured her over with a friendly wave.

"Good afternoon, sir," Amelia said, knuckling her forehead to both of them as she stepped up next to Blackwood. "Captain."

Riverton glanced down quickly, almost dismissively, from the pair of screens before her. "Quartermaster."

Her sharp features were set in a casually neutral expression—polite and collected, but hardly welcoming. Amelia suppressed a shiver and turned her attention to Blackwood.

"Sir, I've completed the underway inventory and reckoning."

He smiled down at her, taking the tablet and scanning it.

"Everything is in order," she said, taking a deep breath, "and I'm happy to brief you on it."

He glanced around the bridge, then gave her his full attention. "Go ahead."

LIAM LISTENED AS PETTY OFFICER VIRTUE LAUNCHED into an efficient briefing of the status of the ship's stores. She guided him through the data on the screen and brought up additional charts with historical information for comparison. It was an impressive briefing, and surprisingly easy to follow.

But so, so, *so* boring. His attention was already drifting back to the tactical situation outside. She was no fool, and she relieved him of the tablet.

"Trouble, sir?"

He glanced at Riverton, then gestured for Virtue to follow him a few steps away from the command chair.

"There's a Sectoid ship out there," he said thoughtfully, pointing out through the clear canopy into the starry blackness.

"What?" Her bright eyes widened, and she immediately leaned in and lowered her voice. "In Human space?"

"Silica is one of those disputed sectors." He sighed. "We claim it and so do they, but there aren't any major worlds from which either side can assert dominance."

"So we both grab what we can before the other side does?" she asked, peering vainly into the starry sky.

He handed her his telescope and pointed down the bearing he knew the ship to be on. She lifted it to her eye with the basic competence of any space-farer, but she scanned too quickly to see anything. He placed one hand on her shoulder and the other on her own hand, which reached out to support the telescope. Steadying her grip, he eased her toward the correct bearing.

"Do you see it?" he asked.

"Um . . . not yet . . . Yes!"

Her sudden delight genuinely pleased him. He left his hands in place a moment longer. She didn't seem to mind his closeness, even leaning up against him slightly as she continued to peer down the telescope.

"She's been slowly overtaking us throughout the day,"

he explained. "We haven't altered course, or acknowledged them."

"We're just another merchant ship plying the lanes, aren't we, sir?"

"With the cargo bays strapped to us, our profile doesn't match any Navy ship, and all our military sensors are on standby." He gestured ahead to where a couple of distant vessels were silhouetted against the bright background of the Cluster. "The other merchants in the neighborhood haven't responded to the hails either."

"Are those merchants in convoy?" she asked.

"No." He gave her a curious glance. "But their courses seem to be converging."

"Not unusual behavior, maybe," she offered, "if they're both heading for the same port."

"But they do seem a little close." He was impressed at her tactical perception. "Well spotted, Quartermaster."

He grabbed a spare telescope from the central console and peered toward the Sectoid ship. The powerful, augmented optics gave him a good view of the distant vessel, all the light down that narrow field of vision focused and computer-enhanced for his eye. He could see the tall, gray form of the bug ship, easily twice the size of a Human battleship—meaning it was one of their minor vessels. "Any hostile activity from the Sectoid?" he asked Brown.

"No, sir, except that she's now inside the control zone for one of our colonies." Brown tapped the chart laid out before her, indicating the red sphere surrounding the nearest planet. "Terrestrial world, marginally habitable for Humans, called Farmer's Paradise."

Liam guessed it was an ironic name. They usually were.

"It's a known hideout for some pirate elements in this

sector," he explained to Virtue, "and a good place for us to begin our hunt."

"There's a collection of tiny Human settlements on this world," Cadet Highcastle interjected. "Mostly stubborn individualists who want to live free from Imperial oversight. We don't usually pay them any mind, but that doesn't mean the bugs can just wander into their space."

Brown kept her eyes on Blackwood, ignoring the cadet.

"I'm more puzzled by the proximity of the two merchants," she said. "The smaller one is definitely closing the larger one."

"We should close the Sectoid," Highcastle said, loud enough for everyone to hear. When no one responded, he repeated himself, stepping closer to the command chair and staring up at Riverton expectantly.

"Mind your station, Cadet Highcastle," Liam finally replied.

Highcastle turned away, face hardening into a sullen glare. He strode back to the central watch station, planting himself at the console right next to Brown. So close, in fact, that his bulk pressed against her, forcing her to sidestep to maintain her balance.

Liam suppressed a sigh. That sort of action was typical of a noble snotter: insolent, but not actively insubordinate. Brown's face darkened. She glared up at the self-absorbed youth, turned back to her displays for a moment, then stepped back.

"Cadet Highcastle," she asked loudly, "what's our estimated CPA on the Sectoid?"

Highcastle stared at her blankly.

Liam watched the two officers stare at each other.

"What's our what?" Highcastle finally responded.

Brown's expression grew predatory. "CPA . . . Closest

point of approach, Cadet. I'm pretty sure that was covered at the Academy. In the first week."

"I haven't been to the Academy yet," Highcastle mumbled, face reddening. "I'll be starting next year."

"Then I suggest you spend your watch listening to Sublieutenant Brown," Liam interjected, stepping toward them, "who *has* attended the Academy and who has earned her qualification to be in charge of this vessel."

Highcastle glanced at Brown and scoffed.

Brown, to her extreme credit, didn't give an inch.

"You still haven't answered my question, Cadet," she said. "What's our CPA on the Sectoid vessel?"

"Obviously I don't know," Highcastle replied, rolling his eyes. "So why don't you show me, Sublieutenant Brown?"

"Well," she said, "let's start with the basics. First, surely you can tell me what our relative velocity is to the Sectoid ship?"

Highcastle flicked his eyes across the command console, no doubt hoping the answer was flashing boldly in front of him. The silence crawled by. Liam sensed Virtue stepping slowly away.

"Too hard?" Brown snapped. "How about you just tell me the distance between us and the Sectoid?"

Highcastle looked at the chart, then fingered his telescope. His lips tried to form a response but failed.

"Something simple, then," Brown said. "What's the name of our ship?"

"What?"

"No, Cadet, it's *Daring*."

The color in Highcastle's cheeks deepened. But Liam had seen enough cadets get publicly torn to shreds on the bridge, and he knew that Brown's towering intellect was just beginning to stir; he didn't really want such a public humiliation to occur with so many witnesses.

"Mr. Highcastle," he interjected, giving the young man a smile and placing a friendly hand on his shoulder. "The bridge crew are about to conduct their hourly rotation. Go and supervise it, if you please."

"Yes, sir," the cadet replied. Liam caught the flash of relief on his face as he strode away to intercept the bosn's mate.

Liam stepped closer to Brown, keeping his smile in place. "Watch your temper with the lordlings, Sublieutenant," he said quietly. "They haven't learned their place yet."

"I'll show him his place," she growled.

"I know. But remember, there was once a time when even you were that clueless."

"When I was ten, perhaps."

He laughed. "I was thinking more seven, but perhaps at that age you hadn't yet learned to sneer."

Her stern expression cracked into a smile. "I can handle the lordling, sir. But maybe after the next port visit, Lieutenant Swift should be given a turn."

"Stars, Charlotte—I want Highcastle alive when we return home."

"Then let Sublieutenant Templegrey coddle him for a while."

"I'll see what I can do. Until then, do your best to turn him into something useful."

"Yes, sir." She glanced down at the chart. "I can probably at least get him doing—"

"Ma'am!" cried one of the lookouts. "Weapons fire between the two merchantmen."

Brown snapped her telescope free from her belt and

raised it to her eye in a practiced motion. Liam did the same. It took him several moments to find the right part of the sky, but then he saw the flashes of short-range cannon fire, brilliant pinpricks of light ending in muted explosions against the hull of the larger merchant. Despite the lookout's initial report, Liam quickly saw that this was no pitched battle between ships.

"The smaller ship is doing all the shooting," Brown said, squinting through her scope.

"It's the pirates," Highcastle exclaimed from his perch near the helmsman. "We should close and engage!"

Liam looked over at the captain. She'd straightened in her chair and alternated between watching the battle through her own telescope and looking down at her tactical array. "Activate optical recording on the battle," she said. "Maximum resolution."

"Yes, ma'am," Brown replied, fingers flying across her console.

"Course, ma'am?" Liam prompted.

"Maintain current course," she ordered.

He scanned the chart, and the relative position of the pirate attack, not sure he understood her thinking. Was she intending to flank? In any case, he had to get the ship ready to fight.

"That stores report," he asked Virtue, "do we have all our assault boarding-party gear ready for deployment?"

"Yes, sir," she said, handing the tablet to him.

"And the boats?"

"Operational, sir." She thought for a moment. "But they're currently rigged for standard sailing. If we're sending an assault party, they'll need to be reset to make room for the extra bodies."

"What does that take? Half an hour?"

"About that, sir."

Liam checked Brown's tactical display again, then turned back to Virtue.

"Drawing weapons and armor, how long until we're ready to send the assault team?"

Virtue paused, clearly considering all the supply components that went into equipping fifteen sailors for close combat and getting them over to another ship.

"An hour, sir, maybe a bit more."

"Make it so, Quartermaster."

Virtue knuckled her forehead and dashed from the bridge.

Liam strode over to the captain's chair.

"I recommend I take a full assault party, ma'am. The pirates will be well armed."

"Regular boarding party," she replied, still manipulating her tactical display. "By the time we get there, the pirates will be long gone."

Liam could read a tactical display as well as anyone. With their current sailing configuration, it would take several hours to close the distance. But he knew *Daring* was capable of greater speed. He was suddenly disappointed in Riverton—she'd seemed so much smarter.

"If we full sheet we can reduce closing time by at least a quarter—and we have the thrusters, ma'am."

Her expression could have frozen a star. "I'm fully aware of my ship's capabilities."

"Yes, ma'am." He leaned closer, considering carefully his next words. "But at our current speed we won't be able to intercede in this attack."

She pretended to ignore him for a moment, gazing through her telescope once more, but eventually she turned to face him again.

"Agreed. Unfortunate, but true. Maintain course."

Words of protest pushed up his throat, but discipline held them down. He stared up at his captain, reading in her stony expression something more than just obstinacy. There was a calculated intelligence there. "Maintain sensor silence as well," Riverton added.

It made no sense, but he had to obey. His mind churned over her words, trying to figure out what latitude they gave him.

"Do not change any outward indicator from this ship," Riverton said. "No course or speed changes, no active sensors, nothing."

He realized with chagrin that she was purposefully hemming him in. She wanted no deviation from her intent, that was clear.

"I'll see to it, ma'am."

He returned to the officer-of-the-watch console, noting with satisfaction as Brown updated their intercept course based on different possible speeds. Highcastle stood uselessly beside her, watching with restless energy.

"Maintain sensor silence," Liam ordered, loud enough for the entire bridge to hear.

"Are we coming to full sail?" Highcastle demanded.

"No. Maintain course."

The young noble suddenly turned to the console, inexpertly tapping in commands.

"We're still an hour away from missile range," he protested. "We need to get closer."

"Maintain course and speed," Liam said quietly to Brown.

"Yes, sir."

"But what about the pirates!" the lad exclaimed.

"Shut your mouth, Cadet," Liam barked. His own frustration was getting too close to the surface. He peered through his telescope again, noting that the firing had stopped and the two ships were now much closer. The pirates were going to board the merchant. His eyes snapped over to Riverton, who was also watching through her telescope. What was she thinking?

"Status of the Sectoid ship?" Riverton asked suddenly.

Her question caught everyone by surprise, and Liam realized that he, Brown, and Highcastle had all tunneled in on only one aspect of the tactical situation. Brown was momentarily flustered as she shifted her thinking.

"No apparent change," Liam reported, after a quick glance at the readouts. "No change to her course or speed, no increased energy levels or emissions that we can detect."

"Very well."

Riverton's calm voice ensured a stillness on the bridge, and Liam forced himself to not pace as he watched *Daring*'s distance to intercept slowly close.

Highcastle was fuming, arms crossed as he stood near the officer-of-the-watch station. Liam could sense the young man's overwhelming frustration—no doubt he was not at all used to feeling powerless.

Highcastle noticed his gaze. After a moment's hesitation, the young man stalked over and leaned in to speak quietly.

"Lord Blackwood, I . . . am most distressed at our decision to not aid that merchant ship." The effort he was making to contain himself was impressive.

"I understand," Liam said carefully, not allowing any of his own frustration to show. "But the captain knows what she's doing. We'll arrive on scene when the time is right."

His last sentence sounded as hollow when spoken as it had in his mind.

"But this ship has missiles, doesn't it? We can fire them from well outside cannon range."

It was an unusual feeling for Liam to agree more with an untrained cadet than with his own commanding officer, but he held his expression firm.

"We do, and we can. But we have very few of them, and they're not intended for use against pirate ships." He stabbed a finger out toward the distant Sectoid. "We need them in case something like that decides to take a run at us."

Highcastle listened in taut silence. Then, finally, he nodded.

"I understand, Blackwood. Still, it's a damn shame."

"It is." Liam hardened his features. "And address me as 'sir,' Cadet Highcastle."

The youth barely managed to suppress his eye roll. "Yes, sir."

CHAPTER 7

One of the ship's boats had been launched from its cradle and was tethered to *Daring*'s hull by a pair of lines and the airlock tube. The two-man crew was already aboard, and the sailors of the boarding party were gathered around her in the narrow passageway.

Hedge and Flatrock were there, of course, their reputations as scrappers well known in the Passagia squadron and their selection for boarding party a given. Amelia didn't know the other two sailors, but they both looked fit and capable. She quickly inspected everyone's space suits and weapons.

Like them, her own belt was heavy with a cutlass and a pistol. The sword was bigger than anything she was used to, and she'd never even fired a pistol before. Her hands rested on the weapon on each hip, trying to get used to the feel of each. The space suit was lightweight, more an emergency escape suit—perfect for mobility but limited in actual lifesaving capability.

The sound of boots approaching caught her attention, and she straightened as Subcommander Blackwood strode into view, flanked by Lieutenant Swift and Chief Sky. All three were suited and armed, faces set in grim determination.

"Quartermaster," Blackwood called out, "are we ready to cast off?"

"Yes, sir. Boat's crew is aboard, medical equipment has been loaded, and boarding party is ready."

Blackwood came to a halt in the middle of the team, his eyes casting around at the assembled sailors.

"This is more likely a rescue mission than a fighting one," he said, "but we know nothing about how these pirates operate and we'll take no chances. Even though the pirate ship itself has fled, they may have left a prize crew on board. We will move swiftly, but cautiously, to secure the vessel."

Chief Sky gave the order to commence boarding, and the sailors swung themselves one by one down through the airlock tube. It was always an awkward motion for anyone, but Amelia winced as she watched her shipmates bumble to get themselves through the passage.

"Might want to schedule some more training with the boat, Chief," Lieutenant Swift commented lightly. "I'd like to get on board before I retire."

"I'll see to it, sir," Sky growled.

Amelia ignored the eyes of the officers on her as she fumbled to maneuver herself into the tube. She did a final check of her gear, then gripped the crossbar at the top of the airlock tube with both hands. Swinging into zero-g was always a minor act of faith, but Amelia felt the familiar yet odd sense of sudden buoyancy as her suited body left *Daring*'s artificial gravity and floated free into the tube. Her trajectory wasn't perfect, but a quick push against the approaching wall corrected her movement, and within moments she drifted through the hardened hatch of the boat. Steadying hands grabbed her on all sides and settled her in the middle of the space.

The boat was large enough for twenty sailors, the deck uncluttered and currently laid out with harnesses along both sides for the boarding party to strap into. She checked the bindings of the stretchers laid across medical equipment in the center of the boat, a grim reminder of what might be waiting for them. The upper half of the hull was transparent and currently facing outward from *Daring,* offering a view of the half-lit, sickly-green surface of Farmer's Paradise. Scattered settlements lit the night side and a few ships were barely visible in the gulf between *Daring* and the planet. The pirate ship was one of them, still being silently tracked as she fled.

Blackwood drifted into the boat and took his seat next to the boat's helmsman, Master Rating Faith. The old sailor gave him a polite nod. "Ready when you are, sir."

"Cast off, helmsman."

The bowsman, Able Rating Hunter, sealed the airlock and released all moorings to *Daring* before taking his position forward in the boat's eyes. With a puff from the ion thrusters, Faith pushed them clear of the ship, passing astern of *Daring*'s bulk. Beyond was the battered hull of the merchant ship *Lightning Louise,* pockmarked from the effects of the pirate cannon. Amelia looked over it carefully, searching for any sign of life, but the ship appeared dark and silent. She felt her heart tighten as she imagined what might be waiting for them.

"Starting our approach," Blackwood signaled over his radio.

"No change in energy levels," reported Brown from the bridge.

If there was anyone still on board, they didn't appear to be reacting. The nearest mast was little more than a stump projecting from *Louise*'s hull, shreds of solar sail still clinging to the shattered post. Without fresh sheets, this ship was dead in space. She was a midsized merchant, easily three times *Daring*'s displacement with vast internal cargo bays.

"Watch for movement," Chief Sky ordered the team. "Any ports opening, any trackers turning."

Their boat was vulnerable as it crossed the gulf between vessels. Its hull was thick enough, but it carried no weapons itself. *Daring*'s crews were manning their firing stations, Amelia knew, but the last place she wanted to be was right between two ships blasting away at each other.

The boat approached *Louise*'s hull, maneuvering to hover as best it could over an airlock that appeared intact. Hunter extended the airlock tube, then crawled into it to manipulate its tiny jets and line up with the lock on the hull. It took no more than a few seconds, but to Amelia it felt like an hour. She could feel the growing knot of tension in her gut, and she focused on keeping her breathing slow and steady.

"We're connected," Sky suddenly announced. "Permission to board, sir?"

Amelia glanced at Hedge, who was staring at the airlock with aggressive anticipation. Next to her, Flatrock's hand slid down to grip his pistol.

"Board the vessel," Blackwood said with a nod.

Hunter reemerged and scrambled up to his position in

the bow. Sky disappeared through the airlock, followed by individual team members until it was Amelia's turn. She unhooked from her seat and floated into the tube, pulling herself along the flexible walls until she felt the consistent pull of gravity start to weigh her down. Her hands hit the deck of the ship and she heaved herself forward onto her hands and knees, fighting the burn in her muscles and struggling to her feet.

The airlock of *Lightning Louise* opened into a narrow corridor. Emergency lamps cast pools of light in either direction, revealing the waiting forms of the boarding party spread down the passageway. Their weapons were sheathed, but Amelia could sense the sudden increase in tension. The merchant ship was unnaturally quiet. No soft thuds of sailors moving along passageways, no distant shouts of command or bursts of laughter. Not even the hum of machinery or rush of environmentals. Only a single creak from one of the masts broke the silence.

Amelia focused on her breathing, adjusting to the new atmosphere. She didn't smell anything unusual—just the typical odors of oil, metal, and wood found in any working ship.

"Sky," Blackwood called, "environment?"

"Temperature and atmosphere both normal for Human habitation," replied the assaulter. "Pressure is lower than normal, and with no ventilation working, I reckon we have limited oxygen."

"Swift, check propulsion," Blackwood said. "Sky, head forward and look for survivors. I'll take the bridge."

The shuffle of suited bodies echoed in the still air as the boarding party split into three teams. Amelia moved into position behind Blackwood, Hedge bringing up the rear. They followed the narrow corridor, passing cargo doors inboard and following the line of the outer hull. Eventually they reached a passageway moving into the ship, lit by the same emergency bulbs that gave only a shadowy suggestion of what lay ahead.

Amelia tensed, listening for any hint of an ambush. She reached down to snap open her holster.

"Keep your pistols away," Blackwood whispered. "We don't know how much pounding the outer hull's taken yet, and I don't want to risk a breach by a stray shot."

Amelia shifted her grip to her sheathed cutlass. It was the unknown that was gnawing at her, she knew. She'd rather just advance and meet whatever awaited them than skulk forward on tiptoe. She stepped past Blackwood. "I'll lead, sir."

He nodded, and she went first down the passageway. Within twenty paces she reached a wider corridor moving fore and aft through the ship. The lighting was still muted, and there was still no sound except for their padded footfalls. The passageway was littered with the debris of broken equipment, indicating either a fight or sheer vandalism. The detritus barely slowed them, but Amelia checked her pace as the end of the corridor emerged from the gloom.

"XO, Assault," Sky called over the radio. *"Signs of weapons fire forward. Mix of Human and Sectoid design."*

Amelia examined a long spray pattern of corroded metal across one bulkhead, suggesting an acidic attack. A moment of fear was swallowed up by a rush of adrenaline, and she felt herself suddenly sweating in her space suit. She shined her light along the tortured, burned metal riddled with bullet holes, then up above their heads. Suddenly it seemed every shadow might hold a Sectoid warrior. Horror welled up within her as all those tavern tales suddenly loomed up before her. She tried to take another step, but her feet refused to move.

"Come on, Quartermaster," Blackwood whispered, nudging her forward.

She forced her legs into action, her hand reaching down to grip the pommel of her heavy sword. Her breathing quickened, her eyes darting left and right, up and down. Up ahead, the passageway terminated.

The airlock to the bridge was a shredded mess of twisted metal and shards. It didn't take much imagination to see how the pirates had used a combination of acid and explosives to force their way in. The hole was large enough for her to walk through without snagging her space suit against the shattered metal framework. There were no lights—just the distant glow of the Cluster shining through the transparent deckhead. As everywhere in *Louise,* there was no movement, no sound.

But Amelia sensed something else. There was a smell in the air.

It was salty, almost metallic, amplified by the close confines of the space and the lack of ventilation. She immediately slipped her blade from its scabbard.

"Sir, I smell blood."

Her torch cast a bright beam across the consoles of the merchant bridge. She panned it carefully across the space, revealing the control panels and seating typical of a civilian merchant. The light continued toward the port bulkhead.

"XO, Sails," came Swift's crackling voice over the cir-

cuit. *"We've found multiple dead in propulsion control. Looks like murder, not combat."*

Amelia's torch paused, frozen on a gruesome sight on the bridge's port side. She moved closer, her heart hardening even as her stomach churned.

"XO acknowledges," Blackwood said beside her. "We have the same here on the bridge."

The bodies of the merchant crew had been tossed in a hideous pile, cleared out of the way while the pirates ransacked the bridge systems. Most of the bodies were clean kills, but the one heaped on the top was hacked with multiple wounds. Shallow wounds, designed to cause pain rather than kill outright. This one man had clearly been made to suffer before he was killed. The deck leading to the pile was sticky with blood, with even a few grisly footprints tracking through.

Booted, Human footprints, she noted immediately. Not bug pads or brute triangles. There may have been Sectoid weapons involved outside, but not in here. Amelia looked around for any evidence, willing this atrocity to have been committed by one of the other races. But the pirates, it seemed, were of her own kind.

Swallowing back an uprush of bile, she glanced at Blackwood. He was gingerly inspecting the top body, his own saber tracking the multiple wounds that had mutilated the poor merchant. His expression, she saw in the dim light, was incandescent with rage. His lips were pursed shut, eyes staring down at the carnage.

Those eyes suddenly shifted to Amelia, pinning her where she stood.

"Our enemy has revealed himself," he said with deathly calm.

"I'll start gathering evidence," Amelia said, fumbling

for her recorder. "We'll need it for when we bring these villains to the Imperial court."

"These bastards will be lucky if they even get to see the inside of a court," he muttered.

Amelia couldn't help but agree.

CHAPTER 8

"Can't find a thing to wear, sir?"

Liam glanced over his shoulder at Swift, who leaned against the cabin door, arms folded, one eyebrow slightly raised. The propulsor was dressed in shabby civilian clothes, a long brown coat hiding the various equipment hidden on his person.

Through the cabin porthole, Liam could see the nearest spar of the orbital station stretching away from *Daring*'s berth. It was time to go ashore and start creating a reputation as a civilian merchant.

"It's not that I haven't an outfit, Sails," Liam said, turning back to his tiny closet. "It's that I have to make sure I clash."

"Clash with whom?"

"Myself."

He was already wearing a riding outfit that was suitably rugged-looking, but that hinted that he was a man of means. The obvious completion to the ensemble would be a short-coat, perhaps with tails, but he knew that would both make him stand out like a toff and make it difficult to hide his weapons. Glancing again at Swift, Liam grabbed a dark blue long-coat. It was a mixing of fashions that would have drawn derision back home but would pass for vaguely successful out here in the cultural wilderness.

He turned to Swift with a slight bow. "Will I pass for a master of this vessel?"

"Yes, sir, in a shabby sort of way." He paused. "I like the stubble."

Liam absently rubbed his unshaven chin.

"Do you know if Sky was able to coach Virtue on what to wear?" Swift asked.

"I think of us all, the good quartermaster will fit in most naturally."

"You're probably right." Swift was still staring at him, but Liam recognized the unspoken question in the propulsor's eyes. "What?"

"You have a lot of faith in our quartermaster, to bring her along on the first clandestine mission, sir."

Liam fastened his long-coat. "You saw her that evening on Passagia—she's more than capable of taking care of herself."

"Agreed. But can she play the role?"

Liam motioned Swift aside so he could leave the cabin, patting the man on the shoulder as he did so. "I think she's full of surprises, Sails."

"Hmm." He heard Swift fall in behind him. "Well, I'm certainly impressed by any woman who can hold your attention quite this much."

He spun suddenly, then glanced down at the deck, embarrassed at how easily Swift had baited him. When he raised his eyes, Swift was staring at him in amusement, eyebrow cocked and arms folded. It was easier to fool himself than his propulsor, it seemed.

"Shut up, Mason," he said finally, fighting down his own smile. He turned back and headed for the ladder.

Just as he reached the first step down, the bridge door opened and Commander Riverton appeared. "Ah, Sub-commander Blackwood. A moment, if you please."

"Head down to the brow and ensure Sky and Virtue are ready," Liam said to Swift. "I'll join you shortly."

He turned expectant eyes to his captain as Swift vanished. She folded her arms and stared back at him. There was silence on the quarterdeck for a long moment. Finally, Liam cleared his throat, wondering if she was waiting for him to speak. "My ashore team is fully briefed and ready, ma'am. We're just about to depart."

"I see you've chosen to play the part of a man with no fashion sense," she said, eyeing him up and down. "Won't that draw attention?"

"Doubtful," he said, smoothing his long-coat. "Most likely no one in this system cares a jot for noble fashion. And if there actually is anyone who recognizes my mismatches, they'll dismiss me for a fool."

"Exactly," she said, lips pursed.

"And that too can be very useful, ma'am."

"In my experience it's best to blend in with the locals and not draw any attention at all."

"What experience is that, ma'am?" The question was mild, but Liam immediately regretted it.

Riverton's eyebrow raised slightly. "I served five years in the Imperial diplomatic corps."

"Yes, ma'am." Liam didn't dare comment further on

the subject. "Will you be dispatching a message of our Sectoid sighting to Lord Grandview?"

"No. At a station this small there would be no way to send such a message without risk of interception. Our mission is to remain hidden, Mr. Blackwood."

"Yes, ma'am." He paused, still uncertain how open Riverton was to suggestions from her executive officer. "But I think this might constitute one of the reasons for breaking our silence: evidence of a Sectoid attack on a Human ship."

"That is puzzling," she admitted after a surprisingly long moment. "Evidence of acid weapons, but you say that the merchant crew were clearly killed by Human weapons."

"Yes, but—"

"Then we don't actually have evidence of Sectoids killing Humans."

Liam might have scoffed, but the focused intelligence of her gaze gave him pause. He considered what he'd seen.

"Perhaps a force of multiple races," he offered. "We know the Theropods sometimes engage in piracy."

"But never Sectoids," she insisted, "to our knowledge."

"True . . ." He studied her, frustrated at his complete inability to read her. "But, ma'am, with war looming, I feel that merely spotting that Sectoid ship still gives us a good reason to break silence: to report a sighting of the enemy."

"And if war is declared then the Sectoids will be our enemy," she replied, frustration hissing behind her words. "But until then we remain silent."

"Yes, ma'am." She had a point, he conceded. And if things got worse and she still refused to break silence, then Liam could always just contact Grandview himself—it certainly wouldn't be the first time he'd gone behind a captain's back for their own good. But Riverton didn't seem like Silverhawk and the others, and for now he was willing to follow her lead.

"On that note," she continued, "keep your local queries focused on the pirate activity—not the Sectoids."

Liam hadn't planned on specifically asking the locals about a lurking alien spaceship, but he hadn't thought it was off-limits.

"Yes, ma'am. Any reason in particular to avoid the Sectoid topic?"

"In my five years in the diplomatic corps, I learned just how unreasonable our people can be concerning the other races. It will inevitably cause rumors and unease in the population, and it will draw unnecessary attention to you."

Fair enough, Liam conceded, nodding blandly to hide his surprise. Her appreciation for the common folk was quite unlike Silverhawk and the others. His estimation of her quietly rose. "Very good, ma'am."

"And no booze," she suddenly said, luminous eyes boring into him.

He froze, fighting down sudden frustration. Did she really think he was incapable of doing his job sober?

"Captain," he said, choosing his words carefully. "I've done this sort of intelligence gathering many times before. More times, I daresay, than you have. Please trust me."

Another moment passed, then Riverton took a deep breath and lifted her chin in what Liam recognized as a court-trained gesture of reluctant submission. It was so natural that he doubted Riverton even realized she'd done it, for when she spoke her voice was as commanding as ever.

"Very well. Good luck, and report to me immediately upon your return." She strode aft toward her cabin.

Liam descended through the decks, shaking off Riverton's insult to his professionalism. He could tell by now that she was smarter than most noble commanders, and genuinely seemed to take her duties seriously—but she sometimes gave the strangest orders.

Not to mention that even after years of service, it was proving impossible to shake the mental images of the slaughter in *Lightning Louise*. Every time he thought about it, he felt a new surge of rage toward Riverton's decision not to intervene. He knew that *Daring* probably wouldn't have been able to save those poor people, even at full sail and thrusters, but at least she could have tried.

He strode forward into one of the airlock spaces where a connector tube now linked the ship to the station. Swift, Sky, and Virtue were all waiting for him, each dressed in the dull, practical civilian clothes of merchant spacefarers.

He absently rubbed again at the unfamiliar stubble on his chin as he sized up their appearances. The chief propulsor had shaved, but with his completely bald head his look was more menacing than military. Sky's usual scowl was in place, but at least she'd let her hair down, hanging in a straight column to her collar. Virtue's own loose hair hung about her shoulders much more naturally; as expected, she easily looked the most civilian of any of them.

"We're heading ashore," Liam said simply. "Swift and Sky, keep your mouths shut and your eyes open. Virtue, you're up front with me."

She stared at him in surprise. "Me, sir?"

"Yes. Our primary mission is to obtain a set of charts,

but we also need to pick up a few things, and you can talk supplies with the best of them. Feel free to haggle. Just remember that you're not in the Navy—Amelia."

"Yes, sir."

"I hate to say it, but you'd do better to call me 'milord' if anything."

"Yes . . . milord."

"And the rest of you are all using first names. Your real first names, just so it's easy to remember."

Virtue's gaze shifted between Swift and Sky, a flicker of concern giving way to quiet embarrassment. He guessed the source of her sudden concern and leaned in to whisper in her ear.

"That's Mason"—he pointed at Swift before gesturing at Sky—"and that's Harper."

It was cute when she blushed, he thought.

"Mason," he said at regular volume, "you're watching for any unusual equipment and, Harper, you're keeping us safe. I'm the noble in exile who's trying to rebuild my fortune and you, Amelia, are the cargo master who's going to do that for me. You and I are going to be the only ones drawing attention."

She nodded, a flash of anticipation in her eyes.

"And remember that our ship's name," he said with a smile, "is *Sophia's Fancy*."

Sky led the way through the hard connector tube, hands lingering near the pistols she had strapped to each hip beneath her coat. As she opened the airlock to the station's interior, the connector was flooded with the stale air of an overworked environmental system, laced with an unpleasant mix of organics and machinery. Virtue coughed in front of him, and he wiped his own eyes to clear their sudden sting.

The orbital platform, known as Windfall, was the largest settlement on Farmer's Paradise, and it was hundreds of kilometers above the surface, connected by a single elevator to a grubby town in the middle of the agricultural plain far below. Navy records indicated that the repair and replenishment facilities here were competent, if overpriced, and while there were no manufacturing capabilities, there was enough trade to supply standard goods. It was trade that kept this station alive, providing just enough work to keep drawing in destitute farmers from the vast, hostile countryside.

The long line of landing berths had transparent sides and the various ships tied up outside the station's hull were clearly visible, bows pointing upward as each ship connected beam-on to the airlock. Each berth had a clear area in front of it, and they opened into a massive interior chamber with soaring walls and as much floor space as a planetary village. Sunlight streamed in from high overhead and there were even a few birds flitting between solitary gnarled trees in garden mounds. The outside walls of the chamber were still metal, but a great deal of effort had clearly once been made to make this central part of the station look terrestrial.

A waist-high fence separated the berths from the main thoroughfare, but there were no guards and Liam pushed the gate aside with barely a nudge. Locals walked past, barely glancing at the new arrivals, but across the street, scattered in front of an assortment of taverns, cafés, and shops, the usual riffraff of port life eyed them with varying degrees of interest.

"I don't see any obvious reception area for new arrivals," Liam said, looking at the Imperial port building directly ahead of them.

"If there even is a customs official on duty," Swift muttered, "he's probably snoozing or drunk."

"Likely both," Liam agreed. "Let's hit the Cup of Plenty."

The Cup of Plenty, Liam recalled from previous visits years ago, was a coffeehouse known for its patronage of merchants. He spotted the sign hanging several doors down on the far side of the street. "Your pistol comfortable?" he asked Virtue as they weaved through the traffic.

"Not really." She laughed, adjusting the lapel of her leather coat over the concealed weapon pressed tight against her torso. "But at least I don't have a giant sword."

He placed a hand on the long dagger on his belt. "I'd hardly call it a sword, but it'll do for today."

"It's beautiful."

"A gift from my father years ago." He cast her a wry look. "It makes me look the part of the faded noble, don't you think?"

"It's more the size of blade I'm used to," she said. Then she flashed him a sudden grin. "If ever you want to trade it for my cutlass on a boarding, I'm in."

They strolled past the first tavern, with its open doors and broad windows occupied by young ladies and gentlemen whose beckoning eyes promised more than just ale, and the second with its beer kegs piled high out front. The third establishment, the Cup of Plenty, was a larger, brick frontage, and from the number of patrons crowding the open patio, was clearly a local favorite. Liam led his team inside, where the café was arranged in neat rows of long tables, each able to seat three a side in comfort, on a dark, tiled floor under a vaulted roof. The rich smells of roasted beans helped to mask the stale air outside, and on the far wall was an entire table of elegant pastries and cakes. Liam needed only a glance at the finer clothing and smaller number of the patrons inside to guess that the coffee was much more expensive if you wanted to drink it here. With a nod of satisfaction, he headed for one of the tables.

AMELIA FOLLOWED BLACKWOOD ACROSS THE SMOOTH wooden floor of the wonderful café, trying to appear nonchalant even as she drank in the sights and smells. About half the tables were occupied, and all were quiet, she noticed; no gales of laughter, no fists thumping tables—everyone in the café seemed intent on their conversations. One or two glances were cast toward her group, but otherwise they were ignored.

She gladly accepted Blackwood's invitation to sit beside him, noting that Swift and Sky took the far side in order to keep their backs to the wall and gazes to the room.

It was all rather surreal, she thought. Here they quietly sat, in an upscale café, when barely two days ago they'd been sorting through bodies on an abandoned merchant ship. Amelia had seen her share of violence, but it had always been the randomness of tavern brawls or petty street thuggery. She'd never seen butchery performed with such brutal intent. The junior boarding-party members were certainly talking about it on the lower decks, but hardly a word had been uttered at her own dinner table. And here she sat, with the three senior members of that boarding party, all lounging casually as if this was just another day on the job. She admired their cool professionalism, but she doubted she'd ever be able to match it.

Blackwood suddenly reached out and gripped her shoulder. She jumped, shaken from her thoughts.

"Amelia, have you ever met one of the other races before?" he asked quietly.

"No, why?" she asked, startled at the randomness of the question.

"You're about to," he whispered.

In the stillness of the café she heard the soft padding of approaching feet, and she forced herself to turn her head slowly.

The server approached in a walking stance, body horizontal over powerful legs and long tail straight out for balance. It was dressed conservatively in a black outfit that covered it from neckline to tail tip, and a brown apron clung to its midsection above narrow hips. Soft, triangular shoes covered each foot, which she knew from pictures ended in three massive, clawed toes. Its small arms were bare, dark stains of coffee grounds visible against pale, scaly skin, and its neck curved up in an S to a narrow, wedge-shaped head dominated by a long mouth, which was kept politely closed. Vertically slit eyes flicked between the new patrons, quickly settling on Blackwood.

The Theropod paused at Human arm's length, rising into its stationary stance, tail dropped to the floor and the body lifted. At full height it was probably as tall as Amelia, but as the guests were seated it lowered its S-neck to meet Blackwood at eye level.

The server's scaly lips parted, revealing rows of teeth as it barked and grunted in its own language.

"Good morning, sir," came the electronic voice from the translator around the neck. "May I bring you a pot of coffee? Would you like something to eat?"

Blackwood met the Theropod's gaze with complete casualness, as if he spoke to other races on a daily basis.

Amelia tried to take her cue from this and not stare, but the creature was close enough to touch. If the server was aware of her fascination, no indication showed in the reptilian gaze.

"Good morning, madam," Blackwood replied. "A pot of coffee, with five cups. No food, thank you."

The translator around the server's neck growled and snorted its words. The head cocked.

"Five cups? Are you expecting another?"

"Actually, I'm hoping you can help with that. My ship has recently arrived here in Windfall, looking for honest cargo to take on."

The head bobbed fluidly on its neck in a decent imitation of a Human nod. "I'll bring you five cups."

It pivoted away in a quick movement that harkened back to its ancient ancestors' hunting instincts, body lowering to a walking stance and weaving around the dessert table as it retreated to the kitchen.

Amelia tore her gaze away, noticing that Blackwood was watching her. His eyes sparkled with good humor.

"Wow," she said, trying to match his apparent ease. "That's not something you see every day."

"Out here it is," growled Sky. "The brutes go anywhere they think they can make money and not pay taxes."

"This place," Swift added, casting a critical eye toward the door, "probably has just the right amount of anarchy to suit."

Amelia took this in, nodding as she glanced back again to where the server had disappeared. "It seemed nice."

"It is a she," Blackwood said. "You can tell by the lack of adornment on the head—the smooth bones of the nose and around the eyes."

"Are we going to see any bugs here too, do you think?"

"Probably not. The bugs hate this sort of remote wilderness—they like crowds."

"Have you ever met one?"

"What, a bug?"

"Yes." Amelia had heard enough stories of the Sectoids—she was eager to hear a firsthand account.

Blackwood frowned thoughtfully. "I've seen Sectoid ships in space, but never come face-to-face with an individual."

She glanced questioningly at Swift and Sky. The propulsor shook his head.

"Once," said Sky. "A scouting party jumped us when we'd crashed on one of their claimed worlds. It's best to aim for the neck or the waist, where the thorax meets the abdomen." She met their gazes and shrugged. "The meeting didn't end well."

The coffee arrived within minutes. Amelia was fascinated to watch the server carry the pot in one small hand and a gaggle of cups in the other, both slung in a mesh frame supported by a flat tray. The Theropod expertly avoided physical contact as she reached between Amelia and Blackwood to place everything on the table and lay it out with quick, bird-like movements. Amelia had to fight the temptation to reach out and run her fingers along the smooth scales of the brute's arm. Were their bodies cold, or hot? Did they need clothing or was it just an affectation for Human clientele? What kind of food did they eat?

"Do you actually like coffee?" she finally blurted, unable to hold back.

The server ignored the translated question at first, clearing the trays and their webbing from the table. But after the moment of silence extended, she stepped back, eyes flicking from Human to Human. She noticed Amelia watching her and lowered her head to stare back. A third eyelid flashed across her vision, then her long lips parted as she growled. Her translator was only a second behind.

"We like the smell. There are a lot of rich textures to it. You're welcome to enjoy the taste."

Amelia could feel a stupid grin tugging at her lips. She was talking to a Theropod! A dozen questions burst to life in her mind to ask, but with effort she pushed them down. The creature stared back at her now in silence, expectation clear even through her reptilian features.

"Thank you," Amelia said finally.

The server bobbed her head and retreated once again to the kitchen.

"Making friends?" Swift commented, taking a sip. His eyebrows suddenly shot up and he looked at his cup. "This is *good* coffee."

"When you live your life based on smell," Blackwood said, "you can mix a pretty mean blend."

"Can we get a few brutes on board as stewards? I could go for more of this."

"So," Sky asked, "what now?"

"We sit and enjoy our coffee," Blackwood replied. "And wait for business to come to us."

Amelia lifted her cup and tasted the hot, bitter liquid. It was powerful, and not unpleasant, but she reached for the sugar nonetheless and spooned in some sweetness.

"I see we have a more civilized coffee drinker at the table," Blackwood said with a smile. "I learned to drink the stuff as a young bridge watchkeeper, and we always seemed to run out of sugar on the bridge. It was down this stuff straight, or find another way to stay awake."

"Sugar was a rarity where I grew up," Amelia admitted. "It was always a huge treat to have some in the market. When I first discovered coffee I thought it was as repulsive as most Navy fare, but then I heard it was acceptable to put sugar in it."

"So coffee is nothing more than a sugar delivery system for you?" Blackwood observed.

"Pretty much," she said smugly, stirring in another spoonful and taking a sip.

"Do you have any idea who we can approach for business?" Swift asked, eyes casually scanning the room.

"None whatsoever," Blackwood replied, leaning back casually in his seat. "But then, as a merchant new to the station, why would I? Anyone watching us will expect me to be haughtily disinterested in the common rabble."

Swift nodded, pouring himself another cup. Sky, Amelia saw, hadn't touched her drink, or even moved a muscle as she expertly watched the room.

"Both of you, relax," Blackwood said, with a touch of exasperation. "Or at least look like it."

Sky slowly sat back in her chair, placing her hands in her lap. Swift managed a wry smile.

"I think you and Amelia need to up your game," he said. "Create a smoke screen of friendly chatter."

Amelia glanced at Blackwood, her mind racing for something to say.

"Do Theropods lay eggs," she asked suddenly, "or have live young?"

Blackwood leaned in with sudden interest, his arm brushing hers. "I'll bite. Which is it?"

"Uh," she stammered. "I don't know—I'm asking you!"

His laughter was deep and musical. "It sounded like you were making a joke, Amelia. I was genuinely curious where you were going with that." His friendly smile robbed his words of any mockery. "But to answer your question, I think they lay eggs."

"They do," Sky added. "Their nests are the only things they get really defensive about."

Amelia nodded thoughtfully, suddenly charmed at the idea of Theropod villages aggressively defending their young. It sure sounded better than the wretched town where she'd grown up.

She glanced at Sky. "Where are you from, Harper?" she asked, curious if the woman's childhood had been similar to her own.

Sky's eyebrows raised at the question, but her expression softened. "Pacifica. A farming village which bored me to tears."

When no further information seemed forthcoming, Amelia turned to Swift with an inquiring gaze.

"I grew up in space," he said. "My family are traders and we worked for several different merchant houses over the years."

"Is there anywhere you might call home today?"

"Passagia, I guess." He glanced at Blackwood. "My lord is kind enough to drag me along to a fancy ball on occasion."

The words were mild, but they caught Amelia off guard. She caught Sky's glance, and saw a touch of envy in those eyes that mirrored her own. Amelia hadn't ever been inside a noble house, let alone attended a ball. It was easy to forget, she suddenly realized, how different Blackwood's life was from theirs when they left their ship behind. Did he even realize that?

"Mason endures my company from time to time in such settings," Blackwood said with a self-deprecating tone, "and for that I'm grateful."

"It's hardly your company that draws me in, milord—it's the good food."

"And drink," Blackwood added, before giving Amelia an appraising glance. "Perhaps you might join us next time, Amelia? It would be more fun than meeting in dark alleys, I think."

Amelia thought about the brawl at the Laughing Boar she'd escaped. "I don't know if I'm ladylike material," she said wryly. He was still staring at her, so she gave him an appraising glance in return. "But I think you might hold your own at the tavern, if you could drop that accent and learn to cuss."

Blackwood's face lit up as he laughed again. She heard Swift snort with good humor, and even Sky chuckled.

"Perhaps you just need to drop *your* accent," Blackwood retorted. "My vote is still for the ball. I'll even teach you how to dance."

"Good luck with that . . . milord."

THE NEXT HALF HOUR WAS UNDOUBTEDLY THE kind of experience Commander Riverton had not wanted them to have, but that Liam had every intention of enjoying. He was in an upscale café on a distant station, drinking fine coffee with an officer and a chief he respected, and a woman who continued to impress him. Virtue's sincerity was a pleasant counter to Swift's dry sarcasm and Sky's blunt responses to any direct queries. She was really a breath of fresh air after so many years of navigating the intrigue embedded in any conversation with a noblewoman, and Liam had to confess that he was actually quite enchanted with this no-nonsense commoner. The Theropod occasionally padded by, checking in as she made the rounds of all her clients. Liam could almost have forgotten that they were on a mission—that this was just a pleasant run ashore—until the server suddenly approached with a Human in tow.

"Sir," she hissed through her translator, "this gentleman would like to speak to you."

The newcomer was a bull of a man, folds of mottled skin hanging from his jawline. His broad face was pale, his skin was weathered by years of artificial environments, and long, scraggly hair hung from beneath his hat. Deep-set eyes scanned the table, lingering on Virtue before returning to Liam.

"Matthew Long," he said simply, "warehouse owner." His deep voice had a liquid quality to it, almost a faint gurgle from deep in the throat. "Welcome to Farmer's Paradise."

"Thank you," Liam replied, allowing his noble accent to emerge as if he was addressing his father. "Please, join us."

As Long took a seat and the server departed, Swift poured the last of the coffee into the fifth cup and sat back.

"I am Julian Stonebridge, master of the merchant ship *Sophia's Fancy*," Liam continued once the man was settled. "I am bound for Silica and have room aboard for legitimate cargo."

"Well, I can get you cargo, but I can't guarantee it's legitimate," Long said bluntly. "How much space do you have?"

"Twenty standard units, as well as secure storage for any handheld items."

"What kind of armament do you carry?"

"I said," Liam huffed, "that we carry legitimate cargo. I'm not interested in moving contraband weapons."

Long's dark eyes watched him carefully, clearly assessing possibilities in his mind. "No, my lord," he said, "I meant how well armed is your vessel? There are reports of pirates in this region."

Liam made a show of considering this. "Well enough, I'm sure. Not that we'll need it, as our speed will keep us clear of any brigands. Which reminds me—do you have up-to-date charts on small objects in this sector?"

The gravitational maelstrom of the Cluster had little direct effect on local orbits this far out in the Halo, but comets, asteroids, and even whole planets were sometimes flung loose from the Hub, causing havoc for navigation. New objects were often discovered only by accident and at close range, and updated charts were a vital—and expensive—tool for the merchant hoping to sail fast.

"Yes, I believe I may, even though they're very hard to come by."

"And do you know a good chandler who can supply us with a few minor engineering parts?"

"Why don't we go to my offices to discuss this further, my lord? It's just down the street."

"Excellent." Liam rose to his feet, dropping a small collection of coins noisily on the table.

Long rose more slowly, and with some effort, eyes resting on Virtue again.

"Your crew are also welcome, my lord."

Liam felt a rush of revulsion for this man, but continued to play his role. He glanced back at his team with a start, as if he'd already forgotten about them.

"Yes, of course. Come along."

With a heavy limp, Long led the way back out to the station's main thoroughfare. Liam fell in beside him, practically shuffling his feet to maintain the slow pace. As a group of five moving slowly, they created quite a large obstacle in the flow of locals moving past them, drawing no shortage of glares. It was hardly the best way to keep a low profile, and Liam scanned the street for anyone who seemed to be paying them too much attention. No shortage of eyes followed their movement, but whether they were motivated by annoyance, simple curiosity, or something more nefarious was impossible to tell.

Long eventually led them down one of the many side alleys stretching away from the main street. As the clearance overhead dropped, Liam felt like he was on a ship again, with the cold metal of bulkheads stretching between the modest business fronts on either side of the corridor. When he reached a sign that read LONG VOYAGES, Mr. Long pushed open the door and entered, inviting Liam and the others to follow.

Within was a modest office staffed by a pair of bored-looking workers, a middle-aged woman and a man who might have been younger but who had clearly led a hard life, if one could draw such conclusions from his weathered skin and the weariness of his expression. Liam was invited to take the only comfortable-looking seat in the semiprivate corner of the office. Long growled at the man to make some tea and at the woman to bring some files.

"What engineering parts do you need, my lord?" he asked, his obsequious tone returning.

"My cargo master can answer specifics," Liam said, waving vaguely at Virtue. "Just direct us to the chandler."

"Tom," Long barked at the man making tea, "sort out my good captain's chandler needs and arrange to have parts delivered to his ship."

Tom diligently finished brewing the tea, delivered a cup each to his boss and Liam, then quietly engaged

Virtue in a discussion about parts. Virtue tried to look serious, but she was clearly enjoying her role pretending to be a civilian merchant. Swift hovered at her shoulder to provide technical expertise. Sky kept her eyes on the whole room.

A thick sheaf of files was brought over by the woman, and Long made a show of sifting through them. "Let me take a look at some of the cargoes which are currently on the station. You say you're bound for Silica, my lord?"

"Yes. But before we discuss cargoes, I want to secure a small-object chart. You did say you have one?"

"Ah, yes."

Plucking a key from his pocket, he reached back and unlocked a safe. He pulled out a data cube and handed it to Liam, pointing out the Imperial date stamp on it.

"As you can see, my lord, this is an official chart issued less than forty days ago—hard to get more current than that." He gestured at the clearly empty safe. "This is my last copy. They are impossible to tamper with and impossible to duplicate, so you can rest assured that this is the genuine article. That does mean that it comes with a substantial price, of course, but it is worth every penny."

Liam examined the cube, immediately recognizing the date stamp as official and seeing no signs of tampering. It was a frustrating reality that small-object charting was too localized and too chaotic for a bureaucratic, centralized organization like the Navy to stay on top of, and this wasn't the first time he'd had to purchase a civilian navigation tool to assist in operations. But this level of detailed knowledge was essential to *Daring*'s mission.

"Tell me about these pirates you mentioned," he said lightly as he handed the cube back to Long.

"Dangerous folk, my lord. Not two days ago they attacked a ship, *Lightning Louise,* within sight of Farmer's Paradise—stole everything and killed the crew." He flicked one of the cargo sheets. "This shipment here was supposed to be for *Louise,* in fact. I could make you a special offer if you're willing to take it out of here on schedule."

"Do the pirates operate mostly around this planet? Should I make all haste to clear to a certain distance?"

"I don't think they're based on the planet, my lord. Most of the attacks occur farther away—this latest one was unusually bold. It's making for uncertainties in the entire sector. As you are clearly brave enough to continue your trade, I think you may stand to do very well."

"We can handle a bunch of rogues," Liam said with the airiness of an ignorant toff, "but I'd rather not risk my crew. If you know of any routes which are safer than others, I'd be quite grateful."

"Likewise, my lord, if you can safely deliver some of my cargo, I will quite grateful."

He was desperate to unload goods, Liam realized. No doubt many merchant captains were simply refusing to ply this sector, and if trade ground to a halt, it would spell disaster for all of the colonies.

"I would like to work together, Mr. Long."

With renewed energy, Long placed the data cube in his terminal and brought up the chart. He marked out every pirate attack location he knew of in the past four seasons, giving what info he could on the results of the attack. Liam listened carefully, noticing a clear pattern of increasing aggressiveness in the attacks—but nothing to pinpoint a base of operations. Long's information wasn't useless, but it was little more than rumor and hearsay. Perhaps further data mining of the chart back aboard *Daring* would provide fresh insight.

Finally, Liam sat back. Long eyed him expectantly.

"Can we make a deal, my lord?"

The man had been of some use, Liam admitted to himself.

"I'll take your chart, but I'll need to consider the cargo options. Give me half a day."

Frustration welled up in the deep-set eyes, but Long kept his face neutral. He handed Liam the cargo manifest that had been destined for *Lightning Louise*.

"I would like to see this shipment moved and I'll offer you a very generous price."

Liam removed the data cube from the terminal, pocketed it, and placed a tidy pile of coins on the table between them. He was probably going to take the offered cargo, he knew, but making the merchant wait was all part of the negotiations.

"As I said, I will consider your offer of the cargo." He rose and looked over to where Virtue was busy writing on a form for Tom. "Have you sorted your needs, Amelia?"

"Yes, milord," she said, eyes flashing. "Tom will arrange for the delivery this afternoon."

"Splendid." He nodded to Long. "Good morning to you, sir."

Long struggled to his feet, his dark expression partially shielded as he bowed his head.

"Good morning, Captain."

Sky led the way back out with Swift and Virtue close on her heels. Liam followed, keeping his eyes on every side alley. No doubt Mr. Long was well connected on this station, and Liam knew his performance as a new, arrogant noble captain splashing money everywhere would start tongues wagging immediately.

"Word will be getting out about us," he warned his team, "and we're a little far from the ship. Keep your eyes open for trouble."

Once they were back on the street, they slipped into the general movement of the crowds. Merchants shouted their wares from a long line of temporary stalls, and young boys darted along and across the promenade.

"Watch those boys," Virtue said, walking beside him. "Where I come from, they're often runners and lookouts."

"I have no doubt we're being watched," Liam replied. "It was my intention. Let's just hope we convinced them that we are who we say."

"Amelia did a fine job negotiating," Swift offered. "I think she saved us a dozen crowns."

"Yeah," she said, grinning suddenly. "That was kind of fun."

The flow of people was quick and they retraced their steps in good time. Liam eventually saw the sign for the Cup of Plenty hanging up ahead and he began to relax. The docks were just beyond, and through the clear canopy he could see the rugged form of *Daring* floating safely.

"Sir," Sky hissed from behind him, "trouble at two o'clock."

He casually turned his head, and immediately spotted the group of men who had just risen en masse from two tables in front of the Cup of Plenty. And they were all looking at Liam.

"Move faster," he said.

He grabbed Virtue's hand, increasing his pace to a jog and slipping through the crowd. The group of men abandoned any attempt at stealth and rushed forward, pouring off of the café's deck and shoving people aside. Liam broke into a run, feeling Virtue match his pace even as she held on to him. He glanced back to see Swift and Sky pushing locals out of their way and into the path of the oncoming thugs. Turning forward, he saw the fence to the docks ahead.

But his path was suddenly blocked by a trio of powerful young men who closed in, shoulder to shoulder. Before Liam could veer off, they were upon him, strong hands grabbing his shoulders. Virtue's hand slipped violently out of his. He shook off his assailant, blocking a massive forearm swinging down at his head. He launched a hook punch into the thug's chest and felt the inner sagging as his blow knocked the lungs empty of air. A sharp elbow to the back of the neck and the thug dropped to his knees.

Swift had already downed an attacker and was wrestling with a second. Sky was grappling with a large man; a sharp twist of her hands caused a sickening crack and he collapsed in pain, desperately cradling his arm. Another man grabbed her from behind in a choke, but she muscled him forward toward Swift then used her own attacker's weight as an anchor as she lifted both legs to deliver a double kick to Swift's opponent. Dropping back, she raked her heels down her attacker's shins and slammed down on his feet. As he staggered she slid sideways, backfisted him in the groin, and pulled loose of his choke to elbow him in the head before knocking him to the ground.

A gunshot cracked through the air. Liam ducked, cursing himself for pausing to admire how dirty Sky fought. The remaining thugs backed away, and Swift and Sky both paused, their gazes darting around for the source of the shot. Screams erupted all across the street as locals ran to clear the area, but within moments a strange quiet had descended.

With growing dread, Liam looked toward where he'd last seen Virtue.

She was being held by a man with a gun. The pistol was still pointed upward, but when he caught Liam's eye, he lowered it. Liam started to move forward, but stopped cold as the thug jammed the pistol against Virtue's skull. She winced in pain. Liam's anger suddenly surged, threatening to overwhelm his cool, tactical assessment.

"Well now," drawled another man, stepping into the several paces between Liam and Virtue. He wasn't as big as the others, but carried an air of petty authority. "There ain't no need for trouble. All's we want is that fancy little chart you're carrying."

He glared at Swift and Sky, then looked toward the inside pocket of Liam's coat, exactly where the data cube rested. Liam guessed they were two paces apart. Swift and Sky were both unencumbered, but the various thugs were slowly picking themselves up from their beatings. There were only a few seconds before the entire group would be combat ready again.

Hiding his anger, he raised his hands and assumed a look of desperation.

"Of course, of course," he said with full noble accent, stepping forward and reaching under his coat. "Have mercy. Please don't hurt us."

"Nobody needs to get hurt," the thug leader said. "I reckon—"

His sentence died on a gargled gasp as Liam plunged the dagger into his heart. His head tried to turn back and shocked eyes faded to darkness even as Liam grabbed him and charged forward into the pistol-wielding thug. A crash of bodies saw the weapon tumble to the ground and Virtue immediately scrambled free and leaped back. Liam pushed until his enemy fell, the weight of the body landing on top of the thug. Then he recovered the dropped gun and pointed it at the remaining thugs, motioning Virtue in close behind him. His free hand gripped hers and he could hear her rapid breathing.

"You have ten seconds until I take it upon myself to determine how many more bullets are left in this pistol," he said coldly, silently daring one of them to give him a reason to fire again.

The thugs ran. As Liam tracked them, he realized with some surprise that he was holding a Navy-issue pistol. Glancing at Virtue, he saw the open flap of her holster visible beneath her coat.

Sky drew her own pistols as she slowly scanned the street. She took the proffered weapon from Liam.

"Everyone all right?" he asked.

Around them, the street activity was already returning to normal. The incident over, locals were quick to continue with their daily routines.

"I'm fine," Virtue managed, her face flushed. "Were those pirates?"

"Local goons," Swift said. "Trying to rough up newcomers."

"They knew exactly where we were," Liam growled, "and where I had the chart in my pocket. We were set up."

"Want me to send a team to pay Mr. Long a visit?" Swift suggested, his face hardening.

"No. I think we made our point. And we still need to be welcome on this station—trashing warehouse offices doesn't seem like the thing an honest merchant would do."

"We're not in a secure position," Sky said, eyes still watching their surroundings. "I recommend we talk on the ship."

"Agreed." Liam wondered if his father would be impressed or horrified to know that his ceremonial gift had actually drawn blood. "Let's get out of here."

He led the way back through the gate and to the airlock, knowing Sky would cover their withdrawal. It wasn't until he reached to activate the airlock that he realized he was still holding Virtue's hand.

CHAPTER 9

"Are you ready for another spin as the plucky cargo master?"

Amelia glanced over at Blackwood, appreciating the good-natured expression on his usually stern face. She didn't mind looking at him either way, and she was embarrassed how many times he'd caught her staring recently. She really needed to focus on their mission, especially now that they'd arrived at a new port of call.

Their eventful visit to Windfall Station was more than a week in the past, and the quiet transit across the outer Silica sector hadn't dampened her enthusiasm for another run ashore in disguise.

"Ready, milord. Let's grind these merchants down with our skillful negotiations."

He clapped her on the shoulder and signaled Swift to open the cargo doors. The touch of his hand sent a rush of warmth through her, but she shook it off. The mission, she reminded herself.

The crates were lined up in *Daring*'s midships cargo

bay, using every lifter on board. Normally she would have mustered the entire ship's company to off-load this amount of supplies, but no merchant ship sailed with a crew that large. So it was just her, Swift, and Blackwood to handle the lot.

The cargo doors clanged to a stop and once again the metallic air of a space station drifted in. Amelia followed Blackwood through the wide gangway connecting the ship to the jetty and got her first look at station Silica 7. Her immediate sense was of open space, but a space very different from the promenade at Windfall. The utilitarian spar was wide enough for a regiment of soldiers to march down, but barely taller than a typical station passageway. *Daring* had taken the single berth at one end and Amelia could see a series of open airlock doors at the other, perhaps a hundred paces away. The long, low, industrial space was lined on either side with cargo caged behind hastily assembled mesh walls, a single tractor rumbling faintly at the far end of the spar as it moved crates. Perhaps a dozen people were scattered across her view, and more than a few eyes turned her way as she stepped across the cargo gangplank and onto the station's metal deck.

One woman was strolling up the dock, a younger man in tow, and her gaze quickly settled on Amelia and Blackwood. She carried a clipboard and the young man trailed a box on wheels behind him. They moved with easy purpose and Blackwood stepped forward to greet them.

"Captain Julian Stonebridge," he said as he extended his hand. *"Sophia's Fancy."*

"Leah Digger," the woman said with a firm handshake before nodding to her companion. "My son Henry. Welcome to Silica 7."

Amelia had already guessed the family connection.

Both mother and son were of average height and fair complexion, with the same piercing green eyes. She caught the lad's eye and smiled. He smiled shyly back before dropping his gaze.

"We have your scheduled cargo," Blackwood said, "plus an extra shipment which I understand was urgently needed." He offered the cargo manifest. They'd eventually decided to take Matthew Long's offer of the *Lightning Louise* shipment, and a bit of aggressive negotiation by Blackwood had convinced the vile tradesman to throw in the extra cargo for pennies. Long had clearly realized that he'd been caught out in his attempted robbery, and Amelia was confident that the crew of *Sophia's Fancy* would be treated to more respect when they next returned to Windfall Station.

Ma Digger—Amelia thought it was sweet to see a family business like this—read the cargo manifest and compared it to her own sheet. After a moment she handed the manifest to her son and instructed him to begin counting the crates that Swift was efficiently off-loading.

"Are you looking for cash payment, Captain, or a trade for new cargo?"

"I'll have a look at what you have to offer," Blackwood replied. "We're heading back to Farmer's Paradise."

The week-long sail had been quiet, but Amelia knew that the pirates who had hit *Lightning Louise* were still in the area and that the captain and XO were counting on their return voyage to Windfall being considerably more eventful.

"When are you planning to depart?" Digger had opened the wheeled box and was already selecting certain cargo lists.

"As soon as possible, Ms. Digger."

"Henry, help this crew unload."

Blackwood nodded to Amelia to go as well. Amelia smiled at the young man again and walked with him back toward the crates.

"Do you do a lot of trade these days?" she asked.

"It depends on the days," Henry said with a shrug. "The last three shipments we was expecting never made it."

Swift arrived with the loader and lowered the crates to the deck. Amelia grabbed one side of the first crate and Henry took the other. Together they heaved it over to the pile already on the jetty.

"I hear there are pirates in this region of space," she said as she and Henry grabbed the next crate.

"Either that," he said, "or nobody wants to come to little ol' Silica 7."

"Why wouldn't they?"

"They says there are spies on this station. For the Emperor, and for the other races." He lifted the next crate by himself, scoffing at his own words. "But I ain't never seen anybody I don't know since I was a boy."

"Are there Theropods living here?"

"Sure, a bunch of families, but they don't cause no trouble."

"Any Sectoids?"

He paused at that, staring at her.

"We're a clean, honest station, ma'am," he said slowly. His young face displayed a mix of pride and challenge. The sincerity of his expression warmed her.

"I hear there's a bug ship in the region, but it don't ever come here," he added. "Folks say that those bugs ain't even really alive—they just keep coming no matter how many pieces of 'em you hack off. Word is they kill anybody they find and feed 'em to their larvas."

"We've sure steered clear of it," she said with a smile, noting that the rumors of Sectoid incursions had clearly reached the civilian population.

"But if they came here, they'd have to deal with the Diggers!" He struck a muscular pose, but his absurd expression and goofy smile robbed the gesture of any seriousness. She couldn't help but laugh.

"Amelia!" Blackwood suddenly called. "Come here, please."

She nodded good-bye to her new friend and jogged over. "Yes, milord?"

"Have a look at these." He thrust the cargo papers at her. "What do you think would be suitable for our return to Windfall? I'd like to do a fair exchange for our off-loaded cargo."

She started reading the files, scanning the various cargoes on offer. She knew they'd spent just over six thousand crowns on Long's shipment, but knew also that it was worth quite a bit more. In trade she reckoned they could acquire at least ten-thousand-worth of new cargo, and she scanned the lists to assess which of Digger's offerings were good value.

As she did, Swift pushed the last of the crates out of *Daring* and then guided the lifter back into the cargo hold. Moments later the cargo doors began to rumble shut. Swift darted through the gap and started unlocking the crates for Henry's inspection. In a very few minutes the lad strode back and nodded to his mother.

"Everything accounted for and in good condition."

"Of course it is," Blackwood said haughtily, playing up his role as the fallen nobleman. "I am an honorable businessman."

"No doubt, Captain," Ma Digger replied. "But with the

increasing pirate attacks we never know what condition a cargo may arrive in."

"I'd like to see those blaggards try and catch my ship."

The Diggers exchanged a glance but made no reply.

"I think, milord," Amelia said as she arranged the sheets of paper, "that these three cargoes would be a fair exchange for what we've delivered."

Blackwood examined her choices. She estimated their combined value at fifteen thousand crowns, but figured there was room for negotiation. At his nod, she indicated her choices to Digger. The merchant shook her head.

"I might give you two of them for your cargo, and even then I'd need a small cash payment to balance the exchange."

Blackwood looked at her expectantly. Amelia suppressed her grin, eager for the thrill of negotiation.

"Perhaps you don't understand the value of what we've delivered," she said cheerfully. "These fine silks can be very hard to secure anywhere in the Halo these days, and their market price has risen considerably. And I challenge you to find another merchant with pottery this durable. Such things carry great value."

"Not so much as to be worth three of my cargoes."

Amelia made a show of looking over the cargo lists again. Then she launched into a rapid-fire explanation of the relative merit of several cargoes, using her years of experience as a Navy storesman to bombard them with a flurry of prices, disasters on this planet or that, the fortunes of different companies, and, of course, the pirate threat. Ma Digger listened and interjected a few times, her face severe and her expression focused. But Amelia had a basket of ready answers, never letting her pleasant expression falter.

"Ms. Digger," Blackwood suddenly interjected, sidling past Amelia and placing a hand on Ma Digger's arm. "You're clearly as intelligent as you are beautiful, and we would like to deal fairly. But surely you realize how much I risk, taking my fine vessel through this pirate-infested sector to keep your livelihood going."

Ma Digger's gaze shifted to Blackwood, and Amelia saw a distinct softening in her posture. He gazed down at her with an open, earnest expression.

"Captain," she replied, "your efforts are much appreciated, by all of us. But I have to make a living as well."

"Of course. I want us all to do well out of this. And hopefully"—his rugged features split into a winning smile—"this is just the beginning of our relationship."

She considered, scanning the cargo lists again.

"Perhaps these two cargoes," she said finally, "plus fifteen hundred crowns."

"Would your son be able to show Amelia these cargoes for inspection?"

"Of course."

At her gesture, Henry started toward one of the lockups, motioning for Amelia to follow him.

She hurried to catch up to him, leaving Blackwood to work his charms.

LIAM HELD MS. DIGGER'S GAZE AS HE LIFTED HER hand to his lips.

"An excellent deal, madam. I look forward to a long and prosperous relationship with you."

The woman was seasoned and hard, he could tell, but obviously hadn't been flattered in a long time. Kind words and a few compliments could disarm even the most jaded professional, if delivered correctly. And a courtly kiss of her hand . . . That had caught her pleasantly by surprise.

"I look forward to that as well, Captain Stonebridge," she replied. "When next you return to this station, do try and schedule a longer visit."

"With certainty, madam."

He released her hand and motioned for Virtue to join him as he started walking back toward the ship. The quartermaster's eyes sparkled with good humor as she jogged up to him.

"Did you invite her to a grand ball, milord?"

"No, but perhaps I made her feel like a lady for a few moments." He gave her a sidelong glance. "Negotiations are best when everyone leaves happy."

He handed her the manifest sheets for the cargoes they'd purchased and outlined the deal.

"I'll remain here on the jetty," she offered, "until we've sorted a time for loading."

"Very good." He paused, and Virtue stuttered to a halt next to him. He looked down at her, appreciating anew how her brown eyes glowed from under their fringe of dark lashes. She stared back, her good humor shifting slowly to curiosity.

"Yes, sir?" she finally asked.

"Fine work, Amelia. It was no doubt your avalanche of information that convinced Digger she was getting a good deal. I just gave her the final nudge she needed."

"It's why I'm here," she said with a modest shrug. But a small smile tugged at the corners of her lips all the same. She gave him a nod and left him at the door to the extended gangway.

Liam stepped through and back into *Daring,* nodding

to Able Rating Hedge, who stood guard inside and out of view.

With his eyes diverted he nearly bumped into Commander Riverton as she strode toward the airlock. She was in civilian clothes, her hair tied back in a neat braid.

"Ma'am." He pulled himself to a halt.

She paused, then politely indicated for him to get out of the way.

"We have civilians on the dock, ma'am," he said. "This might not be the best time to step ashore."

"I'm heading onto the station. I won't be more than an hour."

"Yes, ma'am," he replied automatically, then he processed her words. "What?"

"Do I really need to repeat myself?" Her expression hardened.

"No, ma'am, but . . . I thought we had an agreement that only my ashore team would be visible to outsiders."

"I have Chief Sky with me," she said, indicating where Sky was standing a pace behind, staring off with apparent disinterest.

Liam's mind raced. This was not what they'd agreed to. But she was the captain of this vessel. If she wanted to leave the ship, he could hardly stop her. "Shall I accompany you as well, ma'am?"

"No, thank you. You need to ensure our merchant activities are conducted properly—"

"Virtue can do that."

"*And,* I require at least one command-qualified officer on board at all times." Her eyes narrowed in sudden anger. "Get out of my way, Subcommander Blackwood, and don't interrupt me again."

Liam shuffled to the side in the cramped airlock,

bumping against Hedge, who was doing her best to be both silent and invisible amid the clash of senior-officer wills.

"May I inquire as to the captain's business ashore?" Liam persisted.

She stepped past him without another word. Sky avoided eye contact as she slipped by and joined Riverton on the dock. Liam watched as they strolled without apparent concern past the pile of crates and past where Virtue was still discussing details with the Diggers. Swift made no movement as he tracked the captain, and Virtue thankfully didn't notice with her head buried in the paperwork.

Riverton and Sky walked all the way to the end of the dock, where they disappeared into Silica 7 station.

Realizing he hadn't moved from his perch in the airlock, Liam stepped back into *Daring*'s interior. "No one goes ashore," he snapped at Hedge.

"Yes, sir," she whispered.

It was unfair, he knew, taking out his frustration on a sailor. But he also knew that young Hedge was going to report this juicy incident to her messmates as soon as she could. Nothing fueled gossip on board a warship more than a perceived rift between captain and executive officer.

He wandered up a deck and found himself pushing open the door to the senior mess. The smell of fresh-brewed coffee lifted his mood immediately and he motioned for the steward to bring him a cup.

Ava Templegrey and James Highcastle were both lounging at the table, uniform coats draped over their chairs and empty cups in front of them. The bags under Highcastle's eyes were heavy and he leaned forward on his elbows. She, on the other hand, glanced up at Liam with an easy warmth.

"Sir, how nice to see you," she said. "With the watch rotation while under sail I find I can go days without seeing another officer for more than a bridge turnover."

"Well, you look none the worse for wear, Doctor," Liam said as he sat down at the head of the table. "It seems shipboard life suits you."

The steward presented a coffee to Liam and refilled the other officers' cups before retreating.

"Oh, it's a fine enough life," she said, stretching lazily. "And our noble duty, this service to the Emperor."

"But . . . ?"

She laughed, spreading her hands in a courtly gesture of innocence.

"You always think there's a 'but'—can a lady not just state a simple truth?"

Various tidbits of inconsequential noble gossip occupied their casual conversation for a few minutes as Liam sipped at his coffee and felt his mood lighten further. Highcastle roused himself from his stupor and joined in, a surprisingly biting wit peppering his remarks. The lad was many things, Liam thought, but stupid was not one of them. Maybe there was hope yet to turn him into something more effective than his peacock of a cousin.

The door opened and Virtue stepped in. Her face lit up as she spotted Liam and she began talking even as she helped herself to a coffee on the side table. "Sir, everything's arranged. My new friend Henry will have our cargo ready for loading in fifteen minutes."

"A new friend?" Templegrey asked interestedly. "Tell us about this Henry."

Virtue launched into a highly entertaining recounting

of their encounter, her accent shifting beautifully as she quoted young Henry's defense of his station's honor. Her enthusiasm was infectious. Liam found himself laughing and Templegrey had turned fully in her seat to face Virtue by the end.

"So what happened?" she asked. "Does he want to marry you now?"

"I think the talk is going to be whether Lord Blackwood is marrying his mother."

Templegrey spun in her seat. "Oho? Do tell, sir?"

"My good quartermaster exaggerates." He gave a dismissive wave of the hand. "I simply followed Amelia's lead in being lovely."

"*You* being lovely?" Templegrey said in mock astonishment, turning to Virtue and wrapping an affectionate arm around her. "I can't see that at all."

"So we made a good trade," Highcastle muttered. "We're well on our way to becoming common merchants. Huzzah."

"It's all part of our cover," Virtue replied.

"We should be taking those pirates down," Highcastle retorted. "And getting some prize money instead of haggling over pennies."

"And we will, Mr. Highcastle," Liam said, irritated at the sudden dampening of the mood. "When the time is right."

"We had a fix on them," Highcastle said with sudden frustration. "We knew where they were headed, but instead we came to this pathetic little station to sell our trinkets."

"We still know where they are—and more importantly we know where they're going."

Highcastle frowned uncertainly.

"A ship that size can't stay out in deep space for long," Liam added. "They need to replenish, and we know the trajectory of the only natural source of water in this corner of the sector."

"Is that the comet nucleus you were all talking about?" Virtue asked. "What you found on that small-objects chart?"

"Exactly," Liam replied. "Space is full of random bodies like that which wander between systems. There are too many variables to track them long term, so we make new charts to record and report them every so often. Another few months and this chunk might not even be in Silica anymore. Or it might loop around for another orbit—we just don't know."

"But how do you know the pirates will go there?"

"We tracked the pirate ship for more than a week after the attack on *Lightning Louise*," he said. "We knew she was heading in this general direction, but that there were no inhabited worlds or stations on her path. As I said, a ship that size needs to replenish, and the only nearby small object with enough useful water is the comet you mentioned—so that gave us an area to search more closely. Three days ago, we intercepted a series of badly coded transmissions which gave us a lock on the pirate ship."

"They're definitely headed for that comet," Templegrey added, "and they'll be there within two days."

"So we had time," Liam concluded, "to complete our scheduled run and start building our reputation as an honest, completely ordinary merchant vessel."

"Just don't be too adorable to the locals," Templegrey said to Virtue with a wink, "or else we'll have them all lining up to vie for your custom whenever we pull into port."

"I'll try and restrain myself," Virtue said dryly.

"It's all well and good to charm the common folk,"

Highcastle said with a sudden predatory gleam. "Let's see how adorable you are when we're hand to hand with pirates."

Virtue blinked, clearly uncertain how he meant the remark to be taken. "I will do my duty," she said carefully, "when the time comes."

"Just make sure to keep your pistol in your own hand, not theirs, next time."

Liam was on his feet, vaguely hearing the clatter of his chair falling backward as he glared down at the cadet.

"James," Templegrey said with a slight edge to her voice, "that was uncalled for."

Silence hung around the table. For a moment it seemed Highcastle would simply remain silent, but finally he offered Virtue a nod. "My apologies."

Templegrey reached out and stroked his hand. "You're tired, James," she said. "Standing the middle watch as regularly as you have can be exhausting to anyone."

"I'm fine." He sighed.

She leaned forward, resting her chin on her free hand as she stared earnestly at him.

"You're not, darling. I'm a doctor, remember? I can see the detrimental signs of fatigue. We're going to be alongside for at least a few hours. Go and get some rest."

After a painfully long moment, he squeezed her hand and rose. He nodded to Liam, ignored Virtue, and walked heavily from the room.

Templegrey turned to Virtue again. "I'm sorry about that. He's young, and exhausted."

"It's okay," Virtue replied, her previous good humor vanished. She downed her coffee and rose from her seat. "I'm going to go and check on the loading details."

———

HEDGE WAS WATCHING BOTH THE GANGWAY AND the open door between brow and cargo hold when Amelia returned to the brow.

"Hey, Hedgie," she greeted, forcing a smile to her face.

"Hey, PO. Everything seems to be going smoothly."

"Good."

"How's life in the senior mess?" Hedge asked suddenly.

"Oh, nothing special," Amelia replied automatically, suppressing a frown. That little snotter Highcastle could do with a smack, she thought, still reeling from his caustic comments. As she looked at Hedge she really wanted to just vent her frustrations, but overall the officers had made her welcome and she didn't want to spread gossip because of one rude young man.

"Same food," she said finally, "but less flatulence at the table."

Hedge laughed.

"Although some of the noble talk might be considered a different kind of it," she couldn't help but add.

Hedge guffawed, covering her mouth to suppress the sound as she glanced out toward the cargo bay. "Don't blow my cover, PO," she whispered in mock admonishment, fighting down her mirth.

Amelia smiled, knowing that there was little truth in her words. Most of the senior staff were actually commoners, and she could find little fault in Ava Templegrey's exquisite demeanor. And Lord Blackwood . . . he was certainly an example of what every young woman believed a lord should be.

Even Highcastle's recent comment had been cruel, but not unjustified. She *had* lost her pistol to an attacker in the middle of a battle, and it had almost been used against her. She knew better than that, and it had been gnawing at her for the entire transit. She still couldn't believe how forgiving Subcommander Blackwood had been about the whole mess. She wasn't sure how the mission would be faring without him—Commander Riverton was so distant and difficult to read that the entire ship would feel like a different and colder place if not for Lord Blackwood.

On an impulse, she reached back to ensure that the sign indicating no access was still hanging on the door. *Daring*'s true military identity was most at risk at moments like these, with civilians in or near the cargo bay, and the last thing she needed was a uniformed crewmember to wander out into full view. It was part of her responsibility, as a member of the ashore team, to maintain their façade as *Sophia's Fancy* and it never hurt to take that extra step. There was another door on the far side of the cargo bay and she decided to double-check it as well, then wandered over to where Swift was checking an open-topped crate of sacks. Henry's heavy loader was rumbling off down the jetty for the next load.

"Looks like we'll be completed within the hour, Amelia," the propulsion officer commented. "But I'd appreciate if we could train up one of your storesmen to act as part of our civilian crew."

"You don't like counting bags of seed?" she asked with a bit of a smirk.

"I just have more important things to do," he replied tartly. "Like ensuring our thrusters are ready for battle."

Fair point, she realized. She was about to offer to take over when she heard Hedge's laughter again from the brow. Frowning curiously, she excused herself from Swift and walked back to the open door. Stepping through, she saw Hedge leaning against the wall, smiling at High-castle, who smirked down at her. He was still in uniform, and Amelia immediately grabbed the door behind her and swung it shut.

"Sir, you shouldn't be out here dressed so." She bit down a few other choice words, reminding herself that she wasn't the senior rank here.

"I did wonder why you were in civilians," he mused, eyeing her up and down with none of his previous contempt. But his gaze quickly returned to Hedge. "I think we should adopt this sort of dress policy all the time—you look so much prettier."

Hedge dropped her gaze, only to lift her eyelashes at him.

"I can only imagine how beautiful you'd be at a gala ball," he continued softly.

"I'm sure you cut quite a dashing figure yourself at a ball," Hedge replied.

Amelia considered her options. She couldn't order an officer—even a cadet—but she had to get him out of here, and fast. Her first, military instinct was to sharply remind him of the rules and send him packing. But she knew from watching his earlier interactions with Brown how poorly he responded to her no-nonsense style.

He seemed to listen to whatever Ava Templegrey said, though, and it was no secret to Amelia how the good doctor manipulated conversations. She sized up the situation. If she could charm young Henry Digger, she could probably charm young James Highcastle. Swallowing down the revulsion in her gut, she turned on the charm.

"It is possible to have two companions at a ball,"

she said with a sudden smile, wrapping her arm around Hedge's. "You do have two arms, my lord."

Highcastle's face twisted slightly in a cross between a smirk and a frown, but his eyes flicked between the two women. Hedge, as Amelia hoped she would, innocently joined in the banter. She snuggled against Amelia's shoulder.

"Oh, yes, two companions would be much better than one."

The young cadet laughed slightly, clearly sizing up the possibilities in his mind.

"We've been friends for a long time," Amelia added, leaning her head toward Hedge's.

"Perhaps I misjudged you, Amelia," Highcastle said.

She reached out and touched his arm.

"You have lots to learn, my lord," she said, disengaging from Hedge. "And we'll have lots of time to teach you, but not right now. Lord Blackwood is on his way back down and I wouldn't want him to see a uniform this close to the jetty."

"Oh, no, you don't want that," Hedge said sincerely. "The XO could jam your next shore leave."

"Perhaps you're right," Highcastle said, adopting a look of indulgent resignation. "I wouldn't want to risk it."

With a wink and a grin he disappeared back into the ship. Amelia immediately turned to Hedge and rolled her eyes.

"He's sweet," Hedge protested softly.

"He's a lordling," Amelia replied. "Mind yourself around his type, Hedgie."

She shrugged, glancing back through the door that Highcastle had failed to close properly behind him.

"I think we're both entitled to a bit of noble attention."

"What do you mean?"

Hedge's lips were curling into a smirk. She nodded toward the open door behind Amelia.

LIAM PASSED HIGHCASTLE ON HIS WAY TO THE BROW. The cadet offered him a friendly nod, apparently in better spirits. But Liam's attention was drawn ahead to the door to the brow—it was hanging wide open. He stepped through, shutting it firmly behind him.

Hedge was still on brow duty, and before he could speak she shot a meaningful glance to Virtue next to her. For some reason, Virtue blushed.

"Keep this door shut at all times," he said to both of them.

"Yes, sir," Virtue replied.

"How are the loading procedures going?"

"Smoothly. But I need to supervise young Digger and his loader."

She opened the door to the cargo bay abruptly and hurried off.

"Captain's returning," Hedge said suddenly, looking out through the gangway to the jetty.

Liam felt his pulse quicken. His immediate reaction was to greet them on the dock, but he had to maintain his public image as the ship's noble master and he forced himself to stay hidden inside, scanning them for any signs of recent trouble. Both women appeared as when they'd left, Riverton strolling up the dock with willowy grace and Sky stalking along beside her.

As soon as they entered the gangway, however, he stepped into view. Riverton regarded him with her usual cool expression.

"Welcome back, ma'am," he said. He wanted to ask more, but held his tongue in the presence of Sky and Hedge.

"Thank you," she replied without expression. "It appears our merchant activities are proceeding well?"

"Yes, ma'am. I anticipate being ready to sail within the hour."

"Good. Have the sailing crews start preparations for departure. We'll slip as soon as you give the word."

"May I have Chief Sky to help in checking manifests?" he asked quickly, suddenly spotting an opportunity. "Lieutenant Swift needs to get below to supervise and Virtue is directing the loading."

"Of course." Riverton nodded to Sky. "Thank you, Chief."

Liam led Sky back into the cargo bay, where a relieved Swift was only too happy to turn over the manifest duties. Sky silently picked up the task, shifting her gaze casually between her stores and the heavy loader.

She also noticed that Liam was hovering.

"May I be of additional service, sir?" she asked, not pausing in her duties.

Liam hesitated. Sky had been one of Commander Riverton's three personal selections for this crew, just as Swift, Brown, and Virtue had been his. He had already grown to respect his assaulter, but he didn't yet know how much that feeling was reciprocated.

"How was your jaunt ashore?"

"Without incident, sir."

"Did you see much of the station?"

"There isn't much to see. The central hub is no bigger than a country amphitheater and the two spokes we saw looked exactly like what they are—former government offices and barracks converted into private living quarters."

"Are there many people about?"

"We saw a few civilians conducting their daily business, but no crowds like on Windfall. No one appeared threatening, or even interested in us—other than a few glances, no doubt because we're strangers."

"Where did you go?"

"To an apartment which the captain seemed familiar with."

Liam waited for more. Sky continued her inspection.

"Did you go inside?" he asked finally.

"I waited in the main room while the captain had a private conversation in the bedroom with her associate."

"Who was the associate?"

"I don't know, sir," Sky said, with a hint of frustration finally showing through. "He was a somewhat older gentleman, with an accent similar to Her Ladyship's."

Liam knew he'd pushed his assaulter far enough. Thanking her, he retreated to watch the last of the cargo loading from the edge of the bay. He almost wanted to laugh. That was hardly what he'd expected from the aloof Commander Riverton, but if the captain wanted to go ashore for a private dalliance, who was he to begrudge her?

CHAPTER 10

The starlight reflecting down off a full sheeting of sails was enough to bathe the bridge in an ethereal glow. As Liam stepped forward into the space, armor clanking, he clearly saw the expressions of the watch as curious gazes turned toward him. High above, the sails of the top mast pressed against a strong and steady stern wind.

The ship was at battle stations and Liam wasted no time as he strode up to the command chair.

"Captain, XO," he said. "I've completed my rounds and all stations are manned. Both boats are ready for launch. All batteries are loaded and charged. Propulsion and medical both report ready."

Riverton slowly turned her gaze toward him. In the ghostly light even her dark skin looked pallid, but her expression was set in a neutral mask.

"Very good."

He waited for more, but she simply turned back to her screens. On one, he noticed, was a navigation display indicating *Daring*'s vector toward their target. On the other was a weapons control board. *Daring* had six beam turrets for close defense and a missile launcher for a big punch, but today the brunt of the battle would be fought with cannon broadsides. It was going to be close and ugly.

Liam turned away from Riverton, pausing in case she called him back. In the silence that followed he decided that she was done with him, and he strode over to the officer-of-the-watch station.

Chief Sky was already there, silently observing as Sublieutenant Brown manipulated her screens, with Highcastle standing idly next to her. Sky was in armor, as expected, but Liam immediately noticed that hers was not a standard-issue set of protective padding. Sky's armor was shaped to her powerful body, smooth surfaces curved to better deflect blows. The plates were a dull green—a subtle color, but Liam knew enough about armor to know that such an affectation didn't come cheap. His assaulter clearly took her own protection seriously.

His own armor was black, polished to a reflective shine and accented with gold filigree. It was expected for a noble officer to display a bit of finery even in combat, but Liam had always understood the very practical purpose of identifying himself, if a battle went badly, as someone worth capturing and ransoming—rather than simply executing.

"Time to intercept?" he asked.

"Twenty minutes," Highcastle replied. His face was alight with excitement.

"We're closing the comet at full sail for another five before we batten down," Brown added.

She looked through her telescope and then pointed out through the canopy toward a brilliant object growing larger ahead of them. This far from the closest star it lacked any halo, but the power of the reflected starlight off its surface was impressive.

"Any sign of hostile activity?"

"The pirate ship is currently on the far side, so we can't observe directly," she said, "but over the last few hours we didn't pick up any unusual activity when it was visible."

The icy comet nucleus was slowly rotating as it tumbled through space. The pirate ship was connected to it, replenishing water, and had been carried out of sight as it moved with its host. It meant both ships were blind to each other, but surprise was exactly what *Daring* needed.

"Do you recommend we proceed?" he prompted.

"Yes, sir." She nervously scanned her displays one last time. "Bridge is ready for battle."

"Let's smash 'em," Highcastle growled.

Liam motioned for Sky to follow him back to the command chair.

Riverton looked down at him again. Her face remained set in an expression of courtly indifference, but he could see the depth of emotions in her eyes. Was it excitement or fear? Having witnessed enough nobles lead their ships into combat, he hoped it was a healthy dose of both.

"Captain, XO. The ship is in all respects ready for battle. Permission to board the boats and proceed with the plan."

"Make sure you board from below," she said. "I'll keep my arcs of fire high, but cannons are a blunt instrument."

"Yes, ma'am. We'll approach perpendicular to your line of fire and latch on to their far side."

"My initial broadsides will be aft and center, but as soon as you latch on I'll shift targeting forward."

"Yes, ma'am." It was exactly as they'd discussed for days. Did she think he'd never done this before?

Or, he suddenly realized, perhaps *she'd* never done this before. Her neutral expression was unmoving, as if she'd purposely locked her features. Except for her eyes, and Liam now assessed there was a lot more fear in them than excitement. He glanced back to where Highcastle was now pacing restlessly, and looked back at his stoic, almost frozen, captain. He leaned in.

"It's going to get messy, ma'am," he said quietly. "But trust the crew to do our job. We're ready for this."

"Tell me again," she said, "why you're not wearing space suits."

"Too bulky for close-in fighting, and they don't offer any real protection against weapons. Plus, they'd get slashed to pieces during close-in fighting—making them useless in the vacuum. We're far better off in armor."

Riverton regarded him for a long moment. If she had more to say she swallowed the words down.

"Proceed with the plan, XO. Good luck."

"And to you, ma'am."

Liam strode aft to the ladder and descended, Sky close behind him.

DARING WAS LOCKED DOWN FOR BATTLE. AS AMELIA stood in the crowded passageway, shifting in her padded armor, she felt uncomfortable in the lack of background noise. There was no air rushing through ventilation, no steady patter of footsteps on the decks, no casual chatter between sailors. All airtight openings were dogged down and everyone was at their battle station. Around her the twelve other members of the assault team stood in grim, anticipatory silence. Some looked like old hands at this sort of thing, while others were clearly putting on a brave face.

They were gathered in the main transverse passageway on Three Deck, which ended in a pair of airlock hatches that were both currently open. Through the flexible connector tubes Amelia could see the crews of each boat waiting for their passengers to climb aboard.

Amelia had seen her fair share of fights growing up, but nothing like the brutality she'd witnessed in *Lightning Louise*. These pirates were vicious killers, and she had no intention of letting them get a shot at her. She fingered the hilt of her cutlass, reminding herself of its reassuring weight. And her pistol on the other hip—she was very aware of it.

Two figures appeared at the end of the passageway—Blackwood and Sky. The assaulter gave the signal to start boarding and Amelia stepped aside to let the first sailors past. She greeted her superiors.

"Teams ready," she said.

"Thanks, PO," Blackwood replied before turning to Sky. "Any last questions, Chief?"

"No, sir," Sky replied. "The plan is clear."

Sky had a job to do, and she was ready to do it. Amelia wished she could project such cool confidence.

"See you on the inside, then."

Sky swung into the airlock tube and floated out of sight. Blackwood gestured for Amelia to precede him into their tube. She swung herself in feetfirst and glided along until she felt hands reach out to grab her legs and steer her into the boat.

The glare of the distant Cluster illuminated the boat and Amelia quickly took stock of her half of the assault team. Eight men and women all dressed in the padded armor issued by the Navy for close self-defense. It was enough to at least slow bullets and blade strikes, and lightweight enough not to impede movement. Each sailor had a pistol and a cutlass at his or her belt.

As the boat's thrusters pushed it away from *Daring*'s hull, Blackwood strapped in next to her. He gave some quick instructions to Master Rating Faith at the helm then leaned in close to her.

"Feeling good?" he asked quietly.

"Yes, sir," she replied. She kept her expression locked down in what she hoped was calm determination.

"If we need to split up, you'll lead the second group."

"Why would we split up, sir?"

"No idea," he said airily. "But battles have a way of quickly changing the plan."

"I'll try and keep up, sir."

He gave her a friendly wink.

Amelia watched as *Daring*'s sails began to furl, her own thrusters firing swiftly as Riverton aligned the ship for the last dash. She looked forward at the lumpy comet that was looming before them. Its white surface was cut with hundreds of thin cracks amid random, jagged outcrops. It was probably a remnant of stellar formation billions of years ago whose long dance through the gravitational chaos of the Cluster had never let it come close enough to a solar system to get caked in dust, and its icy purity made it a prime target for deep-space replenishment.

As the surface of the comet rolled by, a particularly large ridge passed overhead. Beyond it, the dark shape of a Human-designed ship stood out starkly against the icy landscape.

"And there she is," Blackwood whispered.

The pirate ship was small—she barely would have rated a sloop in the Navy—and with her masts retracted she resembled a bullet with her rakish bow and smooth lines. She hovered just above the gleaming surface of the comet, two long arms extending from her hull into the ice.

Amelia leaned forward, feeling the adrenaline course through her. The pirates were vulnerable, and were blind to their approach as the tiny boat blended into the dark backdrop of space behind her. She looked off to port and saw Sky's boat keeping pace with theirs. Up ahead, beyond the pirate ship, she scanned for any sign of *Daring*.

There! Just skimming the final ridge, she spotted the bulky form of the frigate as she sailed into view. Her bow was pointed at the target, but even as Amelia watched, *Daring* began to turn. Her momentum still carried her toward the pirate ship, but now her full broadside was brought to bear.

Blackwood grabbed a telescope and searched the pirate hull.

"No sign of ports opening or weapons charging," he said. "But we're probably inside cannon range now."

Amelia gripped her straps tightly, suddenly feeling very exposed in this open-topped, unarmed boat.

"Increase speed," Blackwood ordered, snapping the telescope down. "Close for boarding."

The gentle push of the thrusters accelerated the boat. Amelia heard a smattering of activity behind her as sailors adjusted their weapons. She scanned the target with her bare eyes. Still no movement.

A flash of light caught her peripheral. To starboard, with a series of flashes rolling across her hull from bow to stern, *Daring* opened fire. Seconds later the first shells struck the pirate hull. From Amelia's distance the impacts appeared little more than tufts of dust, but she knew the thunder that was rolling through the interior of the target.

"Steer twenty degrees down," Blackwood said.

The boat dipped to aim beneath the pirate ship. Another rolling sequence of fire erupted from *Daring*'s flank, and another wave of impacts pounded the target. Explosions burst outward from the pirate ship. For a moment Amelia thought that *Daring*'s shots had penetrated the outer armor, but then she saw the first tufts of smoke against *Daring*'s hull.

The pirates were returning fire.

THE PIRATE SHIP WAS LOOMING LARGE THROUGH the boat's canopy, and Liam scanned it for airlocks.

"There," he said, tapping Faith on the shoulder and pointing at the bulky hatch that extended out from the pirate ship's quarter, far enough aft to be in line with the bridge. "That's where we're locking on."

"Yes, sir."

The boat glided up onto the quiet side of the pirate ship, sheltered from the thunder of cannon fire as *Daring* drew all the attention. A surprise attack always caused a few minutes of panic and confusion: now was their chance. With a rush of thruster power, the boat killed its speed and thumped up alongside the ship. Able Rating Hunter dived into the airlock tube, stabilized it over the pirate airlock, and latched on.

"We're on!" he shouted up.

"Board the vessel," Liam commanded.

The first sailor clambered through. Moments later Liam heard the clank of the airlock opening and felt his ears pop as pressures equalized. The second member of his team boarded, then the third. He heard the shouts of alarm and the clang of steel even while he still waited in the boat, but his sailors kept piling through. Finally, he grabbed the hatch and yanked himself down into the airlock.

"Signal *Daring* that we're aboard," he shouted back to Faith.

His feet thudded down as artificial gravity took hold. Moving forward through the airlock chamber he drew his saber and scanned ahead. His team was formed in a defensive semicircle beyond the airlock, covering a junction of three passageways. A pair of pirates had already been taken down, their bodies strewn across the deck. But Liam saw one of his own sailors down too. The deck shook as another barrage of cannon fire struck the far side of the hull. Moments later the thunder of the pirates' cannons blasted their answer.

The sailor, Master Rating Flatrock, was hunched over, grasping his side as the medic ripped out a thick bandage and pressed it against the wound. Blood oozed from the slash wound, and Flatrock's face was ashen. But there was no fear in his expression.

"I'm sorry, sir," he gasped. "Bastard got in a lucky strike."

Liam quickly assessed the wound. It was survivable if they could get this man to safety, but he was already weakening. He was in no shape to continue the attack.

"Not to worry, Flatrock," he said with forced good cheer. "Well played for making my choice of boat sentry easy. Guard the airlock with your pistol and get the boat's crew to get this scratch sealed up."

Flatrock's expression suggested an impending protest, but Liam could see the strength already fading from his eyes. Still hunched and cradling the bandage against his side, he shuffled to the airlock door and settled against the bulkhead. He drew his pistol.

"Boat's crew!" Liam called back. "Bring Flatrock some fresh bandages, and a double shot of medicinal rum!"

Flatrock's eyes lit up at the order. Medicinal rum was laced with powerful painkillers made from poppies—and was a damned potent drink in its own right.

Turning back, Liam assessed his team, now reduced to seven including himself. They were sharp, on a razor's edge of aggression.

"To the bridge," he said, striding into the center corridor as he activated his radio. "Assault, XO—we're aboard and moving on target."

"Assault," came the curt reply. *"Aboard and engaged with hostiles."*

Amid the pounding of cannon fire, Liam could hear shouts and clatter in all directions. Chaos and confusion were his friends right now, but neither would last long. Up ahead was another junction, likely with the main fore-and-aft passageway of the ship. He increased to a jog, drawing a pistol into his free hand and rounding the corner without slowing.

Half a dozen pirates were running toward him in the dim light, still strapping on their weapons belts. He fired at the closest, then swung his saber down in a lightning strike as he crashed into the crowd. His blade sliced through flesh and struck bone as he slammed into another body. His momentum carried him forward, and he wrenched his sword free as he turned.

A dagger blow glanced against his armor. Liam slashed back, unable to see his opponent amid the quick movements. A heavy blade swung at him from the left and he barely managed to parry, staggering back at the force of the blow. He ducked back against a return swing and fired his pistol at chest level. The shots pinged against the bulkhead. Where was the attacker?

Liam stepped back, trying to spot his opponent in the shadowy melee. The giant sword swung at him again from the right. It was low, and he caught the blade on his own saber, forcing it down. As the sword scraped across the deck, Liam stabbed out at where his opponent should be, but again hit only air.

Frustrated, he stepped back again, gaining room.

Then he finally saw his opponent. Not a man at all, but a brute. Low to the deck in a fighting stance, teeth bared in fury.

The Theropod pirate pounced forward, powerful legs rearing up. Dagger-like claws slashed at Liam's breast-plate and he stepped back again, banging into the bulk-head behind him. The Theropod thumped down on the deck, body low as he shifted his weight. A heavy blade was strapped to his long tail, which whipped around with crushing force. Liam dropped his pistol and gripped the saber with both hands, taking the brunt of the swing and crashing backward against the bulkhead. The Theropod shuffled for a second blow, but Liam finally knew where to attack; he chopped down at the brute's back, the two-handed strike snapping through the thin plates of armor and into the spine. The Theropod roared in pain and staggered back, but Liam pressed the attack home. Ignoring a rake of claws down his leg, he swung again at the brute's neck. The blade sliced through the delicate creature's bone and flesh, the long, bony head dropping to the deck in a final spasm of shock and pain.

Liam lifted his sword in a guard as he crouched down to retrieve his pistol. He swept the gun through a surveying arc, just in time to watch the last pirate, a Human, stagger back.

Virtue danced forward, knocking the pirate's blade spinning, and with one quick thrust, her cutlass entered his heart.

The pirate collapsed. Amelia tucked into a crouch and did her own scan, finally noticing Liam staring at her. Her breath was quick and her eyes were wild, but she eventually managed a grimace.

"Back home you usually just have to cut the street thugs and they run away," she gasped. "These bastards are tough."

Liam straightened, surveying the carnage in the passageway. Virtue and the five sailors were gasping and panting, but they were all still standing amid the scattered bodies.

"Well done, PO," he said to Virtue, before raising his voice. "We'll come back to search this lot, but for now we press on."

Momentum was everything, he knew. The pounding from *Daring*'s cannon continued to rock the ship, but the pirates would surely know by now that for all its sound and fury, *Daring*'s attack was merely the distraction. Although still catching his breath, Liam hustled forward into a jog again. The clatter of his own armor was matched by the dull thudding of his sailors behind him. He spotted a ladder heading up and, without slowing, sheathed his sword and pistol. With both hands free he scrambled up without pause, trusting in his armor. Hedge was right behind him.

Bullets cracked against his backplate as he found his footing on the upper deck, then on his breastplate as he swung around with pistols in his hands. He returned fire rapidly, stepping forward in the dim light to where a trio of pirates hunkered behind consoles. Light shone down through the uncovered bridge canopy, the brilliant reflection of the icy asteroid bathing the space in a cold, twilight glow.

He heard Hedge scramble up the ladder as he stepped forward. Shots from her pistol joined his, and one of the pirates switched his aim. The sound of bullets ripping through soft armor was followed by Hedge grunting in pain as she scrambled for cover. Hedge hunkered down behind a console, one hand pressing against her torso as she struggled to reload her own pistol.

Liam stepped forward, drawing the enemy fire. Both his pistols clicked empty. He slammed them back into their holsters and drew his saber, running to close the distance. One pirate pistol appeared over a console and Liam slashed down. The pistol and the hand that held it tumbled to the deck. Liam grabbed the screaming pirate and threw him down, resting one armored foot heavily on the man's neck, pinning him. His other sailors fanned out, weapons drawn. The two remaining pirates, one Human and one Theropod, rose slowly from their positions, hands in the air.

Liam scanned the bridge. It was smaller than *Daring*'s, with a single command chair in the center and a trio of matching consoles forward. Another trio of consoles was aft, two of which were now sputtering smoke and riddled with bullet holes. The canopy overhead was still uncovered, and low enough that Liam could almost have touched it at a stretch. The curved outer hull of the ship was very apparent in the rounded upper plates that sloped down to the deck.

"Assault, XO," he said into his radio, "bridge secure."

"XO, Assault," said Sky. *"Propulsion secure. Indication that someone is trying to jettison cargo from Three Deck, port side aft."*

Seizing cargo was key, Liam knew. Every sailor in *Daring* knew that there was prize money for them if the mission was successful.

"Secure propulsion," he ordered, "and send a team to stop that jettison. I'll send a team as well."

"Yes, sir."

Liam studied his remaining sailors. Hedge was sagging noticeably, and blood seeped from her torso armor. The other five watched him expectantly. He motioned to the medic.

"Able Rating Song, you stay here and do some patching on Hedge. Petty Officer Virtue, take the others and get down to Three Deck, aft. Somebody's trying to jettison cargo—stop them. Sky's sending a team as well, so watch for friendlies."

"Yes, sir." Virtue motioned the three sailors to follow her down the ladder.

Liam lifted his foot off the pirate he'd pinned, to a grateful moan and deep breaths. He rested the point of his saber on the man's back, watching the other two, who still had their hands raised in surrender.

The next question on Liam's agenda was to figure out who the captain was.

AMELIA LEAPED DOWN THE LAST LADDER, LANDING in a crouch on Three Deck and scanning both ways for pirates. Flatrock was down, and now Hedgie, and Amelia was ready to mete out some punishment on these criminal thugs. She readied her cutlass and advanced.

The pirate ship's corridors were low and tight, and

poorly lit. The thunder of *Daring*'s cannon impacts still rocked the interior, but the return fire was becoming less frequent. Amelia staggered aft as the deck shook again, hearing her three sailors jumping down behind her. Down the narrow passageway she saw furtive movement.

Without hesitation, she charged forward, raising her cutlass. The passage was only wide enough for one person at a time, and she heard her shipmates behind her. As she neared, the movement resolved itself into two Human pirates desperately stuffing strongboxes through an airlock hatch. At the sound of her approach they turned, wide-eyed. The nearest gathered his wits faster, lifting his sword and lunging forward. Amelia brought her blade up, knocking the blow aside as her body crashed into his. He was as solid as a brick wall, unmoving against her charge and blocking the entire passageway. His powerful arm grabbed at her neck, but she ducked down, feeling a sharp tug on her scalp as her hair slipped through his grasp. She stomped her foot down on his, then drove her elbow into his groin. He staggered, but managed to get a grip on her hair with his free hand. His sword glinted in the gloom.

Amelia slashed low, her blade shattering his knee. With a roar of pain, he sagged, struggling to raise his sword again. Another cutlass swung over her head from behind, the heavy blade driving into flesh and bone. The hot, salty spray of blood splashed across her face.

She pushed past the pirate's collapsing form, just in time to see the other pirate drop her sword and raise her hands in surrender. Amelia threw the woman up against the bulkhead, sword to her neck. The woman's eyes were hard, but as they stared into Amelia's, they filled with fear.

Amelia felt the power coursing through her, felt the

pressure of her blade as it started to press against the pirate's skin.

"I'll take that prisoner," boomed a strong, female voice to her side.

Still pinning the pirate, Amelia glanced back and saw Chief Sky striding forward, flanked by her own team of sailors. The assaulter loomed into Amelia's space, her dark gaze calm and authoritative. Slowly, slowly, Amelia lessened the pressure of her sword, then drew it back.

Sky immediately grabbed the pirate and pushed her expertly to the ground, binding her wrists in a swift, practiced motion.

"Check the cargo," she ordered.

Amelia moved to open the airlock hatch, but the controls failed to respond. Then she noticed the red alarm of vacuum beyond. Peering through the porthole, she saw nothing but empty space through the narrow opening beyond.

"She jettisoned it," Amelia hissed.

"Well," Sky said slowly, pressing her knee down on the pirate's back, "that makes me very unhappy."

"Can we retrieve it?" one of her sailors asked, stepping forward.

"No," Amelia said, scanning again through the porthole. "Stuff that size . . . It's gone."

The force of the air blast out of a breached airlock would have rocketed the cargo outward at tremendous speed, Amelia knew. And with no gravity from the tiny comet below to slow them down, the strongboxes would already be past escape velocity and headed for the Abyss. Nothing that small, in the vastness of space, would ever be found.

"Damnation," she whispered.

LIAM'S INITIAL QUESTIONS TO THE PIRATE PRISON-
ers had so far been met with stubborn silence. Hedge
was covering them with her pistol as she leaned heavily
against a console. Song opened his medikit and unwound
the bandages. Liam glanced at the bridge displays, looking for clues, his saber still at the ready.

Song eased the gauze up under Hedge's armor. She
gasped as a new torrent of blood splashed down on the
deck, dropping her pistol with a clatter that echoed in
the silence. Liam's gaze flickered over to where Hedge
collapsed against Song.

The Theropod leaped to his feet with lightning swift-
ness. Liam's saber flashed up in a guard and he interposed
himself between the attacker and his crew. But the pirate
bounded away from them, landing at a console where
his nimble fingers began frantically tapping commands.
Liam instinctively drew a pistol and fired, only to hear the
awful click of an empty weapon. He flung the pistol at the
brute, forcing the pirate to raise his hands as a shield, as
Liam raced forward, saber raised.

The pirate ignored him for the seconds it took him to
cross the bridge, eyes still focused on the console. Then,
with a flush of blood to the horned ridges above his eyes,
the Theropod swung with his mighty tailsword. Liam
parried the blow, but the force made him stagger backward. He readied for the backswing, but the brute merely
raised the sword in a guard and kept working the console.
With a bellow Liam knocked the blade clear, then bashed
down against the pirate's head with his armored fist. The
blow was barely a glance, but the brute finally abandoned
his efforts.

The tailsword slashed down, crushing the plate on
Liam's shoulder, numbing his sword arm. He swung his

left fist again, desperately trying to keep a grip on his weapon. But then the tail suddenly dropped to the deck, and the brute's legs kicked upward, talon claws slashing at Liam's legs.

He punched again, swinging wildly, and his fist finally connected with the brute's skull. The pirate sagged against the console. He tried to raise his tailsword, but was too slow as Liam stabbed down with the saber. The pirate's last hiss faded into a gargle as he slumped off the console to collapse on the deck.

Liam staggered up and stepped on the tail to ensure it was pinned. As his gaze raked the console, he watched the last of the ship's memory core vanish, the data completely erased.

He looked up at the bridge. Hedge was barely conscious, leaning against the console, and Song had his pistol out, covering both remaining pirates.

He looked again at the console, then down at the dead brute by his feet. Only the most senior crewmembers on any ship had the codes to wipe a memory core: Liam guessed that he'd identified the pirate captain.

"Damnation," he muttered.

CHAPTER 11

Liam winced as he slipped out of his shirt, noting the red spots where blood had leaked through his bandages. The pain in his shoulder was still sharp, standing out against the dull aches nearly everywhere else in his body.

Templegrey pulled the garment free of his arm and dropped it in his lap. Her hair was tied back in a tight bun, several medical instruments slung around her neck. Her white coat was spattered with stains from the last few days and she moved with a steady efficiency.

"I've told you to rest more," she scolded him with the hint of a smile. "But I see you've been ignoring me."

Her eyes lacked some of their usual gleam, and fatigue slowed her movements. In the days since the attack on the pirates, the doctor had been busier than most. Liam sat on a bed in sickbay, and five of the other beds were occupied by sailors who'd fared less well than he had. Flatrock lay across from him, propped on his uninjured side. Hedge was in the next bunk, talking quietly to him. Three of Sky's team were asleep or unconscious, having taken the brunt of the battle as her team fought through the pirate gun crews and their propulsors. For all his aches and a troublesome shoulder, Liam had gotten off lightly.

"I'll get more rest," he said, "now that we've finished with the pirate ship."

"Any luck retrieving the lost data?" she asked as she began unwrapping his shoulder bandage.

"No, unfortunately. But the coxn and assaulter have been questioning the prisoners."

"Wretched bunch," she said, shaking her head. "I inspected them for any acute wounds, but there's nothing I can do for the consequences of their hard living. None of them will see old age."

"After what they've done, none of them deserve to."

"Agreed, sir. Let's just hope we can get what we need from them before they expire."

The prisoners were being fed the bare minimum of rations, and the lights were always kept on in their cells to encourage sleep deprivation. It was all in support of the interrogation efforts. Many of the pirates were already weakened from the battle, and with no further medical help authorized, it was doubtful if all of them would survive to see trial. Liam wasn't troubled at the thought.

The door to the passageway opened and Highcastle peered in, entering when Templegrey gave him a nod.

"Anything I might do to help, Doctor?" he said rather loudly.

"Everything is quiet, Mr. Highcastle," she responded as she dropped Liam's bloody bandages into a basket at her feet. "But thank you for asking."

"Been to the wars, Lord Blackwood?" he said with a smile.

"Barely a scratch," Liam replied.

"You should join us next time, sir," Flatrock interjected with a toothy smile.

"I might just, Rocky," the cadet countered good-naturedly, sitting on the edge of Hedge's bed. "But you keep living and not opening a spot for me."

Flatrock laughed. Highcastle took Hedge's hand in his own and glanced down at her. "All right there, Hedgie?"

"Yes, sir," she responded weakly. "Quite all right, thank you."

Liam was surprised at his gentle tone and his clear desire to keep morale up in the sickbay. It was not what he would have expected from a lordling.

"Are we resuming regular watches?" Templegrey asked, drawing his attention back.

"Yes, with the dog watch. I've slated you for the mid-watch, unfortunately," he said somewhat apologetically. "It's your turn."

She gave an elegant shrug before starting to rewrap his shoulder. "At least young James will get some rest." She cast Highcastle a mock-withering look. "He is rather beastly right now."

Highcastle wrinkled his nose at her reprovingly. "Well, why not? Those blaggards ejected our prize money out the airlock. These fine sailors deserve their reward."

He patted Hedge's leg and nodded to Flatrock.

"It is frustrating, sir." Flatrock sighed.

"If only I'd been unleashed on those pirates for the interrogation," Highcastle added. "Then you'd have seen beastly."

"You're not an interrogator?" Flatrock asked.

"No." Highcastle sighed. "Apparently Sublieutenant Brown needs me far more on the bridge."

Liam knew the truth to be rather different. Chief Petty

Officer Butcher had quite rightly refused Highcastle's demand to question the prisoners, which had caused the lordling no small amount of outrage. The coxn, in turn, had taken rather poorly to a cadet trying to impose his will. It was always a difficult dance between senior sailors and junior officers, and when high nobility was mixed in, things could get volatile. He didn't want to add the mob opinion of the crew to this issue.

"Speaking of which, aren't you due on the bridge rather soon?" Liam asked with a certain firmness.

"Yes, sir. I just wanted to check in on our brave casualties." He rose from Hedge's bed. "Fear not, my friends, I'll be keeping you safe for the next twelve hours."

"Appreciate you coming by, sir," Flatrock said.

"Thank you, sir," Hedge whispered.

Highcastle departed. Hedge drifted off to sleep in moments, and Flatrock closed his eyes as well.

"You know," Templegrey said quietly to Liam as she pressed down fresh dressings and started to overlay them with a bandage, "we could help the fatigue problem by switching to a one-in-four watch rotation. We're in deep space, and even just a few days of a more relaxed schedule would help everyone catch up on their rest."

"But who would be the fourth officer of the watch?" he replied, barely above a whisper. "The captain's gesture that first night was a one-off, and I'm not really interested, Ava."

"James could stand his own watch," she said, pausing her work on the bandage to meet his gaze. "He's learned basic navigation and watch routine, and he could be given explicit instructions on when to call for assistance."

He stared back at her. "Are you mad?"

She laughed. "No, sir. But I do see the impact of fatigue

on the entire crew. You know that deep-space watches are uneventful, and that James could handle it, especially with a senior sailor assigned to support him."

Her arguments actually had some merit, he admitted to himself.

"I think being given his own watch," she said as she resumed dressing his shoulder, finishing quickly, "would go a long way to settling James's sense of self-worth. His confidence has been taking a beating these past few weeks, and he doesn't know how to handle it. If the captain were to extend some confidence to him, I think he would rise to the challenge."

Liam couldn't disagree with her position—being challenged was how any sailor grew. His instincts had been correct in throwing Amelia Virtue into a higher rank and position: she'd absolutely thrived. What was to say Highcastle couldn't do the same? Was it his connection to Silverhawk that had clouded Liam's judgment?

"You make a compelling case, Ava. I'll speak to Commander Riverton about giving Highcastle his own watch for this next deep-space transit."

She offered him a warm smile. "Thank you, sir. The entire crew will benefit."

Liam worked his shoulder through a range of motion. He was able to move it without wincing, but he knew not to push it. For the next few hours he needed to appear as implacable as a rock.

HE DESCENDED FROM SICKBAY ANOTHER TWO decks, passing a few crewmembers on the way. Each greeted him with a respectful knuckle to the eyebrow and he could clearly see the brighter expressions and energy in their movements. The battle against the pirates had gone well, and combat always inspired a deeper cohesion of the crew. All the frustrations of the past had been swept away in this new sense of forward momentum.

Down on Four Deck, he made his way to where a small gathering of sailors clustered at the end of a side passageway. Four of them were armed—two standing sentry and the other two hovering near Virtue, who was shifting restlessly, fiddling with the bag on her shoulder.

"Good afternoon, everyone," he greeted. "Are we ready to continue?"

"Yes, sir," Virtue replied immediately.

At his order, one of the sentries unlocked the door and quickly scanned the space beyond before holding it open. Liam stepped through, followed by Virtue and two guards.

The brig was a converted cargo container, specially kitted out prior to their departure from Passagia for precisely the purpose of holding prisoners. Reinforced, beige bulkheads had been welded to allow for a wide central passageway, and on either side there were five heavy doors leading to cells. A pair of ladders led up to a narrow catwalk where a second set of cells awaited future guests. The single lantern was cold and harsh.

This sort of interrogation was hardly Liam's favorite activity, but it was essential if they were going to make headway in their overall mission. As he stepped toward the first cell, he forced himself to remember the carnage aboard *Lightning Louise,* and that it had been these scumbags who had done that.

Liam glanced through the tiny window. The inhabitant sat crouched on his haunches, head dipped. But as the lock shifted with a heavy creak, the Theropod's head snapped up, eye ridges flaring weakly. He was dressed in coarse prisoner garb that had been made for a Human body. The leggings only reached halfway down his calves and the sleeves draped ridiculously over his short arms. The seat of the pants had been slit to allow his tail to extend outward. It was no doubt awkward for the Theropod to move and he remained motionless in his crouch, weight leaning back against the tail.

Liam stepped inside, nodding to Virtue, who came forward and handed over a translator. The brute extended his neck to slip his head through the looped string, letting the translator fall against his chest. Reptilian eyes flicked between the two Humans.

Virtue took another step closer, crouching down to his eye level.

"We recovered a few personal items from your ship before we destroyed it," she said. She reached into her bag and pulled out a book. Its cover was a hard paper encased in resin, scratched with the runes of the brute language. "I believe this is yours."

"It's no use to us," Liam snapped, maintaining a cold expression.

The Theropod's third eyelids flicked sideways, and he shuffled to free a hand from the folds of his sleeve. He reached for the book, but Virtue held it back.

"I'm sure having something to read will help you pass the time," she said, "but I'm hoping you can give us something in return."

The hiss from deep in the brute's throat needed little translation, but the device dutifully produced intelligible words. "Die in the Abyss."

Metaphors didn't always translate accurately, and Liam remembered to speak clearly to ensure the translator caught his words.

"I told you this was a waste of time," he said to Virtue. "Just burn it with the rest of the rubbish."

Virtue held up a hand, sighing deeply. She looked at the brute again. "It was hard enough for me to convince them to offer this mercy. It would be a shame to destroy this, but you're not helping me. I just want to ask you a few questions."

The ridged eyes locked on to the book, then snapped between Liam and Virtue.

"I want more than just a book," came the words just after the growl.

"This is all I have," she said. "For now. We're planning to burn the rest of the personal effects today, but . . . you never know what I might find."

"What do you want to know?"

"How many pirate ships are there in your band?"

"Just one. And you took us out."

Liam stepped forward menacingly, raising his hand and threatening to strike. "Don't lie to us, brute," he warned.

"Let me say my question a different way," Virtue continued. "How many pirate ships are there in the region?"

"More than you can count."

"I can count pretty high."

"More than I can count, then." The growled speech ended in a short bark that might have been a laugh.

"Use your fingers."

"Use yours—you have more of them."

Virtue smiled wryly and placed the book on the deck between them. She lifted her hands and spread the fingers wide.

The Theropod glanced at her, barking again.

"About that many," he said, nodding his long head toward her hands.

"They can't stay in space all the time, though. Where do they go to replenish?"

"You saw for yourself."

"That's just water. Where do you get food and supplies?"

"Somewhere in the dark."

Liam chopped down with his hand, striking the brute at the back of the skull, right behind the ridges, where he knew it hurt. "This is a waste of time," he snapped. "We're done here."

Virtue sighed again, retrieved the book, and stepped back. She looked up at Liam and shook her head sadly.

"He can rot in here until he starves," Liam said stonily, turning to leave.

"Wait," came the growl behind him.

Virtue turned, but Liam purposely waited a beat before looking back. Virtue took a single step toward the prisoner. "Can you tell me where the base is?"

"I don't know, truthfully. I'm just a gunner. But it's somewhere away from any star."

"That's no help," Liam lied with venom. "Let's go."

"Listen," the Theropod continued, voice rising to almost a roar. "There are seven pirate crews that I know of. Seven."

"And the base?" Liam demanded.

"I don't know." The reptilian body slumped. "Somewhere in the dark."

"I told you," Liam said to Virtue. "A waste of time."

She looked back at the prisoner and then spoke in her best pleading voice, holding up the book. "At least let me give him this."

"Why?"

"Because it's the merciful thing to do."

He made a long show of considering, then assented with an angry wave of the hand before striding out of the cell.

Virtue emerged from the cell moments later and shut the door.

"I think that went well," she said quietly.

"Yes, but that was just the warm-up," he reminded her, resting a hand on her shoulder. "A brute can't read our facial expressions and our tone of voice is lost in translation. A human prisoner will be much more aware."

"Well, if it helps, I thought you were truly beastly. Keep it up and *I'll* be afraid of you by the end of this," she said with a little half smile.

"I find that extremely hard to believe," he said with a grin. Then he reminded himself that he needed to stay in character, schooling his expression back to haughty indifference and reaching for the next cell door. "You ready?"

"Ready, sir—let's do this."

The man behind the cell door was pale and gaunt, curled up in the far corner. When the door opened, he glanced up, scanning between Liam and Virtue. From the few records they'd been able to recover from the pirate ship, this Human appeared to have an unusual position on board. He had no official rank, but apparently enough authority to issue orders.

Liam moved to the other side of the cell, keeping his eyes trained steadily on the man. The man returned the gaze warily before switching to Virtue as she crouched down in front of him.

"How are you feeling?" she asked.

"Held prisoner by a corrupt tyranny," he spat. "At least when I die it will be as a martyr."

"We didn't tell you to attack the *Lightning Louise*," she said evenly. "We just need to stop you from doing that again."

"You can't stop us. Even if you silence me there are many more out there."

"How many more?"

"Legions."

Amelia's eyebrows shot up at this, and she looked over at Liam. He nodded.

"So," she said, "you *are* in league with the Sectoids. Why?"

"We're not in league with those scum." His expression revealed shock and horror, which Liam assessed as genuine. "How dare you question my loyalty to my species."

"Attacking honest merchants and killing civilians doesn't strike me as loyalty," Amelia retorted, "especially with Sectoids and their acid."

"You understand nothing," he scoffed. "We take what weapons we can get, and we're fighting for a cause you don't understand."

"Don't lie to us," Liam interjected. "You're nothing but a band of thugs, preying on the innocent."

"And what do you know," the prisoner suddenly shouted, "about preying on the innocent?"

His voice echoed off the cell walls as he shuffled painfully up to his feet. Virtue stepped back a pace, but the prisoner made no move to come forward. He leaned heavily against the wall.

"I can hear your accent, *milord*. And I can see the casual disregard you have for our lives. If anyone preys on the innocent, it's you."

"I beg to differ," Liam said, stepping forward as his fists clenched. "I saw what you did to the crew of the *Lightning Louise*."

"Necessary casualties. They were killed quickly."

"Not all of them."

The prisoner's face darkened, and as he looked straight at Liam it twisted into a cruel sneer.

"Yes, the ship's patron. He got what he deserved."

"Why did he deserve to be tortured?" Virtue asked. "What did he do?"

"Are you nothing but a puppet, girl? Can you not see what people like him are doing?"

"I see an honest merchant, nothing more."

"Then you're blind."

Liam took another good look at this man. His hair was cut short, and his clothes were of a city dweller from farther in toward the Hub. His speech was precise, though common, and his gaze burned with a zeal not typical of a pirate.

"So you're the one who tortured and killed the patron," Liam said quietly, reaching for his sword.

"I'm not saying I did it," the prisoner responded. But Liam saw the uncertainty that flickered across his features. "Only that I think he deserved it."

"A petty distinction," Liam replied, slowly starting to draw the saber.

He felt Virtue's hand on his, pausing the motion.

"You need to explain to us why you think that," she said. "If there's some legitimate grievance in this sector which needs to be addressed, we need to know about it."

The prisoner considered this for a moment, then scoffed.

"The grievance . . . is you."

"Me?" Virtue asked, her eyes wide with shock.

"No! You, the Navy, your Imperial masters. You're all just puppets."

"And I suppose," Liam said, keeping his sword sheathed but resting his hand on the pommel, "your little band of pirates is going to make everything right."

"Justice will prevail," he said with a knowing, anticipatory look, "when the dark star rises."

"What is that?" Virtue asked. "The dark star?"

"Something you should learn about."

"It's their pirate plan," Liam muttered. "Steal all the money, buy all the weapons, and then impose their own kind of tyranny on Silica."

"You know nothing."

"I know plenty of people like you. Lawless, selfish types who don't want to live by the rules of the Empire, and who make up some perceived grievance as moral cover for their own atrocities."

The prisoner fell silent for a moment, staring at Liam. Then he slumped back down into a crouch. "This is pointless. I have nothing to say to you."

Liam made to turn away, but he gave Virtue a tiny nod.

She reached into her bag and pulled out a gold pendant.

"We found this in your ship," she said, holding it up for him. "I was going to give it to one of my hardworking shipmates, but I sensed it might have sentimental value for you."

He glanced at it, clear recognition lighting up his eyes. But then he looked away.

"Tell me more about this dark star," she said, "and you can have it back."

"Keep it," he said, expression hardening. "I won't be bought."

"Remain silent and you'll hang for sure," Liam pronounced. "But if you cooperate we might be able to work something out."

"The promises of an Imperial lord," the prisoner scoffed, "are worthless."

"And clearly," Liam countered, "so are the words of a pirate murderer."

"Talk to me," Virtue said again, holding up the pendant. "There's no need to make things worse."

"Things can't get any worse." The prisoner turned to face the far wall of the cell.

Virtue sighed, and glanced up at Liam. He motioned for her to follow him out.

He had a feeling they would get no more out of this man tonight.

THE LACK OF STARLIGHT SHINING IN THROUGH THE portholes of the captain's cabin told Liam that *Daring* was on the starboard tack again. She'd been struggling against this head wind for days and was making slow time back to Windfall.

"The interrogations produced some results," he said. "It appears even pirates can respond well to kindness."

Riverton sat back in her chair, crossing one leg over the other. She'd discarded her uniform coat and her white shirt and trousers stood in stark contrast to her dark face and hands. Despite her relaxed posture, however, there was a new intensity in her eyes. "Do tell."

"This crew is clearly not the mainstay of the pirate force. There are at least half a dozen ships, operating with some independence, but with overall coordination. And this is definitely more than a band of rogues—there is a bigger force behind them. Something called the dark star. We weren't able to confirm what that is."

"Perhaps a base on a distant planet?"

"That would be my guess, ma'am, or maybe a very large ship."

"Oh?"

"Several pirates let slip that their main base is far from any sun. And we do have a Sectoid ship lurking in this sector."

"I don't think that ship would be this dark star they speak of," she said smoothly. "You did ask the pirates if they were connected to Sectoids?"

"Yes, ma'am, and they denied it. But we do have that acid damage in *Lightning Louise*."

"Puzzling," she said, nodding. "But hardly definitive evidence to set us against the Sectoid vessel."

"But, ma'am . . ." Liam was honestly at a loss for words. Why was she ignoring what was clearly staring them in the face? "Surely we should consider the possibility."

"Consider all you want," she snapped. "But our mission is to support the fleet in case of war. Our mission is not to *start* that war."

"Yes, ma'am."

Liam stood in silence for a moment, watching Riverton's expression and posture expertly slip back into her usual cool serenity.

"Do you think the pirates have larger ships?" she asked mildly.

"I think that the ship we took is one of the smaller ones, but I would suspect few of them are larger than a frigate. Amelia managed to get one ship name out of a prisoner: the *Golden Wind*."

"Is it in any of our records?"

"No, ma'am. But when we put into Windfall we can do a search through the Imperial archives and I can ask around. I'm sure my new friend Mr. Long will be willing to share info if I offer to take more cargo off his hands."

Riverton leaned forward. "Yes, about that. This trip we specifically took low-value cargo. For our next, I'd like to reverse that."

"A high-value shipment," Liam asked, following her reasoning, "in order to attract attention?"

"We had a lead on this pirate ship we captured, because we happened to witness its attack. I don't expect to be that lucky again. We need to make our own luck."

"By drawing an attack on ourselves." Liam nodded his approval.

"It's the fastest way to get more information, more prisoners, and more prize money," she said, rising to her feet. "I'm impressed at how well we fought and I'm confident that we can repeat our success."

She'd had her first taste of victory in command, Liam knew. And now she wanted more. It was a natural reaction, but the fact that she'd considered it for this long before voicing her idea gave him confidence that she'd thought the plan through. More and more he was seeing real ability in her, and he realized that for the first time he actually thought of her as someone worthy of command. It was an odd feeling, these days, but a welcome one. Now he just had to figure out how her mind worked.

"I'll look for the most valuable cargo I can find, ma'am."

She nodded, pacing in the tiny space between her desk and dining table. "Any thoughts on where the pirate base might be?"

"Only that it's not in one of the solar systems. We'll have to keep studying the small-objects chart to see if there's anything large enough to support a permanent settlement that's within range of the known attacks in this sector."

"Damned shame we lost the memory core of the pirate ship."

"Yes," Liam said, frowning as he thought of the Theropod captain who had managed to best him. "Next time we'll prioritize its capture."

She stopped pacing, facing him full on. Her large eyes seemed to assess him anew, and a glimmer of a smile brightened her features. "Well done, XO," she said simply. "Carry on."

CHAPTER 12

Normally it was a relief to get off the ship after an extended period in space, but as Amelia stepped across the brow and onto Windfall Station, she wrinkled her nose at the stale air. As much as sailors liked to complain about life aboard ships, out here in the Halo worlds, there were plenty of worse fates. As her eyes scanned the promenade she felt the same sadness she had felt during their first visit. Once upon a time somebody had really put some effort into making this station a nice place to live, with the wide-open space under a vaulted ceiling, and even real trees to cast shadows across the line of storefronts. But years of either poverty or simple neglect had diminished what could have been a happy place.

At least she was in comfortable civilian clothes. She stole an admiring glance at Subcommander Blackwood as he strode forward in his riding trousers to greet Matthew Long and his assistants. The XO's voice carried across the docks as he played his role of the impatient noble, and she had to suppress a smile at his chameleon qualities. Captain Julian Stonebridge was quite a change from the beggar she'd taken pity on that rainy night, and neither was even close to the real man himself.

"Sightseeing," she heard Swift growl behind her, "or lending a hand?"

She tore her eyes from Blackwood, answering Swift's wry expression with a quick, embarrassed grin before reaching down to take one end of the crate. Together she and Swift heaved it onto the waiting cart. Mr. Long's associates didn't seem that interested in helping, standing off to the side of their boss while he reviewed paperwork with Blackwood. After she'd tossed down the second crate, she paused to catch her breath, motioning for Swift to pause as well.

"Hey there," she called over to Long's assistants, "we could use a couple of big, strong lads to help us out."

They couldn't help but look back at her, but were slow to move. She put on her best pouty look, then flashed them a big smile. As expected, that inspired them to action and they came over to help unload cargo. It wasn't easy for her to keep the smile on her face as they chatted her up, but she was pleased when the final crate was secured on the cart. Why couldn't people just help out because it was kind? Did there always have to be the promise of some reward?

Blackwood returned with a new pouch of money, nodding curtly and motioning for Long's men to take the cart away. Once they were clear, he motioned Amelia and Swift closer.

"Mr. Long says he has some very valuable cargoes," he said quietly, "but they're not stored in his usual warehouses. We'll have to go with him into the station to inspect them."

"I'd really rather stay here," Swift replied. "We have a lot of work to do on the masts."

"And the captain wants us out of here in less than a day," Blackwood finished, agreeing. "I'd take Sky, but she's escorting the captain."

"Where to?" Swift asked.

Blackwood shrugged in what Amelia could tell was a show of indifference. When he spoke, his voice was carefully casual. "So I guess it's just us, Amelia—care for a stroll in the station?"

"A tour of Windfall," she said with a smirk. "It's every girl's daydream."

"And every young gentleman's," he replied wryly before turning back to Swift. "Get the cargo doors closed up and get to your work. Set a senior sailor as brow's mate and ensure no one goes ashore."

"Yes, milord."

Amelia moved to Blackwood's side and walked with him back to where Long waited. The heavyset man gave her a slow nod then turned to Blackwood.

"If you'll accompany me, my lord, it's a bit of a walk to the secure storage."

Long led the way with his limping shuffle, and Amelia was forced to slow her pace. The promenade was quieter than it had been during their last visit, but enough people were moving in both directions to keep her wary. She felt the pressure of her pistol strapped under her shoulder, knowing that the only person who was going to get their hands on it was her. Her muscles tensed as she watched each passerby, almost wanting one of them to try to grab at her.

Blackwood's hand brushed against her arm. She glanced up at him, held by his inquisitive gaze.

You okay? he mouthed.

Forcing her shoulders to loosen, she nodded. He watched her for a moment longer, then gave her a friendly wink. She raised an eyebrow, then playfully knocked his hand away.

"This way, my lord," Long said, turning to indicate a set of stairs leading up away from the promenade. "Please precede me—my old bones need more time to make the ascent."

Blackwood in turn gestured for Amelia to go first. "After you."

If someone was going to be looking at her butt, she decided, she'd rather it be Blackwood than Long. She stepped up onto the stairs, listening as the XO followed her at a respectful distance and Long huffed and puffed along behind. At the top of the stairs a mezzanine spread out before her in a half-moon, with clusters of chairs and half a dozen doors leading through the rounded, reinforced wall. Beside each door was a small window, and a pair of sword-wielding toughs stood guard over the entire area.

Blackwood stepped up next to her, scanning the scene. "I guess this is where they keep the good stuff."

It took Long another minute to reach the top of the stairs, and he pulled out a moist handkerchief to mop his brow. He simply stood and breathed for a long moment, dark eyes skirting irritatedly over the lean and healthy bodies of his guests. Finally, he motioned toward one of the doors.

"I have a cargo in my secure stores which I think might be just what you're looking for, my lord. Alas, visitors are not allowed into the vaults, but if you make yourself comfortable here, I will bring you a sample and a full manifest."

"Yes"—Blackwood simpered—"splendid. And have them send out some wine."

Long frowned, but made no reply other than to nod before limping toward the middle door.

Amelia sat down in the nearest chair, which overlooked the promenade below. Blackwood sat down facing her, his own eyes gazing down at the wide walkway.

"The air seems a bit fresher up here," he commented.

"I don't think there are too many crowds coming up this way," she replied. "Not too many valuable cargoes passing through, I'd guess."

She glanced up as an elderly man hurried over with a tray balancing two glasses and a decanter of what looked like red wine. He set it down with a smile and retreated. Blackwood expertly poured them each a glass.

"I'm curious about what counts as valuable cargo here at Windfall," she mused, taking a sip of the wine.

He stifled a gag, face screwing up as he peered at the wine in his glass. "I certainly hope it isn't this vinegar."

She took another sip. It was bold, to be sure, but hardly undrinkable. Was he just playing the part of a spoiled dandy, or was he really offended?

"Well, all the more for me, then, my lord," she offered.

His expression was still pained, and he cast startled eyes over to her. "Are you serious?"

She still wasn't sure if he was playing a role or not, and with a glance at the distant guards she leaned in across the table. "Sir, do you really not like it? I think it's okay."

He started, then quickly composed himself. He leaned in, so that their noses were almost touching. "Julian Stonebridge can't abide it, but of course it's not that bad."

He leaned back and, eyes on her, took another small

sip. His lip wrinkled but otherwise he displayed no reaction. "You see?"

"You think it's piss, don't you?"

"Not at all, Amelia. A rich, fruity varietal with earthy undercurrents and a bold finish."

"You're full of it . . . milord."

He sighed, gently replacing the glass. "Watered down beer I can drink. Back-shed moonshine I can drink, but I've never been able to acquire a taste for cheap plonk."

"Well, the stuff in the senior mess is certainly better than anything I've ever tasted in my life," she said, taking another sip, "but I haven't lost my taste for the plonk."

"My apologies, Amelia, I meant no disrespect."

His concern for her honor was actually quite touching, she thought. The nobility might be a collection of ignorant snobs, but they did have manners. And as he stared earnestly at her across the small table, she was struck at how much she liked his attention.

"None taken," she whispered. "None at all."

"And if you think the wine in *Daring* is good," he added, leaning back casually in his chair, "just wait until you try some at one of Lord Grandview's balls."

She nearly spit out her wine as she fought down the laugh that burst from her lips.

"What?" he asked.

"Sorry," she said, wiping her mouth with the back of her hand, "that just sounds like something Highcastle would say." She put on her best imitation of a royal accent. "By Lord Grandview's balls, that's a capital idea, eh, Blackwood?"

He failed to swallow down his own guffaw, covering his mouth as he shook. He glanced toward the guards then back at her, eyes alight. She'd never seen a nobleman giggle before, and she grinned as he tried to get himself under control.

"Well played, Amelia," he finally gasped. "I shall have to tell my father that one."

She toasted him and took another sip of the wine. He took the decanter and refilled her glass.

"Is your father in the Navy as well?" she asked suddenly.

"No. I think he wished he'd been, but he inherited our family estate quite young and had to take up his lordly duties even before he married."

"He must have been quite a catch . . . Young, handsome, and already a seated lord."

Blackwood shrugged. "He apparently wasn't in a hurry; he was in his thirtieth year before he finally wed my mother."

"Too many hearts to break, so little time?"

"Perhaps," he admitted, eyebrow arching, "but in fact a lord's marriage is as much about politics as anything. No doubt he was busy maneuvering to secure the most advantageous match."

"He didn't carry your mother's favor at the jousts? Win a tournament to win her love?"

"You really don't know how the nobility live, do you?"

She laughed, tapping her fingers on the hand he rested on the table. "It all just sounds so glamorous to us common folk—we can't keep all the fairy tales straight."

"I assure you, my father never jousted." He pondered for a moment. "I'm not even sure he can ride—I've never seen him take anything other than a carriage. But then, I've really only known him as an older man."

He'd said that it was strange for his father to have married as late as thirty, but surely the XO himself was already beyond that age. Must his own wedding bells ring soon?

"And in these noble schemes of marriage," she asked carefully, "does the family make the decision or the individual?"

A cloud passed over his features, so quick she would have missed it were she not watching him so closely. He shifted in his seat.

"For the firstborn, dynasty is everything. My brother has been paraded around since he could walk as my parents lobbied other noble families. A match that seems to have pleased everyone was made a few years ago, and the happy couple have obligingly produced an heir and a spare to the Blackwood line."

"And for the secondborn?"

"I have considerably more latitude," he said with a breezy wave of the hand, "and far less pressure."

He rose from his chair suddenly, stepping briskly away from the table. Her gaze followed and she saw Mr. Long shuffling over with an elaborate box in his hands. The two men exchanged quiet words, and she watched as Blackwood lifted a gold pendant for inspection. Even from this distance Amelia could see its exquisite workmanship, but she kept her seat and awaited Captain Stonebridge's command. Blackwood replaced the pendant and looked through a few papers, then nodded decisively to Long. The merchant bowed and retreated.

"A collection of gold and jewelry," Blackwood said quietly, retaking his seat across from her. "Very rare to see that sort of quality this far out in the Halo, and

Mr. Long has an established relationship with a jewelry merchant in the Iron Swarm. It's a bit out of our way but the perfect sort of high-profile cargo to draw attention."

"I hope he doesn't expect us to carry that back to the ship," she said, scanning the promenade below.

"No, no, he'll arrange for delivery. I think after that last little scuffle, we've established an understanding with dear Mr. Long . . . What?"

Amelia's gaze had wandered across the crowds and shops below, but now she was staring at a strangely familiar figure.

"Or," she said slowly, blinking to ensure she was seeing clearly, "we could always ask Chief Sky to escort us."

"The chief is with the captain," he said, confused.

"No." Amelia nodded down to where a powerful female figure stood at the edge of an alleyway. "She's right there."

Blackwood turned slowly in his seat, his eyes scanning. Far below, Sky was watching the street but hadn't yet looked up. She suddenly turned to glance down the alley, then was joined by a tall, willowy figure in a shawl. Together the two started back toward the docks.

"Was that the captain?" Amelia asked.

"It was," Blackwood murmured, his face furrowed in thought. "How very interesting."

"What does she do when ashore?"

"Say nothing of this to anyone," he said sharply. "Not a soul. Understand?"

"Yes, sir."

His expression was melting into one of careful unconcern, but he couldn't quite hide his puzzlement, or his worry.

CHAPTER 13

The quiet transit back to Windfall had been a welcome relief for the crew, but the lack of activity was starting to wear on them now. As Liam conducted his daily rounds of the ship, he noticed the first signs of carelessness. A piece of equipment not properly secured for storms; a section of cleaning not completed; a pair of sailors caught up in fisticuffs on their mess deck. Nothing to cause concern on its own, but Liam had led ship's companies for long enough to see the first signs of a slackening of discipline.

The fact that no one had been allowed ashore during their latest, brief stop in Windfall was a source of resentment, he knew. Often an XO would authorize extra rum rations and reduced working hours for those confined to ship during a port visit, but *Daring*'s stop in Windfall had only been a few hours. There had been no downtime to offer the crew, and extra rum rations would have been a bad idea with the ship putting out into space again so quickly.

Any thoughts of lingering at Windfall had been quashed

by Commander Riverton. After her mysterious trip ashore, she'd reported that a squadron of Navy ships was expected at the station within a day. *Daring* was to clear out and disappear before she was accidentally identified.

And now, four days out, Liam had heard the first of the grumblings. Or, more accurately, he'd heard from the senior sailors about the grumbling. No one would dare cross the executive officer, a fact that most lordly officers appreciated, but one that Liam recognized as a limitation on his ability to do his job.

Cadet Highcastle, however, for all his foppery, seemed to have developed a common touch. Liam often saw the young lordling chatting and laughing with the crew. Highcastle's own grousing at the senior mess dinner table every evening was Liam's best glimpse into the minds of his sailors. And while the cadet tended to dress every issue with puffed-up importance, Liam recognized the mood as one primarily soured by boredom. Although the lack of prize money so far was potentially a more serious issue, as common sailors loved to dream about wealth, and so far they'd seen very little of it.

But that was about to change.

Liam descended the ladder to Four Deck and strode down the main passageway, getting used to the weight of his armor again. Usually the quietest deck, this lower level of the ship was currently abuzz with activity. Three sailors wheeled trolleys of ammunition past him, the sweat on their brows revealing that they'd already been loading cannon for some time. They were followed by another trio of sailors carrying powder bags and spare plungers. He saw that one of the internal cargo-bay doors was open and he stopped to poke his head inside.

Virtue was inside, eyes up at the rows of shelving as

she counted. Liam watched her for a moment, admiring her lithe form and the way her dark hair framed her face. He couldn't put his finger on what, precisely, about Virtue fascinated him so, but it was a feeling he could no longer ignore.

She turned suddenly, seeming to feel his gaze. When she saw it was him, she smiled.

"Everything secure?" he asked automatically, embarrassed at being caught staring.

"Our high-value cargo is," she said, pointing back at the locked safes lining the deck. "Enough gold to outfit a princess, and still give earrings to the entire crew. I just figured I'd check our emergency rations while I was here."

Liam followed her gaze back to the shelves, where crates of freeze-dried food waited in case the regular stores ever ran out. Liam had eaten enough emergency rations over the years to know how important it was to restock fresh food in each port visit—even one as brief as their last stop in Windfall.

"Don't take too long," he said. "I expect you'll be needing to get your armor on soon."

"Yes, sir."

Turning away, he trekked down the side passage that led to the brig. Two armed sailors stood guard as usual, and he briefed them on the importance of maintaining their post no matter what happened in the next few hours.

"I realize it may be frustrating," he concluded, "having to stand down here and do nothing while there's action elsewhere. But you are what's keeping our prisoners where we need them—locked up. The last thing we need is six angry pirates loose inside our ship."

Having reassured himself that the guards would do their duty, Liam began the climb back up to the bridge.

Three Deck was crowded with propulsors as they brought packets of spare sails to propulsion control, ready to hurry up the masts when required. One Deck was rich with the smell of powder as the cannon crews readied their weapons. *Daring*'s crew was only big enough to man one side at a time, but both port and starboard cannon batteries were loaded and primed.

Liam climbed the last ladder to the bridge. Starlight flooded through the canopy from starboard, illuminating a full crew at their stations. Two sailors manned the propulsion controls, overseen by the coxn. Another two manned the tactical station with Chief Sky looming over them in her deep green armor. Sublieutenant Brown had the watch and Cadet Highcastle stood at her side, looking far less useless for his recent two weeks of having charge. Both were facing aft, telescopes out. One entire side of the sky was lit up by the thousands of stars in the Hub, but even in the glare Liam could easily see the reflecting surfaces of a dozen or more vessels in this shipping lane.

Liam nodded to Brown and approached the command chair. He read Riverton's displays and then turned to look upon their pursuer.

The ship was similar to the pirate sloop they'd captured, but larger, with a sleek bullet form unencumbered by external cargo pods. All four masts were at full sail on a port tack, their taut sheets glimmering in the light of the Hub. At this range the patterns on the sails were visible, a mishmash of colors and designs obviously cobbled together from a wide variety of sources. Most honest merchants either flew custom-marked sails provided by their wealthy owners or chose a single color and stayed with it. This patchwork of sails alone was enough to mark this approaching vessel as suspicious.

"Still no hails," Riverton said suddenly. "They've just been closing us at full speed for over a day."

"Is it time to end the charade, ma'am?" Liam asked.

Riverton turned forward in her chair and gestured for Liam to examine her tactical screen.

"I wanted to engage them at a far enough distance from other ships to hide our actions," she said, "but in lanes this busy that's proven impossible. By staying on this tack, we've opened the distance to the big merchants trundling along, but these two ships"—she indicated a pair of vessels that looked like fast cutters silhouetted against the Hub—"are still within easy visible range."

Liam nodded. Maintaining their identity as a civilian merchant was of utmost importance. "There will be nothing unusual about cannon fire," he offered. "We're just a merchant defending ourselves. When it comes time to board we can maneuver *Daring* to block the insertion, just in case anyone's watching."

"I suppose it's a risk we have to take," she said. She shielded her eyes and looked toward the glare of the Hub.

Daring had spotted the Sectoid vessel again on the second day out, but it was at the very edge of detectable range. Its purpose for loitering in this sector for so long remained a mystery, but Liam had his suspicions. The original pirate attack they'd seen on *Lightning Louise* had used Sectoid acid. His interrogations had revealed that the pirate base wasn't in a solar system, and despite the protests of that prisoner, Liam had his own suspicions. Was the pirate base in fact the Sectoid ship itself? Was it the dark star?

"If only we still had tracking on the Sectoids," he muttered. "We could finish this."

Riverton stiffened, and slowly turned her head to stare at him.

"We will do nothing rash, XO. Is that clear?"

"Yes, ma'am," he replied, surprised at her sudden intensity. She was readying herself for battle, he figured, and wanted no distractions.

"Shots fired from our pursuer!" cried Brown.

Liam spun to look, surprised to see the pirate ship still at full sail, bow aimed at *Daring*. Whatever they'd fired was no broadside. A second later, movement caught his eye and he glanced upward, watching with surprise as two of the top mast's sails split. The pirates had lobbed the first salvo now, and he could feel the familiar, prebattle rush of adrenaline course through his veins. Two more sails tore a moment later, and he just caught sight of the chain shot tearing through them.

"They're trying to slow us," he said to Riverton.

"Furl all sheets," she ordered. "Stow the masts!"

At the coxn's direction the pair of sailors at propulsion control began issuing instructions to Swift and his team below. But it took time to respond, and even as Liam saw the first of the mainsails begin to retract, more chain shot punched holes through the membranes.

"Is the hostile within cannon range?" Riverton barked.

"Not yet," Brown replied. "But we're losing speed and she's gaining fast."

Liam grabbed a spare telescope from Brown's station. Tufts of flame every fifteen seconds indicated more shots from the pirate ship's trio of bow guns. As the sails began to disappear into the lanyards Liam heard the first distant clang of the chain striking one of the masts. Cunning bastards, but they had no idea what was in store for them.

"Recommend we turn to open our starboard cannon," he said to Riverton. "It'll also shield the port and bottom masts."

"Do it," Riverton said to Brown.

"Coxn," Liam barked, "prioritize mast stowage as top, starboard, bottom, port."

"Yes, sir," Butcher replied.

Liam scanned visually. The last of the sails were still being furled on starboard mast, but a heavy creak through the ship indicated that top mast was unlocked and beginning to lower against the hull. He watched as the thick metal column loomed closer in his view, even as Brown ordered the bridge canopy shielding deployed. The visual world disappeared behind the armor plating, but the thump of the top mast settling against the canopy gave hint to the progress outside.

On the screens of the officer-of-the-watch station, Liam watched the pirate ship come into view as *Daring* turned with her thrusters. Her main direction of motion through space was now "sideways," but with no sails to propel her she was free to turn as required for battle.

The huge sails of the pirate ship now came into full effect and she closed the remaining distance swiftly. Too swiftly, in fact. With full sheeting it was going to take several minutes to withdraw her sails and stow her masts, but *Daring* had no intention of waiting.

"The bastard's in range!" Highcastle crowed.

"Starboard broadside," Riverton roared, "fire!"

The deck shook as sixteen cannons unleashed their opening shots as one. On the screens Liam saw the pirate bow shatter with the impact, splinters of hull careening off into space. The bullet nose held, but the chain guns didn't fire again.

"Fire at will!" Riverton ordered.

Liam felt the rumble as each cannon on One Deck fired, reloaded, and fired again, as fast as their operators could move. Tufts of dust riddled the pirate ship, hull plates flying off and the last of the sails flapping madly as cannonballs punched through them and their rigging. The pirate ship began to turn, her port mast slowly retracting to free her own guns.

"Full thrusters forward," Riverton said. "Concentrate fire on their bow."

Daring surged ahead, trying to stay aligned with the pirate's bow and avoid her arcs of cannon fire. The bullet hull was already riddled with craters and dents, but Liam could see that most of the damage was superficial. It was going to take a lucky shot or, as Riverton was doing, a continued concentration on one part of the hull to eventually score a breakthrough.

The ships continued their slow dance for some minutes, *Daring*'s guns blasting away as the pirate vessel desperately tried to turn. Turning a ship was faster than maneuvering one, however, and slowly the pirate ship was able to bring *Daring* into the arcs of fire of its lead cannon. Gouts of flame burst from the pirate hull and Liam felt the first thuds of impact against the starboard quarter. Another minute and fully half the pirate guns were in line.

"Shift target," Riverton said. "Hit their gunports."

The orders were relayed down by the weapons controllers, and within moments the tufts of impact moved from the shattered pirate bow toward the single line of flashing cannons. This was where pitched battles got dangerous. One lucky shot straight through an open gunport could wreak havoc on a ship's interior.

Liam checked the damage-control console. *Daring* was at full airtight status, meaning every gun was isolated in its own compartment and the ship itself was honeycombed to minimize air loss. Every spaceship had some degree of airtight capability, but he doubted the converted racer these pirates were driving could match the structural integrity of a Navy warship.

A sudden rush of orange flame from a pirate gunport gave hint to their first success. Liam zoomed in and saw that the square port was ragged, smoke racing outward into space for a few seconds before a still blackness settled over the wound.

"They've lost gun number two," he reported.

"And eleven," Highcastle echoed triumphantly.

The pounding of cannon fire continued as both *Daring* and the pirate made small maneuvers to disrupt each other's aim. As they drifted ever closer, though, the required position shifts became larger and more difficult. More cannonballs hit their targets. Liam staggered and grabbed his console as a shudder rippled the entire deck.

"We've lost guns three and four," Sky shouted. "Took 'em both out with a single shot!"

Liam looked up at Riverton. She steadied herself in her chair and nodded.

"Maintain broadside: prepare for boarding."

"Beat to quarters," Liam ordered, gesturing for Sky to follow. "Broadside boarding stations."

As Liam raced through the aft door of the bridge he heard Brown sounding the drums through the ship and repeating the order. Gripping both handrails, he flew down the ladder to One Deck, and into a haze of gun-powder and smoke. Up ahead he could see two sailors pressing emergency airtight panels against the twisted starboard bulkhead of the main passageway. Guns three and four were beyond that tortured metal, Liam knew, destroyed along with their crew by a lucky pirate shot. The smoke was streaming toward cracks in the bulkhead and a sailor smacked down yet another airtight patch as his partner nailed it into place. Around them, other sailors still passed fresh ammunition along the passageway, sliding it through the box-sized airlocks to the gun crews firing on the other side. The constant thunder of cannon fire shook the deck.

Liam steadied himself against a sudden pitch, then dropped to Two Deck. Staggering forward along the main passageway, he saw his boarding team assembling mid-ships. Virtue was already in padded armor, directing the issuance of weapons.

"Get the boats ready," he ordered Sky as she stumbled up behind him.

Virtue handed over the last weapons belt and turned to knuckle her forehead. "Boarding party ready, sir!"

"We're going in hot," Liam said to the assembled team. "We'll take out the gunnery teams first, then move on the bridge together. Their masts are stowed, so propulsion can wait."

The deck shook, throwing Liam against the bulkhead. He pulled himself up, helping Virtue to her feet as another series of thumps rattled the deck. They felt different from the continual cannon pounding, but Liam knew this wasn't the time to question. He needed to get those boats loaded and over to the pirate ship. Sky emerged from one of the airlocks.

"Both boats ready," she reported, stepping clear to make room for the first sailor to swing into the airlock tube.

"Board the boats," Liam ordered.

Another blast rocked the entire deck. Among the clatter of tumbling bodies Liam heard a distant scream, then the whoosh as a fireball exploded out of one of the airlocks. The flames washed over him for a second before disappearing, but behind them came the ominous rushing of wind.

"Breach!" he shouted.

Sky grabbed the airlock hatch and slammed it shut, silencing the roar and stilling the air. Liam climbed over his fallen sailors to help Sky seal the opening. Through the porthole he caught a glimpse of the ship's boat tumbling free, broken in half and still sparking as it tore apart.

The two sailors manning the other boat suddenly appeared through their airlock, scrambling back into the safety of the ship.

"Enemy ships," one shouted. "Port side!"

"Shut that hatch!" Virtue shouted, climbing forward to help secure the second airlock.

Moments later, the hatch creaked as pressure disappeared on the far side. Virtue was frozen in shock, staring through the porthole. Liam moved to her side, looking through the cracked glass to where the second boat was spinning away madly as it broke apart.

"Damnation," he hissed. He ran for the nearest comms station and punched up the command station.

"Captain," came Riverton's voice through the scratchy circuit.

"Captain, XO," he gasped. "We've lost both boats. Boarding is impossible."

"You lost them?" The shock in her voice filled him with a sudden dread.

"Smashed by enemy fire." The deck shook again under a series of impacts. Liam remembered that they were on the port side, the opposite side from where their quarry lay. He gripped the handset tightly. "What's going on up there?"

"We're being flanked." She broke off to issue orders.

The hull shook as another blast struck the ship. Liam heard only hissing on the circuit.

"XO," Riverton said suddenly, "are you still there?"

"Here, Captain."

"Deploy to repel boarders," she snapped.

The circuit went dead. Liam stared at the panel for a second, still processing her order. Boarders. As in, pirates were going to board them. He struggled to hang up the phone, steadying himself against the bulkhead. Fear gripped his gut like an iron weight. Pirates were outside the hull, looking to break in. He scanned the passageway, and his own crew still sprawled across the deck from the impacts. They hung on as another series of blasts rocked the ship. Riverton said they were being flanked—that meant more than one enemy ship. How many more? The fear weighed him down anew, but he'd felt it before, and he knew how to use it. Fear could fuel action if directed properly, and it was action that was needed now. His mind reengaged to process the new situation: it was still a battle, just now on his ship instead of theirs. He pushed himself up and breathed deeply. So be it, pirate scum.

He spun to face his crew, who were still picking themselves up from the deck.

"Chief Sky," he ordered calmly, "we need to deploy to repel boarders."

Sky stared at him for a moment, then nodded. Her expression didn't falter as she surveyed the sailors in front of her.

"We'll need four teams," she said, gesturing to separate the boarding party into rough groups, "split fore and aft on Two and Four Decks. Virtue, get the other medic from sickbay, get yourself a medikit, and split your section between the defense teams."

"We need to brief the prisoner guards," Liam said, his mind racing through all the needs of his ship. "And get reinforcements to the bridge."

"I'll do the guards," Sky snapped. "Sir, you guard the bridge."

Liam nodded, grabbing two extra braces of pistols. Another series of concussive blasts rocked the deck. He took a few steps toward the after ladder, noting Sky already in motion. But the rest of the boarding team were still staring in shock, some not even on their feet.

"You heard the assaulter," he roared at the sailors. "Man your stations, and defend this ship!"

He grabbed Virtue by the arm and hustled her down the passageway. Through two airlocks and they reached sickbay, where Sublieutenant Templegrey and Able Rating Song were bracing themselves against the steady thunder of battle. As Virtue collected two medikits, he handed one of the pistol sets to Templegrey.

"We're repelling boarders and all three medics are needed forward. You can remain here and defend sickbay"—he nodded to the pistols—"or you can come with me to the bridge."

Templegrey's pale skin was a sickly shade of gray. But she knew she was being watched by the common sailors and pulled herself up to her full height, wrapping the pistols around her white medical frock.

"I will remain at my station, sir," she said.

Liam steadied her shaking hands and fastened the buckle for her. She looked down at the weapons as if they were parasites crawling up her hips.

"Stay down," he said quietly. "Our sailors might bring wounded to you, so look before you shoot. But if you're sure, shoot to kill. You've got four shots in each pistol—make them count."

She clasped her hands together to still the trembling.

"Yes, sir."

Liam moved to the door, where Virtue had already dispatched Song and was hovering. She looked up at him, almost expectantly. He stared back, suddenly aware that they were alone. The entire ship lurched, throwing him against the bulkhead. Her armored body crashed against his. She righted herself as the deck vibrated again, collecting the medikit she'd dropped. She looked up at him again.

"Sir . . ."

There was no time for this, but he couldn't tear himself away. He stared down at her, feeling her hand grip his arm as the ship rocked again. He leaned toward her.

"Amelia, I . . ."

The clang of an airtight door opening interrupted him. He straightened as Virtue's hand dropped away and she called out to the pair of armed sailors. She tossed one of the medikits down the passageway to them, then glanced back over her shoulder at him one last time.

He swallowed the words he wanted to say, and the surge of emotion he hadn't expected. "Good luck, Amelia."

Her normally sparkling eyes were dark with fear as she gave him a look he couldn't decipher. "And to you, sir."

She hurried away, following the sailors. Liam grabbed the rungs of the ladder and hauled himself up the two decks to the bridge.

Riverton was still in her command chair, but ramrod straight as she barked orders for maneuvering. Even as he approached her station, Liam could make out the grim tactical situation; three vessels now swarmed *Daring*.

"Captain, XO. My team is divided into four squads to cover the main airlocks, and I've maintained the two guards at the brig." He handed her the last brace of pistols, gasping to catch his breath. "You might want these, ma'am, just in case."

"I'm trying to steer us clear," she said, ignoring the weapons, "but they're surrounding us."

Liam examined her tactical screen more closely. The pirate ship with which *Daring* had been exchanging broadsides was pulling back, but two new ships were even now retracting masts and starting to pound *Daring* from ahead and behind. Riverton was turning the ship to open her broadsides against one of them, but the enemies were quick.

"Where did they come from?" he asked.

"It's that pair of fast couriers," she said. "They must have been watching, ready to support if the initial attack didn't go well."

"I guess we're not the only ones disguised as merchants."

"And now they're launching boats against us."

Liam saw the symbols on the display, revealing no fewer than eight small boats separated from their mother ships and approaching *Daring* from all sides.

"Propulsion," Riverton barked. "Extend top and bottom masts, full sail!"

"Ma'am, what are you doing?"

"I need to get our top and bottom masts extended," she hissed in frustration, "to get some speed."

Even at full thrusters, Liam could see *Daring* wasn't moving fast enough to leave the boats behind. It was only a matter of time before they caught up to her.

And then pirates would be aboard their ship.

"The sails will be shredded before we can clear," Liam warned. "We're going to lose propulsors if they try and re-rig during battle."

Riverton's stern expression faltered, just for a moment. She stepped down from her chair and took the brace of pistols still hanging in Liam's hand. As she buckled them on, she leaned in very close to him. Her dark eyes burned with something close to panic. He'd seen it too many times in battle, when noble officers truly grasped their own mortality.

"I welcome your advice, Subcommander Blackwood," she said, with barely a quaver in her voice.

"We can't outrun them," Liam replied, mind racing as he surveyed the battle again. "And with cannon only we can't outgun them. I recommend we engage with military weapons."

"If we do," she said, "our identity is compromised."

"If that many pirates get aboard us," he countered, "we could lose everything. Ma'am, I assess our ability to repel that many boarders as unlikely."

"If I destroy those ships, we lose any hope of gaining intelligence from them."

She was too focused on the big picture, he realized furiously, and was ignoring the deadly reality right in front of them. He stared into her dark eyes, realizing with sudden clarity that for all her intelligence, for all her cold and decisive manner, she was inexperienced and needed his help. And at least, unlike the other fops, she knew when to ask for it.

"And it would be unfortunate," he agreed quietly. "But we can always start over."

She braced herself against the chair as the deck rocked again. The two masts were half deployed and already being targeted by the circling pirates.

"If I destroy those ships," she said, "we may fail in our mission."

"If we're destroyed or captured," Liam said, "we *will* fail in our mission."

Liam could practically see her thoughts jumping from one option to the other as she weighed the command decision. Finally, she nodded. "Make it so."

"Weapons control," Liam ordered across the bridge, "you are free to engage with all armaments. Turrets, target the pirate boats!"

The pair of sailors manning the weapons consoles on the starboard side of the bridge began frantically manipulating their controls. Liam heard the faint whine of the lasers spooling up, then watched the display as *Daring*'s six turrets opened fire on the small craft closing in. The powerful beams were designed as self-defense against military missile attacks, and they made short work of the boats.

"Target the three pirates with missiles," Liam ordered. "Salvo size one per ship."

Three dazzling rockets launched forth from *Daring*'s missile battery. The first lanced through the blackness and impacted the first pirate ship seconds later. It had no military defense weapons and the missile crashed into its hull before exploding. The vessel reeled, spurts of flame and shrapnel erupting into space as its entire port side broke apart. The keel snapped and the remains of the ship broke in two.

The two smaller ships fared even worse. The missile impacts were enough to tear their hulls completely apart. Within seconds, nothing remained but two chaotic clouds of debris.

Liam stood in the center of the bridge, watching the results in grim assessment.

All threats were eliminated. His ship was safe. But at what cost? Was *Daring* intact? How many sailors had been lost? And had his decision just compromised their entire mission?

"Huzzah!" cried Highcastle. "That gave them the what for!"

Liam pressed a steadying hand against the command chair, fighting down the savage desire to run that ignorant fop through. The desire to fight still coursed through him. He rolled his fingers to ensure no shaking, then took several deep, calming breaths.

Brown wiped sweat from her brow as she continued to hunker over her consoles, directing ship activity even as she plotted a new course. Highcastle stood beyond her, arms folded triumphantly as he surveyed the scene.

"Steer us in toward the wreckage of the first ship," Riverton ordered. "Subcommander Blackwood, prepare a boat to search. If we're lucky, their mainframe survived the attack."

"We have no boats, ma'am," he reminded her softly. "They were both destroyed."

"Then get a team suited up and ready to search," she snapped. "We'll get in close enough that they can use tethers."

"Yes, ma'am."

EVEN WITH THE AWKWARD TETHERS AND BULKY space suits, it took Liam and his team less than an hour to search the wreckage of the pirate ship. With half the vessel obliterated, access to every remaining compartment was simply a matter of clambering over the twisted remains of bulkheads now open to the vacuum. There was no power to run the ship's main computer, but the team was able to extract a few memory drives that appeared intact enough to possibly provide data. The expedition very quickly became little more than a scavenge for supplies. Based on what they recovered, these pirate crews were mostly Human with a few brutes thrown in. No sign of Sectoids on board.

Back on board, Liam barely had time to shed his space suit before receiving a summons to the senior mess. As he stepped through into the familiar room he was surprised to see most of the senior staff seated around the table, including the captain.

"Lord Blackwood," Riverton said with a gesture to the head of the table, "please take a seat."

She had positioned herself at the foot of the table, and he appreciated her respecting his position as head of the mess. He took his seat, not doubting for a second who was really in charge of this meeting.

"Propulsion," Riverton said without preamble, "report status."

"All four masts are operational," Swift replied. "Three of them have taken damage, but it's nothing that will stop us from sailing. I'll want to take a closer look at them whenever we next put into port. Sail inventory is at sixty-five percent. Thruster fuel, though, is at ten percent. It'll be enough to get us alongside, but not much more."

"Doctor," Riverton continued, "crew status."

"I have five wounded who are in stable condition," Templegrey said. "And three deceased. All gunners."

"Coxn, prisoner status."

"All six alive and accounted for, ma'am."

"Quartermaster, stores status."

"Enemy fire damaged three of our main holds," Virtue said, leaning forward with concern. "The leaks weren't discovered until after the battle and we lost a great deal of water and compressed air. Food stores are fine, but water is at fifteen percent and air is at thirty percent. All three of those holds are compromised until we can repair them, so maximum storage of air and water is no more than fifty percent."

"Assaulter, combat status."

"We lost both boats, so no boarding capability. All six turrets are operational, cannon ammunition is sixty percent, and missile inventory is five remaining."

"XO." Riverton turned to Liam. "What did your excursion uncover?"

"Very little to salvage. We brought back some data drives to examine, but the ship's memory core was destroyed. And we discovered the ship's name: *Golden Wind*."

Riverton's fist thumped the table, her frustration finally showing through.

"But that was our only lead!" Highcastle protested. "Tell me there's something useful on those drives."

"Watch your tone, Cadet," Liam snapped, unable to contain his own emotions.

Riverton was silent for a long moment, and all eyes eventually turned to her. She looked back at her senior staff impassively.

"Lieutenant Swift," she said finally. "Does Windfall Station have the facilities to make our required repairs?"

"They have the facilities," he replied, with some hesitation, "but they're short on manpower. I'd probably need to use our own crew to effect repairs, getting supplies and tools from the station."

Silence descended again, Riverton's expression hardening. She looked at Virtue.

"We don't have the supplies to reach any major port beyond Windfall, do we?"

"No, ma'am."

She stood suddenly. Everyone at the table scrambled to rise.

"Subcommander Blackwood," she said, "set sail for Windfall Station, best speed. Impose maximum air and water restrictions. Prepare a list of requirements for repairs and restocking—I don't want to spend an extra moment alongside."

"Yes, ma'am."

Riverton strode from the mess without another word.

Liam sized up his officers and senior sailors. They were all still dirty and harried from the battle, and new fatigue hung over all of them.

"You heard the captain," he said, giving them an encouraging smile. "To your duties."

Butcher and Sky moved for the door first, their faces set and grim. Templegrey was close behind them, gesturing silently for Highcastle to follow. Virtue was watching him, as if she had something else to say, but eventually she nodded and left.

That left Swift, who had sat back down in his chair. He eyed Liam expectantly.

Liam stared back for a moment, then sighed and retook his seat.

"That did not go well, Sails."

"It was a battle," Swift said with a curious frown. "There are always casualties, and always damage. Compared to some, I'd say it went pretty well."

"Sure, because I broke our cover and expended nearly half our heavy weaponry on a bunch of pirate ships which we desperately needed to take intact."

Swift cocked his head. "So it was your order to fire the missiles?"

"The captain was actually trying to maneuver us clear so that we could keep engaging with cannon and conceal our true identity." Liam rested his chin in his hands. "She was focused on the mission—I just wanted to keep us alive."

"That's no bad thing," Swift offered.

"No." Liam glanced around the empty table. "But since when have I been one to play it safe?"

"You set a trap, like you always do. And it worked. Except this time, we had three pirate ships instead of one enter the trap." Swift shrugged. "Sometimes the trap works too well—and we needed an escape plan.

You saw that we were in over our head, long before the captain did, and you acted accordingly. I see no fault in that, sir."

"We should have seen them coming—should have spotted the threat beforehand."

"I don't think that was your job," Swift said carefully.

"No, it was Riverton's!"

His last words hung in the mess for a long moment. Swift drew a tired hand across the back of his head.

"I want to put my faith in her," Liam said finally, "but I'm struggling. She doesn't have the experience to lead this kind of operation."

"The crew don't know what to think of her."

"What do *you* think, Mason?"

Swift let out a long breath. "She's better than some. At least I don't expect her to get us killed racing to a grand ball. But I think she's more of a courtier than a warrior."

"Yes." Liam had been coming to very much the same conclusion.

"Which is why she needs you," Swift added bluntly.

Liam nodded. He wanted to leave it there, but another thought, one he had been trying to suppress to no avail, bubbled to the surface and he finally had to voice it.

"But I don't need her."

Swift's eyes widened, and for a moment he couldn't find his voice.

"Oh, I'm not talking mutiny, Mason: she has my loyalty, to my dying breath," Liam clarified quickly. "But at times I wonder . . . is she just getting in my way?"

Relief visibly washed over Swift as he realized they weren't contemplating the ultimate crime, and his usual frown settled into place again.

"Most of us feel that way about our superiors," he said thoughtfully, "at some point or another. But at least with this mission, if we succeed, we'll all be rich enough to chart our own courses. So let's accomplish this mission, and worry about who's in our way afterward."

Liam considered that for a moment, and could see the wisdom in Swift's advice. He nodded, feeling like a weight was lifted from his shoulders. "Let's accomplish this mission," he repeated.

CHAPTER 14

Amelia turned carefully in her space suit, trying to reach her tool bag without getting caught up in her tether again. Moving outside the ship in zero-gravity was an acquired skill, and one that she hadn't practiced in a long time. Since leaving the airlock, she'd kept her movements slow and steady, gliding along the curving surface of the hull. Even the slightest wrong push could send her sailing away into the blackness, and no tether was guaranteed unbreakable.

Retrieving a small spray can from her tool bag, she inched forward again and scanned the hull through her faceplate. She could tell by the pattern of cannon impacts that she was close to the breach, but the blasted thing was proving devilishly hard to find. The once-smooth surface of *Daring*'s hull was dented and chipped from cannon fire. Up ahead, the towering form of the starboard mast rose away from her, the sails shimmering in a blustery solar wind. She skirted around the shattered remains of a sensor pod, wondering idly what aspect of the bridge was now blind for its loss.

"Okay, Able Rating Massive," she said into her circuit, "I'm in position. Release the spray."

"Yes, PO," came the reply from her storesman in the cargo hold.

As she waited, Amelia marveled at the oddities of perception. Massive was little more than five paces away from her, just on the other side of the battered hull against which she now floated. In other circumstances they could have reached each other in seconds. But here, with her bundled in a space suit staring down the Abyss, and him inside a pressurized hull wearing just his duty uniform, they might as well have been on different worlds.

"Spray released," he reported. *"It's moving toward the hull, topside."*

She turned herself to look over the hull toward the top part of the cargo hold, readying one hand to push forward while holding the spray can in the other. She waited, eyes scanning the battered surface.

There! A tiny cloud of rapidly freezing liquid emerged against the metal. She pushed off, sailing over the hull to intercept. The fluid had been specially treated to crystallize upon freezing, making it easy for her to spot. She slowed over a dent in the hull nearly as wide as her arm span and watched as the fluid seeped through the tiny crack. Reaching down with her own spray can, she smothered the metal surface with sealant.

"That ought to do it," she said. "I'm coming inside."

"Yes, PO."

Grabbing her tether, she pulled herself back to the airlock and started the depressurization sequence. In those few seconds of waiting, she looked out away from the ship, marveling at the vastness of this ocean of nothingness in which *Daring* sailed. The brilliant swell of the

Hub was visible past her feet, millions of stars lighting the sky in all directions. Above her the Halo began to fade toward the Abyss, but there were still too many stars to count even in that direction. She wondered how many other tiny objects were out there, invisible and lost, like the jettisoned cargo of that first pirate ship. The airlock door signaled ready and Amelia heaved it open, having no desire to become one of those lost objects herself.

It took more than ten minutes to get back into the ship, call the bridge to report she was in, climb out of her space suit, and get everything stowed. Able Rating Massive came up just as she closed the locker, asking if there was anything else she needed.

"Give the outer sealant an hour," she said, "then do another test with the fluid to ensure there's no remaining leak. Until then, see if they need a hand in the galley."

"I hear we got some provisions from the pirate wreckage?"

"Yeah, and some of it might actually taste good."

"Shame we didn't get much else."

It was a common complaint these days. With the lure of prize money dangled before them, this entire crew was becoming obsessed with anything Amelia kept in her stores.

"I'm just glad we all kept our skins, Able Rating," she said, a bit more harshly than she'd intended.

"Yes, PO," he muttered, walking away.

Beyond him, the main passageway of Two Deck was alive with activity. A pair of propulsors were hunkered against one of the internal airlocks, pounding at the doorframe to realign the seal. Massive bumped into another one of the storesies coming up a ladder, laden with supplies, and took some of the burden as they headed for the galley. A train of gunners was passing ammunition up the after ladders, no doubt replenishing all the cannon shot so recently used. And through it all, a lone ordinary rating was diligently sweeping the deck on his cleaning rounds. A busy ship was a happy ship, she'd often heard said.

Since the battle, she'd certainly lived by that motto, running from one task to the next in every waking moment. But with the last hull breach finally isolated and contained, she wondered if she might not make a bit of time to stop in on Subcommander Blackwood. No doubt he could use a status report—she smiled to herself as she started down the passageway—or maybe just a friendly chat.

She'd barely made it five steps when she noticed a sudden hush at the after end of the passageway. The gunners all stopped passing ammunition and cleared the ladder up to One Deck. A pair of white-uniformed legs appeared, and the willowy form of Commander Riverton emerged, her blue uniform coat in stark contrast to the grubby work clothes of the crew.

Amelia couldn't remember the last time she'd seen the captain down on Two Deck. Those gunners still on the deck knuckled their foreheads to the captain and the ordinary rating abandoned his broom to do the same. Massive struggled to put down his armload in time to offer a salute. Riverton simply strode forward, eyes locking on to Amelia even from a distance.

An eerie silence descended as Riverton came to a stop in front of her, staring down with her usual frosty expression. Amelia knuckled her forehead, resisting the urge to bow her head.

"Were you able to secure that leak, PO?" Riverton asked simply.

"Yes, ma'am," Amelia replied. "The sealant will hold until we return to Windfall Station, and the bright color will make it easy for repair crews to spot."

"Good." The captain cocked her head slightly. "Isn't hull repair a propulsor's job?"

"Normally, ma'am, but they're busy. This leak was in one of my cargo holds and I want the space back, so I coordinated with Lieutenant Swift and did the job with my own department."

Riverton nodded, her face inscrutable.

Amelia stood frozen, wondering if she was expected to say anything else.

"Well done, PO," Riverton said. Then she turned and strode back down the passageway.

Amelia remained motionless, ignoring the stares from the two propulsors. The entire passageway seemed paused in a tableau until Riverton returned to the after ladder and ascended out of sight.

Then motion resumed, with the gunners collecting their ammunition packs and the ordinary rating retrieving his broom. Still, no one spoke as Amelia slipped past them.

Massive was handing stores through the door to the galley, but he looked up as Amelia approached.

"Excuse me, PO," he said hesitantly. "This box needs to go to the senior mess—could I please trouble you to take it there so I can help in the galley?"

She saw the small wooden box of coffee bags by his feet and scooped it up, noting how nervous he appeared, though the favor was such a small one. She offered him an easy smile and nod, and saw a trace of relief cross his features.

When she reached the senior mess, she found Subcommander Blackwood seated at the table, work spread out in front of him. He glanced up, face brightening.

"Wow," he said. "Not ten minutes from a spacewalk and now you're delivering coffee. Is there anything you can't do, Amelia?"

She laughed, not even trying to tamp down the sudden rush of happiness she felt. She handed the box to the steward on duty and leaned against one of the dining chairs. "Well, apparently I've also mastered the persona of being a mean old petty officer. You should have seen how nervous Massive was, asking me to carry that box down the passageway."

"Get used to it." He sighed, leaning back and stretching. "As a senior sailor, you are now, in the eyes of the crew, officially part of the problem."

"What problem?"

"Any problem. It's always our fault, whether it is or not."

She glanced to where the steward was doing his best to be invisible, silently unpacking the coffee into a cupboard.

"What are you working on, sir?" she asked, taking the seat next to him.

"I'm studying the small-objects chart we bought—and kept—from our friend Mr. Long." He gestured to the large viewers spread out on the table. "It's best to look at large screens, and my cabin is pretty tight. Here I can spread out—and actually have a bit of Human contact."

His tone was casual, but his eyes danced as they met hers. She felt her heart flutter just a bit.

"Just what are you looking for?" she asked, holding his gaze.

He blinked, lips parting as he considered an answer, until she nodded down at the charts.

"Oh," he said. "Er, there are only certain kinds of objects in space that would be useful to the pirates. I'm pinpointing them to try and narrow our search."

"Long-orbit comets?" she ventured.

"Mostly. Anything with water, really. There are plenty of rocks floating around out there which could serve as a base, but if they don't have water they're not much good for the long term." He shrugged. "At this point we don't have a lot of hard data to go on, so I'm just trying to give us some direction where we can focus our search efforts."

"Can I help you?"

He glanced at the steward, then gave her a little smile.

"Much as I'd normally appreciate it, this is rather technical, detailed work and it's best for me just to focus on it without distraction." He reached down and gave her hand a quick squeeze. "Another time."

"Another time, sir." She rose and headed for the door. When she glanced back, he was still looking at her.

Butterflies were rioting in her stomach, but she tried to temper her excitement. He was a nobleman, and they were notorious for charming young sailors all the way to heartbreak. He was also the executive officer of this ship. The Navy had no formal ban on relationships within a crew—centuries of space travel had proven the impossibility of stopping people in isolated, close quarters from seeking each other out—but when it crossed ranks there was always the risk of trouble.

But he was just so damn cute. And intelligent, and courageous.

She forced herself to take a deep breath. She just had to be careful.

The gunners were still loading ammunition, passing what seemed like an endless stream of heavy sacks up from Three Deck and then up again to One Deck. Sweat soaked their uniforms and chests heaved as the sacks were handed up. Just to the side of the ladder was a pack of what looked like tools, which struck Amelia as an odd place for it to be. The master rating who stood on the deck between ladders noticed her approach and called down the hatch for a pause.

"Do you need the ladder, PO?" he gasped, reaching for his canteen.

Amelia suddenly realized that she wasn't sure where she was going. So many little distractions had come up in the last five minutes she'd lost her sense of purpose. Not wanting to appear indecisive in front of the crew, though, she latched on to her latest thought. She pointed down at the pack of tools.

"Is this yours? It seems out of place, here."

"Oh, that's for the crew repairing Gun Five," he replied. "We'll get it to them eventually, but right now I've got this ammo train set up and I don't want to mess with it."

"I'll take it up for you," she offered on impulse.

"Would you, PO?" he asked gratefully. "That would be much appreciated."

She hefted the pack, waited for the gunner perched on the ladder to climb down, then scooted up. The hatch on One Deck was also crowded with hardworking gunners, clearly appreciating the break in efforts. Amelia stepped past them, noting the two open gun compartments on either side of the hatch where ammunition was being stored. There were sixteen gun bays on each side of *Daring* and she headed to Gun Five, third from forward on the starboard side. It was immediately recognizable from the bent bulkhead and buckled door. A temporary airtight door had been mounted in the passageway but it was open.

As soon as Amelia stepped through she felt the temperature rise. Half a dozen lanterns were placed around the space to provide strong light and her eyes were immediately drawn to the pale brown metal of the temporary hull plate bolted onto the far end of the space. This was where a pirate cannon had breached the armor and hit the gun's own ammunition. The explosion had killed the gun crew instantly and blasted an entire piece of the outer hull away. The temporary hull plate was airtight, but it wasn't treated to properly hold out the solar radiation from the thousands of nearby stars.

Three sailors were crouched around the dismantled components of the main cannon. They were stripped to the waist in the heat, all eyes down as they worked together to slide a heavy piece of machinery back into place in the gun's pivot mechanism. The blond ponytail identified Hedge. Next to her was the thick, hairy form of Master Rating Flatrock, and across the gun, muscles flexing under a sheen of sweat, was Cadet Highcastle.

Amelia waited in silence as the three finished their delicate task. Despite herself, her eyes lingered on Highcastle's sinewy form. His sandy-blond hair fell over his forehead, and his sharp features were locked in a determined grimace that relaxed into a grin as the piece dropped into place and he sat back.

He was the first to notice Amelia standing there,

and she blinked and blushed as she realized she'd been staring.

"Ah, Quartermaster," he greeted with a friendly wave. "Come to bring us refreshments?"

"More tools, actually," she replied, stepping forward and dropping the pack on the deck next to Flatrock. The senior technician used the top of the pack to wipe the sweat off his brow, then flipped it open to look inside. He grunted approvingly.

"I'm surprised to see you here, Cadet Highcastle."

"I find I quite enjoy this technical work," he said breezily, glancing at Hedge. "And I have excellent teachers."

"Are we going to be able to rebuild the breech, now?" Hedge asked Flatrock, smiling her appreciation at Highcastle. She untied her ponytail and flipped her long hair from side to side, stretching back her shoulders in a way that, given the fact she was in only a practical bra, left little to the imagination.

Amelia could see Highcastle's eyes dip down over Hedge's chest. Her first instinct was disapproval—but then she remembered her own thoughts just minutes earlier about the other nobleman officer on board. And Hedgie was smart and spirited—maybe a handsome toff was exactly what she needed. Amelia's eyes wandered back to the young lordling's taut frame. One could do worse. Too bad he was a self-centered little prat.

"Yeah," Flatrock finally replied, his breath slowing. "This is the stuff we need."

"Obviously very important," Highcastle mused, "for the quartermaster herself to be charged with delivering it."

"Oh, I just had a spare moment," Amelia answered, sitting down cross-legged in their impromptu circle. "Not many people have that luxury right now."

"Yeah, it's been a tough go," Hedge agreed. "I just wish we'd got something for it."

"I told you," Flatrock muttered. "We picked that wreck clean. There was nothing left of value."

"Perhaps the decision to use missiles was a bit hasty," Highcastle offered. He took a slow sip of his water and surveyed the sailors. "But we were under attack by three ships. I don't blame the captain for panicking a bit."

"She panicked?" Hedge asked.

"No, no," he said with a dismissive wave of the hand. "That's the wrong word. It was a stressful situation on the bridge—as it was everywhere on board—and she had to act quickly to get us out of danger."

"Well, I for one approve," Amelia said quickly. "We weren't boarding anybody at that point. Not with both boats destroyed."

"I don't know why we didn't board sooner," Flatrock said. "If we'd launched right away, we could have been aboard *Golden Wind* and then *Daring* could have laid waste to the other two ships."

Hedge and Highcastle both nodded.

"But at least we're in one piece," Amelia said. "And a quick stop back at Windfall will see us in fighting shape again. I was just—"

"And all our coffers will be emptied into those greedy shipwrights' hands," Highcastle interrupted. "Of course, I don't need the prize money. But I care about all of you."

"That's thoughtful of you," Hedge said, turning the full charm of her doe eyes on him.

"He has a point—we're basically back to square one," Flatrock observed with a frown.

"No," Amelia countered. "As I was saying, I was just talking to the XO"—she ignored Hedge's raised eyebrow—"and he's narrowing down likely positions for the pirate base. We aren't going to have to search the entire sector—we'll have just a few places to focus on."

"On the bridge I've been tracking errant signals from time to time," Highcastle added. "It gives me clues to where there might be pirate ships operating."

"Really?" Hedge asked, leaning forward with interest. "How do you do that?"

Highcastle gave an elaborate shrug. "Officer stuff."

Hedge reached over and smacked him on the bare chest.

"But seriously," Flatrock said suddenly, looking at Amelia, "how much treasure do we have stored away right now?"

"We have a prince's ransom of gold," she said matter-of-factly. "But it's scheduled for delivery to the Iron Swarm."

"So they're paying us to deliver the cargo?"

"No. We buy it from the merchant in Windfall, and then we sell it for a higher price to a merchant in the Iron Swarm. In this case, the cargo is very valuable and we'll make a huge profit when we deliver it."

"Like, how much?"

"Enough for all of us to retire, and for you to drink yourself to death."

Flatrock grunted appreciatively.

"Why don't we just keep the cargo?" Hedge mused. "Split it between us all."

Amelia was too startled by the question to answer, and she instinctively looked to the officer. But Highcastle offered no help, his expression bland and unresponsive.

"Because," she said finally, "it was Navy money that bought this cargo, so if we scarpered with it then we'd be pirates and the Navy would hunt *us* down."

"Yes"—Highcastle weighed in—"let's focus on our task of capturing the real pirates. There'll be plenty of booty for everyone once we finish our mission."

"But didn't you say the Sectoids are involved?" Hedge nibbled her lip, worry clouding her features.

"Without doubt," Highcastle replied. "We've seen the acid weapons used by the pirates, and that damn ship is always lurking in the darkness."

"Damn bugs," Flatrock agreed, his massive frame shuddering.

"We don't know if they're involved," Amelia said carefully. "There haven't been any on the pirate ships we've seen."

"No," Hedge exclaimed, pointing vaguely outward beyond the hull, "they're out there, in their giant ship, watching us. And pretty soon they're going to decide to take us out."

"I've heard enough stories," Flatrock muttered, "that I don't ever want to fight the bugs hand to hand—or whatever blasted appendages they have."

"Chief Sky has fought them," Highcastle commented. "She's told a few grim tales over drinks of an evening."

"How are we going to fight them?" Hedge persisted.

"I'm not sure yet, but I'll figure it out," Highcastle replied intently. "I have every confidence in this crew."

There was an unspoken meaning in his sentence, Amelia could tell, and she caught a return glint of something in Hedge's eyes. Suddenly this friendly discussion felt supremely uncomfortable. She rose to her feet. "Good luck with your repairs," she said lightly. "I'm off to solve my next crisis."

"Shaving the coxn's back?" Flatrock asked, to a sudden burst of laughter.

"Or the assaulter's legs?" Hedge threw in.

Amelia couldn't help but laugh as well as she headed for the door. Her uniform was already slick from the heat and she tugged at it. "As delightful as that sounds, I think a cool washdown might be next on my priority list."

"Just use water the captain's touched," Hedge said. "It's sure to be cold as ice."

Hedge snorted, and their laughter echoed behind Amelia as she exited the gun bay. All harmless fun, she told herself. Just sailors complaining as usual—and it was nice to be counted as one of them.

So why did she feel so uneasy?

CHAPTER 15

"I know we're here to work," Virtue said, "but I almost feel like we're coming home."

Liam paused beside her as they gazed up at the soaring chamber that was the Windfall Station promenade. It was bustling with activity, with a cluster of new market stands crowding the central thoroughfare and competing with the established facilities for the sudden surge in patronage. Bright Navy uniforms mixed with the dull clothes of civilians, and there was a festive quality to the air. He watched the movement of Navy personnel for a moment.

"We have to keep a very low profile," he said, speaking past Virtue to where Riverton and Sky stood, "and stay clear of the Navy. Drunken sailors aren't fussy about who they cause trouble with."

"I'll be no more than an hour," Riverton said. "How long do you need?"

"To make arrangements, probably the same." He gestured back to the airlock that led to *Daring*. "But we'll have to bring a few crewmembers out when we load stores."

They'd taken the most distant berth on the station. It helped to keep their ashore activities out of view from the main promenade, and it also physically shielded *Daring* from the squadron of Navy ships tied up at the prime berths. With her battered hull and external cargo holds, she bore little resemblance to the sleek, modern warships, but Liam knew it took only one sharp eye to spot her true form through the disguise and start asking questions.

And with those sleek, modern warships as slashed and cratered as they were, the Navy was hyperalert to anything unusual. There had been a skirmish between this squadron and a single Sectoid mother ship, and from the damage he could see through the clear berths even from here, Liam doubted the Navy was calling it a victory. The festive air on the promenade had a grim undercurrent to it, as sailors drank, whored, and gambled away their cares. If war was coming, this might be the last respite any of them had.

"The crew will stay aboard until then," Riverton said, "without exception. I think I made myself clear earlier?"

"Yes, ma'am." The captain's announcement to the ship's company had been made in no uncertain terms— anyone caught ashore unauthorized would forfeit their share of the prize money.

Riverton adjusted the scarf on her head and started forward, Sky close behind. It was another mysterious outing for the captain, and one that again she'd felt no need to explain.

But at the moment Liam had bigger things to worry

about than Riverton's assignations. He motioned for Virtue to follow him.

Once they were past the waist-high gates guarding the jetty, the mass of Humanity closed in immediately. The arrival of the Navy certainly supplied a large number of boisterous new bodies, but in addition, an entirely new ecosystem of products and services seemed to have materialized to support them. The brothel windows were empty, he noted, the lads and ladies he'd seen before advertising their wares now no doubt busy inside. The taverns were brimming over with laughing sailors, and the new market stalls were laden with trinkets and snacks for purchase. Overall the mood was buoyant, but among the civilian locals Liam also saw a cool sense of purpose. This Navy visit was a rare opportunity to bring fresh currency into their lives, and they intended to get it, by whatever means necessary.

His left hand slipped down to touch the hilt of his dagger, and his right reached out to take Virtue's. Her slender fingers wrapped around his and he sensed her moving closer to him. Her presence reassured him, and steeled his own nerve as he swore to himself that she would come to no harm. He glanced down. She gave him a serious expression and subtly tapped her coat where the pistol was hidden.

The Cup of Plenty stood out clearly with its red-brick frontage, its patio crowded with tables, patrons packed close together with their coffees and treats. Liam skirted around chairs, carefully scanning the Navy uniforms for any familiar faces while trying to avoid eye contact. Virtue's hand remained pressed in his, and as far as he could tell no one paid them any mind.

Stepping into the café brought welcome relief from the cacophony of the street, and Liam's eyes swept the room in search of Matthew Long, lingering on a section of tables that had been draped in green.

A Theropod dressed smartly in black and gold stood there, small hands expertly shuffling and dealing cards. Most of the patrons were Human, a mix of Navy officers and well-to-do locals. There was a focused hum in the room, with most of the gamblers playing in silence and the nongaming patrons leaning close over their coffees in hushed conversation, until one Navy officer threw down his cards in disgust.

"Damnation," the man hissed. He snapped his fingers at the nearby waitress. "Brute, get me another cup."

His back was to Liam, but there was no mistaking that broad back and sandy-blond hair, nor the rank of captain on his shoulders. Liam squeezed Virtue's hand and immediately led her back out onto the patio. Amid the sudden resurgence of noise, he had to lean down to hear her question.

"What's wrong, sir . . . milord?"

"It's Captain Silverhawk," he muttered, discreetly checking the patio anew for any officers who might recognize him.

"Oh . . ." She swallowed down her first choice of word. "Damnation."

"We can't stay here, but we need to meet Long." Liam assessed the street beyond quickly. "Silverhawk won't recognize you. Get in there, find Long, and bring him out to that stall over there, the one with the juices for sale. I'll be waiting."

She nodded and slipped back through the doors. Liam edged his way past the seated patrons and eventually cleared to the main thoroughfare. He joined the line at the juice stall and did his best to blend in. The juices on offer were all local fare, and Liam listened to the orders of those in front of him to reveal the most popular choice. When the merchant finally cast questioning eyes at him, he paid for the pale yellow beverage and was provided a cup without a second glance. He moved to the side, eyes once again on the doors to the Cup of Plenty.

To his relief, he spotted Virtue emerge onto the patio, the wide, shuffling form of Matthew Long behind her. As they cleared the crowd and approached, Long's hooded eyes revealed more than a hint of annoyance. Liam cared little if he inconvenienced this petty kingpin, but reminded himself that right now he needed Long's help.

"Mr. Long, milord," Virtue said as they met. "I explained your distaste for gambling."

Her excuse to get Long out here. Liam appreciated her not bringing the Navy into her reasoning. He assumed his usual air of foppery.

"Yes, ghastly habit—ruins households." He nodded to Long. "I appreciate your indulgence, Mr. Long."

"Of course, my lord," he said with a slight bow. "I am here to serve. But I confess your message took me by surprise—I wasn't expecting to see you return to Windfall for at least several weeks."

"A storm caught us unawares and caused some damage. Very disruptive to our schedule, and I'd like to get back under sail as soon as possible."

"I'm very sorry to hear of such misfortune, my lord. How can I help?"

Explaining the need for air and water was easy, but it took several minutes to explain the technical requirements for effecting repairs to *Daring*'s hull and masts. Long listened carefully.

"Those facilities do exist, my lord, but it may be several days before the yard is ready to receive your ship." He gestured at the heaving crowd around them. "With this visit by His Imperial Majesty's Navy, many resources have been diverted."

"My own crew can do the work. I just need access to the equipment and materials."

"An excellent suggestion, but there may be some difficulties. Our shipwrights are very protective of their trade. They will resist the idea of someone else doing their work." He paused as if in thought. "You are clearly an honorable man, my lord, and I know you would normally give this work to the yard. But this is a unique situation. I know the guild leader well—I would be happy to speak to him on your behalf."

"Your assistance will be much appreciated, Mr. Long. I wish to set sail as soon as possible in order to deliver your very valuable cargo."

"It is your cargo, my lord, and I wish you every success with it."

Liam realized his misstep. He'd already paid Long in full for the gold—the merchant had no interest in its fate now. He switched tack.

"And I hope to be able to return for future cargoes. If I prove I can deliver, I'm sure you and I can build quite a reputation for high-value goods."

"Quite right, my lord," Long said with an easy smile. "And as I said, I am happy to speak to the shipwright guild master to support you. But the master may take some . . . convincing to rent you his equipment."

Liam didn't pretend not to understand. "How much convincing?"

While Long made a show of considering, Liam quickly retallied the reserves he had, knowing that *Daring*'s supply of currency was quite low—most of their prize money to date was currently tied up in the gold shipment locked on board.

"I would suggest ten thousand, my lord, to secure the equipment and materials and to ensure that the guild master sees the situation our way."

It was an effort to keep from showing his frustration. That amount would wipe out his hard-currency reserves. He didn't relish the idea of asking any of his noble officers if they could spare some cash.

He raised a brow. "That's outrageous, Mr. Long."

"The shipwrights are very busy right now," the man said with a slow shrug. "And so am I."

Virtue lifted her hand to rub it against Long's arm. "But surely, Mr. Long," she said with her most charming smile, "you must know that we don't have that kind of currency on hand."

He turned his entire, jowled head and gave her a simpering smile.

"I am sympathetic, Amelia, and open to finding a solution. Perhaps some other arrangements could be made to offset the costs?"

A true bolt of anger shot through Liam, catching him by surprise. "I will assess my hard currency," he interjected coldly. "But for ten thousand, I want the air and water included in the deal."

Long glanced at him, but then turned his attention back to Virtue. She was still smiling, but she nodded at

Liam's words. "I think my lord has an excellent suggestion, Mr. Long. A fair compromise?"

The big man hesitated for a moment, then finally offered a bow. "Let me contact the guild master, my lord, and see what I can organize. But I will need to deliver payment before any work can commence."

"I will return to my ship at once. Meet me there as soon as you've arranged for discussion with the guild master."

Long departed with purpose, his limp barely slowing him as he disappeared into the crowd.

Liam and Virtue headed back toward the docks.

"You know that's all our money, right, milord?" she commented.

He sighed. "Yes. But I don't see that we have any choice. We have to get out of here before someone in the Navy recognizes either us or the ship. And we have that damn gold to deliver and get paid for."

"This isn't going to go down well with the crew," she warned with sudden seriousness. "I think I could have negotiated the price down at least some."

Liam bit down his response, annoyed at his own reaction to Long's lasciviousness toward Amelia. He understood well her warning—if the crew found out, the grumblings to date might turn into something more dangerous.

"I think my compromise is about as much as we could hope for with the pressure we're under," he said shortly. "And it gets us everything we need in a single go."

She gave him a sidelong glance, but didn't say anything more than "Yes, sir."

They returned to *Daring*'s berth without another word. The next few hours were a strange dance of frantic activity mixed with cloak-and-dagger operations. When Long arrived on the ship as promised, Liam assigned Mason Swift to accompany the merchant with the strongbox of ten thousand crowns, both to assure the money went to where it was intended, and also for Swift to get exactly the equipment and materials he needed.

The work began quickly enough to patch *Daring*'s hull, but the propulsors were limited to no more than six outside the hull at any one time. A merchant ship like *Sophia's Fancy* would run on a skeleton crew, and if dozens of sailors were to suddenly emerge from within her, any observers would conclude that she was either a pirate or a military vessel. Progress was going to be slow.

"SO WE'LL BE ABLE TO MAKE SAIL IN TWO DAYS? That's not bad, considering." Riverton was unusually animated, pacing her cabin. She'd finally returned, having been gone much longer than her intended hour, and Liam was briefing her on the status of the repairs.

"I'll use the time to further investigate the pirate data we recovered—try to pick up some new clues. I'll work out an alternate route to Silica, as I want to keep clear of that Sectoid ship."

"They have extremely long-ranged sensors," Riverton said, head cocked slightly. "I'm not sure we'll be able to hide from them."

"We know what region she was in before, so I'll estimate from her last known position."

"Sectoids employ remote drones as well, all linked to the central mind. They're small and slow-moving—they can be very hard to spot until it's too late."

Liam had heard of such things, but never experienced them in person. He considered this new information.

"My point," Riverton continued, "is that hiding from the Sectoids may be too difficult. I want you to focus your attention more on finding the pirates."

Liam knew his captain well enough to recognize when her words were an order, no matter how softly she said them.

"Yes, ma'am. I'll track outgoing messages from Windfall as well; see if there's anything unusual."

"What sort of things would you look for?" she asked suddenly, stopping to stare at him.

"I'm not sure," he said with a shrug. "Unusual things. Is there something in particular you'd like me to search for, ma'am?"

She shook her head, resuming her pacing. "Just be mindful that with the Navy here, there will be a lot of encrypted comms, and more traffic than usual heading out of the station."

"Are we running out of time, ma'am?" Open talk of war was everywhere on the station, Liam knew from his visit, and Riverton's shift in expression didn't fill him with confidence.

"Yes," she said finally. "We need to find out what this dark star is, reveal the true source of the pirate strength, and destroy it."

"I'll have Sublieutenant Brown start the searches immediately, ma'am."

"Do you think your friend Mr. Long might be feeding information to the pirates?"

"It's a possibility." He considered the idea further for a moment. "But a remote one, I think. He genuinely makes money with his legal merchant activities, and the pirate activity is hurting this. He's a petty thug and local kingpin, to be sure, but I think the pirate threat is separate from his local brand of crime."

"I agree. The pirates are operating with a sophistication I didn't expect." Riverton stopped. "We have our work cut out for us. Thank you for stopping by."

Liam recognized the dismissal and with a slight bow retreated. Riverton had turned to her main console and was bringing up information before he'd taken three steps, and seemed to hardly notice as he departed her cabin.

The ship's interior was bustling with activity as propulsors ferried new hull plates up to where the repairs to the gunports were under way. The gunners themselves were busy refurbishing those weapons that had been damaged in the battle, cannibalizing what they could from the guns that were beyond repair. Liam looked into several gun bays and noted with satisfaction the industrious activity, but the view into one of them stopped him short. Amid a trio of sailors, stripped to his shirt and sleeves rolled up to reveal grubby forearms, was Cadet Highcastle. The lordling muttered something too quiet for Liam to hear, but the sailors all burst into laughter.

Highcastle suddenly noticed Liam in the doorway and rose to his full height, absently wiping his hands with a dirty cloth.

"Good afternoon, Lord Blackwood."

The sailors started, scrambling to their feet and knuckling their foreheads.

"Relax, gentlemen," Liam said as he stepped into the compartment. "It's good to see you learning all aspects of shipboard life, Mr. Highcastle."

"I think it's important to understand my ship intimately," he said, before grinning and smacking one of the sailors with his cloth. "Next week perhaps I'll go swinging with the mast monkeys."

"Stick with us, sir," the sailor growled with good humor.

"This is where the glory is," said another with more seriousness, patting the breech of the long cannon. He then looked at Liam. "Are we going to get more ammunition, sir?"

"We're well stocked already," Liam replied. "Once the hull repairs are made, and you lads have all your guns in order, we'll be setting sail again."

"Well, if you need anyone to go ashore for supplies," he said, "I'm in."

The other sailors echoed him.

"Hardly anyone's going ashore for now. We have to keep our cover as a merchant ship." Liam offered a wry smile. "And trust me, you're not missing much by missing Windfall Station—except an interesting set of smells."

"Still," Highcastle chimed in, "it would be smashing just to have a change of scenery. Stretch the legs, so to speak."

"Understood. But with Navy ships in port right now, we have to be especially careful to maintain a low profile."

"The Navy's here?" Highcastle asked, new light in his eyes. "Why don't we just request help and supplies from them?"

"It could have saved our prize money from being spent," muttered a sailor.

Information spread quickly on a ship, Liam knew. He sensed a shift in the entire atmosphere of the room as the crew continued to look at him.

"As I said," he emphasized softly, "we need to maintain our cover. If we don't, we'll never accomplish our mission, and there'll be no prize money for any of us."

"But we've destroyed four pirate ships already," Highcastle protested. "Surely that's accomplishment enough for us to claim victory."

"Not when there are twice as many still out there, plus a base coordinating them."

"That's the Sectoid ship," a sailor said with certainty. "And we'll need an entire squadron to take her down."

Nods and murmurs revealed to Liam that the crew was drawing their own conclusions.

"We don't know that," he said. "But as we gather more information it will become clear."

The tinny voice of the bosn's mate over the loudspeaker interrupted any further discussion. *"Captain Stonebridge requested on the jetty."*

"Time to play your role again, sir," Highcastle said with a bow.

Liam took another look around the room, noting the mix of resentment and frustration on the faces of his sailors. Maybe a bit of a perk was in order for the crew.

"Good work, lads," he said as he headed for the passageway. "An extra tot of rum for each of you after dinner." It was the best he could do for now. He hoped it would be enough.

Able Rating Flatrock was on the docks when he emerged; in his shabby civilian clothes he looked and sounded every bit the merchant sailor. With him was a civilian, whom Liam recognized as Tom from Matthew Long's office. He greeted Liam with a polite knuckle to the forehead.

"Captain Stonebridge," he said, "Mr. Long would like to invite you and your cargo master to dine with him this evening at the Rooster's Perch."

Where he would no doubt ply Virtue with wine to see where things went, Liam thought immediately. But to refuse an offer to dine at the finest restaurant on the station would seem very odd, and he had to maintain appearances—especially to Matthew Long. But such an invitation certainly gave him enough freedom to stack the deck in his favor.

"Mr. Long is very kind. I would be happy to attend, but please let him know that we'll be accompanied by my second mate as well, who has been working tirelessly and who deserves this welcome break."

"Of course, my lord. Mr. Long will expect you at eight."

Liam retreated into the ship, doubting that Chief Sky had any other plans for the evening.

AT TIMES IT WAS DIFFICULT TO MAINTAIN THE façade of a fallen nobleman, but as dinner dragged on at the Rooster's Perch Liam felt increasingly comfortable in his role. Mr. Long had arranged for a back room to ensure privacy, but the close quarters made the deficiencies of the station's air system that much more apparent. The food was well prepared, but the quality of the ingredients was questionable. Virtue and Sky both ate with gusto, and Liam conceded that the food was a step up on the rations served up after *Daring* had been in space for a while, but a Passagia gala dinner this fare was not. It was easy, Liam found, to express a general distaste for his surroundings even as he kept up polite conversation.

Long had ensured that Amelia sat next to him, with the shipwrights' guild master, a Mr. Carpenter, on her other side. The wine flowed freely, and Liam was pleased to see Long's frustration at the fact that Virtue kept her consumption to a trickle, keeping her wits about her as she verbally parried the increasingly less subtle advances of the two civilians. Liam was disgusted at how these men so completely objectified Virtue, but actually found himself admiring how nonchalantly she handled them. It was both painful and fascinating to watch.

The dinner lasted the obligatory several hours, but finally Liam was able to extract himself and his crew. Long and Carpenter were thoroughly drunk, but happy enough simply to have enjoyed a pleasant evening. They both made elaborate farewells involving long hugs of Virtue, then staggered off down the promenade.

"Well," Sky muttered dryly, "that was a lovely evening."

"I think I need a thorough wash," Virtue replied.

"Thank you both," Liam said. "That was a necessary activity to build our relationship—I'm sorry that you in particular, Amelia, had to endure it. Now let's get back to the ship."

Despite the hour, the promenade was bustling with activity. All the market stalls were still open, and the patios of the drinking establishments heaved with merrymakers. Navy uniforms easily outnumbered the civilians, but Liam felt confident they could slip through the throng. Sky led the way, her stern face helping to part the crowd before them, and Liam tucked in behind Virtue to cover the rear. She reached back and took his hand, pulling him steadily forward.

He appreciated the gesture, and the warm embrace of her hand in his. Tucked in close behind her, he couldn't help but notice her silky hair falling past her neck.

But now was not the time to be distracted. First, they needed to get back to the ship.

He kept his head lowered into the high folds of his collar, but in truth was carefully watching their surroundings. Most of the uniforms were young sailors intent on revelry, none of them even glancing his way. The occasional flash of gold indicated a group of officers, but no one Liam recognized. They passed the Cup of Plenty, where the gambling tables were barely visible through the open doors for all the patrons crowded around them. As they slowly weaved past the doors, Liam spotted Captain Silverhawk. The nobleman was on his feet, and appeared to be arguing with the Theropod table master. He looked quickly away.

In front of him, Sky suddenly halted and pivoted. Amid the noise of the street Liam and Virtue both leaned in close to the assaulter. She subtly pointed toward one of the nearby taverns.

"Sir, it's one of ours," she muttered.

Liam followed her gaze and, with a sinking heart, spotted the tall, sandy-haired figure of James Highcastle. He strolled with the easy confidence of a man well into his cups, his glazed expression a mixture of curiosity and disdain. His eyes passed over the tavern he was passing, then fixed with new interest on the Cup of Plenty.

"Darkness and damnation," Liam hissed.

Even from the crowded promenade, Liam could hear the rising voices of conflict inside the Cup of Plenty. Curious stares were already turning from all directions, and he spotted a junior officer moving with purpose through the crowd back toward the Navy berths, calling for guards. Highcastle sensed the new focal point of attention as well, and quickened his pace.

"Come on," Liam said, abandoning stealth to push through the crowd and intercept Highcastle.

The lordling didn't notice his approach until Liam physically stepped in front of him and placed a hand on his chest. He stopped, looking down in outrage before recognition kicked in. But whereas Liam might have expected fear or at least guilt on the expression of a sailor caught ashore by the executive officer, Highcastle simply smiled conspiratorially.

"Ah, Lord Blackwood. No, wait . . . Stonebridge! Care to join me for a turn at the tables? Some ruffians back that way told me there's gambling at this Cup of Plenty."

"What are you doing ashore, Cadet?" Liam said, leaning in close.

"Oh, don't worry—I won't spoil our disguise. I just had to stretch my legs, you know."

Liam sensed Sky tensing to forcibly control Highcastle, but he gripped her arm firmly. The youth seemed to have decided that military ranks only applied inside the hull of the ship—to try to apply discipline in this moment would only cause indignant, and possibly violent, protest from the drunk lordling.

"How did you get ashore?" Liam was genuinely perplexed—he'd given the brow's mates strict instructions.

"I just waited for Hedgie to be at the brow," he said, as if they were a pair of mates. "Butter up a girl and promise her the worlds, and you can get whatever you want."

Liam didn't have time to be angry at Able Rating Hedge, or with Highcastle, for that matter. A commotion had broken out in earnest within the Cup of Plenty.

He could see armed soldiers already deploying along the docks, being directed by the young officer who had hurried back. Looking back at the café, Liam knew that Silverhawk could emerge at any moment. He had to get Highcastle away from here.

"Come," he said quickly, pushing the cadet toward the tavern they stood in front of, "let's have a drink. Let that trouble in the gambling hall boil over and then we can visit."

"Yes," Virtue said, taking Highcastle's other arm, "come have a drink with me, my lord."

Together they led Highcastle through the doors to the tavern. The large room within was dimly lit by lamps on each table, dark pillars rising from the floor to meet matching beams overhead. The air was thick with the smell of greasy food and a haze of smoke lingered over everything. There was no Navy in here, and many a glance passed over Liam and his group as they found their way to an empty table. The tavern noise continued without interruption, though, and no one seemed to take any particular interest in the newcomers.

"I say"—Highcastle frowned as he ran a finger across their greasy table—"this is a bit rough, Blackwood. Do you usually slum it when ashore?"

"It depends on the port, James. Sometimes this is all that's on offer."

Highcastle rolled his eyes and scanned the room. Liam did as well, noting the clothing of the patrons and guessing that this was a tavern frequented mostly by sailors and dockworkers. Merchants would be a rare sight in here, and the Navy was clearly not welcome. In short, it was the perfect place to hide for a while.

Sky appeared with four tankards and placed them on the table.

"Let me sit there please, my lord," she said to Highcastle, "so that I can better view the room. It's my job to keep you safe."

"Gladly," Highcastle scoffed, rising and moving to a seat with his back to the room. He suddenly seemed to notice Virtue next to him. "I can think of much more pleasant things to look upon."

"Is that what I am to you?" she said with a smirk. "A thing?"

"No, not at all, Amelia," he replied. "I think you're an amazing individual—very talented, and beautiful."

Liam had always been amazed at how easily most aristocrats could slip into flattery, but the apparent sincerity in Highcastle's words was in its own class.

Virtue, to her credit, wasn't so easily convinced. She patted her coat where the pistol was hidden. "Talented enough to stay armed through an entire port visit."

He looked at her for a moment, then dropped his gaze with a nod. "I truly apologize for what I said those weeks ago, Amelia. It was uncalled for and completely out of line. I was very tired and not behaving as a gentleman should." He reached out to take her hand, looking her in the eye. "I beg your forgiveness."

She shook her head, but she couldn't quite keep the smile from her face. "Thank you," she said. "I'm sure you can understand the challenges of learning a new profession."

He returned her smile, making some self-deprecating remark that Liam found irritating, mostly because it was genuinely funny. Virtue laughed appreciatively, and

Liam, who didn't really want to watch her flirt with the lordling any further, turned to Sky.

"Does the room look secure to you?"

"Yes, sir," she said, eyes still moving in a slow sweep. "No one's paying us any attention, but I'd recommend getting this snotter back to the ship before he takes it upon himself to impress Virtue with his bravery or some other stupid stunt."

"Agreed. I'll take a look at the street in a few minutes to see if it's clear."

"Yes, sir."

He sat back and took a sip from his tankard. The beer was thick and dark, and packed quite a wallop. Glancing over, he saw Highcastle had already drained half his cup.

"How was your visit ashore with the captain today?"

"Without incident, sir."

"Where did you go?"

"We went to the upper levels of the station."

"Did you meet with anyone?"

Sky paused, then turned her gaze fully on Liam.

"Sir, I don't appreciate these interrogations. I am loyal to Commander Riverton and I will not betray her confidence."

"I'm loyal to her as well," he snapped. "But I'm also the second-in-command of our vessel. I need to have the full picture, in case anything was to happen to Commander Riverton."

"Then ask her yourself, sir."

Liam felt a rush of frustration, mixed with embarrassment as the truth of the situation became clear. Riverton apparently trusted her assaulter more than her executive officer, and now both of them knew it.

Virtue laughed at another of Highcastle's jokes, swatting playfully at his chest. It was suddenly too much, and Liam rose from his seat. When all eyes turned to him, he took a moment to straighten his coat. "I'm going to see if it's clear. Be ready to move if it is."

Despite his frustration, he was careful to meander through the tavern, taking care not to rush or seem perturbed in any way. All around him the drunken conversations of sailors continued without pause. The talk was mainly gripes about ship conditions, half-baked theories about local politics, or tales of romance, real or imagined. In short, much the same as would happen among Navy sailors.

He reached the front door and peered out to the promenade. The augmented military presence of armed sailors still lined the docks, but the commotion around the Cup of Plenty had quieted. He saw a group of Navy officers clustered just outside the café's patio. Captain Silverhawk was easily visible, towering above the rest, and even from this distance Liam recognized his mood as one of petulant frustration. The mood of the officers was calm, though, and he suspected that the incident was winding down. He'd have to keep Highcastle out of sight for another few minutes at least.

Looking back at his table, and Highcastle flirting away with Virtue, Liam wondered if it might be less unpleasant just to wait here at the door. But, he knew, that would eventually draw suspicious glances and with one last look out to the street he turned to make his way back. He took his time, though, idly listening to the chatter around him.

". . . happened to *Golden Wind* . . ."

He froze, then forced himself to take another step, turning his head with enforced casualness to where he'd just heard those words. The table to his left was large enough for six, but only three sailors remained, practically shouting at each other across a brewery's worth of tankards littering the wooden surface.

"She's overdue," one of the sailors griped. "And Red still owes me twenty crowns! And now we have to sail—when am I going to get paid?"

"From what I hear," drawled another from across the table, "she joined a pack to jump some fast courier with gold bullion. When we meet them next Red'll have enough to pay you double what he owes you."

"If not, I'm gonna thump him."

"Whatever—drink up. We have to get back to the ship."

Liam kept moving, sliding into his seat and leaning toward Sky.

"See that trio of sailors—one of them has a blue-and-white bandanna, the other with that silly mustache?" he said.

"Yes." She straightened, hearing the urgency in his tone, and her eyes narrowed toward the table.

"They're pirates. We need to follow them back to their ship."

"How clear is the street?"

"Not very, yet."

"I can slip out unnoticed."

"I'm coming with you. Two sets of eyes are better than one, and this is our only lead."

She nodded. "Virtue can keep our youngster in here."

"So long as he doesn't know why we're leaving. If he hears it's pirates, we'll never contain him."

"Agreed."

They watched the trio of drunken sailors finish the last of their beers then stagger up and head for the door.

Sky slipped from her seat and began to move for the exit. Liam rose a second later, leaning in to Virtue and Highcastle.

"The chief and I are going to check the street again and see if everything is clear." He gave Virtue an imploring stare. "Don't move from this table, either of you. We'll be back in a few minutes."

"We'll be here," she replied. She seemed to want to ask more, but taking in his expression, turned back to Highcastle and resumed their conversation.

Within moments he was outside, lengthening his pace out to the promenade, where Sky was already following the three drunks at a nonchalant distance. Their rambling chatter softened to muttering as they noted the Navy guards along the docks, but their shuffling progress soon took them well clear of the military berths. Half a dozen ships floated beyond the jetty shielding, and it was to a bulky, nondescript tub that the pirates staggered. A lone watchman greeted them at the brow with a caustic joke, and with hearty replies the three drunks disappeared through the airlock.

"Berth Ten," Liam noted quietly. "We'll have to set a watch to discover when she slips, and be ready to follow."

"I can suit up and float over for an external look," Sky replied. "I'd like to know what we're up against this time. Now, during the night watch, would be the best time to do so."

"Make it so, but take someone with you." He looked back down the jetty, to where the armed Navy presence was starting to thin as sailors were stood down and recalled aboard their ships. "Looks like things are getting quiet here. I'll retrieve the other two and see you back on the ship."

"Yes, sir."

Liam left his assaulter and strolled back to the tavern. The group of officers outside the Cup of Plenty had dispersed, and Captain Silverhawk was nowhere to be seen. Liam felt a moment of panic as he imagined the lord wandering into the tavern and finding Highcastle, but he reminded himself that a man of such noble birth would never willingly debase himself in such a common place. As he entered the tavern once again, a quick scan revealed that his instinct was correct—no Silverhawk.

But what he did see stopped him dead. Highcastle and Virtue were still at their table, but it seemed the time for flirtatious chatter had ended. She was practically in his lap, arms wrapped over his shoulders as she kissed him. His hands roamed hungrily across her figure, and even as Liam pushed forward across the room it looked like the cadet might lift Virtue right up and lay her out on the table.

Liam grabbed them each by the shoulder and wrenched them apart. Virtue stumbled back into her own chair and Highcastle looked up in shock. As recognition dawned, though, the shock gave way to a smirk.

"I say, Blackwood, there's no need to butt in."

Liam's fist collided with Highcastle's face before he even knew it was flying. The force was enough to upend the cadet's chair, sending him sprawling back across the wooden floor. Liam stepped forward, grabbed the youth by the collar, and hauled him up.

"We are going back to the ship this instant," he hissed, "and if I hear one word of complaint I'll run you through."

Highcastle's eyes were glazed from the blow, and in stunned silence he steadied himself against the table. Liam turned his gaze to Virtue. She was also on her feet, her expression one of regret—but regret at what she'd done or regret at being caught Liam couldn't tell.

"We're going back to the ship," he said to her.

"Sir . . . milord," she began, but Liam was already turning away to direct Highcastle's unsteady form toward the door.

There were a few glances that followed their progress through the tables, but Liam suspected that bar fights and lovers' quarrels were hardly uncommon in this establishment.

He knew it was hardly his best effort to maintain a low profile, but hopefully no damage was done. Except to Highcastle's face, which he was immeasurably pleased about.

CHAPTER 16

The silence in Riverton's cabin was broken only by a creak in the outer hull as *Daring* leaned into a freshening wind. Liam stood beside the captain, staring across at the table where Highcastle and Virtue both stood at attention. His anger at their conduct still smoldered, but it was nothing compared to the rage Riverton had just unleashed. He'd had no idea her voice could be so deafening, and her usual, icy demeanor had melted into a white-hot fury.

Her last words of contempt still hung in the cabin. Virtue withered in her stance, unable to lift her eyes. Highcastle stood perfectly straight, gaze fixed and unmoving on the far bulkhead.

"I'm very tempted," Riverton finally continued, "to have you both publicly flogged. Perhaps I need to make an example of you in case anyone else in the crew is thinking of jeopardizing our entire mission for their own selfish desires."

Liam remained still and silent. Often, as executive officer, he would speak to support his captain, but this time he had no idea what was going on in Riverton's mind.

"But I need my crew focused on our upcoming assault," she concluded, "and not whispering about illicit activities ashore. Both of you are docked one week's pay, and you are forbidden to discuss this incident with anyone. Is that clear?"

"Yes, ma'am," both replied.

"Get out of my sight."

Virtue practically fled the cabin, with Highcastle only a few steps behind. The door shut behind him and Liam turned to the captain.

"As for you," she snapped before he could say a word, "I'm furious. You disobeyed my order of no alcohol ashore, and you left two inebriated sailors alone. And don't use the fact that you uncovered a new pirate lead as an excuse for your actions. That lead is the main reason why I'm not taking disciplinary action against you, but it doesn't change the fact that you displayed poor judgment. You risked the safety of two of my sailors, and also the integrity of our mission."

She crossed her arms and stared at him. Her expression suggested that he was allowed to speak.

"When I discovered Highcastle ashore," he said carefully, "I had to act fast to get him out of sight, and the tavern was the only refuge. We ordered the drinks to fit in, but we sipped at them—except Highcastle, who was already drunk when we found him."

"From the sounds of things, Petty Officer Virtue was also fairly intoxicated."

"Yes," Liam said, his anger quietly rising again. "Her behavior was . . . disappointing."

"You've lectured me in the past about the unpredict-ability of missions ashore," she said, her gaze penetrating. "I suggest you listen to your own words and take better care with the Human variables. Ours is not a profession where personal feelings can intrude."

His gaze flicked up at that. Riverton continued to stare at him with the intensity of cold fire.

"We can't afford any more mistakes," she continued, "and I need you free of distractions. Including personal distractions. Sort yourself out, Mr. Blackwood. Now."

The anger in his heart mixed with fear, and even a bit of shame, as he endured his captain's stern gaze. He forced himself to meet that gaze, and in her dark eyes he saw wisdom, and even a touch of compassion. Despite her youth and lack of battle experience, this was no oblivious noble dandy who commanded him. He still didn't know really what she was, this enigma named Sophia Riverton.

"Yes, ma'am. You can count on me."

"Carry on."

Liam left the cabin, hesitating in the passageway outside as he faced the door to his own cabin. He was tempted to seek refuge there, but Riverton's words rang in his ears. He needed to sort himself out and time was not on his side.

Daring had slipped her berth first thing that morning, before Windfall Station had really awoken. Liam would have liked to have left earlier, to stay close in the wake of the pirate ship *Bluebird,* but Swift had argued desperately for more time to finish at least the most basic repairs. Abandoning any attempt to disguise the size of the crew, Swift had his propulsion team crawling over *Daring*'s hull like ants throughout the remainder of the night, sealing breaches and rebuilding shattered gunports while air and water supplies were continuously pumped on board.

Farmer's Paradise and its orbiting station were now behind them, and the bridge was tracking the distant form of *Bluebird* in the darkness ahead. *Daring* was more or less intact, but even now, at full sail, Liam knew that Swift and his crew were still making repairs. The propulsion officer had made his displeasure at their sudden and hasty departure fully known, but then had pushed his department to accomplish the impossible. Even so, as Liam moved forward he listened to the steady creaks as the ship strained against a strong stern wind. His ear could easily discern that they were not the usual groans of a ship in motion, which was not a good sign.

Climbing down a ladder, he saw Highcastle in conversation with Able Rating Hedge. Her eyes widened as soon as she saw the XO, and Liam hardened his expression into a frown of disapproval. She knuckled her forehead to him and moved off, almost breaking into a run.

"I was just telling her that we shouldn't be seen together," Highcastle mused. "Poor girl."

"She's in a lot of trouble," Liam warned, "and don't think you aren't. She's had her brow's-mate ticket revoked, and the coxn is considering laying a charge."

"Lesson learned," Highcastle said, raising his hands in confession. "I regret that I caused her such trouble. But you have to admit, she's one of the most darling of the crew."

His easy manner was grating. This was all a big game to him, and the loss of a week's pay was in his mind just a point scored against him. He had no idea that Hedge's career was in jeopardy. It made Liam want to knock him on his backside again, but he knew too well the mind-set of the nobility. Highcastle was genetically incapable of taking responsibility for his actions.

"As officers," Liam finally said, as mildly as he could, "we really should avoid fraternizing with the crew. You've already seen what trouble it can cause."

Highcastle nodded, assuming a look of sage resignation.

"There are plenty of wellborn ladies worthy of your attention," Liam added. "Save your efforts for them."

"Yes, of course. But these sailing voyages can be long, and as men, we need a distraction." He gave Liam a questioning look. "Is it all right for us to amuse ourselves with petty officers?"

"Stay away from her."

Highcastle retreated a step, sudden surprise on his features. Liam only then realized that he'd stepped forward, and he carefully unclenched his fists.

"Oh, my apologies," Highcastle said with a slight bow. His expression was knowing in a way that set Liam's teeth on edge. "I assumed you were dallying with Ava. I'll keep clear of Amelia."

The shallow disregard of his words was shocking in its sincerity. People were nothing more than objects to him, playing pieces in a game of one-upmanship, and he truly saw nothing wrong with thinking that way. Liam fought down his contempt for the entire Imperial aristocracy and forced his words to be casual.

"It's best for all of us to stay clear of shipboard romance, Mr. Highcastle. It complicates things. While we're under sail, focus your efforts on your professional development. When we get back to home port you can then impress all the ladies of any rank with your exploits."

"You speak wisdom," he said. "I think I'll go and help out with the gunnery repairs before my watch."

Liam watched the cadet stride off, wondering if he'd been such a toff himself at that age. He doubted Highcastle would actually follow his advice, but Liam knew that he, as an older and wiser man, had no excuse for ignoring the advice his own superior had just given him. He needed to sort himself out, and that meant speaking to a woman who might want nothing to do with him right now.

But it couldn't wait any longer. One way or another, for the good of the ship and for the good of them both, this had to get sorted, now. But first, he decided as he headed for the senior mess, he could at least prepare a peace offering.

THE SENIOR MESS WAS QUIET, EMPTY BUT FOR CHAR-lotte Brown with a series of screens laid out on the table. She glanced up at his arrival.

"Good afternoon, sir. I'm glad you are here, as I was just planning to come find you. I've been searching the transmissions from Windfall Station during our stay, and I've got something unusual."

"Something from the *Bluebird*?" Liam asked as he poured a cup of coffee and fumbled with the sugar.

"No, she was completely silent. It was from the station, but what caught my attention was the encoding. It was Sectoid-style encryption."

"Sectoids on the station? I'm surprised we didn't hear about that. We certainly didn't see any."

"It was sent from the upper levels, so a bit out of your way."

"Hmm." Something twigged in Liam's memory, but it was too fleeting to catch. It would come to him later, he was sure. And he had other, more pressing things to take care of now. He headed for the door, coffee in hand. "Good work, Charlotte. Keep digging and let me know what else you uncover."

Liam's instincts about his crew told him exactly where to head next. Sailors reacted differently to disciplinary measures. Some went straight to the bar to drown their sorrows, some went straight to their racks to hide away. And some buried themselves in work. As he poked his head into the supply office, he wasn't at all surprised to see Amelia Virtue seated at her console, working furiously.

He stepped inside, shutting the door behind him. She looked up, her shoulders stiffening at the sight of him. After a moment she made to rise, but he motioned her back down and took the seat next to her. He handed her the coffee.

"I don't take sugar," he said with a smile, "so I had to guess how much you like."

She took the drink, breathing in the steam before trying a sip.

"Not bad, sir. Thanks."

He sat back, folding his hands in his lap. She didn't meet his gaze, busying herself with the coffee for a few moments before finally setting it down. Her complexion was pale, he noticed, and her shoulders sagged. But she collected herself and forced her eyes up.

"What can I do for you, sir?"

What indeed? A few things leaped to mind, but he forced himself to sit back and keep distance between them. Her physical presence was intoxicating, and the way she looked at him, even now, made his heart melt. Romance aboard ship was an accepted reality within the

Navy, but senior officers were supposed to be above such things—duty to the Empire, and all that. The silence stretched uncomfortably in the supply office. Liam knew he needed to speak, and with a titanic effort he made his decision and forced the words from his mouth.

To the Abyss with duty.

"Amelia, I'd like to speak without ranks."

She stared back at him, struggling to keep her expression neutral.

"All right," she said.

"Let's put aside the captain's reaction to the incident ashore, and let's put aside the punishment. I don't want to talk about that." The words stuck in his throat, and he pushed them out. "I want to talk about how I feel."

New emotion welled up in her eyes, but she said nothing.

"I'm not happy about you kissing Highcastle."

"I'm not too pleased about it either."

"Really?" The sudden delight he felt was surprising for its intensity.

"I don't like having a week's pay taken from me." She shrugged. "And now I assume Cadet Highcastle is going to be pestering me."

"He won't. I'll make sure of it."

She folded her arms and sat back, eyeing him intently.

"And why is that, sir?"

"No ranks, Amelia."

She hesitated, clearly struggling.

"Why are you protecting me . . . Liam?"

"Because I think you're a wonderful person," he responded simply.

A touch of her old grin flashed across her face. It gave him confidence.

"And," he continued, "I'd like to think that our relationship might be more than professional."

Her expression softened, but she clearly wrestled with conflicting emotions. "I'd . . . like that too," she said carefully. "But, Liam . . . I don't know if it's worth the trouble."

"The incident with Highcastle is different. It was a silly mistake, caused by alcohol."

She blinked, her expression hardening. "No, it wasn't," she said flatly. "He wanted to get up and follow you. You gave me orders to keep him at that table. I didn't have a lot of other ways to distract him."

Liam was as surprised by this revelation as he was by the cold calculation behind it.

"Yes, but . . . surely you could have restrained yourself to flirting."

"I'm not trained in your courtly ways," she snapped with sudden anger. "I don't know how to dance, or prance, or whatever it is you people do."

"What do you mean—we people?" His tone sharpened. "I've watched you flirt with every civilian from the merchant kings to the loading boys."

"Yes, and it works, doesn't it? I've learned from the best!"

They stared at each other for a moment, neither giving ground. Then she sighed.

"I've watched our little world in this ship. Apart from the captain—who no one understands, by the way—we have five officers on board. Four of them, including you, lead with charisma and charm, and yes, flirting when it's necessary. Only one officer focuses entirely on getting her job done. And while Charlotte Brown may be the most competent officer on board, she's also the least liked. I'm just following the lead of my superiors. *Sir.*"

"So . . . this is all just a game?"

"You tell me."

He paused, searching for the right words.

"It's a game for some," he admitted. "For Highcastle, definitely. For Templegrey, most likely. But not for me."

A long silence hung between them. "I'll admit you do seem a little different," she finally said. She didn't seem angry anymore, but a touch wary, as if she wasn't quite sure what to make of him. She studied him a moment longer. "So," she said finally, "what do we do now?"

He met her gaze with new confidence. "I'd like to get to know you better, with no ranks."

She relaxed visibly, a smile playing at her lips. "That seems like a good plan to me."

"Just do me a favor?" he said. "Stay clear of Highcastle."

The beginnings of her smile faded. "I will, with pleasure. But I'm sure you understand that if he wants me physically I don't have much choice."

"You always have a choice."

"Oh, really?" Her face contorted in sudden contempt. She stabbed a finger in his chest. "You think, as a commoner, I have a choice when a nobleman decides to have his way with me? If Highcastle had been determined to lay me out on the table in that tavern, do you think I could have stopped him?"

"What?" Liam was stunned by the sudden outburst, and by her implications. "Of course you could. We have regulations against that—and our Empire has laws."

"Do you believe those regulations and laws truly apply

to nobles?" she scoffed. "He could have done whatever he wanted to me—and nothing would have happened to him. More likely I'd have been blamed. So thank you for returning when you did—and thank you for clobbering him—but don't tell me I have a choice."

Liam reached out and put his hand over hers, struggling to find the words.

"Amelia, you're always protected. I'll ensure that."

"Why, because I'm yours?" She withdrew her hand, crossing her arms defensively. "Is this all because Lord Highcastle tried to storm your little estate? Are you, Lord Blackwood, intending to require physical services from this common sailor?"

He felt like he'd been struck. Her anger was visceral, and deep, and it burned into him.

"Of course not," he managed to say. "Amelia . . . this has nothing to do with rank, or noble title."

"Yes it does! You just don't see it because you wield both with such unconscious familiarity. Do you really think Lord Highcastle would be punished if he raped a sailor? Do you think you would?"

She sat tensed in the chair. Liam suddenly realized that she was ready to defend herself. And with good reason, he admitted, recognizing with new clarity the vast difference between their positions in society.

"I'm not going to demand anything from you," he said firmly.

She stared at him, eyes searching his. She took a deep, shuddering breath and relaxed back slightly.

"I'm sorry," she said. "I'm being unfair to you. You've always been a perfect gentleman."

"But I know that my fellow gentlemen don't always live up to their titles."

"No," she whispered.

"*I'm* sorry." He knew as he said them that words were inadequate. "For . . . for our entire society."

She laughed a bit at that, then reached out and took both his hands in hers.

"Thank you for coming to speak to me. And for bringing me a coffee."

Her hands were warm in his, and he was very aware of her closeness.

"Amelia," he said in a low voice, drawing back slightly. "I'm not going to force anything here. I want you to be comfortable, and—"

She closed the distance between them, and then her lips were on his.

CHAPTER 17

"Excellent work, Sublieutenant Brown," Liam declared, loudly enough that the entire bridge could hear.

If what Amelia said was true, and Brown was the least-respected officer on board simply because she was the least charming, Liam was now determined to make a habit of publicly recognizing her for her strengths. And she had many.

Not only had she isolated that mysterious Sectoid signal from Windfall Station, and not only had she figured out how to identify the Sectoid drones lurking in the blackness, but she had even managed to find an interior layout for the class of ship to which their current prey *Bluebird* belonged. Projecting the image from her officer-of-the-watch station, she had just finished describing it to the boarding party.

It was unusual to have the entire team assembled on the bridge, with the clatter of their armor as they shifted their stances, but this was an unusual mission. Visible dead ahead was the lumbering pirate ship, sails fluttering in an uncertain beam breeze. *Daring* had been intercepting for more than a day, tacking back and forth to maximize speed even though efficiency suffered. Swift had advised that the hull really wasn't up to another pitched battle, and the steady maneuvering had put audible strain on the starboard mast.

"We'll be boarding here and here." Liam indicated a pair of emergency airlocks at *Bluebird*'s stern. "The target for both teams is the bridge, and the ship's memory core. We must hold this entire deck"—he pointed at the highest afterdeck—"to ensure our escape route. Once we have what we need, we withdraw."

Chief Sky took over the brief, reminding everyone of their specific roles. Liam watched the restless anticipation of his boarding team, and noticed several glances from both Flatrock and Hedge toward Highcastle. When Sky concluded and asked for any questions, it was the cadet's voice that broke the silence.

"I think there'd be a handsome amount of booty on a pirate ship that size," he said. "It would be a shame to leave it behind."

"We fully expect the pirate crew to move to defend their cargo," Liam replied, "and that will play to our advantage. For this mission, our goal is information, not booty."

There was a rustle among the boarding party, but no one spoke.

"I'd like to think we could do both," Highcastle sniffed. "It'd be a shame to leave all that cargo for the Sectoids to collect at their leisure."

It was no secret that at least two Sectoid drones were nearby, and no one doubted that the Sectoid ship itself was still in the sector. Liam understood the crew's frustration, but what was frustrating him personally was the fact that this noble toff seemed to be growing into the crew's spokesperson.

"Well," Liam said with a smile, "if the information we recover indicates Sectoid involvement with these pirates, we'll know exactly where to go to get the cargo back."

This drew a few laughs, and silenced Highcastle.

"Get to the boats," Sky commanded, "and make sure you take the right seat. These civilian tubs are laid out differently."

The boarding party began to gaggle toward the ladder. With a single glance at Virtue, Liam turned back to Brown.

"Where are the Sectoid probes?"

"Here"—she pointed at her chart—"and here. Both are more or less matching *Bluebird*'s course and speed."

"So likely they know where she is."

"Yes, sir."

He approached the command chair, where Riverton had been watching the entire brief in silence.

"We're ready, ma'am. But we can't guarantee that the Sectoids won't see this."

"That can't stop us," she said, glancing at her own display. "We need this information."

"Permission to board the pirates, ma'am?"

"Granted. Good luck."

Liam took one final look at the looming form of *Bluebird* ahead. The pirates hadn't altered course, but were no doubt aware of the merchant ship that had been slowly gaining on them. It wasn't unusual for ships to meet coincidentally in deep space, especially in the trade lanes, but *Daring* was now getting uncomfortably close.

The pair of boats Swift had managed to secure at

Windfall were larger than *Daring*'s originals, with wide beams and a lower canopy. Small storage compartments were built into the deck and the boarding team were scattered in seats squeezed between empty fixtures. These had been yard boats, Liam guessed, hardworking tenders that were capable of taking a pounding. As he felt them push off from *Daring*'s hull and thrust out into the open space between the two sailing ships, he hoped they were up for a new kind of work.

As *Daring* fell astern, Liam watched the squat stern of *Bluebird* for any change. The big ship appeared unmoving in the abyss, her sails fluttering in the unfavorable winds. Her masts showed no signs of retracting—a dead giveaway to hostile intent—and no signs of activity changed the face of her hull. Looking back, he saw that *Daring* had nosed to starboard as if on another tack but also opening the bearing for her foremost gunports. The beam turrets were manned, he knew, but in low power so as not to alert any possible sensors lurking within the pirate ship.

The pirate hull loomed ahead. Liam scanned closely for any signs of opening ports or emerging gun barrels. Merchant ships this size often had both bow and stern cannon, to guard against precisely this sort of attack. But he saw nothing.

A bang suddenly shook the boat hull. Liam searched *Bluebird*'s stern anew, but saw no movement or flashes. A pair of impacts, smaller than the first, struck the clear canopy.

"There!" Virtue shouted, pointing up at the very top of the stern.

Quick movement revealed at least three suited figures moving on the hull, each carrying weapons. As Liam watched, one of them took aim and fired. Another pair of slugs rapped against the boat's canopy, and this time a shard of discoloration began to seep across the clear surface.

"Get us alongside," Liam roared.

The boat's thrusters went to maximum, pushing Liam back in his seat, but the lumbering civilian vessel had none of the quick response Liam was used to. More shots struck the canopy, and new slivers began to appear. He heard the first, ominous snap of air pressure against weakening glass. Master Rating Faith rolled the boat, presenting the strong hull to the pirate shooters as an increasing volley rained down. Liam watched the now-inverted form of *Bluebird* approach, and he strained to catch a glimpse of the other boat as it fired its thrusters to slow and pivot against its target airlock. Flashes of fire bounced off its hull, then canopy, as it maneuvered into position.

Liam gripped his chair and hung on as his own boat swung violently, lining up its hull with *Bluebird*'s and barreling in. The thrusters fired again, pushing him down until the boat slammed into its target. Shots peppered the canopy, and cracks were visibly appearing. Without waiting for an order, Hunter ripped open the boat's hatch and snapped open the airlock. The awful hiss of escaping air flooded the boat.

"Go, go, go!" Liam shouted.

His sailors piled through the airlock with practiced efficiency as more shots cracked down on the boat. Liam felt his ears pop and saw a new crack spider out from an impact.

"I don't have a seal," Faith cried. "I can't hold up snug for long."

The boat shuddered as the thrusters pushed it hard

against the hull, and Liam heard creaking as the metal in the airlock twisted under the strain.

A flash of energy blinded him. He blinked it away in time to see another energy beam cut across *Bluebird*'s stern and blast one of the shooters. He glanced up, back to where *Daring* was turning again, both forward beam turrets picking off the pirates. It was enough for a reprieve, but as the last of the boarding team disappeared through the hatch, Liam grabbed Hunter and Faith.

"This tub won't last—you're with us!"

Another, larger slug smashed into the boat's gunnel, visibly buckling the metal. His boat's crew needed no further encouragement, scrambling through the airlock. With a last glance at Sky's boat—which looked intact— Liam was close behind them.

The wind was strong in the airlock tube as air escaped. As he crossed from boat to ship Liam saw the cracks in the casing, and he kept blinking to clear his vision. The glow of the thruster exhaust beyond lit his way, but then faded into darkness. Even as he watched, the cracks started to grow wider, and as his boat began to drift away he felt the frigidness of deep space claw at him. With his own eyes he glimpsed the distant stars in the Abyss.

Then hands grabbed him and hauled him through the disintegrating tube. A hatch slammed shut and he collapsed to the hard deck, gasping for air. Thunder filled his ears as pressure returned and he wiped away the ice on his cheeks and eyelids where tears had fought to protect his eyes against the vacuum. He struggled to rise, disoriented by the lights and sounds all around him.

Something big slammed into him, and he crashed against a bulkhead. Still clearing his vision, he caught a glimpse of a Theropod snout, then a padded Human fist smacking it back. A sword slashed down and the Thero-pod squealed in pain as it collapsed in a bloody heap. An-other face filled his view.

He realized it was Virtue.

". . . keep going?" she was asking him.

He pulled himself up, instinctively drawing his saber. Beyond Virtue, his boarding team was in close-quarters fighting with what seemed to be a wall of pirates, in a wide passageway that extended both left and right. Flashing back to Brown's diagram of *Bluebird*'s decks, he realized where they were: inside the port airlock and straddling the main athwartships passageway near *Bluebird*'s stern. Sky's team was barely three dozen paces to the right, the route to the bridge between them.

His team was hemmed in in a semicircle, with pirates pressing in on both sides. Liam drew his pistol, took care-ful aim through his own sailors, and emptied his rounds at the pirates to the right. Three Humans and a Theropod went down, giving his team an opening.

"Press to the right," he ordered.

His team surged into the passageway, pushing back the two remaining pirates. Liam moved forward with Virtue, joining the rear guard and holding the flank as the team steadily advanced toward the center of the ship.

"Assault, XO," he gasped into his radio, "we're fighting our way from the airlock toward the midships passageway."

"On our way," replied Sky.

Liam took another step back, giving ground to furious blade attacks. These pirates were hardly expert swords-men, but any fool could swing a blade enough times and eventually hit someone. He parried another swing, deflecting the sword down and flicking his own saber up to slice open the man's throat. The gargled scream distracted the next pirate long enough for Liam to slash down and take his hand clean off. A sword clattered to the deck as the pirate grasped desperately at his severed wrist and staggered back.

"Sir," shouted Flatrock behind him, "we're clear to advance."

"Roundly, then," Liam bellowed as he stepped up his own backward shuffle, blocking the next strike.

"XO, Assault." Sky's determined voice sounded in his ear. *"When I say 'drop,' hit the deck."*

"Understood." He repeated the order to Virtue on his left and Hedge on his right.

"XO, Assault: drop."

"Down," he hissed, dropping to a crouch and lifting his saber in defense.

Shots rang out and the attacking pirates jerked and fell backward as bullets ripped through them. Liam stayed low, motioning Virtue and Hedge to keep backing away. He assessed the enemy for movement and saw nothing.

Rising, he moved through his sailors to meet Sky at the intersection with another passageway heading forward.

"We lost our boat," he said, wiping at the sweat on his brow. "It's going to be a staggered withdrawal, but we don't need to protect that route."

Sky took the news with a grim expression, her mind quickly adjusting to the new tactical reality.

"I had my boat decouple and go for cover," she said. "We'll have to call it back when we need it."

Liam nodded his approval, then turned his attention to the next challenge. The passageway forward extended no more than twenty paces and ended in a solid, metal door. The bridge.

With the entire boarding team crowding the route, Liam found himself a long way back as the leading elements reached the bridge door. Hand signals reported back that it was locked and he motioned to bring up explosives. The sailors set their charges and backed off. Everyone hunkered down.

The door exploded, flying forward out of its frame as smoke billowed through the passageway and beyond. The first sailors charged forward and Liam rose to his feet with the rest of the boarding party. Over the clatter of armor, he could hear the ringing of swords clashing and the screams of the dying through the obscuring cloud.

Pushing through the smoke, he had to step carefully over the shattered metal and bodies. He drew his second pistol and held his saber up in a parry. Virtue stayed at his side, mimicking his defensive stance with her own weapons.

There was no need, though; the clanging of blades quickly diminished and an eerie silence descended over the bridge. Watching every corner for movement, Liam swept his gaze around the space.

This merchant bridge was large, with excellent visibility on all sides through the broad canopy. The top, port, and starboard masts were all still deployed, sails fluttering gaily. Soft, comfortable chairs and ergonomic consoles indicated a premium for crew comfort, but most of the deck was uncluttered and clear. This ship must have been quite a prize when the pirates captured her. But now the bridge was a slaughterhouse, with half a dozen pirates dead and two of Liam's own sailors down. He glanced over at one of his own casualties and saw the unmistakable burns of Sectoid acid across his face and armor.

Sky noticed Liam's gaze and closed in.

"Bastards were waiting. Took out our first pair with that acid."

"I don't see any Sectoids," Liam replied, examining the bridge again.

"They had it contained in hand-sized pods," Sky said, a mix of confusion and fear etched across her face. "They threw them and the damned things exploded against us."

"But where'd they get the acid in the first place?"

Sky nodded, her gaze shifting nervously. That was the key question.

Liam gave quick orders to secure the route back to Sky's boat and to tend to the casualties. Then he sat down in the broad chair at the command console, which was still active. A quick glance revealed standard civilian displays. A navigation display showed the ship's intended route—to what looked like an empty part of space—and a damage-control display gave a quick summary of the internal condition of the ship. There were several red markers just aft of the bridge, but otherwise the interior was intact and open.

"Virtue," he said, "see if you and one of the propulsors can lock down all the internal airlocks. I'd like to contain the rest of the pirates where they are."

"Yes, sir." Virtue motioned for one of the sailors to join her at the main damage-control panel on the starboard side of the bridge. They began manipulating controls, and doors and hatches began to shut throughout *Bluebird*.

Liam removed a data drive from one of his waist bags and inserted it into the command console. He started copying the entire navigation library while he scanned through the ship's log. It didn't take long to realize just how much information he wanted to take back. As soon as his first data drive indicated it was full, he swapped it out for a second.

"Sir," Virtue called, "a couple of internal doors have been opened locally."

Liam looked over to where she was pointing at airtight doors two decks down. Even as he watched, another two doors, farther aft, opened.

"Can you lock them down?"

"We're trying," she said, "but there are local overrides at each door."

"Chief Sky, prepare for an attack. Keep that route to the boat open."

"Yes, sir." Sky disappeared through the blasted bridge door and aft down the passageway.

Half a dozen sailors still held the bridge, but the rest of the team were strung out along their escape route. Liam knew that it was a poor defensive position.

He climbed out of the command chair and pulled off an access panel for the command console. The main memory core was a brick-sized device, secured firmly in an antiradiation cage with three robust data leads extending from it. Liam turned to size up the sailors at his disposal. Hedge was a junior electronics tech—not ideal, but the most qualified here to do this job.

"Hedge," he snapped, "get this memory core out without damaging it. We're taking it with us."

She moved in immediately, not meeting his eyes but pulling out her tools and starting the delicate process of freeing the precious memory core.

"Doors opening on One Deck," Virtue warned.

Only a single deck away. Liam retrieved the second

data disk, hoping that he'd captured the most important data. He handed both disks to Virtue.

"Guard these with your life. You're going back with the first boat ride. When you get on board, give them straight to the captain."

She took them and slipped them into an inside pocket of her armor. Then she lifted questioning eyes to him.

"What about you?"

"I'm bringing the memory core," he said, jerking a thumb back to where Hedge was reaching deep into the console. "You and I can't be in the same boat, in case something . . . goes wrong."

She nodded in sober understanding.

"I guess I should get going."

"Good luck, Amelia."

"And to you, sir."

She strode from the bridge. Liam watched her go, losing her in the hazy air just as she drew her sword once again.

"Assault, XO," he said into his radio. "Have the boat hook up—the first team is going. Virtue has the data which needs to get back to the ship."

"Yes, sir."

Liam examined the damage-control board again. There were airtight doors open at three places on the deck below. The pirates were encircling the bridge.

"Assault, XO, attack imminent on all sides."

"Understood. How long until you abandon the bridge?"

"Hedge, how's that core coming?"

"Almost got it, sir," she mumbled, reaching in up to her elbows.

Another set of airtight doors indicated open below. He heard the distant sound of feet on deck. He dashed over to Hedge and surveyed her frantic work.

"Sixty seconds," he replied to Sky.

Liam reloaded his first pistol, then hefted both weapons in his hands just as Hedge triumphantly pulled the memory core free.

"You carry it," he ordered her, moving to her side. "The rest of you, form up fore and aft around us. This core has to get back to our ship."

Liam moved with Hedge over the bodies and shrapnel and into the smoky passageway. Two sailors moved forward ahead of them, and two covered their rear. Up ahead, he could hear the clangs and shouts of combat. As they emerged from the last wisps of smoke he saw two of his own sailors dash through the T-junction ahead, swords out.

"Step it up," he ordered.

His group quickened to a jog, round the T-junction to the left. Ahead, a melee of blades filled the passageway.

"Sir, behind us!"

He swung around, spotting the first pirate emerging up through a deck hatch. He fired, and the pirate collapsed backward. But another pirate was right behind. Liam's next shot pinged off armor. Two more bullets finished him off, but the pistol clicked empty. Liam slammed it back into its holster and drew his saber, ordering his group to back away. More pirates spilled up through the hatch. Liam fired his second pistol, slowing the advance, but not enough. He bumped into the sailor behind him. Turning, he realized that his team had met the rest of the boarding party, with pirates ahead and behind. He motioned Hedge behind him, and stepped forward to join the battle line.

A Theropod leaped at them, swinging his mighty tailsword across the width of the passageway. Liam arched back, dodging the blow, then slashing down at the brute's back. He nicked cloth, just enough to upset the tail's back-swing. The massive blade flew high and Liam stabbed, driving the point of his sword into the pirate's leathery hide. The brute recoiled, off balance, and Liam stepped forward, stabbing again with a flick to tear open the wound. Thick blood oozed across the pirate's shirt and he retreated with a hiss.

Two Human pirates took his place, though, both swiping down at Liam's head. He caught both blows on his saber, stepping back as his team engaged, slicing at the pirates' exposed torsos. Liam felt the enemy blades fall away and he struck out with a flurry of slashes to finish the attackers off. But more were coming.

Liam glanced over his shoulder. His sailors behind him were cut off from the boat. In all, he had six members of his team clustered in a defensive huddle, surrounded. Hedge was in the middle, clutching the memory core.

"Leave that with me," he said, grabbing the core from her and switching places. "Hold the line while I clear a path to the boat."

She drew her sword and filled his space in the corridor, immediately blocking a blade strike. Liam pulled out a pistol and slapped in its final reload of bullets. Through the chaos he could just see the junction that led to the airlock and their surviving boat. But a mob of pirates blocked the way. It was a dangerous business, firing his pistol into a melee, but his sailors could only fight so long before exhaustion took them all and the sheer numbers of the enemy overwhelmed them. He aimed and fired. One pirate dropped. Another stepped in, sword swinging. Another shot. Another pirate down.

"Acid!" screamed Hedge.

Liam spun, and saw a pirate pulling a ball-sized object out of a strongbox. One acid blast and his entire boarding team would be down. He thrust his pistol over her shoulder to clear his own line and fired. The shot struck the acid-wielding pirate, but he staggered forward, hefting his deadly cargo. Liam fired his last shot. The pirate stumbled back, the ball flying from his hands. It sailed into the air as other pirates fled down the passageway. The bomb traced a deadly arc down to the deck, barely three paces behind the line of pirates pressing in on Liam's team. It struck, and an explosion of black acid sprayed across the passageway.

The pirates took the brunt of the blow on their backs, and they collapsed in screams. The awful hiss of burning cloth and flesh filled the corridor. Hedge staggered, tearing off her armor as drops of acid ate away at the thick padding. One of Liam's men collapsed forward, desperately clawing at his disintegrating face and neck. He was dead before his body hit the deck. Liam felt heat rise past his chin and edged back as drops of acid burned across his own breastplate. For six paces down the passageway, all the surfaces sizzled as the black ooze burned. Liam pulled Hedge and his other surviving sailor away, turning them to face the second front of pirates. They pressed the attack as Liam quickly examined the memory core at his feet. No acid had reached it, and aside from being knocked over, it appeared unharmed. He loaded his second pistol with its final set of bullets and watched the passageway beyond the acid for a counterattack.

"XO, Assault: boat away," Sky suddenly reported over the radio. *"Virtue aboard with the package."*

"Understood," he replied. "We're in the cross-passage, fighting to your position."

"We're holding the airlock, but hemmed in."

It was going to be a brawl to get to that airlock, Liam realized. With four blades in action, his sailors were pushing the pirates back, and he was tempted to help clear the path with his pistol, but a glance back down toward the acid explosion reminded him that those four remaining bullets were needed to defend against grenade throwers.

A single pirate head peeked around the corner of the distant T-junction. Liam pointed his pistol and the head disappeared.

"Fall back," he heard suddenly. But it was a voice he didn't recognize.

Looking forward, he saw the pirates clearly backing away, still blocking attacks but definitely retreating. Farther ahead, he saw another group of pirates shuffle into view, holding their position at the T-junction until their comrades joined them. Consolidated, the pirates continued to back away, allowing Liam's team to join up with Sky's.

Hefting the memory core and dragging the body of his fallen sailor, Liam hustled to reach the airlock. He grinned viciously at Sky.

"I guess we're too much for them."

Sky didn't return the humor. "They had us contained. Why pull back?"

"They were fighting on multiple fronts—this way they only have to defend against us from one direction."

"Or trap us," Sky muttered, nodding to the airlock. She examined the door for a moment, then grabbed a small handle and wrenched it down, locking the controls. "Nobody's ejecting us remotely."

Liam peered out through the airlock portal, surprised at how close *Daring* loomed. The frigate's masts were retracted, thrusters firing to keep pace with the still-sailing *Bluebird*. The boat was racing to cross the open gulf between ships, and even from this distance Liam could see the sparks of weapons fire striking it. He tried not to imagine Amelia as she clung on to her seat. If that canopy shattered . . .

When the boat finally disappeared behind *Daring*'s bulk, he exhaled, suddenly realizing he'd been holding his breath.

"Boat's made it to mother," he reported to Sky.

She repeated the report loudly enough for the rest of the team to hear. Visible relief washed over the eight remaining sailors.

"How many did you send in the first boat?" he asked Sky.

"Virtue, your boat's crew, and the wounded or dead," she replied. "I needed every able fighter just to hold this position."

He nodded. He would have preferred for more of his team to have been on that boat, but he couldn't argue with his assaulter's calculus. He looked back out through the porthole, and saw the boat reemerging from behind *Daring*. It immediately came under renewed fire, and *Daring*'s energy turrets flashed to life in response. The boat surged across the gulf, but the impacts were relentless. *Daring*'s turrets fired repeatedly at targets but quickly went dark as they needed to recharge. And the onslaught of impacts on the boat continued.

Liam guessed why the pirates had pulled back from the close fighting. Why risk lives trying to attack with swords when you could just destroy the escape mechanism?

The boat grew larger in his view, not even bothering to try to evade the barrage, but making the quickest run it could across open space. Liam could even see the boat's crew, the bowsman frantically applying sealant to the cracks on the canopy as the coxn hunkered over his controls. The boat's thrusters fired anew and it began to roll, pitching upward to face its hull toward the airlock. The battered gray surface filled Liam's view, closing in at speed. It shuddered mightily, tipping askew, but still approaching quickly. Too quickly, he suddenly realized. And no retro-thrusters firing.

He leaped back from the airlock, staggering as the boat crashed into the outer door. The impact buckled the gateway and the boat careened off. As it spiraled away, Liam saw the shattered canopy and lifeless interior. The bowsman was gone, but the coxn was still hunched forward in his seat, hands flash-frozen to the controls as the icy vacuum of space consumed him.

Tearing his eyes away, Liam saw that the entire boarding party was looking back at him. They'd felt the bump, heard the wrenching of metal.

"Hold your ground," he said instinctively, even as his mind raced frantically. Without the boat, what options did they have left? "The pirates may try another assault."

That focused them, and turned their attention forward again.

Sky crouched down, pulling out her pistol and checking her bullets. She eyed him questioningly.

"Boat was destroyed," he said, low enough for her ears only.

She nodded, holstering her pistol. "How many reloads do you have left, sir?"

"None." He patted his right holster. "And this one's empty."

She stepped forward, reaching for the belt of the casualty laid out on the deck. Grabbing a cartridge, she handed it to him.

"Load up, and stay in the rear."

"I fight with my sailors, Chief."

"You accomplish our mission," she said firmly, pointing at the memory core. "You find a way to get that back to the ship."

"With respect, I'm probably the best swordsman on the team. You want me up front."

"With respect, sir"—she leaned in close, running her fingers across the acid burns on his breastplate—"I want you alive. If you go down, they lose all hope. If you're alive, they believe that there's still a way out of this."

He made to protest, but her detached professionalism dampened any sense of misplaced honor. She was brutal and unsentimental, but she was right. No one doubted his courage, but what they needed now was inspiration. He needed to think. Where were *Bluebird*'s boats? Could they fight their way down and steal one? And even if they did, how would they get past the snipers on the outer hull?

He glanced out through the porthole again, wondering crazily if they could use space suits and swim across the distance? If they could capture even a couple of personal thruster pods, could the rest hang on and . . . ?

His wild train of thought dissipated as he noticed that *Daring* was visibly turning. She'd been keeping up her chase all this time, her two bow turrets staying in play while protecting the bulk of her hull. But now her aspect was clearly shifting, her starboard beam coming into view. Liam saw the first shot from her top midships beam turret, followed seconds later by the bottom midships turret. Then, moments later, both stern turrets fired. By shifting to a beam aspect, Riverton had opened the arcs on all six of her turrets, and the weapons lanced out at targets high above him on *Bluebird*'s hull. Each turret could fire only so much before recharging, but between the six, they maintained a constant rain of fire on the pirates exposed outside their ship. It was clever, but it also exposed *Daring*'s full hull to counterattack. Ships in battle only presented their full hull if they were planning on . . .

Down the length of *Daring,* cannon ports swung open. Liam felt his jaw drop. *She wasn't.*

Fire rippled down the hull as *Daring* unleashed a full cannon broadside. He felt the deck beneath him shake under the impact.

"Covering fire from the captain," he shouted back over the din. "Stay ready for a renewed attack."

His team braced themselves as best they could, hanging on as the ship rocked under a second round of impacts. Distant alarms sounded, and Liam knew the pirates were in trouble. Their own cannons were pointed port and starboard, useless against a foe behind them. With no one on the bridge, even turning *Bluebird* would be a challenge— let alone maneuvering her for battle. *Daring* had free rein to pound away. The frequency of impact slowly increased as Liam looked out the porthole again.

Daring was closer than she'd been before. Even with *Bluebird*'s sails propelling her forward, she was being overtaken by the broadsided warship. Liam could see the glow of *Daring*'s portside thrusters as they, incredibly, pushed the frigate closer. Cannon fire rippled again. Ship-wide alarms now sounded within *Bluebird,* and Liam guessed there was an uncontained breach on the decks below. *Daring* was essentially in a shooting gallery, pinpointing every shot against the helpless pirate vessel.

He could hear the blasts of cannon impact below him and could still see the flashes of turret fire above him. *Daring*'s bulk now filled Liam's entire view; her starboard thrusters fired, slowing the imminent collision of ships, but Liam made ready to order his troops to run.

Then, to his astonishment, he saw one of *Daring*'s main airlocks open. A standard gangway tunnel extended, just as if the ship were coming alongside a Navy dock. The tunnel bumped against the wreckage of his outer airlock, sealing down. *Daring*'s own inner airlock opened, and he saw Lieutenant Swift frantically gesturing for them to move.

He jumped to his feet, slammed up the airlock override level, and smacked the controls. The airlock hatch slid open. He heard startled shouts from his team, cut off midexclamation as they saw what he saw. He grabbed the memory core.

"Withdraw!"

Sniper shots thumped against the gangway and he knew there was no time to waste. He sprinted down the passageway and cleared into *Daring*'s hull. He glanced back to ensure his team was following, waiting long enough to see Sky bringing up the rear. Another broadside thundered. But this time it was the reassuring roar of fire, not the ominous crush of impact.

"Nice plan," he gasped at Swift. "Yours?"

"The captain's," Swift answered, running his hands over his shaved head as he watched the perilous retreat. "You owe that icy bitch a kiss, I think."

Too relieved to take offense, Liam patted his propulsion officer on the shoulder and raced for the nearest ladder heading up.

The bridge was thick with tension, the focused quiet

broken only by the steady pounding of the guns. Riverton was sitting forward in her chair, eyes flicking between displays, but her gaze shot up at Liam's approach, her dark eyes luminous in her stony face.

"Do you have the memory core?" she asked.

He held it up, struggling to control his breathing.

"Gangplank detached," Brown reported. "We're clear."

"Full thruster starboard," Riverton ordered. "Maintain broadside attack."

The ship rocked as the thrusters fired again, opening the distance from *Bluebird*.

Liam noticed Amelia hovering at the back of the bridge, watching the battle over the shoulder of the damage-control crews. She caught his gaze, and the relief in her face sent a spark of warmth through him. But aside from lifting the two data drives for him to see, she remained motionless. He nodded to her with a tiny smile then turned back to the screens.

"Casualties?" Riverton asked him suddenly.

"Five dead or wounded. Most came back with the first boat—with the boat."

"What sort of pirate strength on board?"

"Heavy. We were under nearly continuous attack the entire time, until the boat left on our first return. They shifted their focus at that point."

"Agreed. We'd had harassing fire only, until suddenly their outside crews tripled in number." She'd been half watching her displays, but now turned her full attention to him. "So would you assess this as a major pirate vessel?"

"Yes, ma'am. Heavily manned, well armed, and probably well supplied with cargo. We never got far enough to really assess that." He lifted the memory core again. "But this will probably tell us."

"We've damaged them," she mused as another cannon broadside fired, "but they're still mostly intact."

"If we can examine this data, we can determine whether to reboard them, and where to target." He stepped forward, gripping her arm gently. "Ma'am, they used Sectoid weapons against us. We didn't see any, but there might even be Sectoids on board. That would be clear proof of Sectoid collusion—if we could capture them."

She frowned down at his hand but didn't move. She examined her screens again, which indicated that *Daring* had opened to the maximum effective range of her cannon.

"What kind of Sectoid weapons?" she asked. Liam described the grenades, watching as her face paled.

"Cease broadside," she ordered. "Ready missile, salvo size one."

Liam stared at her in shock.

"Ma'am, even a single missile could destroy the entire ship."

"Optically target the shattered stern," she said to Brown. "I want maximum damage."

"Yes, ma'am," Brown said, manipulating her controls.

Highcastle was beside Brown and clearly saw the implications of the order as well. He cast Liam a desperate look.

"Captain," Liam said quietly, "this ship may have more intelligence for us to gather. Not to mention much-needed supplies."

"You can pick through the wreckage if you want," she said. Her voice was steel, the touch of friendliness vanished from her manner. "And get your hand off me."

"Missile ready," Brown reported.

"Fire," Riverton said.

Liam watched on one of the external screens as a blazing pinprick of fire rocketed away from *Daring,* clearing the distance in little more than a second before vanishing into the shattered stern of *Bluebird.* The pirate ship cracked like an egg under the sudden force of the internal explosion, breaking apart as wreckage flew in all directions behind the rush of fire.

Silence descended on the bridge. Highcastle's fists clenched, and he again looked at Liam.

Liam kept his face impassive, not meeting anyone's eye.

"Secure from general quarters," Riverton said to Brown. Then she tapped Liam on the arm. "Good to have you back, XO. Well done."

Her words were light, but her expression was as dark as the Abyss. She climbed out of her chair and strode aft for her cabin.

He nodded mutely at her retreating form, not daring to speak.

CHAPTER 18

Liam took his seat at the head of the table, surveying the grim faces down both sides of the broad oak. Riverton had just sat down at the opposite end and nodded for him to begin. Liam had sent the stewards down to the galley for the next hour to avoid any junior ears eavesdropping and gossiping to the ranks. This conversation was for the senior staff only. Templegrey had the watch on the bridge, but otherwise everyone was here.

"This is a command meeting," he said simply. "The captain needs to know the facts—all the facts, good or bad—to help her make the best decision. Your expert opinions are also welcome, so speak freely. There will be no repercussions for dissent around this table."

He indicated the chart spread out before them, showing their local corner of space out to thirty days' sailing.

"I've had the chance to analyze the pirate navigation records and logs, and I've pinpointed several journeys over the last twelve months which seemed to end in the middle of deep space." Four fine lines traced across the chart, each one stopping and then doubling back. "Comparing these to our small-objects chart, I matched these journeys to a large comet nucleus on a wide orbit around the Silica system. This particular comet is far enough out to have a fairly stable orbit and has been circling Silica for centuries."

"Ideal for a permanent base," Chief Butcher commented.

"Exactly, Coxn. The location of this comet in its orbit ties into other pirate activity we've pulled together over the past few months, suggesting that multiple ships are using it as home port." He leaned forward, clasping his hands on the table. "I think we've found our target."

"It looks pretty far," Swift said. "A good fifteen days' sailing. How are we for supplies?"

"Food supplies are fine," Amelia replied. "With emergency rations we have over forty days stocked. Air is between thirty and forty days, depending on usage. My real worry is water—we only have fifteen days. Twenty-five if we really ration."

"It's that far just to get back to Windfall," Brown exclaimed.

"I recommend we sail for Windfall immediately," Swift said, looking first at Liam and then at the captain. "Our hull repairs need more work, if nothing else to stop the leaks, and then we can resupply and set out in strength."

"I agree," Butcher added, pointing at the comet on the chart. "The pirate base isn't going anywhere."

Liam recognized the advice as both sound and reasonable, but he looked down the table to Riverton. She straightened in her chair.

"We can't go back to Windfall," she said. "We haven't

the money to pay for further repairs or resupply, and we'd use up everything we have just to get back."

"I hate to suggest it, ma'am," Butcher said, "but couldn't we use the prize money to pay for it?"

"We already have," Riverton replied, "for the last set of repairs and supply."

"There's nothing left?" Swift blurted, unable to keep the shock from his face.

"Not enough to restock for a voyage out to the pirate base."

"What about the cargo we're carrying? All that fancy gold and jewelry?"

"There's no one willing to buy it at Windfall," Amelia explained, "and no one at Silica 7 with enough money to do so. That shipment is intended for a specific dealer in the Iron Swarm—she's the only one with the cash to buy it."

"Well," Highcastle said, "damn it all. If it's just money we need, I'll pay for it!"

Riverton turned curious eyes to him.

"Do you have the money on board, Mr. Highcastle?"

"Of course not. But I'll just arrange for a credit note at the local bank. My family's name is well regarded."

"That would give away our identity," she replied, already turning away.

"It would bring too much attention to us and our ship," Liam added, "alerting the pirates to our presence and making it impossible for us to sneak away again."

It would also, he and Riverton both knew, send a strong message to the admiralty that *Daring*'s mission was failing and was becoming a potential embarrassment. With so many Navy ships in the area, it would only take a single offended captain—such as the idle Silverhawk—to commandeer *Daring* and ruin everything.

"We're already halfway to the pirate base," Riverton continued. "At the moment we have the advantage of surprise, as the pirates won't yet know of *Bluebird*'s fate, and possibly not even that of the *Golden Wind* and her sisters. As news of their lost ships starts to trickle in, though, the pirates will increase their guard, and perhaps even abandon their base. We won't get a better chance to strike."

Her words filled the room. Liam watched Sky nodding to herself, and Butcher silently accepting the decision with new resolve. Swift and Amelia both looked concerned but they remained quiet. Highcastle's brow furrowed in thought. It was Brown who finally spoke.

"We still have that Sectoid ship out there, and it appears to be closing us. What do we think its involvement in all this is?"

"What do we know for sure?" Riverton asked in response.

"We know the pirates have Sectoid acid, and we've seen the Sectoid ship nearby during several pirate attacks. We know there was a Sectoid-encrypted signal from Windfall before we sailed, and we intercepted at least one other from the Sectoid ship when we were chasing down *Bluebird*." She glanced at Highcastle for confirmation.

"We think it was aimed at *Bluebird*," he added, "though there's a chance it might have been aimed at another target further down our bearing."

"But based on strength, we think it was aimed at *Bluebird*," Brown concluded, "strongly suggesting collusion between Sectoids and pirates."

Riverton's expression remained impassive.

"And," Highcastle interjected, "we have traces of another signal with the same encryption, sent just before we attacked *Bluebird*. It might have come from the pirates." He paused. "It also might have come from *Daring*."

Liam stared at him in astonishment. What was Highcastle suggesting, precisely?

"We don't know that," Brown interrupted, raising her hands to quell the shock rising around the table. "We just caught a trace echo, and it was after the fact. With the ships as close together as they were, it's impossible to pin down exactly where the signal originated from."

"But it's important," Highcastle said with a glare at her, "to report all information."

"Yes"—she glared back—"but the captain asked what we know—not what we *guess*."

"That's fine," Riverton interrupted calmly. "We will continue to monitor for any other signals. If one originates from *Daring* now, we'll know for sure."

Liam struggled to keep his own expression as stoic as the captain's, but he didn't quite succeed. Could it be possible there was a spy aboard *Daring*? That one of their crew had betrayed them?

No, he reminded himself. There was just an uncertain piece of information.

Still, the tension in the silence around the table now was palpable.

"Anything else?" Riverton asked, looking around the table.

"Hull integrity is good," Swift said. "We're in solid enough shape to see action, but I'm concerned about taking cannon fire to the starboard side—I can't guarantee that our fixes will hold as expected under that kind of assault. I recommend we fight with port broadsides only."

"Very well." Riverton nodded.

"The boarding team is understrength after the last attack," Sky said, looking at Butcher. "I'll need to draw from the remaining crew and start training right away."

"We'll look at the watch rotations right after this," the coxn replied.

"And we have no boats," Sky added simply.

Liam frowned at the reminder. Inserting a boarding party without boats was a challenge he'd already spent time trying to solve. Unsuccessfully.

"We'll take that into account when we draw up our battle plan," Riverton said.

"I recommend level-two air and water rationing commence immediately," Amelia suggested. "But let's keep the regular food coming—nothing kills morale faster than emergency rations."

"Agreed."

Liam waited for any other comments, then offered his own observation.

"Crew morale is good, although there has been a growing feeling of uncertainty about the mission. Our last pair of engagements have been indecisive, and the crew is well aware that prize money earned to date is minimal." He couldn't help but glare at Highcastle as he spoke. "I think the idea of striking the pirates' base will focus the crew and raise morale."

The cadet picked up on the silent accusation immediately, straightening in his seat.

"Yes, I speak to the crew," he said defensively. "I feel it's important as a leader to maintain a close relationship with my people. In fact, sometimes I think I'm the only one here who feels that way."

Liam's own indignation was clearly reflected in the

expressions of the other senior staff. Butcher's face darkened, but he glanced at Liam before speaking. Liam quickly noted Riverton's quick headshake, and motioned Butcher to stay silent.

"Go on, Mr. Highcastle," he said quietly.

"Crew morale is not good," Highcastle said, his voice rising. "Your observation is correct that they are feeling uncertain, but I disagree with your statement that they will be cheered by news of this new mission. They are clever people, and they will see as clearly as I do that this plan is reckless. Our ship is damaged, we are low on supplies, we are understrength, and we have no blasted boats! And there's the possibility of a spy on board, not to mention a Sectoid ship steadily bearing down on us."

"I gather you've never been to war," Sky said. "This is hardly the worst it can get. Far from it."

"But if we have the option to withdraw, gather our strength, and then strike later, why not do so?"

"Because we *don't* have that option," Riverton said firmly. "The fleet is depending on us to solve this pirate problem, and they won't wait for us to limp back every time we get a bloody nose. Thank you for your input, Mr. Highcastle."

Liam was impressed at her resolve. He honestly hadn't expected it.

"Even if we survive the attack," Highcastle pressed, "how are we going to cross the gulf with no supplies?"

"We'll replenish from the pirate base," she said. "No doubt they're well stocked."

"And what if we can't take the base?"

"Then we're dead, and it doesn't matter."

Liam had seen battle enough times to not be afraid of

dying. But even he was chilled by the seeming indifference in Riverton's words. She stared down her youngest officer with unflinching certainty. A weak scoff of disbelief escaped his lips . . . but then he dropped his gaze.

"Anything else?" she asked the table, cocking her head. No one spoke.

"Thank you, Captain," Liam said finally. "We'll begin preparations for the base attack."

THE NEXT FEW DAYS PASSED UNEVENTFULLY. Level-two air restrictions meant a minimum of exertion even for routine tasks, but Liam knew there was a lot of restless energy in the ship. He'd already dealt with a couple of fights, but instead of imposing the usual punishments, he'd quietly implored the guilty parties to just behave. The number of romances on board also seemed to be climbing, and he was determined to turn a blind eye completely to that. Riverton probably wouldn't approve, but she spent all her time either on the bridge or in her cabin and likely hadn't even noticed.

For himself, Liam knew of several ways to keep his spirits up and his restlessness down. One he'd just finished: another tour of the ship—keeping his finger on the pulse and ensuring the crew saw the senior leadership regularly. And a second he hoped to start right away. He knocked on one of the cabin doors at the after end of Two Deck.

The door opened, but he kept his face completely neutral until he saw who greeted him. Amelia peered up at him around the door, unkempt hair tumbling past her shoulders. She was dressed in a white shift with the top three buttons undone, one bare leg visible where she balanced herself. He opened his mouth to speak but she shook her head fiercely and indicated with her eyes back behind the door. Her cabinmate, Chief Sky, was home.

"Thanks, Able Rating," she said. "Take it down to stores and I'll see you there in a minute."

He stepped back in silence as she shut the door, then made his way casually down to the stores office. It was locked, of course, and he made a show of examining the firefighting gear mounted on the bulkhead across the passageway. Quick steps announced the approach of a sailor, but he purposefully kept his eyes on his apparent task.

"I think that particular set of hoses," said a familiar, lovely voice, "is the best-inspected piece of kit in the whole ship."

He turned, watching as Amelia unlocked the stores office and stepped through. She was in uniform, although she'd left her coat in her cabin and the white shirt clung to her figure.

"I do try to run a tight ship," he mused, following her in.

She shut the door and locked it, stepping right into his waiting arms. Her lips pressed passionately against his, hands gripping his shoulders and running hungrily down his back. Both hands squeezed his butt.

"I like it when you keep things tight," she breathed in his ear.

He laughed, nuzzling against her neck. "I like it when you talk so crassly."

"Too much for you, my delicate duke?"

Everything about her was more than he'd ever known in a woman. She was absolutely intoxicating.

"I'm not a duke, silly." He pulled back slightly to gaze

down at her beautiful face. "But I'd joust for your favor any day."

She scoffed, wrapping her arms around his neck and kissing him firmly.

They simply enjoyed each other for a while, delicately exploring as they got to know each other more and more. It was the noble way to love, and while part of him always wanted to follow her initial instincts and tear each other's clothes off, he'd always found that titillation and anticipation were far more powerful aphrodisiacs.

As quartermaster, she'd easily been able to secure a blanket for the floor and a couple of pillows. With only the glow of the computer screens to light the office, it was about as romantic as a compartment on a ship in space could be. After a while they lay side by side, she tracing a finger across the fabric of his unbuttoned shirt while he played with her long, silky hair.

"So what do you do when you're bouncing around at Lord Grandview's balls?" she asked.

"Hobnob," he answered, to a burst of laughter. He thought for a moment, casting his memory back to more carefree days. "For the first while everyone stands around, drinking and looking for the best people to talk to. There's a lot of vapid conversation, and a lot of gazes not really looking at you. Eventually the guest of honor will arrive, to much ado and huzzahs, and his or her usual first act is to try the food. This then opens the food tables for all the guests—who are ravenous by this time—to get their snouts in the trough. The food helps to soak up some of the alcohol, so by the time the dancing starts, most of the guests have both the courage and the coordination to take the floor."

"I think it'd take an entire bottle of cheap plonk to give me either of those. Can I bring my own bottle?"

"Dancing is actually rather easy. You have to learn about a dozen different steps, and then it's just a matter of knowing which combination to move in. And as a lady you'll always have a gentleman to lead you."

"I'm not used to that," she said, leaning her head on his chest.

"Not much dancing in the taverns?"

"No." She lifted herself to stare down at him with luminous, dark eyes. "I mean I'm not used to relying on a man to guide me."

He stared up at her, realizing suddenly just how little he knew of her world. He'd spent enough time on missions to be able to blend into the common world, but he was never really a part of it. What was to him just a gallivant before returning to the comforts of home was an entire lifetime for her. The Navy was what they had in common.

"I doubt you've ever needed one," he said. "I think you've cut your own path with remarkable fortitude."

"Thanks," she said, smiling before she laid her head on his chest again.

"But dancing well," he continued, tracing his fingers down the bare skin under her shirt, "is a different sort of challenge altogether. One which requires true skill and dedication."

"Are you saying I don't have that?" she asked with a dangerous expression.

"To be a dancer you need to know your body"—his fingers continued to slide down her back—"and you need to know your partner's body. You need to know every strength"—his fingers slid to the spots on her waist just above her hip bones—"and every weakness."

He stabbed her only tickle spots and she screamed her laughter, fighting to squirm free as he wrapped an arm around her and continued to poke. With impressive strength, she wrenched herself free, climbing on top of him as he lay back.

"You stop that—what do you call it?—that tomfoolery right now, Liam." Her eyes were afire, but they were also starting to smolder. She pressed her weight down on him and leaned in for a kiss.

CHAPTER 19

Amelia realized how long she'd been staring at the screen when it switched itself off due to lack of input. She blinked, then sat back and rubbed her eyes. The dim lights of the stores office made viewing screens easier, but didn't help her maintain concentration. That, and her mind kept drifting to the other series of far more interesting encounters she and Liam had recently been enjoying down here. Sighing, she tapped the screen again, hating this netherworld of fatigue that made her too tired to work but too wired to sleep.

Liam—she smiled to herself—would probably come down to look at stores reports *in order to* fall asleep. He'd finally admitted to her just how dull he found her job—although she'd suspected it for some time. It was sweet how long he'd tried to keep up the façade, but his own fatigue was wearing him down as well.

In the ten days since that command briefing to the captain, she didn't think anyone had slept well. The crew had indeed been re-energized by the news that they were sailing to attack the pirate base, but Amelia could sense the undercurrent of uncertainty. At least one sailor stopped by every hour during the day, asking her how their supplies were holding up. She always had a reassuring response, but it was clear that somebody else was feeding negative information to the crew. At least now, in the middle of the night watches, she got some peace.

"Hey, PO."

She turned, suppressing a sigh of frustration. Her mood lightened, though, when she saw Hedge standing in the doorway. The young technician was definitely on the mend from her battle wound, even if her old infectious enthusiasm hadn't yet returned in full.

"Hey, Hedgie—what are you doing up?"

"Couldn't sleep. And I'm on watch in two hours anyway, so I figured I'd just take a stroll. You?"

"Just checking on our burn-through of food," Amelia said, gesturing at her screen. "You guys eat a ton."

"Not me," Hedge said, stepping in and taking the other seat. "I hardly feel like eating anything."

"Well, that'll save rations and make my job easier."

Hedge didn't laugh. She looked pale, Amelia noticed, and she glanced back at the passageway every few seconds.

"Hedgie, are you okay?"

The younger woman looked up at her with pleading eyes.

"PO, do you think we're going to survive this mission?"

Amelia sat in silence for a moment. It would be a relief just to share her own fears with a friend, but she was very aware of her position as a senior sailor and the responsibilities that brought.

"We've survived everything up until now," she said with a forced smile. "I don't think the pirates will have anything worse to throw at us."

"We haven't been hit by the Sectoids yet." Hedge shuddered. "I don't know if I'll be able to handle that."

Amelia couldn't disagree. She'd heard Sky mutter enough things about the bugs to know that the chief was afraid of them, and that terrified Amelia.

"I think when it comes to fighting bugs, we just stand off as best we can and hit them from range. Our bullets shoot further than their acid."

"And what about that huge ship chasing us?"

The Sectoid vessel was out there again, and seemed to be gaining on them. But so far it hadn't done anything provocative.

"From what I hear, our missiles out-range their weapons."

Hedge folded her arms, almost curling up on herself. And her eyes still darted toward the door.

"I just wish we could have a way out of this. I don't think we're going to survive if we keep going the way we're going. And I'm worried about what's going to happen."

Amelia reached out a tender hand to grip Hedge's arm.

"I'll be here for you," she said. "No matter what happens."

"Really?" The relief in Hedge's eyes was obvious.

"Of course."

Hedge uncurled and leaned forward, wrapping her arms tightly around Amelia. She buried her face in Amelia's shoulder and squeezed even tighter. Amelia held her for a long moment. Then she noticed movement at the doorway.

It was Flatrock. He met Amelia's gaze for a moment, but then dropped his eyes.

"Hedge," he said quietly, "it's time."

She disengaged from Amelia, wiping her eyes. She looked intently at Amelia, a brief smile lighting up her wan face. "The PO should come with us," she said to Flatrock.

The big sailor considered for a moment, then nodded.

"Where are we going?" Amelia asked.

"To the bridge," he replied. "We've been summoned."

Off-watch personnel getting called to the bridge rarely meant good news, Amelia knew as she rose from her chair, especially when it was the middle of the night.

She followed Flatrock and Hedge up the ladders. The ship was as quiet as expected, with all off-watch personnel in their bunks, but Amelia could sense the tension in both Flatrock and Hedge as they silently ascended to the bridge, and it made her uneasy.

She glanced around, on high alert as they stepped out onto the dim open space under the canopy, but she saw nothing immediately unusual. There was no gathering of senior staff, or a group of specialists prepping for a mission. There was just the officer of the watch, Highcastle, and his three regular bridge crew.

The young cadet spotted them immediately, motioning them over with barely contained nervous energy. His gaze lingered on Amelia and his brow furrowed in confusion.

"The PO should be here," Hedge said, noticing his look. "She's dedicated to us and to the ship."

Amelia was puzzled by the statement, but before she could question it, Flatrock spoke.

"Have you got something, sir?"

"Oh, yeah," Highcastle said. "We've got her dead to rights. Listen to this."

He pressed a button on his console, and the recording of a crackly signal echoed through the bridge. It was a mechanical voice, a translator over the clicking of Sectoid speech.

"Human warship *Daring,* this is the Sectoid warship Two-Seven-One. We will connect. I am here for Sophia Riverton."

As the sound of the recording faded away, Amelia felt her insides twist. One glance at the other sailors was enough to see their horrified glances matched her own.

"So," Flatrock said finally, "she's a traitor."

"That's what we're going to find out," Highcastle replied firmly, before pushing another button on his console. "Captain, ma'am, officer of the watch."

"Captain," came Riverton's sleepy voice from her cabin.

"Request you come to the bridge, please."

LIAM STARED UP AT THE DARK LANTERN IN THE center of the ceiling. Starlight through the portal over his bunk always cast a soft glow through his cabin, but *Daring*'s current aspect to the distant stars of the Hub directed the illumination onto the lantern. It swayed almost imperceptibly as the steady winds pushed *Daring* forward into the darkness. In times past he'd often used the steady swinging motion to clear his mind and lull him to sleep, but the past few hours of staring upward had brought no respite.

Contrary to Highcastle's immature prediction, the crew had responded well to the news that *Daring* was en route to destroy the pirate base. Sky had selected her new boarding team members, and no one had complained at the extra drills. Swift and his team had battened down as best they could, and Amelia had brought out the best food to keep spirits up.

But Liam knew it was all a conspiracy of optimism. This was a do-or-die mission and the weight of responsibility was exhausting him. And that, perversely, was robbing him of sleep. It had been ten days since the command team meeting had set them on this course and not one of those nights had brought rest.

Commander Riverton was showing the strain as well, despite her best efforts—Liam had watched her mannerisms shift subtly from the cool military commander to the haughty noblewoman. She was tired, and falling back on instinctive behavior. She'd asked him three times about the loyalty of the crew. Clearly her own confidence in her command decisions was less than rock-solid. He'd assured her that the crew was fully onside, even as his own doubts in her ability to see this mission through wisped into his mind.

Adjusting the thin sheet thrown over him, he wished for hardly the first time that Amelia was here with him.

She shared a cabin with Sky, and he wondered if fear of awkward questions from the assaulter might also be a motivator for her not sleeping elsewhere.

A sudden knock at his door startled him. For a wild minute, he hoped it was Amelia—that for some reason, she had changed her mind . . .

"XO, sir, Assault," came the voice through the wood.

Wrong cabinmate—he sighed to himself—climbing off his bunk and throwing on his white uniform shirt. He flicked on the desk lantern and sat back down on his bunk.

"Come in."

Light from the passageway silhouetted Sky's broad figure as she slipped in and shut the door. She eyed his bedraggled state impassively.

"I'm sorry to disturb you, sir."

"No, not at all," he said, indicating for her to sit at the desk chair. "I have no doubt this is something important and timely."

"Yes, sir." Sky sat, folding her hands in her lap. Her gaze darted aimlessly around the room for a long moment.

Liam watched her curiously. He'd never seen his assaulter like this.

"Chief?"

"Sir." She took a deep breath. "You know how you've asked me in the past about my shore excursions with the captain. I've not betrayed the captain's confidence by answering you, but I feel that there are some things you should know."

"You've been very loyal to her," he said carefully, "and I respect that."

"But ultimately I'm loyal to the Emperor, to the Navy, to the ship, and to our mission. And at the moment I find my loyalty to the captain in conflict with that." Her eyes beseeched him, revealing her internal struggle.

"You've committed no disloyalty, Chief. Right now you and I are just talking. There are no consequences for a chat."

"It started three days ago, when I went to sign out our confidential book on Sectoid ships and their capabilities. With that bug ship gaining on us, I wanted to know what we were up against."

"I had the same thought yesterday," he mused. "I guess

the captain had too because the book was signed out to her."

"Yesterday, and the day before, and the day I first wanted it." Sky stared at him with new intensity. "And it's still signed out to her today. I checked and it's been signed out for ten days."

"Since the command brief."

"Yes. Two days ago, I sent a request to have the book, but she's ignored it."

And all this time, Liam knew, the Sectoid ship had been on an intercept course. It was close enough to see with the naked eye now, and through a telescope its massive petals of sails were clearly visible, grabbing every gust of solar wind.

But Liam refused to leap to conclusions.

"Perhaps she's forgotten that she has the book," he offered. "She is very busy, and tired."

"That's just the first thing," Sky pressed on. "And it got me thinking. You remember that Sectoid-encrypted signal sent from Windfall Station that Brown sniped? I talked to her, and she said it was sent from the station's upper levels."

"That's right." Liam nodded, remembering how that fact had lodged in his brain for some reason.

"The captain and I were in the upper levels." Sky glanced down for a moment, then met his gaze again. "And at her meeting, the subject of discussion was Sectoids."

"Who did she meet with?"

"I don't know him, but I gathered from their greetings that they knew each other from the diplomatic corps. He was an older gentleman, quite handsome, very well dressed—I remember he had more lace on his wrists than our dining table."

Liam sniffed a laugh, but a sudden memory triggered.

"Did this gentleman have a gold sash?"

"There was one laid out across his surcoat," Sky said after a moment's recollection. "I noticed them on the dressing table."

"Did it have a symbol on it?"

Sky described the seal of the Imperial diplomatic corps.

"I think this man was Lord Redfort," Liam concluded. "One of our senior diplomats."

"The captain never introduced me to him. They kept their speech formal in front of me, but they seemed quite familiar with each other."

"So, naturally you assumed it was a dalliance with an old lover?"

"That's what I assumed, sir. As I did with our first visit on Silica 7. After initial pleasantries at that meeting, the captain started asking about Sectoid movements in the sector. It seemed to me like friendly shoptalk, and when they disappeared into the other room I purposefully tuned out."

"Understandable discretion, Chief."

Sky bit her lip. "But has it now cost us, sir?"

HIGHCASTLE WAS OPENLY PACING THE BRIDGE NOW. Flatrock and Hedge both stood to the side of the officer-of-the-watch station; he was stoic, staring straight ahead, but she kept glancing around, unable to keep her hands still. She looked to Amelia often, but Amelia had nothing to offer. This situation was spiraling out of control and she saw no good ending to it. She wanted nothing more than to disappear—but professional duty held her in place. One way or another, she needed to know what was going on. She bumped against one of the rear weapons consoles, unaware that she'd been slowly stepping away from the action.

After a seeming eternity of silent, tense waiting, Amelia heard the soft thump of the door at the after end of the bridge. It was with a mixture of relief and fear that she spotted Commander Riverton striding forward. The captain stood tall, her uniform impeccable as always, and her face was set in stone. Her eyes flicked over once to where Amelia stood—freezing her in place—and then to Flatrock and Hedge, before she settled her attention on her officer of the watch.

"Report, if you please, Mr. Highcastle," she commanded.

"We received a signal from the Sectoid ship, ma'am," he said, before playing the recording once again.

Riverton listened without reaction.

"What are we going to do, ma'am?" Highcastle asked, a dangerous edge creeping into his voice.

Riverton climbed smoothly into her command chair.

"Shorten sails, Mr. Highcastle, and prepare to receive the Sectoid ship."

"What?" Highcastle gasped. He glanced back at his sailors. The faces of Flatrock and Hedge reflected his shock—and his growing anger.

Amelia stepped silently around the console, searching desperately for a comms button.

"I think, Lady Riverton," Highcastle boomed, "you have some explaining to do."

The captain's entire frame tensed, but she kept her voice low.

"Every moment you are on this ship, *Cadet,* you will

address me by my military rank and demonstrate the proper respect."

"And I would be happy to do so, were I not questioning your loyalty to the Emperor."

Riverton's eyes swept the bridge. Her gaze lingered on Flatrock and Hedge, and then moved to Amelia.

"Why are these extra people on the bridge, Mr. Highcastle?"

"Because they, like me, and like the entire crew, wish to know the truth." He stabbed his finger at the console where the recording had played. "Explain yourself, Lady Riverton. Explain why a Sectoid ship known to be in collusion with pirates has hailed us by our real name, and asked for you personally."

LIAM RUBBED HIS CHIN, STRUGGLING TO TIE THESE disparate thoughts together. The captain had twice gone ashore, and twice met with people to discuss Sectoids.

"Maybe she didn't send the signal," he suggested. "Maybe Lord Redfort did after you'd left."

"I checked the timings," Sky replied glumly. "It was sent while we were in those apartments."

"But we don't know if it was sent *from* those apartments . . ."

"Why did the captain order the destruction of *Bluebird*?" Sky suddenly asked. "Especially right after you reported the presence of Sectoid weapons on board."

"She wanted to stop the pirates from signaling their base." It sounded like a weak defense even as he said it, but after days of thought, he hadn't come up with a better reason.

"They were too far out to signal anyone! And we could have done it after a second boarding for more intel."

Images of the vicious fighting aboard *Bluebird* flashed through Liam's mind.

"Did you really want to try another boarding, Chief? With no boats?"

"No, but . . ." She sighed. "Fair enough. But what about that signal sent to the Sectoids from *Daring*?"

"We don't know if it was from *Daring* or *Bluebird*."

"Have you ever fought the bugs, sir?"

"No."

"If you thought *Bluebird* was tough," she said, fists clenching, "you haven't seen anything."

The sheer size of the Sectoid ship was enough to fill Liam with dread. If the bugs decided to make trouble, *Daring*'s only option would be to run.

"And why didn't the captain ask the Navy for help?" Sky asked suddenly. "I'm sure we could have made a few discreet inquiries without alerting the civilians on Windfall."

These questions were suddenly starting to make her sound suspiciously like Highcastle.

"Are there others on board talking like this?" Liam asked.

"There are mutterings," she admitted. "No one says them to me directly, but I have ears."

Liam considered this. He knew the reason why Riverton was keeping clear of the Navy—any sign of failure might see the entire mission canceled, with her shouldering the blame—but he doubted any common sailor would sympathize with that. Better to see a few nobles disgraced than an entire crew killed in action, they'd say.

"I'm sensing a spark of discontent," Sky added, "and it's being fed by someone."

He nodded. But his thoughts were interrupted by the

ring of a tiny bell at the head of his bunk. It was a call
from the bridge. He leaned over and activated the link.

"XO."

"Sir, it's Amelia," came a whispered voice. *"Come to
the bridge, now."*

LIAM'S SHIRT WAS BARELY TUCKED IN AND HIS COAT
was undone as he stepped up onto the bridge, Sky right
behind him. He buttoned his coat as he stepped forward,
realizing that in his haste he'd left his belt behind.

Nothing appeared out of order at first glance. Highcastle stood at his officer-of-the-watch station and the
crew was seated at their consoles. Commander Riverton
was in her chair—a bit unusual, considering the hour—
but there were no alerts sounding, no visible threats
through the canopy. Liam's pace slowed as he struggled
to uncover the reason for his summons. Then he saw
Amelia by one of the rear consoles, and two other sailors
standing several paces from Highcastle.

Surprise flashed across Riverton's face, followed for
an instant by what looked like relief, before her usual icy
demeanor solidified again.

"XO," she said, "what good timing. Please take the
watch from Cadet Highcastle."

The cadet, Liam saw at this close range, was flushed
and tight-faced. He glared at the captain, then turned
pleading eyes to Liam.

"Don't listen to her," he said. "She means to doom
us all."

"Stand aside, Cadet," Liam ordered automatically.
Still, something in the young man's face kept him from
moving forward.

"Listen to me!" Highcastle stabbed at his console, and Liam heard a crackly signal of a translator over the distinctive clicking of Sectoid speech.

"Human warship *Daring,* this is the Sectoid warship Two-Seven-One. We will connect. I am here for Sophia Riverton."

"They've been signaling that for the past hour," Highcastle exclaimed, pointing at Riverton. "She's working with them."

Liam's eyes shot to Riverton. Her expression was as unreadable as ever.

"As I have already explained," she said slowly, "Sectoid speech is very limited. What he is really saying is that he wants to talk to me."

"They know her," Highcastle accused. "She's working with them. How else could they know our ship's real name?"

"I am tired of arguing with you, Cadet," Riverton stated. "You are relieved of duty."

"I am not," Highcastle said, placing his hands defiantly on his hips, "going to let you hand His Majesty's sailing ship over to the bugs."

"Executive officer," Riverton said loudly, "you have the watch. Shorten our sails and prepare for the Sectoid ship to come alongside."

Liam caught Sky's glance. The assaulter's face was twisted with uncertainty, and the faintest touch of fear. Beyond Highcastle, Flatrock had stepped forward, eyes intent on Commander Riverton. Hedge was frozen in place. Amelia was still behind her console several paces distant. For an awful moment the bridge was frozen in tableau.

Then Liam stepped into the officer-of-the-watch space.

Highcastle retreated a step, but his expression hardened. "Don't listen to her," he warned.

"Sailing control," Liam called out, "shorten all sails and maintain maneuverability. Inform propulsion that we will be retracting the port mast."

"Belay that order!" Highcastle drew his officer-of-the-watch pistol and pressed it against Liam's head.

Liam stilled, cursing himself for forgetting his belt and the sword that hung on it. Sky too was unarmed. On all the bridge there was only one weapon, and it was in the hands of a self-righteous lordling.

"Lower that weapon immediately," Riverton ordered, in a voice that could have cut glass. Liam couldn't see her, but he heard the creak as she stepped down out of her chair.

Highcastle stepped back again, shifting to aim the pistol at the captain.

"Lady Sophia Riverton," he declared, "I hereby relieve you of command. As the ranking lord on this ship, I assume authority to deliver us to safety."

"Don't do this," Liam warned.

The pistol swung back to him. Riverton appeared at his side. And then she stepped in front of him.

"Don't make yourself a murderer," she said, slowly closing in on Highcastle.

His scoff was laced with fear, but the pistol didn't waver.

"Chief Sky," Highcastle ordered, "seize Lady Riverton."

Sky moved to where Highcastle and Riverton faced each other, barely a pace apart. Liam watched his assaulter as she tensed, her eyes flicking back and forth between the two officers. She placed a hand on Riverton's arm.

Liam doubted he could actually take down Sky in hand-to-hand combat, but he tensed, ready to move.

Sky suddenly flung Riverton backward, launching herself against Highcastle. The towering youth stumbled back. A shot thundered in the close air. Sky and Highcastle toppled to the deck. Liam leaped over the staggering Riverton and grabbed the pistol as it clattered free. He swept it in a covering arc around the bridge. The crew was frozen in their seats. Flatrock had stumbled backward against the bulkhead with Hedge, hands up. Sky had pinned Highcastle on his stomach, arms bent back, and Amelia was down next to her wrapping his wrists in her own belt.

Riverton was struggling to her feet by the officer-of-the-watch station. Blood smeared the deck, and dripped down to splash at her boots. Liam spotted the growing stain of dark red liquid seeping through her coat.

"Medical team to the bridge," he shouted. Moments later the order was repeated over the general broadcast. Nodding his gratitude, he held the pistol out to Sky, and she pressed it to Highcastle's temple.

Liam moved to Riverton, who was leaning heavily against the console, pressing her hand against the wound at her side. He hooked her arm over his shoulder and helped her back to her command chair just as Amelia appeared with a medical kit. He tore aside her coat and blouse, pulled out a thick bandage and pressed it against the pulsing wounds. Entry and exit holes, he saw. The bullet had glanced her, but blood was pouring out.

She panted, dark eyes afire with pain, her face pale.

But she was still lucid, gaze darting from the pinned Highcastle and back.

"Thank you," she gasped.

She might pass out at any moment, Liam knew. That meant he'd be in acting command, and there was a looming Sectoid ship to deal with.

"You have my loyalty, Captain," he said. "But I need you to tell me everything."

She pressed her hand over his against the wound, nodding as her eyelids drooped.

"That Sectoid-encrypted signal," she whispered through painful breaths, "was from us. It was from me. I know who commands that Sectoid ship and I needed to get a message to him. And this is why."

Liam leaned in, and listened.

CHAPTER 20

It took the Sectoid ship six more hours to close *Daring,*
its massive gray form filling half the sky as it retracted
several of its masts and drifted into position alongside.
Liam stayed on the bridge during the approach, but as
soon as he received word that the two ships were aligned
for boarding, he made his way down to One Deck. He'd
chosen the airlock closest to the bridge for this—no need
to reveal *Daring*'s interior any more than necessary. At
every junction he'd placed armed sailors, with more providing defense in depth down every passageway. He was
in his armor, which had been polished to try to hide the
acid burns spattered across the breastplate.

Swift and Sky waited at the airlock. Neither looked
happy, and each had added a second pistol to their belts.
Before he could speak, the sound of rapid footsteps caught
his ears. He turned and saw Amelia jogging up.

"Brig is secure," she reported. "Our . . . new guest isn't
happy, but behind all those doors no one can hear him."

Having Highcastle under lock and key removed one

variable from play. Liam acknowledged her report with a nod.

"All security teams are in place," he said to Swift and Sky. "Are we on full ventilation lock-down?"

"Yes," Swift replied. Sectoids were known to use ventilation trunking to swarm a ship.

Liam gave all three of them a long look.

"Are you ready?"

Sky actually shuddered, but she nodded. Swift frowned and placed his hands on the controls. Amelia took a deep breath and smiled with a touch of excitement.

At Swift's command, *Daring*'s airlock door hissed open. Liam stepped into the gangway tube, hearing Amelia and Sky fall in behind him. The tube was fastened to the Sectoid ship not ten paces away.

The hull of the Sectoid ship was a dull gray, with a rough, unfinished texture almost like coarse sand. There was no obvious control panel, or even an outline of a door. As Liam stepped up to its cold surface he wondered if they'd placed their gangway in the right place.

Suddenly the surface of the hull split open, dilating back to create a circular gap. A rush of musty, earthy air washed over him. The space beyond was dark, lit only by the small lanterns from *Daring*'s own gangway. Liam stepped through, carefully finding purchase on the curved deck. The entire passageway was circular, he realized, with no flat surface to stand on. It was more like a tube than a corridor, wide enough in diameter for two Humans to stand head to foot. Sliding down the curve that dropped away from the airlock, he fumbled in the near darkness, finally securing himself by spreading his legs and planting his feet on opposite sides of the curve beneath him.

As he breathed deeply, he felt a rush of invigoration.

The atmosphere on the Sectoid home world had a much higher oxygen content than Humans were used to. For short exposures it caused no harm, but after less than an hour it would start to have intoxicating effects. Liam hoped this meeting would take much less time than that—it was surreal enough without getting drunk on the air itself.

Amelia bumbled in behind him. The sounds of her movements echoed down the passageway and Liam felt the subtle vibrations through his own feet. Sky stayed on the gangway, her flat deck level with Liam's chest. Beyond the dim pool of light from the gangway, the passageway—or tunnel, really—extended in both directions in utter darkness and silence.

The Sectoids didn't need light, he knew, and hearing was one of their secondary senses. His feet felt another, rumbling tremor. The bugs' primary form of communication was touch. With their fumbled steps, he and Amelia had just done the equivalent of shouting at the top of their lungs. The rumbling of the deck continued, now accompanied by a skittering that was growing louder.

"Stand your ground," he said to Amelia, recalling Riverton's instructions. "Let them come to you."

He felt her body bump up against his, back-to-back. She took a deep, shaky breath.

Then, at the edge of the darkness, a form appeared. It was on the ceiling—although direction had no meaning in this alien world—a dark mass of body and limbs that twitched and jittered. Another shape emerged on the side of the passageway, paused, then skittered down to face Liam at his level.

The Sectoid was almost as tall as he was, head perched on an upright torso that pivoted from the abdomen. Four narrow legs held it up, bulbous thorax extending back-ward. Two massive arms were currently held close to its torso, dozens of fingers twiddling down each length to the elbows. The head nodded left and right, pincers clacking as it lowered its antennas to softly pat Liam's head and shoulders. The feathery touch passed in barely a second, and Liam fought down a shiver. He could hear another Sectoid examining Amelia behind him, and she pressed back against him.

The bug in front of Liam tapped its feet and snapped its pincers. He heard what must be a response from the creature facing Amelia. Then his Sectoid moved one of its long arms down, several of the fingers manipulating what Liam suddenly recognized as a translator. The bug tapped and clacked again, and Human words sounded from the mechanical speaker.

"You are not Sophia Riverton."

"Sophia Riverton is in our ship," Liam replied care-fully, keeping his sentences as simple as possible. "I will take your speaker to her."

"You will take us into your ship."

The bluntness of the statement surprised him. Then he realized it might actually be a question. Keep things simple, he reminded himself. Sectoids don't do nuances.

"Yes. Your speaker and two guards."

The bug switched off its translator and snapped its pincers anew, feet dancing out an intricate rhythm. Liam heard a response behind him, and then another from the darkness in front of him. Another Sectoid appeared, mov-ing along the side of the tunnel toward Liam. It was mar-ginally smaller than the others, its skin distinctly brown instead of the usual black.

"I am the speaker of vessel Two-Seven-One," it said through the translator. "I will follow you."

"Yes," Liam replied simply. He pulled himself back up to the airlock, then helped Amelia scramble off the curved tunnel. They withdrew into the gangway and waited.

The Sectoid who had greeted Liam leaped up to the airlock with frightening speed. It stepped forward gingerly, antennas tapping at the air. In the full light Liam could now make out the natural armor of its carapace over torso, abdomen, and thorax. Beneath its antennas there were two small eyes mounted on the sides of the head. Its pincers extended from the sides of its mouth, which opened and closed as it tasted the new air.

Sky backed carefully along the gangway, her hands resting near her pistols and her eyes never leaving the alien. Liam sent Virtue first, then motioned to the Sectoid to follow him, in what he hoped was a friendly gesture. The brown bug hopped up into the gangway, followed by another black guard.

Moving through the ship, Liam saw the expressions of fear and disgust on his sailors' faces, and he motioned to each one of them to stay calm. The tapping of Sectoid feet behind him was enough to send chills down his spine, but he forced himself to walk at a leisurely pace, ascend the ladder, and step clear. The hatch was too small for the Sectoids to simply jump through, and Liam heard gasps behind him on the bridge as first the long arms appeared, fingers pressing down on the deck, then the antennas, the head, and the rest of the body. Liam knew there were plenty of weapons ready to unleash if anything went wrong and he turned his attention away from the spectacle, moving forward to the command chair.

Riverton sat rigidly in her chair, body straight but head resting back. She was wearing her dress uniform, long blue coat with gold trim wrapped tightly around her. A pillow was wedged in the seat next to her, not so much for support as to hide the bloodstains that hadn't yet been cleaned. Her dark complexion had regained some of its color, but her eyes were still glassy. She blinked several times and focused her gaze on the emerging Sectoids, taking long, deep breaths.

Templegrey stood next to the command chair. Liam moved to her side.

"How's she doing?"

"Stabilized, but a patient should be sleeping after surgery—not conducting interstellar diplomacy."

"If we'd stalled any longer, it apparently would have been suspicious."

"This better not take long, then."

Liam cast a glance up at his captain, who was forcing a smile across her taut features as she faced their guests.

The three Sectoids were on the bridge, the smaller brown flanked by the blacks. Sky, Swift, and four other armed sailors had climbed up behind them. The Humans all kept a respectful distance, but there was no hiding the fact that the three aliens were surrounded.

"Welcome, Speaker," Riverton said loudly. Her translator converted the words into snaps and clicks. "It is good to see you again."

The brown Sectoid stepped forward, head turning left and right as it approached the command chair. Riverton gripped her armrests and gently lowered her face toward the antennas that reached up. She accepted the light touches serenely, then straightened back against her seat again. A wince flashed across her face, accompanied by a soft, quick grunt of pain.

"It is good to feel you, Sophia Riverton," the brown replied through the translator. "It has been a long time."

"I hope the Queen is healthy."

"She is. I hope the Emperor is healthy."

"He is."

"Thank you for your messages. Your species does not often communicate with ours in this region."

"There are many uncertainties."

"Many dangers."

"Have you been in a ship for a long time?"

"No. Almost a Human year. Since the first pirate attack on our kind."

Liam glanced at Templegrey in surprise. From everything they knew about this alien race, it was impossible for a Sectoid to lie. They simply didn't know how.

"I am sorry," Riverton said. "The pirates do not represent the Human species."

"We know. They are anarchists."

That was a supreme insult from a Sectoid, Liam guessed.

"Are there Sectoids among the pirates?"

"No." The pincers vibrated for a moment, then sounded again. "There may be prisoners."

"The pirates have used Sectoid acid against us."

Both black aliens tapped their feet at this. The brown stomped its own feet and the blacks stilled.

"The pirates are extracting our venom," the brown said. "That is very bad."

"Extracting the venom from prisoners?"

"My species cannot survive the extraction of venom."

Riverton nodded, her cheeks paling. She slumped for just a moment, then straightened.

"My ship is trying to stop the pirates," she said with new determination.

"We guessed that this is so. We would do it but we cannot find their base."

"We know where their base is."

Both black bugs started tapping their legs at the same time. The brown tapped back.

"We want to know this," it said finally.

"I will tell you, but I need something from you in return. Oxygen and water."

"We can provide this."

Liam watched the range of expressions flash across his crew: surprise, relief, distrust.

"The pirates have many ships," Riverton said. "It will be difficult to get past them to attack the base."

"We are prepared for many losses," the brown replied, "if it will end this threat."

"My ship is going to attack the pirate base," Riverton declared.

The brown paused, head shifting from side to side.

"But how can a ship this small do such a mission?"

Riverton stole a look down to Liam. He nodded.

"I think, Speaker, that we can do it together," she said.

There was a rustle around the bridge as sailors reacted to the incredible suggestion. Liam took a single step forward, glaring in each direction for silence.

The brown Sectoid turned its head left and right, antennas testing the air.

"Because it is you speaking, Sophia Riverton," it said finally, "I will listen."

———

LIAM LEANED AGAINST THE DOOR OF THE STORES office, unable to keep a smile off his face as Amelia regaled him with her visit into the Sectoid ship. Long past any fear, she had obviously been fascinated by the alienness of everything on board, and her face was alive with excitement as she spoke.

"And their water tanks! They hang down from the deckhead in these great bulbs that swing with the motion of the ship. The purity sensors are up at the very top, where the pipes punch through into the deckhead, and I had to ride one of our hosts up to check them."

Liam couldn't contain a revolted shiver at the thought. "You *rode* one of them? Were you drunk?"

"On that air, probably. They use these cargo harnesses to carry stuff around inside the ship, so I just tied myself into one and rode along."

"Right up the wall?"

"Up the wall, onto the ceiling."

"You were upside down?"

"Twenty paces above the deck. I don't know how they can grip like that, especially with my weight strapped on."

Liam smirked, and glanced around to ensure no one was nearby. He stepped in and placed his hands affectionately on her waist.

"You're light as a feather. I'm sure your host didn't even notice."

"You're a wonderful liar." She gave him a quick kiss on the cheek before stepping away and sitting down. "But before you dazzle me with your wit and charm, I have a neat idea."

"Tell me."

"Sails and I were examining the Sectoid boats, but they're too big to attach to *Daring* for our assault."

"Yes, Swift already briefed me on that. It's a shame—I still don't know how we're going to get to the surface of the comet."

"I realized," she said, spinning in her chair with excitement, "that we already have large, detachable, self-contained vessels connected to *Daring*."

He thought for a moment. "The external cargo containers?" he offered uncertainly.

"Yes!" Her face lit up triumphantly. "They're airtight, they have their own power, their own airlocks, and they even have their own maneuvering thrusters. I wouldn't trust those thrusters to get me down to a planet . . . but to a comet with tiny gravity they might just do."

He crossed his arms. "Are you suggesting we land our assault team on the pirate world in a cargo container?"

"Call it an attack barge," she suggested. "We have spare boat sensors in stores which could be bolted on to give the pilot some degree of control."

"And you think that would be safe?"

"All it has to do is get us down from *Daring* to the surface." She shrugged. "Hey, I'll be in it too, so I'll make sure it's safe."

It was a crazy idea, he knew, but . . . not without merit. And this entire mission had already dived deep into the realm of absurd.

"Talk to Swift and Sky," he said. "And tell them you have my full support."

"Thank you, sir."

"And, Amelia, when we get home I'm taking you to a grand ball."

She wrinkled her nose at him. "That's very kind, sir, but you know I can't dance."

"Can't, or just never learned how?"

"It wasn't a skill I needed much growing up."

"Well then"—he leaned closer to her—"I'll just have to teach you in private before we go."

"Now *that* sounds like fun," she said, and something in her gaze made his breath catch.

As he stepped back into the main passageway he felt a spring in his step, and he couldn't contain his grin. Those sailors he passed clearly noticed, and as they knuckled their foreheads he even saw a few smiles in return.

He climbed the ladders to the bridge, where Templegrey had the watch. She strolled back and forth along her console, fingers running along the screens. At his approach she glanced up long enough to meet his eye, but quickly looked down again.

"Good afternoon, Dr. Templegrey," he said, forcing himself to climb into the captain's chair.

It was a very comfortable seat, but never once did he enjoy sitting in it. It was still Riverton's chair, even if she had passed acting command to him.

"Good afternoon, sir," she responded. "Water replenishment is nearly complete—we're on the final tank and it's at fifty-three percent full."

Movement caught his peripheral, out beyond the canopy. He instinctively reached for a telescope and peered outward. His view of the stars was suddenly filled with a dark mass of limbs, very close. He snapped down the telescope, spotting the black form of a Sectoid scuttling across the top of the hull. It was encased in a dark space suit that left its legs exposed. Its long arms were sheathed, but multiple fingers pushed through a flexible membrane to grip tools.

"And hull repairs?" he asked.

"Proceeding well," she said, determinedly not looking

up. "I hope they've finished their work before my next watch."

The ability of the bugs to move easily in both zero-gravity and a vacuum was astonishing, but it also meant that serious work to repair *Daring*'s many cracks could be done here in deep space. The sight of Sectoids crawling over his ship still made Liam tense, but these past five days had shown nothing but honesty and goodwill from the alien race. *Daring* was restocked with air and water, and her hull was being prepped for battle. The Sectoids had also offered food supplies, but even Amelia hadn't been tempted to bring aboard such revolting fare.

"How was the captain, when last you checked on her?"

"Resting, thankfully, and getting stronger because of it." She gave Liam an appraising smile. "Knowing that you're in charge has certainly helped her let go of her responsibilities."

"It's just for a few more days," he said quickly. "The captain will be back in this chair in no time."

"I think I'll be the judge of that," Templegrey said with a raised eyebrow. "We need her healthy, and that requires rest."

"We need her here," Liam said, pointing at his seat. "We need the crew to see her, and to know that she's in control of this crazy alliance with the Sectoids."

"There are mutterings," she admitted. "I haven't heard much support for your stated reason of why the captain destroyed *Bluebird*."

"To put any Sectoid prisoners on board out of their misery? I think it was a necessary decision, now that I understand it."

She shrugged. "Prejudice runs deep, I guess."

"I guess so."

Templegrey moved closer, glancing forward to ensure the bridge crew was out of earshot.

"I'm embarrassed about young Highcastle," she whispered. "His despicable actions bring dishonor to the Navy, and to his family."

"I quite agree." He watched Templegrey for a moment, knowing there was more she wanted to say.

"What's going to happen to him?" she finally asked.

"That's for the Navy to decide." If it was Liam's decision, the blaggard would hang, but he knew enough about the politics of the great houses to guess that a less permanent punishment would be meted out.

"I had nothing to do with it," she said suddenly. "He never told me anything about his plans."

Her admission surprised Liam—there was no evidence to suggest any involvement by her. Even Amelia and the two sailors had really just been dragged along unwittingly. So why did Templegrey feel the need to say that?

"Not to worry, Dr. Templegrey," he said. "You're not under suspicion. The young fool acted rashly and alone."

Relief flashed across her features. She nodded her thanks and returned to her station.

Liam cycled through the various reports available on the command displays, bringing himself up-to-date on all aspects of ship operations. Suitably informed, he climbed down from the command chair and headed aft.

At his knock on her cabin door, Riverton bid him enter. He slipped through into the darkened space, seeing her in her usual seat at the dining table. He had been giving her as much space as he could, but they had arranged for one regular meeting each day in the afternoon.

A yellow shawl covered the shoulders of her uniform

shirt, and her long, black hair fell loosely over the silk. She was leaning forward on her forearms, but her posture was more upright than it had been yesterday. Her dark eyes regarded him with much of their old strength, no longer clouded by pain.

"XO," she greeted him with the hint of a smile. "Please sit down."

"Captain," he said, taking the chair across from her. "Operations are proceeding well."

He gave her a brief on all aspects of the ship, answering her few questions. The update took barely five minutes, but he sensed that she was in no hurry for him to leave.

"Is there anything I can do for you, ma'am?"

"You're doing an excellent job," she said. "Simply accept my thanks."

"I'm merely preparing the ship for your return to full duty—which I suspect will be very soon. You're looking much better today, ma'am."

"I'm feeling better, no doubt thanks to Dr. Templegrey's efforts."

"The doctor would appreciate hearing that, I think," he said, then relayed his recent conversation on the bridge.

"She knows that we consider her and Highcastle to be close." Riverton sighed. "They know each other through their family connections."

"But that's completely unconnected to her performance in this ship."

"Yes, but the high nobility don't make that distinction. In their world, family connections count for everything. Ava is worried that we're going to lump her in with that little traitor through mere association." At Liam's silence, Riverton offered a smile. "I don't intend to do that."

"Ava is a loyal, competent officer," Liam said, feeling an unexpected flash of relief. "I assess she had no hand in Highcastle's scheme."

"I agree. And I notice you've pressed no charges against the three sailors he brought with him to the bridge."

"Petty Officer Virtue was simply caught up in events," he said quickly. "To her credit, she's the one who called me to the bridge."

"No, I'm not worried about her." Her eyebrow arched slightly. "Don't worry."

"The coxn has interviewed Flatrock and Hedge, as have I. It's our opinion that they were both merely caught up in Highcastle's populist charm and hoped that he might make their lives easier. They saw in him a champion for the common sailor—but they never expected him to attempt mutiny. I saw it in their faces when Highcastle made his declaration, and neither of them moved to help him in the moment of crisis."

"To think a spoiled, selfish, wealthy toff could be seen as a champion of the common person," Riverton scoffed. "Ridiculous."

"It's interesting how some people perceive things," Liam replied. "When considering either a noble or an officer, they often just follow whoever they personally like best."

"As both a noble and an officer," Riverton said, leaning back and folding her arms, "I've never sought popularity. It's best to lead through competence."

"As a noble and an officer, I agree," Liam said carefully. He stared across the table at her for a long moment, then forced himself to continue. "But as a captain, one is held to a higher standard. A captain has to do more than lead—a captain has to inspire."

The silence in the cabin stretched on. Riverton's dark gaze was unchanging. Liam felt the heat rising under his uniform.

"So, you are saying," she said finally, "that I do not inspire the crew."

"You have their loyalty, absolutely. They will follow you into the Abyss and back."

"But they will do so out of duty to the Emperor, not to me."

Liam tried to judge her expression, but it was as inscrutable as ever.

"You are seen as . . . a distant figure, ma'am. The crew don't know you, nor what to make of you."

"A certain distance between a commander and her crew is valuable, I would think."

"Yes, ma'am. But ideally there is a connection despite that distance. It's always a fine balance, as you know. Highcastle took it too far one way."

"And I take it too far the other?"

"It is not for me to tell my captain how to command her ship."

She laughed out loud, her entire face brightening. "And yet, you have just done precisely that."

"The crew is loyal," he reemphasized, "but there is also a lot of talk. Everyone knows about the attempted mutiny, and your wounding; such events always shake a crew. Your absence from view these past few days, while necessary, has unfortunately not helped matters. I've heard reports that some of the crew are openly wondering if you're even still alive."

"What?" Riverton seemed appalled by his words.

"There was a rumor floating around—which we have quashed—that you'd died from your wounds and we're just pretending you're still alive to keep the Sectoids from attacking us."

Riverton considered this in silence.

"And I suppose," she said finally, "that to the crew I am hardly martyr material."

"I would recommend, ma'am, that as soon as you feel up to it, you do an informal tour of the ship. Perhaps when Templegrey is off watch so that she can accompany you. She is popular with the crew and can handle any situation."

"No, if I walk around with an attendant doctor, it will only fuel rumors about my health." She thought for a moment. "Arrange for Virtue to accompany me. She has a common touch, and if I'm seen touring the ship with one of the so-called mutineers, it will send a strong message that no grudges are being held."

"An excellent suggestion, ma'am," Liam said with real sincerity.

"Please don't sound so surprised," she said with a new smile. "I was in the diplomatic corps, after all."

"Yes, ma'am."

"And on that," she said suddenly. "Has anyone other than you been communicating with the Sectoids?"

"Only senior staff, in the course of their duties. Virtue for stores, Swift for engineering."

"Communicating effectively with the other races takes a very specific skill," she said. "Speech must be simple and clear—no nuances, no hidden meanings."

"Yes, ma'am." Liam had no criticism to offer of Riverton's diplomatic skills, especially now that he fully understood everything she'd been doing in the background while still commanding this mission. All those secret meetings ashore, feeding vital intelligence about the pirates to build the case to the Emperor that the Sectoids were *not* the enemy everyone assumed they were. Trying to find evidence that the Sectoids were interested in exactly the same things as the Navy—stopping the pirates and protecting their own people.

No regular Navy officer, Liam included, would have ever dreamed of pursuing such a theory. But Sophia Riverton, diplomat and captain, had supposed the unthinkable and gone on to prove it.

"I'll reiterate your instructions, ma'am."

"Diplomacy with the other races is a very different game from diplomacy between our Human worlds and noble houses." She nodded thoughtfully to herself, then eyed Liam. "I suppose I have to work harder at dealing with Humans. In many ways we're more complicated than any of the other races."

"You were obviously an exceptional diplomat, ma'am," Liam said, gesturing vaguely toward where they both knew the Sectoid ship loomed nearby. "We would never be here were you not."

"Yes. But now I need to become a better captain." She looked squarely at Liam. "And I've had an exceptional example to emulate."

He sat back, truly surprised.

"Thank you, ma'am."

CHAPTER 21

The view from the bridge was very dark. One half of the sky was clearly visible, with thousands of distant pin-pricks of starlight heading out into the Abyss. But the other half of the sky—the one where the reassuring glow of the Hub should have been—was nothing but a black wall of Sectoid ship. At this range the hulking vessel easily blocked the light from the millions of stars, casting *Daring* into a deep shadow.

Which was perfect, Liam thought, checking the range to the comet high above them. This was the second distant orbit the two ships had made of the pirate base, and no doubt pirate observers would by now have noticed the giant bug ship moving over them. But no one would be able to spot the tiny Human ship hidden in the shadow. It had taken some skilled sailing to maintain this station on the Sectoid vessel through two huge orbits, and Liam was proud of his crew.

"We're approaching the edge of our sector, sir," Brown reported. "I'll be coming left to open and fall back."

"Very well," Liam replied. Years of habit forced him to check his own display to confirm Brown's assessment, but as always, the young sublieutenant was right. She had taken over the watch from Templegrey thirty minutes ago, and she would likely not move from her station for the next half day. Liam couldn't think of a better person to entrust the ship to.

The view through the canopy shifted as *Daring* steered to port and fell slowly back in relation to the Sectoid ship, dropping deep into the shadow once more.

He pulled out his telescope and scanned the distant comet again. So this was the dark star they'd been hunting. The pirate base was clearly visible as a white scar on the dark surface where structures had been dug in and had displaced the thin surface of black dust. Careful observations had revealed at least four ships in low orbit with short sails.

On the first pass Liam had reported *Daring*'s discoveries to the Sectoid ship and asked for confirmation, but the response had been simply an acknowledgment. Then a question asking how *Daring* could detect such things. It was an interesting bit of intelligence on how limited the Sectoids' visual sensors were.

But on this second orbit, the Sectoids had launched a pair of drone ships to half the distance. They had reported four heat sources on the surface that appeared separate from the main base, strongly indicating four more ships docked. Nothing *Daring* had on board could have detected those ships, and any smugness Liam might have felt at his race's superior eyesight was dashed.

"Signal from the Sectoid," called one of the crewmen from his station. "They are starting their descent to the comet."

"Send acknowledgment," Liam replied. "Ms. Brown, maintain station for the descent."

"Estimate one hour until breakaway," she reported.

Both ships were moving out of sight of the pirate base, but unlike the previous orbit, where they maintained their distance, now they were sailing inward to close the comet. Across the blind side of this little world, the new allies would separate and commence their individual attacks.

It was time to inform the captain and start final preparations. He reached for his comms panel.

"Summon the crew to the bridge," said a new voice behind him.

He turned. Riverton was in her full uniform, taking slow but steady strides across the bridge. Liam smiled, amazed at the uncanny ability of a good ship's captain to know instinctively when to go to the bridge.

As Brown repeated the order to gather all hands, Liam climbed down from the command chair, offering Riverton his hand to help her up. Surprisingly, she took it.

"How are you feeling, ma'am?" he asked.

"How do I look?" she replied simply.

In her full uniform she cut an impressive figure, and with only her face and hands visible, the pale undertone of her dark skin was barely noticeable. Her eyes were as bright as ever.

"Like a captain who is in command," he said.

The crew was mustering in the open deck behind the officer-of-the-watch station, all eyes on Riverton. No one spoke as more sailors climbed up the ladder and joined the crowd. Soon all but the barest skeleton crew in propulsion were gathered. Liam couldn't help but seek out Amelia's smiling face, and while nothing more than a glance passed between them, he felt his spirits lift.

Riverton turned her chair to face the crew. She sat straight, knees together and hands on armrests.

"Men and women of His Majesty's Sailing Ship *Daring*," she said, her voice carrying easily across the entire bridge, "this is a great day. Today we will achieve what no one else has been able to do. Our own Navy couldn't do it." She gestured at the hulking Sectoid ship. "The other races couldn't do it. Only we, the men and women of *Daring,* were able to find this base. And now we are going to capture it, and take the spoils of war."

A few nods and approving glances rippled through the crew.

"Our plan is unorthodox," Riverton continued, "but I think you're all used to that by now. We will outsmart the pirates and, when the time comes, outfight them. We will take back what they have stolen, and we will make it clear to all in this sector of space what happens when you challenge His Majesty's rule of law. We will reassert the authority of our Empire and bring honor both to ourselves and to our ship."

More nods, and even a few smiles.

"This is our time, to prove what we are really made of. Everything we have worked for has led us to this and— despite what one former member of this crew said—this is exactly where I intended us to be." She pointed up at the distant comet.

Her words brought new determination, Liam could see, and even relief on a few faces.

"All past differences are behind us," she declared, "and all doubts are gone. We are one crew, with one purpose, and this is our moment to prove to all who we really are.

"We must be brave. We must be bold." She smiled. "We must be *Daring*."

A roar of laughter filled the bridge, followed by a ragged cheer.

With a nod from Riverton, Liam stepped forward.

"We're an hour from deployment," he called out over the hubbub. "Propulsors, man your masts. Gunners, ready your broadside. Everyone else, prepare the attack barge. Let's get ready to give them a surprise!"

SWIFT HAD MANAGED TO RIG A COLLECTION OF SENsors from the boat stores, but Liam felt uncomfortably blind as he hung on to the back of the single seat. The boat coxn, Master Rating Faith, was hooked into the seat, thruster controls mounted on both sides. His hands hovered over those controls, his eyes glued to the basic information being fed from the sensors lashed to the barge's outer hull.

Liam watched the numbers count down as the barge started to get a solid return on the surface of the comet below. The rate of descent was within the mission parameters, but lacking his usual instruments, Liam felt like the numbers were flashing by awfully quickly.

"Approaching drop point," came Brown's scratchy voice over the circuit.

Faith glanced up at Liam, nodding with determination.

"Ready to release," Liam replied.

The barge shook as *Daring* released all clamps. Liam swiveled the camera mounted forward and saw the bulk of the frigate emerging into view as Faith nudged his thrusters to clear the ship's hull. The barge had been connected on the ship's starboard quarter, and as *Daring* receded the bright glow of her sails was clearly visible.

"We're pulling up to begin covering fire," Brown reported. *"Good luck."*

Daring soared upward in the field of view as the barge continued to drop. Liam rechecked the altitude. Another few seconds of free fall.

All around him, the walls of the converted cargo container were covered by crewmembers in space suits, held tight against the metal by their webbing. In the dim light it looked like his sailors were victims of an attack by giant spiders, and with so much time spent recently with Sectoids, the image was truly unsettling. He shook it off and focused again on the sensor readings.

Faith gripped his thruster controls, easing them open. The deceleration was gentle at first, just a pressure against the deck, but the altitude was still dropping fast and the boat coxn didn't waste time in pushing the thrusters to full. The barge shuddered against the force. Liam turned the camera to look ahead, spying the white scar of the pirate base against the comet's surface. There was only one ship still docked, the rest having already sailed to defend against the Sectoids high overhead. Then the view disappeared as the barge dropped behind a ridge.

The thrusters roared. New rattling shook the hull as dust and debris from the comet's surface blasted up and bathed the barge in a dirty snowstorm. With a thump, the barge touched down. The thrusters went silent.

As his assault team disengaged from their webbing, Liam panned the camera across the dark landscape. Seeing no movement, he lumbered forward in his space suit to the forward airlock. He peered out through the window, scanning as best he could. Sky joined him moments later.

"Clear as far as I can tell, Chief," he said.

"Unless they're waiting right outside, sir, they can't hit us—pistols don't work in a vacuum."

"Teams of four through the airlock, then."

The rest of the sailors had assembled behind them. Swift had been assigned to the assault team, bringing its total to sixteen, divided into teams of four led by Liam, Amelia, Sky, and Swift. Flatrock and Hedge were both back to full duty, but they were separated today. Liam was keeping Flatrock close, and Sky had Hedge.

"Remember," Liam said, "chaos is our friend today. Do as much early damage as you can to their outbuildings—try to make it look as if we're much bigger than we are. And keep moving. Don't let them pin you down. If you have to retreat to get clear, do so, then reapproach from another direction. Between our four teams and *Daring*'s top cover, those pirates should be running confused and scared."

Sky's team went through the airlock first. As soon as the outer door opened they fanned out, swords drawn, then bounded for cover, skipping across the dusty surface in the minimal gravity. Swift's team was next, followed by Amelia's. As the airlock repressurized for a final time, Liam glanced back at his one-man boat's crew. Faith was still seated at his controls, weapons on his belt.

"Keep the thrusters warm," Liam said. "You're our only way out of here."

"Good luck, sir," Faith said with a knuckle to the forehead.

"And to you."

The inner airlock door opened and Liam led his team in. Flatrock, the medic Song, and his old bowsman Hunter crowded close in their heavy space suits. They all wore armor underneath, with swords and pistols strapped to their outer belts, as well as grenades stuffed with compressed air and the same black powder that the ship's cannons used. Flatrock carried a small battering ram, Hunter an electronics tool kit, and Song a medical pack.

Helmet visors snapped down. Liam waited until the air was pumped out, then activated the outer door. He stepped out of the barge's gravity, testing his footing against the alien surface. There was ice everywhere around the barge, melted by the thrusters and then flash-frozen again in the frigid vacuum. He pushed off from the barge's side, sailing forward several paces before touching down amid a small cloud of dust. Looking back, he saw that his team was moving to follow him. He hand-gestured for the other teams to advance. Sky began to ascend the ridge in front of them. Amelia headed to the left and Swift to the far right.

Liam started up the ridge.

IT TOOK SEVERAL PACES TO GET COMFORTABLE moving, but Amelia finally settled into a long, bounding stride that kept her low. A big risk on a world this small was jumping too high and never coming down again. All around her, she saw her team bumbling forward unevenly as each sailor found his or her rhythm.

She slowed as the ridge top approached, eventually dropping to a crawl as she eased up to the lip of the hill. Beyond was the sprawl of the pirate base. There were half a dozen buildings scattered around the brilliant white surface and two large docks that extended up in space. The last ship was just thrustering free of her mooring. The dock structure plunged down into the comet's surface, and Sectoid thermal scans had indicated that the pirates had built a subterranean network. A single, massive crater cut through the open space between surface buildings—

an opening shot by the Sectoids to start this battle and draw the fire.

High above, the flashes of cannon fire were clearly visible against the stars. The giant Sectoid hull was ringed with sails, and smaller vessels were harrying it on all sides. The last pirate ship was intending to join that fight, but it would never get the chance.

Over a ridge to Amelia's left, the magnificent sight of *Daring* under full sail hove into view. The flash of a missile streaked away from her hull. Seconds later the pirate ship erupted into flame, crashing against her dock and tearing apart. Half her hull tumbled slowly down to pound the icy surface in a plume of dust, while the other half wrapped around the dock and disintegrated. Clouds of debris rained down across the base in a silent, slow-motion whirlwind of destruction. *Daring* unsheeted the port mast and began retracting it, steering a high, circular course to bring her cannon to bear.

"All teams advance," Liam barked over the radio. *"Cause maximum damage to the outbuildings and then get into the base to press the attack. Unleash chaos!"*

Amelia gestured her own sailors forward. As *Daring* circled overhead, cannon fire raining down on the central docks, Amelia and her team bounded for the first surface building. It was a square metal box with no windows, but a locked set of double doors. No airlock. Able Rating Fence, her biggest sailor, hefted his battering ram and pounded at the doors. On the third strike the doors buckled inward. Amelia glanced in. The dark space was piled high with barrels of fuel for surface vehicles. Certainly useful for long-term pirate operations, but worth little on the open market.

She hefted one of her grenades and each of her sailors followed suit. They pulled the pins, threw the grenades through the broken doors, and bounded away. With no atmosphere, there was no sound or shock wave, but Amelia saw the snow at her feet suddenly glow orange as the grenades detonated and greedily consumed as much fuel as they could before their air ran out. She slowed to pause behind an icy outcrop and glanced back. The base of the fuel building was a blackened shard, and a metal rain of roof fragments and unexploded barrels was drifting down all around.

A FLASH OF FIRE TO HIS LEFT CAUGHT LIAM'S EYE. An outbuilding was disintegrating in an explosive halo of debris. He smiled. Amelia and her team were making their presence known. His smile faded, though, as he saw new flashes on the landscape. Small but steady, these bursts of fire pointed upward: cannon fire. He looked up to where *Daring* was still circling, focusing her broadsides on the central docks. Even as Liam watched he saw the puffs of impact on her hull as the pirate guns struck home.

His team had gathered around him and he quickly surveyed the landscape. The nearest battery of surface cannon was directly ahead, a short dash across an open field of snow.

"All teams, this is the XO," he signaled, "priority target the surface cannons."

He peeked out from behind the outcrop, assessing the target. The battery was dug into the surface, the four cannon barrels pointing upward. Each one fired individually, taking an average of thirty seconds between shots. He motioned his team forward. They bounded across the open snow, each stride lifting Liam high enough to get a glimpse of the battery top. It was a transparent surface with flexible seals around each cannon to allow some freedom of aiming. Each cannon fired once in the time it took to close the distance. Liam slowed his approach, skidding along the slippery surface to finally stop within an easy throw of the battery. He lobbed a single grenade. It landed on the transparent surface, rolled backward, then detonated. As the flash cleared Liam saw that the battery surface was scarred but still intact. He frowned, judging whether another grenade would do enough damage.

"Sir," Flatrock signaled, "I have an idea. I'm going in."

Flatrock trotted forward carefully, a grenade in his hand. He reached the battery surface, shuffling right out on top of it. He was completely exposed to the pirates below, but Liam suddenly realized that there was nothing they could do to stop him as long as he avoided the barrels. Flatrock inched forward, pausing. Then, just after the nearest cannon fired, he lunged forward and dropped his grenade down the exposed barrel. He pushed himself off and sailed clear of the battery, touching down in the snow in a tuft of crystals.

Liam was already advancing, Hunter and Song at his flanks. He saw the fire of a full explosion in atmosphere beneath the transparent surface, followed by another. By the time he slid to a stop and crawled to the lip of the battery, there was nothing visible beneath but thick smoke. The cannons had stopped firing. He signaled the ingenious tactic to the other teams, then scanned the terrain for their next target.

Up ahead was a small but heavily reinforced shack. One side of it sloped down and the other was perfectly upright. A patch of ground had been cleared and leveled on the upright side. Liam approached and his suspicions were quickly confirmed—this was an airlock leading down into the main base.

"All teams, this is the XO," he signaled. "I am starting my assault into the base itself."

AMELIA STEADIED HERSELF IN FRONT OF THE AIR-lock door and tried the controls. Unsurprisingly, they were locked. She motioned Able Rating Green forward with his tool kit; he pulled out a small encryption pad and plugged it into the airlock controls. His movements were clumsy in the thick space-suit gloves, but he carefully tapped in commands and his pad started its work.

Amelia kept watch on the surrounding battlefield. One of the two towering docks was tipping dangerously under the constant barrage of *Daring*'s cannon fire and flashes from a single gun emplacement on the far side of the base still peppered the frigate as she circled overhead. She saw movement to her right, but recognized the suited figures of Liam and his team as they advanced toward another airlock more than a hundred paces away. She pulled out the rough map created by the Sectoid thermal scans. Everything in the subterranean base appeared to be inter-connected, so whichever airlock the teams used to gain entry should allow for an eventual meet-up. But it was going to be a lot of guesswork. Chaos was their friend today, she reminded herself.

Green tapped her suit, indicating that the airlock was depressurizing and would open in moments. He stuffed his encryption pad back into the tool kit and drew his sword. The outer door opened and he led them into the tight space. Stairs descended along a narrow tube as nor-mal gravity slowly took hold, and they paused at another door. This one was unlocked and opened into a long metal passageway, wide enough for two abreast, stretching away to a distant set of doors. Lanterns rested at ten-pace intervals, casting stark white light to combat the heavy shadows. Crates and barrels lined one wall.

Amelia lifted her faceplate, wincing at the cold. It was uncomfortable, but not dangerous—and there was plenty of air. She moved up to Green's side and pointed her cutlass toward the distant doors.

"They might be waiting for us," she said. "Be ready for an ambush."

LIAM AND HIS TEAM HUSTLED DOWN THE PASSAGE-way, feeling the extra bulk of their space suits in the full gravity. Reaching a set of doors, they paused long enough to test them, then, at a nod from Liam, threw them open.

The passageway beyond was much the same, only with more light and fewer stores. It stretched away to the left and right, with occasional doors cut into the walls. Liam saw movement to the left—three Humans and a Theropod. They were armed and armored, and their expressions of shock upon seeing him quickly twisted into anger. They charged forward.

Liam returned the charge, Hunter at his side with the others close behind. One of the Human pirates closed in on him, longsword already raised for a deadly swing. Liam raised his saber for a parry as he thundered forward. He watched the pirate's arms tense, then, just as the longsword began to sweep down, Liam dropped to a slide and stabbed upward. His saber drove up into the pirate's body. Flatrock's cutlass followed through above, the force of his charge knocking the pirate backward. The Theropod behind him staggered under the deadweight and Liam slashed out from below, slicing the brute's foot off at the ankle before swinging again at the next Human target.

The Theropod screeched in pain, hopping backward on one foot as blood poured across the floor. It turned as if to flee, but then swung with its tailsword. Liam staggered back as he blocked the huge blade. He thumped against the wall and struggled to gain his footing. The brute's sword pressed against him, pinning him in place. Small reptilian hands reached into a belt pouch and pulled out an acid bomb. Liam struggled to back away but the force of the tailsword held him fast. Both his hands pushed on his saber to hold the blade clear of cutting his space suit.

The brute raised the acid bomb with a hiss.

Liam shifted his weight to one leg, lifting the other to kick at the Theropod's only functional knee. With a crack the joint snapped sideways. The brute toppled backward, desperately juggling the acid bomb as he fell. The bomb gently hit the floor and rolled away. Liam stepped forward, slashing down at the base of the tail. He stabbed again and the brute collapsed.

Raising his saber, he turned back to the battle, just as Flatrock buried his blade into the final pirate. Liam scanned the passageway in both directions, then quickly examined his sailors' suits. There were no obvious gashes.

"Everybody okay?" he asked.

Amid the gasping for breath, he received three affirmatives. He activated his headset.

"Assault, XO: What's your status?"

"In the base," Sky replied, *"and seeking targets."*

"Propulsion, XO: What's your status?"

"Topside," came Swift's scratchy response, *"making our way to the last cannon emplacement."*

"Quartermaster, XO: What's your status?"

There was no response. Liam repeated his query.

"Inside," Amelia finally answered, voice curt. *"Heavy resistance!"*

Liam tensed—he had to help her. Quickly visualizing where he was in the base, he recalled that her team had been to his left. They had to be somewhere ahead down this passageway.

"Remain defensive," he said. "We're coming to you."

He motioned his sailors into a run. Four sets of heavy footfalls thumped along the passageway as they abandoned any attempt at stealth. Liam drew one of his pistols, scanning each closed doorway they passed. Many were blue and marked with names, suggesting this was a barracks area, but they passed two black doors and one heavy red one with danger markings on it—an airlock.

They reached a T-junction, pausing long enough to peek around both corners and assess their position. The right passageway extended for a hundred paces, the left for only ten before turning again to the right. Liam turned left.

From around the corner ahead a Theropod face popped out then retracted. Liam sensed a trap but knew they couldn't back away. He burst into a sprint, seeing a reptilian hand emerge long enough to lob an acid bomb. It sailed harmlessly past his running sailors, splattering down just behind them in an awful hiss. He skidded around the corner as he raised his pistol. Half a dozen pirates swung into view, poised to strike. He emptied his magazine into them and charged forward, swinging. The first three had collapsed under his hail of bullets, but the others were unafraid as they raised their blades.

Liam met the first strike high, parrying the sword to

the right and smashing the butt of his pistol into the pirate's face. It was enough to stagger the man back. Liam flicked his saber into an uppercut and slashed the pirate across the chest. Flatrock pressed forward, engaging the next pirate. Liam stepped back from the fray.

"Quartermaster, XO," he signaled. "What's your status?"

"Joy and Green are down," she gasped. *"Fence and I are retreating to the airlock."*

"Get topside," he ordered. "They can't follow you there."

"Yes, sir!"

Flatrock, Hunter, and Song were pressing the pirates back, but Liam could see more on the way, funneling down the passageway from what looked like a large, central space. Beyond, he just caught a glimpse of pirates running by in space suits. He pursed his lips in grim assessment of the situation. His team of four would never be able to fight through to Amelia.

But there was an airlock not thirty paces back.

Song dropped the last of the nearest pirates. The next group was still ten paces away, advancing hungrily with swords up.

"Withdraw," he ordered his sailors as he unhooked his last grenade and threw it over their heads into the middle of the attacking pack.

He ran back around the corner, his sailors close on his heels. The blast from the grenade rocked the entire passageway. Shrapnel clanged against the wall behind him and a rush of hot air knocked him forward. He staggered but kept his feet as he ducked down the passageway to the right, retracing his steps until he found the red door.

It opened at his command and he motioned his sailors up the steep stairs. He stepped through, shut the door, and started the depressurization process. Moving under his full weight of armor and space suit was exhausting, and it was blessed relief as he stepped through the outer airlock and back into the comet's natural gravity.

Song did a rapid check of everyone's space suits, slapping down several adhesive patches where blade strikes had cut through the outer layers. Flatrock's suit had taken the most damage, but it would hold together for now.

Liam paused while his eyes adjusted to the ghostly light of the surface again. One of the docks had collapsed down in a twisted, blackened heap and *Daring* was still circling, broadsides tearing up the surface of the comet as Riverton targeted the main power generators. Looking down the slope, Liam could see the airlock where he and his team had first entered, but the way to Amelia was hidden behind a ridge of dirty ice. He bounded up to the edge, looking down to where another small outbuilding suggested where Amelia's escape route would be. It was deep down in a flat-bottomed basin. The landscape between rolled with icy formations that looked like a flash-frozen sea, with some outcrops five times the height of a man. It was going to be tough going.

"We have to get to that airlock," he told his sailors, pointing at the outbuilding. "Let's go."

AMELIA BACKED UP ANOTHER STAIR, STABBING HER sword over Fence's shoulder. The big sailor had done well against half a dozen attackers, but he was clearly exhausted. His blade did nothing but parry attacks now. She stabbed again, catching the pirate in the ear. He stumbled back, losing his footing on the narrow steps and tumbling down into his compatriots, who were still surging up the airlock.

"Let's go!" Amelia said, grabbing Fence by the shoulder.

She turned and ran up the last few steps, punching the switches to open the airlock. The panel flashed red at her, refusing to comply. She tried again, but the panel continued to flash at her: POTENTIAL BREACH.

"What's wrong?" Fence asked.

"The inner airlock door is still open," she said, pointing down to where the pirates had wedged the lower door. "The airlock won't activate until it's closed."

The gaggle of pirates had picked themselves up and were already starting to climb the stairs again. Fence pulled out a grenade, but Amelia grabbed his arm.

"If we damage this passageway the whole airlock will lock down, and the outer door will never open."

"Can you override the fail-safe?"

"Maybe."

He handed her the grenade, raised his sword, and started down to meet the pirates.

"You figure it out," he called. "I'll hold them off."

Amelia examined the console, desperately searching for some sort of manual override. The mechanism was civilian design, easy to use for basic functions but maddeningly bereft of any emergency capabilities. She heard the clash of swords as Fence engaged the lead pirate, and the jeers and shouts of those coming up behind. She searched for an access panel she could remove. Then a united cheer from the pirates wrenched her attention down the passageway. Fence's suited form slumped down, sword dropping from his lifeless hand.

She felt the sting of tears, but she pushed them back. Then she looked down at the grenade. One throw and that entire band of thugs would be wiped out. But then the airlock would be destroyed and she'd be trapped. And there were plenty more pirates crowding the lower airlock door, just waiting for a chance to kill.

All crowding close, she realized. With the lower door propped open.

Oh, she thought to herself, you poor bastards.

She pulled the grenade pin and dropped it right next to the upper door. She snapped her faceplate closed then ran down the steps to grab Fence's sagging body. She pushed him onto the nearest pirates, keeping their blades at bay just long enough for her to clear a few more steps down.

The blast wave hit her back, but it was reversed almost immediately by the thunderous rush of air escaping up through the exploded outer airlock door.

LIAM CRESTED ANOTHER ICY RIDGE AND ASSESSED his distance to Amelia's airlock. Almost there. Just one last descent and some flat terrain to cross before the long descent into the basin.

He blinked at a sudden flash, just catching a glimpse of a red door spinning away from the outbuilding. A second later he saw a small, suited figure come rocketing out, flailing madly as it rode a frosty plume of escaping air. More bodies spat out the shattered airlock and a great cloud of crystals spread like a fog as moist air spilled out into the frigid vacuum.

Liam looked down at the flailing suited figure, immediately recognizing two things. The person in that suit was clearly still alive. And the blast velocity of the escaping air was probably enough to launch her clear into space. She was still below him, but rising out of the basin fast, tracking right to left in front of him. Ahead of him were two dozen paces of rugged ice before the drop-off.

He burst into motion, bounding down from his vantage point and across the rough ice. Her white suit was clearly visible against the black surface below. At the edge of the drop-off he leaped out, sailing free through the airless sky. The figure had slowly rotated, bringing them face-to-face, and through the visor he saw Amelia's stunned expression.

Liam extended his arms as they approached and she did likewise. Her suit slammed into his. He grabbed on to her and felt the pressure of her arms against him. They spun together, the outside world flashing by in circles around them as they clung on. Gently, carefully, he extended his legs outward away from her, slowing their spin enough that he could look down at the landscape clearly.

They were drifting high over the dark basin, level with the lip but slowly descending. A reasonably flat patch of ground awaited them several hundred paces away. Far below, a fog of frozen air was hanging over the wreckage of the airlock, still growing as more atmosphere gushed through an uncontained breach. That was probably going to finish off the bulk of the pirate threat.

He could just make out his three sailors staring up at him from the top of the cliff.

"Flatrock, this is the XO," he called. "Signal the other teams to regroup at the barge. We'll meet you there."

"Yes, sir."

He realized Amelia was staring at him, and he smiled at her through their faceplates pressed together. Her face burst into a grin.

"I accept your invitation, Lord Blackwood," she said, her voice reverberating through the faceplates.

"To what?"

She nodded to their suits intertwined in a slow rotation over the landscape.

"To our first dance."

He laughed, and settled in to enjoy the moment.

CHAPTER 22

The morning sunlight streamed in through the tall windows of Admiral Lord Grandview's study, sparkling through the glass sails of the decorative battleship on his desk: the mighty *Vigilance* at full sail. It was always an impressive sight, but Liam found himself less impressed by it than he might once have been.

"Still dreaming she might one day be yours?" Riverton asked behind him.

He turned, offering a smile to his captain.

"Not at all, ma'am. I've developed a bit of a liking for old frigates hiding under cargo containers."

She sat back in her chair, her former grace restored after getting some true rest on the long voyage home. Her black hair was swept up in a striking new fashion that drew attention to her elegant neck, and the weight of gold rank on both her shoulders.

"Yes," she said. "Especially when they come home in one piece."

"Or mostly one piece. Lieutenant Swift hasn't stopped growling since we left the pirate base."

"Nor do I expect him to," she said with a raised eyebrow, "until one day we decommission *Daring* into retirement. And then I expect him to cry."

He laughed at the thought.

"And how's our quartermaster?" she asked suddenly.

Conflicting emotions suddenly welled up in his heart. Silly joy at just hearing Amelia referred to, mixed with trepidation as Riverton's gaze fixed on him.

"She's fine," he said simply.

"Good." She continued to stare at him, but he finally felt he knew her well enough to sense a hint of softness in her expression. "I value my crew, and I want them to be happy. But I also need discipline to be maintained."

"Yes, ma'am."

"So, do you think you can make one of my crewmembers happy and still maintain discipline?"

It took him a moment to understand the meaning behind her words. But when he did, a great weight of conflict lifted from his heart.

"Yes, ma'am. You can count on me."

"Splendid, XO," she said with a warm smile. "Splendid."

Her eyes suddenly snapped past Liam to the door, and she rose to her feet. Liam turned, stiffening to attention as Admiral Grandview strode into the room, a pair of junior officers visible just outside. His broad face was alive with good humor, and he gestured for everyone to sit.

"The final audit of your cargo has been completed," Grandview said without preamble, "and my team has confirmed the tally of your quartermaster. To the penny, I might add. An impressive haul, Commander Riverton."

"Thank you, sir," she said. "May I order the disbursement of prize money to my crew?"

"Yes. I've chosen my wealthiest underling to coordinate, who hopefully won't be too shocked over how much money we're handing over to common sailors. Lieutenant Lakeblue"—he nodded toward the door—"will supervise with your quartermaster."

"Very good, sir."

"I'll arrange for crew payments this afternoon," Liam added. "We want to be seen to deliver on our promises quickly, sir."

"Quite right," Grandview said. "And I'm sure there will be more than a few boisterous sailors in town this evening—please keep an eye on them."

"Yes, sir." Liam already had plans to spend the evening with Amelia, but he was sure the coxn and Chief Sky could be tasked with keeping the crew out of trouble.

"Good." Grandview glanced at the info pads laid out on the table between them. "And now that we've dealt with the most important issue of prize money, let's wrap up these minor details of the mission."

The admiral was in exceptional humor this morning, but then, as the senior officer responsible for this mission, he was entitled to one-eighth of the prize money. Liam glanced at the glass statue of *Vigilance,* and wondered if a new model of *Daring* might find its way into the admiral's collection.

"Lord Redfort has informed me of your tireless efforts to uncover the truth," Grandview said to Riverton. "If it wasn't for you, we'd probably be at war now."

"And with this revealed truth," Riverton replied, "I hope the Emperor can see that we indeed have an ally in our fight against criminal elements who threaten the peace."

"Don't expect too much," Grandview cautioned. "But yes, diplomatic ties with the Sectoid grand hive have been reestablished."

"Their people were captured and tortured for their venom," Riverton blurted out. "Their presence in our space was just them trying to rescue or seek retribution."

"And it was Humans who did it," Liam added.

"And because of you, everyone now knows this. So there will not be war, but don't expect there to be peace quite that easily." Grandview made a show of looking through the info pads.

"Those prisoners you brought back," he said, "will prove valuable. The intelligence they offer will vary, but even having them behind bars will make the Empire a safer place and will send a message to those who still wish to counter our laws."

"On that subject," Riverton said carefully, "there is one prisoner of particular interest to us."

"Yes, damned shame, that." Grandview glanced over his shoulder to ensure his staff were out of earshot, but still leaned in and lowered his voice. "What an idiot that young Highcastle was. No different from his cousin."

"He attempted a mutiny," Liam said with as much force as he dared. "That is a hanging offense, sir."

Grandview sighed, his gaze dropping to the table.

"What is to be Highcastle's punishment?" Liam persisted.

"He has been placed under guard and is currently being shipped to the home world, where he will be handed over to the Imperial court. They will decide his fate."

Liam held his tongue as Riverton's hand pressed down on his knee.

"I have," she said quietly, "some doubts as to the efficacy of the Imperial court to properly assess the military implications of this crime. Sir."

"And those doubts are not misplaced," Grandview rumbled, "but you both know well that the law is . . . interpreted differently on occasion for the higher nobility."

"Yes . . . ," Riverton almost hissed the word, dark eyes deep in thought, "sir."

"So, let's focus on the things we can control," Grandview said, leaning back and raising his voice again. "The data you captured at the pirate base was considerable, and your crew is to be commended for taking the base with so little damage to the memory cores."

"We conducted as much analysis as we could while in space," Riverton said, gesturing to the pads, "and I was astonished at the complexity of the pirate organization. This was no simple band of buccaneers, sir."

"Agreed," Grandview said. "My team has been adding to your analysis with intelligence gathered from a dozen sectors, and the results are disturbing."

Liam glanced at Riverton. Her eyes narrowed.

"While the open pirate activity was restricted to the Silica sector," Grandview continued, "there are other criminal elements we've been tracking across Human space. None of them seemed connected, until we started noticing names from across the Empire showing up in the memory core of the pirate base you captured. Names of petty kingpins, of local gang leaders, and the odd political troublemaker. The sort of common thug usually of concern only to a local constabulary. But now, it seems, there is a connection between them all."

"That is indeed disturbing, sir," Riverton said.

"We found no pirate leader, as such, at the base," Liam added. "Just a collective of fighters. But they clearly took orders from someone higher."

"We assumed that the pirate leader was killed aboard one of his ships in the battle," Riverton said. "Do you think otherwise, sir?"

"We don't know," Grandview admitted. "But a single name keeps coming up in communications, often used as a threat but, very occasionally, appearing as the source of direct instructions: Dark Star."

The name hung in the silence.

"One of the prisoners mentioned that," Liam recalled. "But at the time we thought it referred to the base."

"It appears that Dark Star is a person," Grandview said. "But there is no criminal connected to that term."

Liam clasped his chin in thought, trying to recall ever hearing that name before. There was, he felt deep down, something familiar about it.

"I don't know that name," Riverton said, looking questioningly to Liam.

"Nothing strikes me," he admitted. "But I'll give it some thought."

"The Emperor would like you to do more than that," Grandview said, his tone strengthening suddenly.

Liam straightened, spotting the new intensity in Grandview's features.

"His Majesty is very concerned at the possibility of some sort of organized criminal element growing in the Empire." Grandview leaned forward, looking first at Liam and then to Riverton. "We don't know how far this element has reached into our society, but there is concern that the Navy itself may be compromised."

Liam felt his chest tighten.

"Traitors, sir?"

"Perhaps just loose tongues and the leaking of information. We don't know. But His Majesty wants us to find out. In particular, he wants *you* to find out."

"Meaning," Riverton asked, "HMSS *Daring,* sir?"

"Are you and your crew up for another challenge, Commander Riverton?"

She sat back, crossing her arms. Liam could detect the smile hovering at the corners of her lips. "I'm interested to hear more, sir."

"You'll be operating outside the Navy, your actions hidden and unreported. You can keep what you capture, and if you succeed you will be rewarded handsomely by His Majesty. But if you fail, there will be no protection or defense from the Empire."

"Sounds familiar. What's the mission, sir?"

"Find out who this Dark Star is, and stop them."

Riverton turned questioning eyes to Liam. He could see the sudden fire in their depths, and realized that he shared it. What was he going to do otherwise—prance around at vapid balls or waste away his days hunting or gambling? This was his calling, he knew. He met Riverton's eyes and nodded.

She rose to her feet, prompting Liam and Grandview to do likewise. She extended her hand to the admiral.

"Lord Grandview," she declared, "my executive officer and I accept this commission."

ACKNOWLEDGMENTS

DESPITE THE COMMON IMAGE OF THE SOLITARY typewriter, no author works alone. I couldn't have produced this book without the following great people: my editor, Vedika Khanna, for steering this project home; my colleague Priyanka Krishnan, for helping me bring this new world to life; my friend Steven Erikson, for his literary advice and anthropological insights; and my agent, Howard Morhaim, for first suggesting that a "fun space-adventure story" might be worth thinking about.

And, as always, my deepest thanks to my beloved Emma, for all her amazing support.